DANGER AT DUNHAVEN CASTLE

ALSO BY NELLIE H. STEELE

Cate Kensie Mysteries:
The Secret of Dunhaven Castle
Murder at Dunhaven Castle
Holiday Heist at Dunhaven Castle

Jack's Journal Versions:
The Secret Keepers
Murder in the Tower

Shadow Slayers Stories:
Shadows of the Past
Stolen Portrait Stolen Soul
Gone

Maggie Edwards Adventures:
Cleopatra's Tomb
Secret of the Ankhs

Duchess of Blackmoore Mysteries
Death of a Duchess

DANGER AT DUNHAVEN CASTLE

A CATE KENSIE MYSTERY

NELLIE H. STEELE

This is a work of fiction. Names, characters, places, and incidents either are the product of the author's imagination or are used fictitiously. Any resemblance to actual persons, living or dead, events, or locales is entirely coincidental.

Copyright © 2021 by Nellie H. Steele

All rights reserved. No part of this book may be reproduced or used in any manner without written permission of the copyright owner except for the use of quotations in a book.

Cover design by Stephanie A. Sovak.

❦ Created with Vellum

*For my goddaughter, Arabella
Keep reading!*

ACKNOWLEDGMENTS

A HUGE thank you to everyone who helped get this book published! Special shout outs to: Stephanie Sovak, Paul Sovak, Michelle Cheplic, Mark D'Angelo and Lori D'Angelo.

Finally, a HUGE thank you to you, the reader!

MacKenzie Family Tree

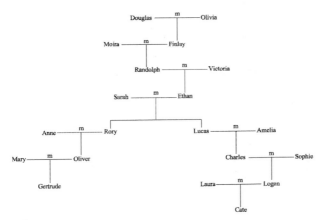

CHAPTER 1

Cate's heart pounded hard in her chest. She puffed with exertion. Her throat parched as she raced down the hall. She risked a glance behind her. The hallway appeared empty. Where was he, she wondered?

She hurried through the doorway into the library. She tugged the train of her gown inside before closing and locking the doors.

Cate backed a few steps away. A loud pounding shook the doors. She jumped and shuddered with each jolt.

"Catherine," a voice growled on the other side. Cate's breath caught in her throat at the sound of his voice. She swallowed hard as she glanced around the library. No escape routes existed. Could she climb from a window, she pondered?

Cate hastened to one window and yanked on the handle. It stuck fast. She struggled with it as the pounding ceased. She spun to face the now silent door. Her eyes widened as the doorknob turned. Would the lock hold? Not for long, Cate surmised.

Her eyes searched the space and she spotted a new

feature. A gaping black hole stared back at her. Cate lifted her skirts and sprinted toward it. She disappeared into the blackness.

Cate knew the space well. Additional light was not needed. She pressed against the stone wall as she crept down the stairs leading to Douglas MacKenzie's secret office. At the bottom, Cate groped the wall in the dim light. Her fingers found the trigger to close the secret passage off to the library. She pulled it. A scraping sound filled her ears as the bookshelf swung closed.

The closing bookcase shut out all light from the room. With the space plunged into blackness, Cate held her breath as she strained her ears for sounds of the library doors being breached. Silence pervaded the space.

After a moment, faint footsteps sounded on the floor above her. Cate's pulse quickened as she glanced to the ceiling. She retreated further into Douglas's office. In the darkness, Cate bumped into his desk. It made a sickening scrape across the floor.

The footsteps halted above. When they resumed, they hurried toward her location. A tear escaped Cate's eye as she rushed to hide.

Light illuminated the space she searched. He had opened the bookcase. "Catherine? Where are you hiding?" he called to her.

Cate held in a sob as she squeezed into a darkened corner. She pressed against the damp stone wall as she sank to the floor. Footfalls sounded on the wooden steps leading down to her hiding place. Cate sucked in air as she struggled to maintain her composure.

The man appeared at the bottom of the stairs, backlit by the light from above. Even featureless, his form was imposing. Cate pressed a hand over her mouth as she strove to remain silent.

The walls around her pushed against her back and side. Were they moving closer to her or was she pressing herself closer to them, she wondered? The man stalked across the room. Had he spotted her? Cate shrank further back. The walls closed in around her. She squeezed her eyes shut as the figure approached.

The damp, cold rock brushed against Cate's skin. When she opened her eyes, the stone wall filled her vision. What happened, she pondered? She felt around, finding stone surrounded her. She pushed against the cold, rough rock, searching for an exit. She found none.

Cate pounded her fists against the wall in front of her. Tears streamed down her face as she fought to escape her prison. "HELP!" she screamed. "HELP!"

* * *

Cate vaulted to sitting. She gulped in air as her heart thudded in her chest. A glance around the space confirmed her location. She sat in her bedroom. Moonlight streamed through the window overlooking the back garden.

Riley, her little black and white dog, popped his head up and stared at her. His dark almond eyes studied Cate with a quizzical expression. Next to him, his dog pal, Bailey, glanced sideways at Cate. "I'm okay, guys," she said as her breathing slowed and her heart returned to normal speed. She reached over and tousled the fur on each of their heads. "Just another nightmare. I'd better write it down."

Satisfied with the explanation, Riley let his head drop onto the bed. With a sigh, his eyes drooped shut, and he returned to sleep. Bailey's eyes closed as he drifted back to dreamland, too. Cate flicked on the bedside lamp and grabbed a notebook and pen from her night table. She flipped it open to the first blank page and began to detail her dream.

After Cate filled in the information, she closed the book, set it on her night table, and switched off the light. As darkness surrounded her, she relaxed back into her pillows. Yet another nightmare, she reflected.

The nightmares had plagued her since early December. Now, almost four months later, they were a growing cause for concern. When they started, Cate assumed they were warning her about something in the library. After she and Jack found a hidden passage leading to the secret workspace of Douglas MacKenzie, the castle's first proprietor, Cate assumed the nightmares would cease. She had been wrong.

The haunting dreams continued for months after they'd located Douglas's office. Shortly after the discovery, Jack suggested the nightmares would taper off. Instead, they had done the opposite, becoming more frequent and more terrifying in nature as time passed.

Cate now spent almost every night chased by a mysterious man whose identity she could not ascertain. After numerous discussions with Jack, he suggested she detail them in a dream journal. Perhaps keeping track of them would allow them to identify the source.

So Cate diligently wrote all the details she could recall upon awakening. In this version, the man chased her through the castle. As usual, they wound up in the library. The gaping hole represented the secret entrance to Douglas's workshop. As Cate sought safety there, the space had somehow morphed into a stone tomb, trapping her inside.

Cate spent another hour contemplating the nightmares before falling asleep. Why had they not stopped after she found Douglas's office? Were they a warning? If so, of what?

Cate pondered the dreams' meaning. In the two months she'd been keeping track, she'd filled half of the thick notebook's pages. Detail after detail from various versions flooded back into her mind. She recalled her heart pounding as she fled through the castle halls, the terror she experienced as the man hissed her name while chasing her, the icy air that gusted from the gaping hole in the library. The damp, cold stone that closed in around her as she hid.

Cate recalled other specifics from prior dreams. In each case, she wore old-fashioned clothing. From the notes Cate described in her dream journal, the clothing appeared to be from the late 1700s.

To the casual observer, this detail may seem nonsensical, typical of a dream. But for Cate, well-acquainted with the well-guarded secret within the castle walls, the clothing seemed indicative of something more. She stared at the timepiece she wore around her neck. At almost a year after her arrival, memories of her first few months in the castle flooded her mind.

A smile crossed her face as she remembered her first glances at her new abode and her overwhelming sense of home. A chuckle escaped her as she recalled the events that occurred over the last summer. From phantom maids to ghostly gardeners, Cate assumed ghosts haunted the halls of her new home. Little did she know she wore around her neck the key to a secret larger than shadowy specters. Imprinted with the warning *ALWAYS KEEP AN EYE ON YOUR TIME*, the golden timepiece interacted with various areas within the castle walls allowing the wearer to travel through time.

Amazed and excited at the discovery, Cate and Jack, who was sworn to protect the secret along with Cate as part of his duty as a Reid, had traveled to the 1850s and the 1920s to help Cate's ancestors solve various mysteries.

The smile returned to Cate's face as she reminisced about meeting her ancestors. After a few fond memories, her mind circled back to her current conundrum. She'd never traveled to the 1700s. She wasn't even aware of a spot in the castle that led to this time period.

Still, the clothing in her dream suggested the terror she lived out nearly every night pointed to this era. Did something or someone call her to that time? Was the man chasing her Douglas MacKenzie? Was he calling for help? The presence always seemed sinister to her. But she couldn't understand why she'd get that vibe from Douglas.

Cate sighed as she stroked the silky fur on Riley's back. She hadn't solved anything thus far, and she wouldn't tonight either. She closed her eyes and drifted off to what she hoped would be a dreamless state.

Red streaked the morning sky as Cate awoke. The sun peeked over the misty moors as she stretched and climbed from her bed. She teetered on the edge, her eyelids still drooping with sleepiness. Her gaze fell to the notebook on the night table. Elements of her dream poured back into her mind.

She frowned at the notebook and turned her focus to Riley. With a large yawn, the little pup stretched and climbed to his feet. His tail offered a lazy wag in Cate's direction as he sidled next to her.

"Good morning, sleepyhead," Cate said as he licked her cheek.

Cate kissed the top of his head as he sank back down amidst the covers for a second snooze while she showered. Bailey stretched as he eyed Cate from his spot. His eyes closed to slits as she plodded to the bathroom.

Cate's mind dwelled on her dream as she adjusted the water's temperature before stepping into her shower. The warm water caressed her skin as she parsed through more details. She came to no new conclusions as she dressed for her day.

Riley shook off any sleepiness the moment the cool Scottish air hit his nostrils. He raced around the portion of the yard closest to the castle. His floppy ears bounced up and down as he bounded around in a circle with his mouth open in a giddy grin. Cate couldn't help but smile at the little pup's exuberance for life. No matter the situation, Riley could always bring a grin to her face.

A bit more reserved than Riley, Bailey trotted around the property, sniffing bushes and following the flight of morning birds venturing from their nests.

Cate collected them after their romp and entered the castle's kitchen for breakfast. Inside, she met her full staff who were preparing for breakfast. Mrs. Fraser, her current housekeeper, bustled about the kitchen as she prepared the morning meal. Close on Mrs. Fraser's heels was her housekeeper trainee, Molly Williams. Cate's former department secretary, Molly, had moved to Scotland a few months ago. When Mrs. Fraser retires, Molly would take over as the housekeeper. That wouldn't be for several years, according to Mrs. Fraser.

Molly bent over the oven, testing cookies with a spatula. "How do they look, Miss Molly?" Mrs. Fraser called over her shoulder as she shook raisins into a bowl.

"Eh," Molly answered, "flat."

Mrs. Fraser finished her task and peered into the oven over Molly's shoulder. "Aye, too much opening of that door and fiddling, that's why. Close it up, girl, and let them bake!"

Molly nodded and pushed the oven door closed. She switched on the oven light and continued to stare at them. "They'll cook in their own time, Molly. Leave them for a few minutes. They'll puff up again.

Cate chuckled at the scene. For months, Molly had begged Mrs. Fraser to teach her to bake the cookies she often supplied everyone with. Mrs. Fraser had finally allowed Molly to try a simple shortbread recipe.

Molly fretted over the recipe for days, afraid her attempt wouldn't measure up. She shot Cate an apologetic glance as she pulled her gaze from the oven. With a shrug, Molly mouthed to Cate, "Hope they're okay!"

"They'll be fine," Mrs. Fraser said without skipping a beat. Cate suppressed a laugh at Mrs. Fraser's almost extrasensory ability.

At the kitchen table, Cate spotted Mr. Fraser and Jack. Mr. Fraser, her head groundskeeper, sipped a cup of coffee as he read a list of tasks for the week. Jack, Cate's estate manager and time-traveling buddy, set his coffee mug on the table as both dogs swarmed him.

"Well, hello, little laddies!" Jack said as Riley leapt into his lap and Bailey stood with his paws planted on Jack's thigh. "Did we have a wonderful sleep last night?"

Riley answered in the form of a lick to Jack's cheek. "Oh, is that right, big fellow?" Jack replied to him.

"Good morning, Lady Cate," Mrs. Fraser said as Cate sat down at the table.

"Good morning," Cate answered. "Putting Molly to work this morning, I see."

"Aye, the lassie has earned her first attempt at the shortbread."

"Earned?" Cate inquired.

"Aye," Jack answered. "She passed her shortbread exam yesterday." He winked at Cate.

Cate chuckled at his statement. "Don't laugh, Lady Cate," Molly said as she placed a glass of water in front of Cate. "He's telling the truth."

Cate knit her brows. "There was a test?"

"Aye, there was," Mrs. Fraser responded. "Had to memorize that recipe. I cannae have the lassie glancing at the recipe card every few seconds. The dough is very persnickety. One moment it's perfect and the next it's ruined. That's what makes my shortbreads the best!

"They are the best," Jack agreed. "When do we get to taste test Molly's?"

Molly peeked through the oven's window, a frown crossing her face. "You may not want to taste mine," she fretted.

"I'll be the judge of that," Jack responded. "You've got to let us try them to know for sure."

Mrs. Fraser peered into the oven again. "A few more minutes," she advised. "See how they are puffy now that you've left them alone?"

A smile crossed Molly's face as she gazed at the baking tray. "Yes, they do look a bit better!"

Mrs. Fraser and Molly finished all the breakfast preparations as Riley and Bailey curled up near Cate's feet. Cate grabbed a bowl as Molly, at Mrs. Fraser's direction, pulled the cookies from the oven. "Set them out and leave them," Mrs. Fraser advised.

Molly nodded and placed the baking tray on the stovetop before retrieving her breakfast. The group sat down for the meal, sharing a discussion about Cate's upcoming one-year anniversary as a countess.

Mrs. Campbell, the town's librarian and president of the historical society, convinced Cate a celebration was in order. With less than three months to go, the massive celebration she planned still required a fair amount of work. Though this time, everyone at Dunhaven Castle fully supported the party since it celebrated their Lady Cate. Scheduled for 6 June, Mrs. Campbell planned an extravaganza that would remain unrivaled for years to come.

"Will we be baking for the anniversary party?" Molly questioned.

"No," Cate responded. "You are GUESTS at my party! Not caterers!"

"Aye, true," Mrs. Fraser responded. "But we will still be baking!"

Cate tilted her head to offer a confused glance at Mrs. Fraser. "But..." she began, when Mrs. Fraser interrupted her.

"Not for the party. I agree, let the caterers handle the scores of people in attendance."

Cate's face blanched. "I hope there aren't scores," she murmured.

Mrs. Fraser continued. "But we shall have our own private celebration for you, Lady Cate! With a large meal and plenty of cookies. And I'd like to make another Scottish Berry Brûlée. The same dessert I made when you arrived."

Cate smiled. "Now THIS is a party I can get on board with! I'll even help with the baking!"

"No, you won't, Lady Cate," Mrs. Fraser chided. "It is a celebration FOR you, so you can't prepare anything for it. And given your tales of woe in the kitchen, I'd rather you didn't, anyway." Mrs. Fraser chuckled.

Cate giggled, too. As she approached her one-year anniversary, she marveled at the change in less than one year. Not only in herself, she reflected, but in everyone around her. When she arrived, Mrs. Fraser detested the idea of a "crass American" running Dunhaven. Now, the woman planned not one but two celebrations in her honor.

Cate glanced around the table. Molly grinned at Mrs. Fraser as they discussed her choice of desserts for the special occasion. Mr. Fraser, always quiet, wore a small grin as he interjected comments about sprucing up the grounds and transforming them for the party.

Cate's eyes rested on Jack, her estate manager and, more than that, her friend. In less than a year, their lives had radically changed when they discovered time travel. Jack, ever the cautious one, always warned against anything too extreme. Even so, he typically gave in to Cate's whims and allowed her to visit and help her family from generations past. He glanced at her from across the table, a wide smile on his face.

Cate returned his expression. She, too, had changed. While she remained introverted, Cate was no longer a wallflower. She transformed from quiet college professor to gracious Countess.

As the meal wound down, Cate considered her next task. With an upcoming meeting with Mrs. Campbell on Wednesday, Cate had many details to review. Orders were due soon on several items, and Mrs. Campbell hoped to have all decisions made within the next two weeks.

Still, with the meeting in two days, Cate could put those decisions off until tomorrow. Instead, she planned to continue her research into Douglas MacKenzie, the castle's builder. Two months ago, they had found his secret workspace. Filled to the brim with journals, sketches, technical drawings, plans and odd devices, Cate had spent the first few months of the new year cataloging and sorting through much of it.

She hoped to learn more about the strange anomaly of time travel encompassed in the castle walls through Douglas's many journals. Unfortunately for Cate, she'd learned nothing thus far. Nonetheless, she was determined to continue exploring options until she made some headway.

After breakfast, she enjoyed a cuppa with Molly and Mrs. Fraser before her usual mind-centering walk around the property with the dogs. With the air still chillier than she'd like, Cate kept her walk shorter than she did in the summer months.

She returned to the castle and navigated the halls to the library. A fire roared in the large central fireplace. Tall bookcases surrounded it, stretching from floor to ceiling. They extended around three of the four walls. The only bare wall contained massive windows adorned with heavy tartan draperies overlooking one of the estate's gardens.

Soon, spring flowers would bloom just outside the window where a massive wooden desk sat. Cate would use them as a distraction from her work whenever a blinking cursor stared at her on her laptop screen. Her book on the castle's history stalled as her research on Douglas dead-ended beyond the standard basics recorded in the history books.

Perhaps Mrs. Campbell could tell her more. They had not discussed Douglas yet. As the town's historical society president, Mrs. Campbell may have information. As the town's biggest gossip, Cate felt certain she would have some tidbit about Douglas to share. She made a mental note to ask during their next meeting.

Riley and Bailey wandered into the library behind Cate. After their walk, a customary nap was in order. Riley wandered toward the fireplace, with Bailey meandering behind him. Bailey curled into a tight ball close enough to feel the warmth of the fire. Riley sprawled next to him, stretching his little body as far as he could before letting his head rest on the thick area rug under him.

Cate smiled at the scene before turning her attention to her target. Her eyes focused on one particular bookshelf across the room. She stalked to the fireplace and pressed the top stone. The square stone retracted, and the customary creak of the hinged bookcase filled the room.

Cate opened the bookcase on so many occasions before, Riley and Bailey no longer reacted to the bookcase's groaning, nor the smell of must that followed. She stepped toward a large cord on the floor and pushed the plug into the wall socket.

Light bloomed from deep within the cavity. The temporary lighting Jack rigged for Cate in the secret lab brightened the dim space. Light filtered all the way to the top of the squeaky wooden staircase leading into its depths. With a deep inhale and exhale, Cate crossed to the opening and peered into the brightened space. What would she find there today, Cate mused?

"Ready to head into your dungeon, m'lady?" Jack queried from behind Cate.

At the sound of his voice, Riley bounded to his feet and dashed across the room. He leapt from the edge of the area rug, flying through the air into Jack's waiting arms. "Did I wake you, little fellow?" Jack asked as he rubbed his head. Bailey meandered over, stretching before glancing up to Jack for an ear scratch.

Cate smiled at the scene. "They were just about to nap," she informed Jack.

"That is a great idea, boys. Probably better than spending your time in the dusty dungeon!"

"It's not a dungeon," Cate corrected. "It would have been easier to assess had it been!"

"Still no progress?" Jack inquired.

Cate threw her arms out with a shrug. "Nope," she admitted. "I'm still sorting through. There's tons of stuff down there, but so far nothing beyond sorting is getting done."

"Perhaps today will be your lucky day, Lady Cate," Jack suggested.

Cate raised her eyebrows as she considered it. "Every day is my lucky day," she responded. "I inherited a castle. Though beyond that, I expect today I'll only find frustration in my dungeon and no answers."

"Why do you do it?" Jack inquired.

Cate inhaled a deep breath as she formulated her answer. "It's Douglas's lab. The man who discovered the time travel anomaly. AND the man who figured out how to control it. The information down there is invaluable. It could teach us so much about the phenomenon. It's worth it even if we glean a tiny bit of information from it.

"If, Lady Cate, if. So far, you haven't deduced anything."

Cate shook her head with a sideways frown. "Nope. So far every book I've found has contained gibberish."

"Perhaps they contain the rantings of a madman. Nonsensical ramblings he scribbled after losing his mind," Jack suggested.

"I don't know," Cate answered with a sigh. "Once I get everything sorted, I'll take more than a glance at the handwritten journals and determine if I can make any headway."

"Well, good luck, Lady Cate," Jack said with a grin.

"Thanks!" Cate answered, matching his expression. "You know, I'm surprised you're so keen on me making any progress! You hate time travel!"

"The longer you spend deciphering those journals, the less we time travel," Jack answered with a grin. Cate shook her head at him. "And I don't hate it. I just don't like it."

"Same difference," Cate contended.

"Not really, but anyway, I don't want to keep you from your gibberish and dust. I just stopped by because I needed your signature on a few items before sending it to Mr. Smythe for payment."

"Oh, sure!" Cate answered. She approached Jack, who passed her a folder. Cate grabbed a pen from the desk. Jack explained the basics of each as Cate signed off.

After collecting the paperwork, he said, "And now, I leave you to your research. M'lady!" He gave an extravagant bow before retreating from the room.

Cate shook her head at the comical display. With Jack gone, the dogs returned to their preferred morning nap spots, while Cate returned to the open passage. She stepped inside and hovered at the top of the stairs. The moment they had first discovered the secret area popped into her mind as she descended each step. They groaned under her weight. Just complaints from aging wood, Jack had told her, after a thorough inspection. Before she continued to traverse them on a regular basis, he insisted on ensuring their safety. With every creak, Cate thanked him.

As she reached the bottom, Cate glanced around the disheveled room. She contemplated whether she'd made any progress. Piles of a variety of items sat in various locations around the room. Cate had sorted them to the best of her ability. She filled the many bookshelves with the odd items which appeared to be inventions or attempts at inventions. In her cataloging, Cate found a prototype of the timepiece she carried around her neck, a rudimentary attempt at a lightbulb, an odd contraption shaped like a helmet and attached to a magnet, and various other peculiarities she could not identify.

In a corner of the room, a wooden staircase led to nowhere. In the opposite corner stood a metal box large enough for a human to stand in, with tubes leading at all angles from it. Next to it sat a large glass ball, stained by watermarks. Across the room, a twisted mass of tubes, beakers and pipettes formed a complicated chemistry setup.

Cate stared at the other piles. She'd used another bookshelf for reference books. In the middle of the floor stood the room's true bounty. A collection of journals written by Douglas MacKenzie. Next to that stood a jumble of technical drawings with his signature.

When Cate and Jack found the space, the journals scattered throughout the room had provided the promise of answers regarding the castle's secret. Cate recalled her heart skipping a beat as she'd read the words "The Journal of

Douglas MacKenzie" on the leather-bound book discarded on the desk.

Only after sorting through them had Cate's hopes been dashed. Journal after journal contained nothing more than gibberish. At first, Cate had searched every page for a readable entry. After the seventh journal, she gave up on the exhaustive examination of each journal's pages. Instead, a cursory glance at the first page, followed by a quick leaf through was all she completed before tossing the journal into the ever-growing pile with the others.

Even the sketches of his inventions were adorned with annotations in gibberish. Cate took her frustrations out by promising to find answers after she'd organized the space. It allowed her to make progress without requiring a search for solutions regarding the gobbledygook in the twelve journals she'd discovered.

Cate's organization goal would soon be met. With one bookshelf left to sort through, Cate estimated she'd finish in the next day or so. She stepped onto the stone floor and made her way to the large structure. She'd cleared the top shelf already, saving herself multiple trips up and down the stepstool today. She focused her energy on the second shelf at her eye level.

Cate pulled the first item from the shelf. A rusty spring the size of her arm, with two cup-shaped objects on either end. Cate rotated the object in her hands. She peered into the cups and placed one to her ear. With both hands, Cate pulled on both ends, stretching the coil before allowing it to snap back. Dust clouded the air as the ancient spring sprung back to shape. Cate coughed and waved at the air in front of her. She shuttled it to an empty spot on her "inventions" shelf.

She continued working her way through all the materials, polishing off two shelves before lunch. Her progress was made slower by her fiddling with each object. Some of them she recalled spotting in technical drawings. She often spent time digging through the pile to compare the sketches to the physical objects. Without any readable text, Cate learned little about any of the items.

"Lady Cate!"

Cate glanced toward the staircase leading to the library. Mrs. Fraser's voice floated down from above. "Lady Cate!" she shouted again.

"Coming!" Cate shouted as she climbed to her feet. She clapped her hands together to remove as much dust as possible before brushing off her shirt and pants.

"Still working in that dusty dungeon?" Mrs. Fraser inquired as Cate appeared at the top of the stairs.

"Afraid so," Cate said. "It's not a dungeon, though. There's some really interesting stuff down there, to be honest!"

Mrs. Fraser lifted an eyebrow at Cate, her eyes sliding up and down Cate's form. "Young Jack says it's a dungeon," she said with a nod. "It's a dungeon. And look at the state you've got yourself in! I dare say we'll not get the dust out of those."

Cate glanced down at her black leggings, now a shade of gray from the powder covering them. Her burgundy tunic hadn't fared much better. A large gray streak of dust adorned her abdomen. Cate pulled her bottom lip into a frown. "Oh, I've really taken a beating already today."

"Aye. You'll clog the drain with the dust in your hair, too, Lady Cate," Mrs. Fraser said with a chuckle.

Cate batted at her hair, attempting to knock some of the dust from it. "You may be right," she answered.

"Well, dusty or not, it's time for your lunch," Mrs. Fraser said as she motioned to the tray on the desk.

"Mmm," Cate responded as she sniffed the air. "Smells wonderful! Is this your famous chicken soup?"

"That it is, Lady Cate," Mrs. Fraser confirmed. "Now, you'd better go wash your hands before you eat."

Cate smiled and nodded as she darted from the room to clean up before eating her lunch. "Thank you!" she shouted behind her.

"You're welcome. Don't dally! It's best-served piping hot!" Mrs. Fraser called after her.

The promise of Mrs. Fraser's famous chicken soup on a chilly day caused Cate to speed through her handwashing and hurry straight back to the library. She leaned over the steaming bowl, inhaling a deep whiff of the fragrant soup. She dug in after blowing on a full spoonful of the broth. Behind her, Riley and Bailey gnawed on soup bones, a treat from Mrs. Fraser. Today, lunch satisfied everyone.

Cate curled in the leather armchair near the fireplace for a few moments after lunch, allowing the dogs to continue their feast. Her muscles protested her return to Douglas's secret office. So did her work ethic. Though nearly complete, the lack of progress annoyed Cate. Perhaps the last two shelves held a breakthrough, she mused.

CHAPTER 2

The promise of a discovery motivated her to return to the space after a brief walk with the dogs. Cate descended the stairs and approached the bookshelf. She knelt on the cold stone floor to assess the final two shelves of unsorted materials. Cate blew on the shelf, sending a dust cloud into the air. She waved it away and began on one end. She removed several unidentifiable items and shuttled them to another shelf.

Underneath two large glass beakers, Cate found another journal. She grasped the thick leather spine and pulled it from the shelf. As she flipped open the front cover, the sound of cracking leather filled her ears. She glanced at the first page. A random assortment of letters adorned it. With a sigh and a shake of her head, Cate flipped through the remaining pages, stopping at random to peruse the contents. None of it made sense.

Another sigh escaped her as she snapped the book shut. A cold, wet nose pressed against her cheek and a warm tongue gave her a lick. Her eyes slid sideways, and a half-smile crossed her face.

"Hey, buddy," Cate said as Riley offered her another kiss on the cheek. "Getting bored?"

Riley stared at her with his dark brown eyes before sniffing the book she held in her hand. "Any thoughts on it, Riley? Can you read this? Maybe it's in dog language."

Cate flipped a page open for Riley to peruse. The pup offered no answers. Instead, he glanced to the page, then to Cate before sliding to the floor and curling near her. Cate scratched his ears for a moment. "Did you leave your brother napping upstairs?" she questioned.

She glanced around the room, spotting a small form peering at her a few steps from the bottom of the staircase. "Did you venture down, too, Bailey? Come on." Cate held her hand out to encourage him. He bounded down the remaining stairs and trotted across the stone floor to Cate. Cate took a moment to cuddle with them both before returning to work.

"What do you say we finish this sorting, boys?" Riley gave her another kiss on the cheek for encouragement.

Cate climbed to her feet and tossed the journal on the top of the pile. She finished moving the additional materials on the shelf. The bottom shelf consisted mainly of laboratory equipment and a few sketches of lab setups. She finished by late afternoon.

With aching muscles, she herded the two dogs up the stairs in search of a much-needed shower. Before leaving the library, Cate pulled the plug on the lab's lighting and closed the secret passage, sealing off the area for another day.

As she crossed the hall and headed toward the main staircase, she ran into Jack. Riley bounded toward him as Bailey trotted behind.

"Any luck today?" he questioned.

She shook her head. "No. But I got everything sorted!"

"Hey! Progress, Lady Cate!"

"Yes, some. Now on to deciphering the information."

"Surely, you can take a few days off to celebrate your sorting feat."

"I'd really like to unravel the information I've found. Not just the journals, but some of those inventions are interesting. I'd love to understand what's written about them, their intended purpose or why he made them."

"I find them creepy."

"They're not creepy," Cate said with a laugh.

"They are! The giant fishbowl? The weird Iron Maiden with the tubes? I don't want to know their purpose, Lady Cate. I'm afraid to find out." Jack shivered in an overly dramatic display of fear.

Cate shook her head at him, a half-grin on her face. "You have no sense of adventure."

"No, I don't, Lady Cate. And I like me just fine that way. If I never find out what secrets the mad scientist's lab holds, I will still live a full and happy life."

"Well, I would like to discover those secrets. Though first," Cate said as she glanced at her clothes, "I would like to discover the shower."

"Aye, you look like you've crawled through a dusty tomb. I shall leave you to your shower. M'lady!" Jack bowed to her as she collected her furry friends and climbed the stairs in search of steamy hot water and clean hair and skin.

* * *

Cate peered from her bedroom window early the next morning. Dense fog covered most of the landscape. Early spring storms rolled through the highlands for most of the night. For the moment, the heavy clouds held the rain at bay. The overnight thunderclaps were enough to send both pups hiding under the covers and pressed against Cate. She laid awake, watching lightning tear through the sky as they huddled against her. The dreamless dozing between storms kept her nightmares at bay.

Cate stretched and climbed from her bed. As she walked the dogs before breakfast, Cate pondered the puzzle awaiting her in Douglas's lab. Could she decipher the enigma? What discoveries lay inside the journals and sketches? Would she learn more about the castle's unique property? Would it provide a better mastery of time travel?

Cate stared into the mists shrouding the moors, her mind searching for answers. A yip several yards away called her attention back to her current situation. Cate glanced around her, finding herself alone.

"Riley! Bailey!" Cate called, not spotting the dogs. "Riley! Bailey!"

Cate heard a grumble from behind a bush in the side garden. As she navigated through the garden, she rounded a row of rose bushes and found both dogs. "There you are! What are you two doing over here?" Cate questioned.

Both dogs studied the ground. Bailey's head tilted sideways as he gave the area a curious look. Riley glanced to Cate before returning his gaze to a grassy patch. Cate stooped to peer closer at the area. Blades of green grass poked from the dirt. She spotted nothing else.

"What is it?" she inquired again.

Bailey scratched the area with his paw twice. Cate shrugged. "I don't see anything, bud."

Riley issued a whine as Bailey raked the patch again with his paw. "You guys are silly. There's nothing there. Come on, let's get our breakfast."

Cate stalked a few steps away. She spun when neither pup followed her. "Riley! Bailey! Come on! Dish!" Both dogs bounded toward her at the mention of their breakfast. Cate shook her head at them, pondering what they imagined they spotted in that grassy patch. Likely a bug, she concluded as they approached the castle.

"Good morning!" Cate called to Molly and Mrs. Fraser as she entered the kitchen.

"Good morning, Lady Cate," Mrs. Fraser answered, followed by Molly.

"Jack and Mr. Fraser already hard at work before breakfast?" Cate inquired.

"Aye, gathering tools for the day and tending to the fires."

"The rain seems to have stopped for the moment. Will they attempt to work outside?" Cate asked.

Mrs. Fraser shook her head. "Storms are expected to continue all day off and on. They're stuck inside. Young Jack will spend most of his day pestering me for biscuits."

"A good day to stay in and learn more baking!" Molly exclaimed as she prepared the oatmeal.

Cate agreed with a nod. "How did your shortbreads turn out?"

"Eh..." Molly murmured.

"For a first attempt, they were quite good!" Mrs. Fraser answered for her. Molly smiled at the compliment. "With a few tweaks, they'll match mine!"

"Looks like we picked the right woman for the job!" Cate answered.

"Aye, I concur, Lady Cate," Mrs. Fraser said with a firm nod.

"Well, I'll be upstairs," Cate said before leaving.

"Dining room?" Molly questioned.

"Yes," Cate confirmed.

"Not in your dungeon?" Mrs. Fraser quipped.

"Not today!" Cate exclaimed. "I finished all the sorting! Now I'm going to move on to Douglas's journals. I hope to find some great information for my book."

"I dare say you will. Interesting man, Douglas MacKenzie. He's a bit of a local legend," Mrs. Fraser answered.

"Local legend?" Molly prompted in a questioning voice.

"Aye," Mrs. Fraser confirmed. "The builder of this old place has quite the reputation."

Cate pursed her lips and narrowed her eyes. "Do you mind if I stay for breakfast and ask you more about him?"

Mrs. Fraser raised her eyebrows at Cate. "All right," she agreed.

Cate smiled at her as she removed the place setting from the tray on the island and placed it on the table. A second breakfast at the servants' table, she reflected. Mrs. Fraser was getting soft.

"And don't you go thinking I'm turning soft, Lady Cate. This is for the sake of your research only!"

"I wouldn't dream of it, Mrs. Fraser," Cate said as she held in a chuckle.

"And today, we will bring your bowl to you. Since this isn't your day off!" Mrs. Fraser declared.

Cate settled herself at the table, not willing to argue. Jack and Mr. Fraser pushed through the door into the kitchen. Riley and Bailey, who had curled near the door, greeted them with tail wags.

"Well, good morning, Sir Riley and Mr. Bailey!" Jack exclaimed. "What are we doing here this fine morning? Still rustling breakfast from Mrs. Fraser and Miss Molly?"

"Lady Cate is joining us again this morning," Molly explained before Cate could.

Jack raised his eyebrows as he scratched Riley's belly. "Again? Why, Mrs. Fraser, have you gone soft?"

Mrs. Fraser harrumphed. "Certainly not, young Jack!" she protested.

"No," Cate defended her. "Mrs. Fraser has allowed me to stay so I can hear the tales of Douglas MacKenzie!"

"Aye, a strange duck, that one," Mr. Fraser added with a nod.

Mrs. Fraser placed a full bowl of oatmeal in front of Cate, along with several toppings. "As I'm sure you discovered in that dusty dungeon," Mrs. Fraser agreed.

Jack filled his bowl and took a seat across from Cate. "The lab of the mad scientist," Jack stated with another dramatic shiver. "It's frightening down there!"

"It's not!" Cate countered. "It's very interesting!"

"He has somewhat of a reputation as a Dr. Frankenstein, yes," Mrs. Fraser admitted as she joined them at the table.

Molly gulped at Mrs. Fraser's description. "Dr. Frankenstein?" she questioned. "What kind of experiments was he doing in that dungeon?"

Mrs. Fraser chuckled a bit. "He didn't build a monster sewn together with dead people's body parts. At least not to my knowledge," Mrs. Fraser answered.

"Perhaps not, but the creepy stuff down there suggests he did some sort of strange experiments," Jack contended.

Molly eyed them each around the table. "What kind of stuff?" she asked with a wrinkled nose.

"Mostly lab equipment and a few odd inventions," Cate explained.

Jack shook his head as he swallowed a spoonful of oatmeal topped with brown sugar. "No. Nope. Strange contraptions, odd apparatus, disturbing devices. It's a dungeon. A torture chamber."

Molly's eyes grew wide.

"It's not!" Cate repeated. "He appears to have been an avid inventor. I'm not sure what everything is, but it seems he tried to invent some form of electrical lighting and perhaps a crude attempt at an early communication device similar to a phone." Cate shrugged.

"Aye, an inventor," Mr. Fraser agreed. "Many describe him that way."

"And I'd bet many more contend he's an evil scientist," Jack suggested.

"Some do, some don't," Mrs. Fraser confirmed. "Some say he toyed with things he shouldn't. Others claim he was an eccentric experimenter with fantastical ideas."

"Hmm," Cate murmured as she pondered the information. "What things shouldn't he have toyed with?"

"They claim Douglas's interests ran toward the occult. Some say he was a devil worshipper. Others claim he investigated the line between life and death, including attempting to restore life," Mrs. Fraser explained.

Molly pulled her lips into a grimace. "Devil worship in the basement of this castle?" She glanced around the room as though searching for signs of the supernatural in every corner.

"And the other side?" Cate inquired.

"They maintain Douglas was nothing more than eccentric. An avid reader and researcher, he fiddled with all sorts of things to pass his time, no more."

"Sounds like typical gossip," Cate replied.

"There is one odd tale that persists through the centuries," Mr. Fraser chimed in.

"Oh?" Cate inquired.

"Aye," Mrs. Fraser agreed. "One persistent rumor has followed that man through the centuries."

"What's the rumor?" Molly choked out, her voice just above a whisper.

Mrs. Fraser leaned forward, her eyes alight with mischief and her eyebrows raised. "That he was a warlock!"

CHAPTER 3

*A*s Mrs. Fraser uttered the word "warlock", lightning flashed and thunder boomed overhead. Both dogs jumped at the loud sound as the sky continued to rumble. Molly jumped with them, shrinking down at the loud roar.

"A warlock?" Cate inquired, a hint of incredulousness in her voice.

"Aye, a warlock," Mrs. Fraser said with a nod.

Molly gulped again. "Wh-Why did they believe that?" she stammered.

"Oh, they presented a whole host of evidence," Mrs. Fraser explained. "Claimed he could appear and disappear at will, summon spirits and he concocted strange potions."

Molly's forehead wrinkled, and she bit her lower lip. "S-Summon spirits?"

Cate cocked her head at Molly's concerned expression. "Oh, Molly, you don't honestly believe this, do you?" she asked.

Molly shrugged. Her eyes darted around the kitchen, glancing from wall to wall and then to the ceiling. "There's usually some truth in rumors!"

"The castle isn't haunted. There are no spirits here," Cate assured her. "And there are no such things as warlocks."

"How do you explain the peculiar equipment in the lab, then?" Jack queried.

Molly glanced between Jack and Cate before focusing on Cate for an answer. "He was a curious guy," Cate answered with a shrug. "In his day and age, people mistook curiosity for witchcraft. Even into the late 1700s, the rumors of witchcraft persisted, particularly in small communities like this one."

Cate glanced at Molly. "It's fine," Cate assured her. "These types of tales exist in every country. They're used to explain away strange behavior people couldn't or didn't want to explain or were jealous of. There's likely a reasonable explanation for all of it!"

"Appearing and disappearing?" Molly questioned.

Cate shrugged again. "It's a large castle. Perhaps they lost track of him or perhaps he used a secret passage, making him appear magical when he was not."

"Smart, Lady Cate," Mrs. Fraser said with a wag of her finger. "Douglas was also known to have a jovial spirit and a good sense of humor in addition to his curious nature."

Cate nodded. "He probably liked to play tricks on people. In a castle this size, it wouldn't be hard to do. Same with the spirits. And his supposed potions were likely his chemistry experiments."

Molly knit her brow further as she considered Cate's explanation. "Trust me," Cate continued. "I'm a historian. These stories persist in every culture across the board. They are nothing more than scary fireside tales! There are no such things as warlocks."

"She's correct, Molly," Mrs. Fraser added. "While you'll still hear that rumor around town, there're no such things as warlocks. It's nonsense! Good for an entertaining tale on a stormy night. That's likely how the rumor took root! Some servants chatting as lightning lit their faces and thunder boomed overhead. Likely embellished for dramatic effect and an interesting yarn. There are no ghosts here. I've lived my entire life on this estate, I know!"

Molly slouched a bit, easing the crinkle in her forehead. She nodded without speaking.

"Oh, Miss Molly," Mrs. Fraser said with a chuckle as she patted Molly's hand. "I was only telling you in jest. It's just a silly rumor! There's no truth to it."

Molly straightened her shoulders and nodded again. "You're right. I'm letting my imagination run away with me."

"Now, we'd better get breakfast cleaned up and start our baking. There are no ghosts around here to do it for us!"

Molly cracked a smile for the first time during the conversation. "I'm glad. I'd rather bake myself. I hear ghosts use too much leavening!"

Mrs. Fraser chuckled at Molly's joke as they began to clear the table. "Well, that's my cue," Cate said. "Good luck with your baking and thank you for the entertaining stories about Douglas!"

"You're welcome, Lady Cate. Good luck with your dungeon."

Cate climbed the stairs to the main level, with Riley and Bailey in tow. Mrs. Fraser's words rung in her mind as she pulled the doors open to the library. Riley trotted toward the fireplace and collapsed in a heap near it. Cate eyed the roaring fire. The flames danced in the fireplace, keeping the damp chill of the Scottish morning air at bay. Bailey meandered toward Riley and curled in a ball next to him.

"I won't be long downstairs today, boys," Cate assured them as she opened the secret passage. "I'm just going to bring the journals upstairs and work here."

Cate plugged in the lighting and peered down the stairs.

As she descended them, her eyes scanned the room. A chill passed over her. She tried to reassure herself it was merely the damp air seeping through the stone walls rather than the haunting words Mrs. Fraser imparted over breakfast.

Cate chuckled. "There are no such things as warlocks," she reminded herself aloud. Her eyes found the stack of journals in the floor's center. She'd focus on those today near the warmth of the fireplace.

She gathered several of the leather journals into her arms. She'd need to make several trips to move them all. After three trips, she'd lugged all thirteen of the journals upstairs and made a pile near her favorite armchair.

Cate sank into it after retrieving a few cleaning materials. She pulled a blanket over her, even though the warmth of the fire reached her seat.

She began by dusting the books before using saddle soap to clean the leather and remove centuries of dirt and dust. Cate stared at the stack of newly cleaned journals. Had she spent the time cleaning to postpone the inevitable?

With a deep sigh, Cate decided she could no longer delay the task of examining the interiors of each journal. She pulled one from the top of the stack. Her first task would be to attempt to order the journals. Cate studied the exterior, searching for a mark or brand indicating the journal's number.

The smooth brown leather displayed no such marks. Cate flipped open the front cover. The front cover's interior contained a table of twenty-five numbers. The values, ranging from one to twenty-five, seemed to be in random order. Cate wondered if they may be some indication of dates, perhaps giving the time period in which the journal was written.

But why five rows of numbers, Cate pondered? And why five numbers in each row? Dates consisted of three pieces of information in most cases: month, day and year. Or in the case of European dates: day, month, year. Perhaps the last number in the row contained the year and the first four contained a range.

Cate glanced down the final column. No, her mind corrected. The years ranged too far apart and made no sense. She focused on the first number on the page. Seven. She'd found thirteen journals. Perhaps this was the seventh of the thirteen.

What the other numbers meant escaped Cate. However, this theory was her best so far. She glanced to the first page after the cover. *Journal of Douglas MacKenzie* was scrawled across it.

Cate flipped to the next page. An array of random letters filled it. Her forehead creased as she studied the writing. She searched for words within the gibberish but found none. Written with careful precision, Cate could not identify anything distinguishable. There were barely any breaks indicating words or other grammatical structures. What was this, she pondered?

She recalled her task of ordering the journals. Instead of searching further in this journal, Cate selected the next book from the stack and opened it to the first page. A similar inscription graced the first page, confirming this book was another of Douglas MacKenzie's journals.

She glanced to the interior of the front cover. A grid of twenty-five numbers was scribbled there. Cate noted the first number on the page was three. Perhaps this was the third journal, she mused. She set it on top of the previous journal and reached for the next in the stack.

Cate peered at the cover's interior. The number twelve sat in the first position of the grid. She set it underneath the journal marked with a seven. So far, so good, she mused. Perhaps her assumption would prove correct.

Cate pulled a fourth journal onto her lap and studied the inside of the front cover. Her heart sank as she read the first of the twenty-five numbers on the page. Twenty-one. There were only thirteen journals. At least that Cate had found. Perhaps there were more journals and Cate hadn't found them all, she ruminated. Or perhaps she was wrong about her theory.

Cate opened all the journals and placed them in order by the first number. If her theory proved correct, she was missing twelve journals. She considered returning to the secret office to search for them but discarded the idea. She'd been over every inch of the space. No other journals existed there.

Cate stared in the air as her mind processed the conundrum. Perhaps the journals were housed somewhere else. She glanced at the bookshelves in front of her. What better place to store journals than in the library, she thought? She pushed up to standing. All the journals shared the same characteristic brown leather with a burned leaf pattern ringing the edges. If other journals were stored here, she could identify them by this characteristic.

Cate approached the first bookshelf and examined each shelf. None of the volumes matched the journals' style. She spent the next hour searching every shelf and book for more journals. None existed.

With a long exhale, Cate sank back into the leather armchair. She stared at the stack of journals. She was missing something.

Cate grabbed the first journal from the stack. She studied the grid of numbers again. Nothing new jumped out at her. Cate moved to the title page. Other than the pronouncement of the journal's owner, no other marks were on the page.

Cate checked the backside of the page, finding nothing. This journal, too, contained a nonsensical framework of letters. Cate tried to read them left to right, right to left, up to down and down to up. No combination spelled anything recognizable as English.

Cate flipped to the next page and found a similar set of markings. She spent another ninety minutes flipping through the more than two hundred written pages. She uncovered nothing.

Cate turned to the final page of the journal. No words were recorded on this last page. Before closing the journal, Cate inspected the back cover's interior. Scrawled in the bottom right corner was a mark. Cate squinted at it and brought the book closer to her face. She identified the symbol as a two.

Did this indicate the order of the journals? Cate grabbed the next journal, pulling open the back cover and checking the bottom right corner. Her pulse quickened as she found a tiny number scrawled there. Cate squinted at it, making out the number seven.

She pulled another journal from the stack and opened it to the same location. The number four appeared in the corner. Cate worked her way through the remaining journals, finding numbers from one to thirteen.

She stared at the new stack of journals next to her, pleased with her work. If her theory proved correct, she had managed to order the journals. Perhaps this achievement would assist her in unraveling the information inside.

Cate glanced at the number grid inside the front cover. The book, marked with the number one on the back cover, contained the number seven in the first spot. What did the numbers refer to, she pondered? She stared at the lattice of numbers, but they provided no answers.

She turned the page and narrowed her eyes at the letters inscribed on the thick paper. Carefully penned in all capital letters, words made little sense. The writing appeared almost to form a grid on the page. Cate counted the letters across the page, finding they numbered twenty-five. What did they mean? Were the letters connected to the numbers on the interior cover? How?

A voice interrupted her thoughts. "That spot looks far more comfortable than your dungeon, Lady Cate," Molly said.

Cate twisted to face her, closing the journal and setting it on the stack. "I'll admit it is much more comfortable," Cate said. "AND warmer!"

"I've got your lunch," Molly said, raising the tray in the air before setting it on the coffee table in front of Cate. Both dogs climbed to their feet to sniff at it.

"Thanks, Molly," Cate answered. "I hadn't even realized the time!

"Just like you, Lady Cate. Once you started working, you'd lose track of everything. What have you got there?" Molly waved her hand to signal the stack of journals.

Cate picked up the first one and opened to the first page. "These are Douglas MacKenzie's journals," she said, showing the inscription on the first page. "I found them in his lab."

Molly shifted her eyes sideways, giving the open bookcase an uneasy glance. "You mean... the dungeon?" she questioned.

"It's not a dungeon," Cate said with a chuckle. "It's just a workspace. It's really interesting! You should take a look!"

Molly peered at the open bookshelf again. She shifted her weight from side to side. "Umm," Molly murmured, her voice an octave above its normal volume, "maybe another time."

Cate stood. "I'll show you," Cate offered. "Come on!"

"No!" Molly answered. "No, no!" She held her hands out to stop Cate's progress. "You've got your lunch and I should be getting downstairs to mine. Maybe another time."

Cate held in a chuckle. "Okay, another time," she agreed as she sank into the armchair again.

"Have a good lunch, Lady Cate. Oh! By the way," Molly exclaimed as she backed to the door, "those shortbread cookies or biscuits if you prefer that term, are my second attempt. See what you think!"

"I can't wait to try them!" Cate called to her. "Thanks, Molly!"

Cate spent her lunch pondering the gibberish contained in the books. Her mind tried to connect the numbers and letters, though she came to no definite conclusions. After lunch, she dodged raindrops on an afternoon walk with the dogs.

As she returned to the library following their walk, Cate ran into Jack. He juggled a few boxes of lightbulbs.

"Lady Cate!" he exclaimed. "Sir Riley and Mr. Bailey, how are you? I'd give you a proper pet, but I've got my hands full."

"I see that! Need help?" Cate inquired as two boxes teetered dangerously on the top of his stack.

"Aye, I believe I do," Jack admitted.

Cate collected several boxes from the top of the pile. "Where are these headed?"

"Ballroom," he answered.

"ALL of them?" Cate questioned.

"Aye, Lady Cate. Those chandeliers have a good number of lightbulbs on each. I've got to climb that massive ladder to change them."

"Ah," Cate exclaimed as realization set in, "so may as well change them all at once."

"You're a smart lady, Lady Cate," Jack said with a wink.

"I don't blame you," she said as they approached the ballroom. "I'll help. You head up the ladder, I'll unbox and hand these up."

"I won't say no, though I hope you don't dock my pay for lack of effort."

Cate chuckled as she shook her head. "Since you are climbing the ladder, I won't."

"Mighty nice of you, Lady Cate," Jack said as he ascended the ladder. Cate stayed below and began to pull lightbulbs from the boxes and hand them up.

"How is your dungeon project coming?" Jack inquired as they worked.

Cate sighed as she pulled another bulb from its box.

"That good, huh?" Jack said as he reached down for it.

Cate nodded. "Yeah, that about sums it up."

"What's the dead-end? Or are you just realizing how creepy that dungeon really is?"

Cate chuckled. "It's not creepy!" she insisted. "I finished all my sorting. I figured the best place to move to is reading those journals we found the first night."

"But?" Jack prompted when Cate didn't continue.

Cate shrugged. "But I can't read them," she responded. "They're gibberish."

"Old English or Scottish?" Jack inquired.

"No," Cate said with a shake of her head as she handed up another lightbulb. "No, I'd recognize that. This isn't English at all."

"Foreign language, maybe?" Jack suggested.

"Could be," Cate answered. "Though I've never seen any language like this before. And another strange thing is it's written in all capitals in almost a grid-like pattern."

Jack climbed down to the floor and dragged the ladder to another chandelier. "Perhaps he was practicing his penmanship." He grinned at Cate.

"I'm really surprised your comedy career never took off, Jack," Cate jested.

Jack climbed the ladder again. "So, it's some form of encryption, then?"

"That's what I'd imagine it is. What specific type of encryption, I'm not sure. I'll need to work on it and dig up some information to decode it. I may even need to ask a few experts."

Jack stopped his work and fixed his gaze on Cate. "Cate, those journals could…"

Cate held up her hand, stopping his speech. "I know, I know," she said. "Information for our eyes only. I can't give the text to anyone, but I may need to consult with a few people from my old university to see if they can suggest any decryption programs to help me."

Jack nodded. "Okay, just watch how much you share with them. We don't need any information getting out that shouldn't."

"I'll be careful," Cate promised.

"Lady Cate promising to be careful, what a leap forward for mankind."

"Very funny, Jack."

"Why not start with something other than the journals?" Jack inquired.

"What else would I start with? I have no idea what some of his inventions are and his sketches seem to be encoded in a similar way."

"So, crack the code on the journals and you'll crack the code on everything, most likely."

"Right," Cate said with a nod. "And since the journals contain the most text, they should provide the most information for decryption."

Jack descended the ladder and collected the empty boxes scattered around Cate. "I wish you luck, Lady Cate. I must admit, I'm rather interested in the contents of those journals."

Cate raised her eyebrows at him. "What's this? Jack Reid interested in something beyond estate affairs?"

"Aye, I'm hoping it contains information that will make us stop time traveling," he said with a wink.

"I'll keep you informed, but," Cate said, clapping her hand on his shoulder, "don't get your hopes up."

Cate's afternoon kept her busy reviewing details for her upcoming meeting with Mrs. Campbell. The work provided a welcome break from her frustrating inability to make progress with Douglas's journals.

Despite that, Cate found her gaze drawn to the stack of books every few minutes. She fought to concentrate on the task at hand. The work took twice as long with her wandering mind. She finished as her dinner tray arrived.

She ended her evening curled by the fire with a book. Written in standard English, Cate was pleased she didn't need to decode it.

*** * * ***

Cate stared at the encoded text in the journal as she sat at the library's desk. The black ink against the cream page stared back at her. The block letters in a neat grid gave her no clue about how to proceed. She glanced outside at the darkened sky. Rain pelted the windows as gray clouds shielded the stars from shining.

Cate yawned as she watched the raindrops slide down the window. She'd given up on sleep hours ago, choosing to rise from her bed and wander to the library to consider her latest conundrum.

Cate glanced back to the page. She swallowed hard. The letters danced across the paper. She blinked her eyes a few times. She must be too tired, she surmised, as she closed her eyes to rest them for a moment.

When she opened them, she was shocked at what she witnessed. The letters ceased their rhythmic motion and melted from the page. Cate pushed the book away as she leapt from her seat and backed away from the desk.

Lightning tore through the night sky and thunder clapped. Cate glanced outside. As the sky darkened again, Cate spotted her reflection in the glass. Her brows knit as she noticed the secret passage open behind her.

She hadn't opened it. But yet it clearly stood ajar in the reflection. As she considered it, the mirror image changed. Cate gasped, pressing her hand over her mouth as a figure formed at the opening.

Cate spun to face it. She inched back step by step.

"Hello, Catherine," the voice growled at her.

"Wh-who are you?" Cate asked, her voice quivering with fear. She squinted toward the opening. The man's features, shrouded in shadow, made him impossible to identify.

The man snickered at the question. His laughter grew louder and louder, roaring through the room.

The desk stopped any further backward progress Cate could make. She stumbled as she bumped into it. Cate clapped her hands over her ears as she sank to the ground. His shrieking laughter threatened to make her ears bleed as the sound howled through the room.

A tear fell to Cate's cheek as she struggled to maintain her composure. The man's chortling died down. She glanced at the opening. Red eyes glowed back at her.

Cate swallowed hard and rose to stand. She squared her shoulders and wiped the tear from her cheek. "Who are you?" she demanded.

"Oh, Catherine," the man's voice chided. He stepped toward her, still shrouded in the blackness of the gaping hole to the secret lab.

The lights flickered before extinguishing. Cate reeled

around, pawing through the desk in search of a flashlight. Her trembling hands clawed through the drawers until her fingertips touched the cylindrical object.

Cate curled her fingers around the base and pushed the toggle button. No light shone from the lens. Cate shook the flashlight and smacked it against her hand. She pushed the button again in a desperate attempt to coerce it to light.

Lightning tore through the sky again, and the room glowed for an instant. As thunder boomed overhead, cold hands grasped Cate's arms. She froze, her muscles tensing, her shoulders rising toward her ears.

Hot breath swept past her neck and a voice whispered in her ear. "I am your worst nightmare."

* * *

Cate gasped for air as she shot up to sitting. Sweat beaded on her forehead. Tears stained her cheeks. Her chest heaved as she sucked in deep breaths of air.

Cate glanced around, finding her surroundings familiar. Soft white moonlight glowed through her bedroom window. She clutched at the bedsheets, drawing them closer to her as her breathing stabilized and her heart ceased to race.

Another nightmare, Cate reflected. She sniffled and wiped at her cheeks before retrieving her journal from the night table. She propped pillows behind her before switching on the bedside lamp.

Cate squinted as her eyes adjusted to the bright light. She paged through the journal to the first blank page and noted the date and details of her newest nightmare. Cate's hairs stood on end and her flesh turned to goosebumps as she recalled the final haunting words the man uttered to her.

After jotting them in her notebook, she snapped it shut, as though this would close the subject. She clutched the journal for a few more moments as she forced her nerves to settle. Cate closed her eyes and breathed in a deep, long breath.

Her eyes snapped open as a cold, wet nose nudged her hand. The corners of her mouth turned upward as her eyes met Riley's sparkling, dark brown eyes. Behind him, Bailey stared curiously at her, his head cocked to the side as he studied her.

"I'm okay, boys, just a bad dream," Cate assured them. She set the notebook and pen on the night table and patted the bed on either side of her. Riley curled in a ball on her right, his head resting on her thigh. Bailey hopped over her legs and nestled into a spot on her left.

Cate flicked off the light, plunging the room into darkness. She rubbed the dogs' heads as she settled back into her pillows. Riley offered her hand a lick before settling his head on her leg.

The calming effect of both boys with her settled Cate back into a dreamless sleep.

CHAPTER 4

"Thanks, Mrs. Campbell!" Cate called as Isla Campbell, the town's librarian, historical society president and party planner extraordinaire, climbed behind the wheel of her car.

After a three-hour meeting to plan details of her anniversary party, Cate's morning was spent. Her mind swam with party nuances, from linen patterns to champagne flutes to hors d'oeuvres. Certain she could not keep track of every minor detail required, Cate appreciated Mrs. Campbell's ability to oversee them all.

"Is the party czar gone?" Jack voiced behind her.

Cate jumped, startled by his sudden appearance. Details of her dream in which the man, who described himself as her worst nightmare, crept into her mind.

"Oops, sorry, I didn't mean to startle you, Lady Cate," Jack apologized.

Cate twisted to face Jack. "No problem and yes, she is."

"Mrs. Fraser sent me up to see if the ninny was gone yet or if she needed to delay lunch."

"No, I just need to gather my things from the sitting room and drop them off in the library and we can head down!"

Jack followed Cate into the sitting room off the foyer. Fabric samples, guest lists, layouts and menus lay scattered across the coffee table. Cate scraped them together, forcing the items into as neat a pile as she could, then stuffed them into a large file folder.

Jack grimaced at the sight. "And what outlandish requests does the party czar have this time?" Jack inquired. "Perhaps she'd like us to move the castle stone by stone to the Caribbean for an island party. Or maybe she'd like us to erect seven stages across the property and invite the world's biggest musical acts."

Cate chuckled at Jack's assessment as she stuffed a few wayward papers into the folder. "Nothing that extravagant," Cate admitted, "though she's definitely scaling this up to be the 'event of the year.'"

Jack slumped his shoulders and closed his eyes for a moment. "Why is every event the 'event of the year' with her?"

Cate shrugged as she pulled the folder to her chest. "Sorry, Lady Cate," Jack continued. "Ever since she asked us to bring in snow machines to ensure snow for the holiday party, I expect her requests to be over the top."

"Oh, this is going to be over the top, all right," Cate replied. "She insisted. Nothing but class, top of the line all the way around. A guest list to rival all other guest lists."

"I didn't expect anything less from Isla Campbell," Jack responded as they navigated to the library.

"You should have seen her face when I suggested an old-fashioned American picnic."

"I'm surprised the woman is still alive, Lady Cate. You could have killed her with that suggestion!"

"I may have come close," Cate admitted, recalling the

shocked expression on Mrs. Campbell's face. It may have been the one time she'd rendered the woman speechless. "Her expression was priceless."

"Damn," Jack muttered. "I wish I'd have been there. I would have loved to have witnessed that!"

Cate pushed the doors open to the library and crossed to the desk. She dumped the party planning materials on it. A chill passed over her as she stood facing the same window she had in her dream. She swallowed hard and glanced at the now-closed bookshelf passage.

"Someone walk over your grave, Lady Cate?" Jack inquired.

"No," Cate said, stifling a yawn. "Recalling the details of yet another nightmare involving this room."

"Another?" Jack questioned.

"Another," Cate said with a sigh. "This time I was working here in the library, trying to translate Douglas's journals. The letters started to run off the page, and I suddenly felt frightened. As I backed away from the desk, I caught a reflection of the room in the window. The bookcase was open, and the figure of a man stood in the shadows."

"Could you identify him? Did he speak to you?"

Cate shook her head. "I couldn't make out his features, but he did speak. He said 'Hello, Catherine.'"

"Same as before," Jack noted.

"Yep, same as before. He always calls me by my full name. In this dream, I asked who he was, and he laughed. Not a normal laugh. It filled the room. It was frightening, almost demonic. Then the lights went out. I raced to retrieve the flashlight, and before I could get it working, he was behind me. He grabbed me and said 'I am your worst nightmare.' Then I woke up."

Jack frowned as he processed the information. "Your worst nightmare? Well, that rules me out."

Cate screwed up her face at him. "What?"

"While I may be the man of your dreams, Lady Cate, I'm not your worst nightmare," Jack joked with a grin.

"That's very funny, Jack," Cate groaned. "It's not you, he doesn't sound like you."

"Douglas?" Jack proposed.

"Perhaps. It would fit. He's tied to the bookcase and the secret room. But why would Douglas be my worst nightmare?"

Jack shrugged. "Who else could it be? Who else would be tied to all this?"

"I'm not sure. Douglas is also my guess, but it makes no sense. Unless it's all just some strange reaction to stress or something and none of it has any meaning."

"These have gone on far too long for them to be meaningless."

"Perhaps when I decrypt the journals, I'll find another clue."

Jack knit his brows, placing his finger on his lips in thought. "It's always been in the library, somehow related to the secret passage. To Douglas's secret office. Now his journals show up. It must be Douglas, right?" He snapped his fingers and pointed to Cate.

"What?" she questioned.

"His accent! You wouldn't recognize his voice. You've never met him..."

"Yet," Cate added.

Jack offered Cate a flat glance. She shrugged in return. "Does he sound Scottish? Like Randolph?"

Cate glanced to the floor and pursed her lips as she recalled the voice. She gave a slow shake of her head. "No," she admitted. She returned her gaze to Jack. "No, his accent isn't Scottish! It's British!"

"You're certain?"

Cate nodded her head as she chewed her lower lip. "One hundred percent certain. That voice... it haunts me even when I'm awake. His 'Hello, Catherine' is so creepy. It rings in my head for hours after those nightmares. It's unforgettable. He's British. Upper-class, well-bred I'd say from his speech pattern."

"Likely not Douglas, then. I'd bet my bottom dollar he had a Scottish brogue, like Randolph. Perhaps not as thick as mine given his station, but nonetheless, Scottish."

Cate nodded in agreement. "That's a likely bet, yes. It doesn't prove it's not Douglas, but it does cast doubt on him."

"That coupled with the question as to why he'd be your worst nightmare, I'd say someone else is haunting your dreams, Lady Cate."

She focused her gaze on Jack. "But..." She paused as her forehead wrinkled. "Who is?"

* * *

The afternoon hours waned as Cate settled in the library. She opened the first of Douglas's journals and stared at the undecipherable text. The conversation with Jack earlier stuck in her mind. Were they correct in assuming Douglas was not the man haunting her? Who else would it be? And why?

Thoughts danced through Cate's brain as she stared blankly at the page in front of her. Perhaps deciphering these journals would lead her to some conclusion. She couldn't see how, but it couldn't hurt.

She opened a browser on her laptop and navigated to Google Translate. Upon closer inspection, she identified small spaces between the letters that seemed to indicate word breaks.

She typed in the first line of the journal. On the off-chance Jack's foreign language idea was correct, perhaps

Google Translate could identify it. The translator came up with nothing. Its closest identified language produced no translation at all.

Cate spent fifteen minutes shifting letters around in case the spaces between words were not where she assumed they were. The translator was not able to offer any additional information.

With a shake of her head, she crossed "foreign language" off the top of her list of theories. She stared again at the first line:

J IDUP ZTHBESL VGPR XDVPMSD YI

Twenty-five indecipherable characters seemed to be broken into six words. Perhaps it made up a simple cryptogram, Cate pondered. She stared at the next line to determine if she could make any headway with this theory.

RIIPXGXVZ SFL DENRHQRF GQ OITLKOCXZDP

The sentence continued to the next line:

BI H QMZYIQ TCP CVJFFEB.

Cate typed on her keyboard and searched for a cryptogram solver. She entered the first sentence into the solver and clicked the Auto-solve button. The solver worked as Cate drummed her fingers on the desk. After a few moments, the results appeared. Cate scrolled through the output. The top-scoring result provided another nonsensical array of letters.

Cate continued down the list. A few solutions contained English words but none of them provided an entire sentence of them. With a sigh, she crossed "Substitution Cipher" off her list.

Cate glanced around the room as she considered her other options to break Douglas's code. Riley approached, stretching as he placed his front paws on Cate's leg.

"Hiya, buddy," Cate said as she scooped him into her arms. She ruffled the fur on his head, tracing the white streak from his nose to between his ears. "Got any ideas on this code?"

Riley leaned back and stretched, offering only a large yawn. "How about you, Bailey?" Cate inquired of the other small dog. He lifted his head from the rug beneath him. "Any ideas on how to break this code?"

The gray and white dog set his head back down on the rug and stared at Cate. He wagged his curly pigtail a few times but offered no other response.

"Well, you two aren't any help! You also aren't far behind me with ideas."

Cate glanced at the page of letters in front of her. "This is NOT my area of expertise!" she exclaimed.

Riley glanced at Cate as she spoke. "Yeah, I know, buddy. When in doubt, research. Which I definitely CAN do." She kissed the pup on his head and set him on the floor. "Can that research wait until tomorrow?" Molly inquired from behind her.

"Already?" Cate questioned, glancing at her timepiece.

"Yep!" Molly announced as she brandished a tray of dinner. "Over there or by the fireplace?"

"By the fireplace," Cate requested. "Thanks. I'm done with this for the day."

"Making progress?" Molly asked as she slid the tray onto the coffee table.

Cate flicked the journal shut and closed her laptop. "No, hence the need for research. I'm stuck!"

"Well, that shouldn't last long," Molly said. "I've never known Dr. Catherine Kensie to be stuck for long."

"We'll see," Cate said. "Decrypting codes is not up my alley. I'm a historian, not a code breaker!"

"What code are you trying to break?" Molly questioned.

"Oh, those journals I found downstairs in Douglas's lab.

They are all encrypted in some way. It looks like the pages were written in gibberish."

"Hmm, that's weird. Why would he write his journals in code?"

Cate shrugged. Though she could elicit a guess, it wasn't one she could share with Molly. "He seemed eccentric. I guess just another one of his eccentricities."

"Hmm," Molly mumbled. "Have you asked Ken Matthews from Aberdeen Math? His expertise is cryptology."

"Oh, right! I didn't know him well. I didn't remember that was his specialty."

"He's a really nice guy," Molly informed her. "I'm sure he'd be happy to help. He'd probably be excited to see a real live cipher in action!"

"If I can't make any headway, I may send him an email and see if he has any ideas."

"Well, it can wait until tomorrow. It's dinner time now!"

"You're starting to sound like Mrs. Fraser," Cate teased.

"She'll be very pleased with that assessment," Molly said with a grin.

"She's already very pleased with you," Cate said. "We're both really happy you're here."

"So am I," Molly answered. "Except now I'm afraid this castle is haunted after all that warlock talk."

"It's not haunted," Cate assured her.

"Yeah, remind me of that when you decipher that journal, and it's full of ghost stories," Molly said with a wink. "Enjoy your dinner, Lady Cate."

Cate thanked Molly again as she eased into her favorite armchair near the fireplace. Molly's words rung in her mind. She was certain Douglas's journals would be filled with such tales. It would be interesting to read his experiences. How had he discovered the anomaly within the castle walls? What incidents had he documented before he realized the circumstances? She wouldn't find out tonight, she reflected with a sigh.

* * *

Cate yawned as she stepped into the foggy morning air with Riley and Bailey. After another nightmare disturbed her sleep, Cate had spent the rest of the night tossing and turning. Between the mysterious journals and the nightmares, Cate's mind could not rest.

As she lay awake, staring at her ceiling, she'd also experienced another odd event. In the quiet stillness, Cate heard the characteristic loud ticking of her timepiece. The noise accompanied the timepiece interacting with a time rip. It indicated the moment when the wearer slipped through the time rip and returned to another era.

Cate grasped the watch and bolted upright. The second hand crept by for a second before returning to normal speed. Cate blinked her eyes several times as she stared at the watch face. She glanced around the room. Both dogs slept on the bed. All her things remained in the room. She hadn't passed through time into 1925, where the rip in her bedroom led.

As she shivered against the chilly morning air, she wondered if she had imagined it? Perhaps she had drifted off and dreamt it. She hadn't been rubbing the timepiece, so the trigger could not have activated.

In the cold light of morning, Cate assumed she imagined it. A trick of her mind as she drifted in and out of sleep, she reflected. Cate stared at the fog in the distance as it shrouded the moors surrounding the estate.

She pulled herself from her pensive mood. "Boys! Boys?" she called. She glanced around her, finding herself alone.

"Riley! Bailey!" Cate called as she searched the area.

A yip came from the side garden. Cate followed the noise.

She found both dogs in the same spot they had been in two days ago. Riley pawed at the ground. Bailey stared at the spot, his front legs flat on the ground with his back end high in the air.

"What are you two doing there again?" Cate inquired of them. Riley glanced to her, then back to the spot. He dragged his paw over it again.

Cate closed the distance between them and peered at the ground. She spotted nothing. "There's nothing there, boys."

Bailey leapt to all fours and let out another yip. Riley continued his mission to paw at the mysterious spot.

"You guys are silly," Cate said. "There's nothing there. Come on, let's go get our breakfast." She stalked a few steps away. Neither dog followed her. "Riley, Bailey, come on!" Both stared intently at the ground.

Cate returned and shooed them away. "Come on, boys. Time for breakfast. Stop that before you're both covered in mud from digging at that spot."

Cate corralled the two small dogs through the castle's kitchen door. After everyone said their good mornings and Cate fed her furry friends, she headed upstairs with the dogs in tow for her breakfast.

After finishing her breakfast, Cate settled at the library's desk with Douglas's journals. She hoped to make more progress today. She began her research with an internet search of popular cryptography methods in the late 1700s.

Cate scanned the list of search results before she selected a few sites and jotted down several notes. As she dug into the fourth site on her search list, a tinkling filled the air. Cate's phone vibrated across the desk's top.

Cate's stomach flip-flopped as she noted the caller: Isla Campbell. "Uh-oh," Cate mumbled as she swiped to answer the call.

"Hello, Mrs. Campbell," she said as the call connected.

"Lady Cate!" Mrs. Campbell's voice greeted her on the other end. "Thank GOODNESS you answered."

"What can I help you with?" Cate inquired.

"The samples I told you about yesterday JUST came across my desk. If you've got a moment this morning, I can run them right up to the castle for you to peek at before you approve."

"Oh, ah," Cate murmured as she searched for a reason to avoid the meeting.

"I just need to toss them into my car. I can be there in fifteen minutes!"

"You know, Mrs. Campbell, I really trust your judgment on this. And if you feel they are the best choice, I'm comfortable approving them sight unseen!"

"Absolutely not!" Mrs. Campbell argued. "This is the single most important party of your year, Lady Cate. We must achieve perfection. And I simply will not feel comfortable approving these choices without you viewing them first."

Cate sighed. She couldn't avoid it, she figured. But perhaps she could kill two birds with one stone. "Okay. I'm available all morning, though I really do trust you."

"A fact that I am aware of and most grateful for. Nonetheless, I shall see you in fifteen minutes!"

Cate ended the call after saying goodbye and stared at her laptop screen. While cryptography was not her expertise and not her cup of tea, she'd rather spend her time with a discussion of mathematics than linen selection.

Still, Cate mused, perhaps she could retrieve some information from the town's historian about her latest research project, the castle's original proprietor.

Cate shut her laptop and stowed her research materials. "You boys stay here," she instructed. "You know how Mrs. Campbell feels about pets."

Mrs. Campbell estimated fifteen minutes before her arrival. That gave Cate ten minutes at best before the woman arrived. After she settled the dogs by the fire in the library, she made a quick trip downstairs to inform Mrs. Fraser and Molly about the latest development.

Mrs. Fraser's eyes went wide as Cate imparted her change of plans for the morning. She placed her hand on her hip as she spoke. "You mean that ninny has invited herself here again? Will that woman's demands on your time never cease?"

"She's particularly excited about these linens, yet she won't order them until I've seen and approved of them."

Mrs. Fraser shook her head. "She'll have you worn out before your party with her antics."

"It's okay," Cate replied. "I plan to use her to gain some information about Douglas for my research." Cate winked at them.

"Well, I suppose that's one thing," Mrs. Fraser admitted. "And she'll make the perfect test subject for your cookies, Molly."

Molly removed a tray from the oven. "Mm-hm," Molly agreed.

"Though dinnae be surprised if she makes a rude comment. That woman wouldn't know how to compliment someone if you gave her a script."

"I'd better head up," Cate said. "She told me fifteen minutes."

"That means she'll be here in seven," Mrs. Fraser said.

Cate nodded as she backed from the kitchen.

"I'll send up the tray of tea and cookies as soon as I've got it ready, Lady Cate," Mrs. Fraser called as Cate traversed the hallway toward the stairway leading to the main floor.

"Thank you!" Cate shouted.

True to form, Mrs. Campbell's car wound down the driveway just as Cate got to the front door.

"Lady Cate!" she greeted her as she climbed from her car. "How fortunate you were available today. Though I can't imagine what else you may be doing."

Cate smiled at her as she considered the statement. "I have the samples. They are simply GORGEOUS," she said as she pulled several items from her car. "Wait until you see them!"

The woman bustled around the car and pushed past Cate into the foyer. "Sitting room, I assume?"

"You guessed it!" Cate answered. "I've got tea on the way up."

"Oh, how lovely. You didn't have to given that the meeting was impromptu. I'd hate to put Emily out. I know how she hates last-minute changes," Mrs. Campbell murmured.

"No trouble at all."

"Wonderful," Mrs. Campbell replied as she plopped onto the loveseat. "I do enjoy a good cuppa."

"And some cookies fresh from the oven from our newest addition, Molly! Mrs. Fraser is teaching her how to bake some of her favorites."

"Oh," Mrs. Campbell answered with a raise of her eyebrows. "There are so many good bakers in the area, I'll bet Molly could pick up lots of new tricks here."

"As long as she picks up all of Mrs. Fraser's, I'll be more than satisfied. She bakes one mean shortbread, and her chicken soup is really the best."

"Yes, well, anyway, we really should get down to business, I suppose," Mrs. Campbell said, changing the subject.

"Sure," Cate agreed. "Oh, and if you have a few moments after we discuss these linens, I hoped to speak with you on another matter."

Mrs. Campbell glanced up at Cate, her eyes narrowed as her mind attempted to guess the other matter. "Of course, Lady Cate, I always have time for you," she replied. "And if it isn't too much, I also had a second item to add to our impromptu agenda."

The opening of the door saved Cate from responding. Molly carried a tray of tea and cookies. "Hello, hello!" she exclaimed as she entered. Molly set the tray on the coffee table between Cate and Mrs. Campbell. "Tea and fresh shortbreads!"

"Thank you, Molly," Cate answered. "Mrs. Campbell is excited to try your cookies."

"I believe these are better than the last batch. They may be closing in on Mrs. Fraser's perfection." Molly held up her hand, flashing crossed fingers.

"Yes, well, thank you, Molly," Mrs. Campbell answered, dismissing her.

"Good luck with your linens," Molly said as she exited. She paused behind Mrs. Campbell and offered Cate a dramatic eye roll before disappearing through the door, her hand covering her mouth as she suppressed a giggle.

Cate poured tea for each of them and offered Mrs. Campbell the plate of cookies. She pulled one from the plate with the tips of her thumb and forefinger. The grimace on her face suggested she preferred not to try one.

"Okay, let's see the infamous linens!" Cate prodded as Mrs. Campbell stared at the cookie with disdain.

"Oh, yes," she answered. She set the cookie down untouched and pulled the linens from her messenger bag. "Here we are. Aren't they simply perfection? The classic look, the classy elegance. It screams Countess of Dunhavenshire."

Cate eyed the linens. Gold with a simple navy-blue pinstripe, Cate wasn't sure they "screamed" anything, but she did agree they provided a classic and elegant look. Mrs.

Campbell's ability to nail down details like these was beyond reproach.

Cate sipped her tea and nodded. "Yes, you are quite right," she agreed. "They are perfect."

Mrs. Campbell held them up and stared at them. She narrowed her eyes at the sample clutched in her hand. "Would a cranberry pinstripe be better? I wonder..."

"Oh, no, I really believe the blue is the better choice."

"Well, navy," Mrs. Campbell corrected.

"Yes. Navy. Navy and gold is a classic combination."

"But is it boring? Classic and classy are not always the same!" Mrs. Campbell warned.

"In this case, they are."

Mrs. Campbell squinted at the fabric sample again. She waved it around, studying it in different lights. Cate took another sip of her tea. "Yes. Yes, you are right. Cranberry simply would not do in this case."

"They really couldn't be more perfect," Cate said.

"Oh, I'm so glad you agree! Well, that was easier than I expected!"

"I'm not too difficult to please!" Cate answered.

"No, though your ideas sometimes differ from mine, Lady Cate." She chuckled a shrill cackling laugh. "Oh, my apologies, I'm recalling your suggestion of... a barbecue." Mrs. Campbell snorted with laughter.

"They are quite popular where I'm from. It seemed like a relaxed idea and the entire town could have participated."

"Definitely a very quaint idea, yes, but really, we need something more elegant and a bit more posh for a countess!"

"I'll be the first to admit you are far better at planning these than I am," Cate answered.

"While I appreciate the vote of confidence, I still prefer that we're both on the same page with all choices."

Cate smiled over her teacup. "Well, now that we are, you

mentioned a second agenda item?"

Mrs. Campbell waved her hand in the air. "I believe you mentioned one as well. Please, by all means, ask yours first."

"Mine may take a bit longer. I'd like to lean on your knowledge as town historian again regarding a former occupant. So, please, go ahead with yours before we move on to that discussion."

"Ah," Mrs. Campbell said, giving Cate a knowing glance. "Moving our interests from Randolph to another proprietor? There's certainly no shortage of tales about any of them!"

Cate was certain there wasn't from the town's gossip. "That tends to be the case in places like this," Cate noted. "Anyway, what was your other item?"

Mrs. Campbell explained. "As president of the historical society, I am a member of an exclusive group of historical society presidents across Scotland. Each year we host a large charitable event, centered around an auction. It occurs in late summer." She glanced to Cate, her eyes narrowing as she considered Cate's response.

"And you'd like a donation?" Cate queried as Mrs. Campbell paused.

"Well," Mrs. Campbell hedged. "In a way, yes."

Cate knit her brows as Mrs. Campbell responded. The woman continued. "Each year, one of the presidents organizes the event, The Presidents' Ball. It really is the event of the year for us, and it is quite an honor to be chosen as the event coordinator. I have tried for it a few times before, but I was always overlooked."

"What a shame," Cate commented. "Your planning skills are excellent. They'd be foolish not to select you."

"I appreciate the vote of confidence and in that way, there is something you can do to help me secure the spot."

"Oh?"

"The president must have a host selected. The host is

really a large part of the selection committee's consideration. In fact, the host can make or break the committee's choice."

A sinking feeling filled the pit of Cate's stomach. She'd hoped to give a donation, monetary or otherwise. Instead, she surmised she'd be offered the role of host. Her personality did not fit well into the circumstances, in her estimation. But...

Mrs. Campbell continued, "And I thought who would be more perfect to host this year's event than our newest Countess? Lady Cate, the American college professor turned Scottish countess! I'm certain with you as our host, the country's latest noblewoman, we'd be a shoo-in for the selection!

"And the boost it would give to the county and town," she babbled. "Not to mention showing off the beautiful castle and the grounds!"

"I..." Cate hedged, searching for an answer. Questions flew through her mind faster than she could process them.

"The historical society would handle everything, with me in the lead. What a thrill it would be for them to work on something like this. It would be the talk of the town for years to come..."

"I'd be happy to," Cate burst. Cate shoved all the questions from her mind. It didn't matter. The event was important to the region, the town and Mrs. Campbell. She'd deal with whatever she had to in order to make it work. With Mrs. Campbell at the helm, she had no doubt the event would be expertly planned and run.

"Oh!" Mrs. Campbell exclaimed. Her voice betrayed her surprise at Cate's acceptance. "Well, I will send our application in today! The moment I leave this meeting, I will prepare it and get it right to them! Thank you, Lady Cate!"

"You're welcome. My fingers will be crossed that we hear good news soon."

"Applications are due at the end of the month, but it never

hurts to be early. We'll hear back by April 3. Oh, so many ideas are running through my head. I'll begin documenting them all, so we're prepared in the event we're selected."

"I have no doubt the event you plan will be outstanding."

"Well, I have my afternoon cut out for me preparing our application! Now, you had a question for me?"

"Yes, I won't take up too much of your time so you can work on the application, but I wanted to gather any stories you had about the castle's original proprietor, Douglas."

Mrs. Campbell's expression changed to coy. A smirk crossed her lips, and she raised an eyebrow. She had a story all right, Cate mused.

"Ahhhh, Douglas," Mrs. Campbell murmured with a nod. "The man who started it all."

"Yes. I began my research for my book with Randolph after our conversation when I arrived. But now I've turned my attention toward Douglas."

"Oh, there certainly are tales," Mrs. Campbell assured her. "Douglas was quite the character."

"So I've heard."

"Of course, the first question on everyone's mind is how Douglas came into his money. Obviously, the MacKenzies before him did not have the wealth to build a castle then suddenly Douglas did!"

"Wise investments?" Cate suggested.

Mrs. Campbell chuckled. "Well, of course, that's what Douglas maintained, but that explanation simply did not add up."

"Were the MacKenzies before Douglas well-off?"

Mrs. Campbell shook her head vehemently. "No. The only thing royal about Douglas's parents was his father's name. Kendrick MacKenzie was a simple town doctor. Douglas left the area early in his twenties and returned home a wealthy earl."

"How?" Cate inquired, encouraging Mrs. Campbell to finish with her yarn.

"No one really knows," Mrs. Campbell whispered.

"Rumors?" Cate questioned.

"There is no shortage of those! Wise investments, as you mentioned, an unexpected inheritance from a befriended nobleman, spying for the crown, alchemy."

"Spying for the crown? Really?"

"Oh, yes, that suggestion was floated! Of course, other suggestions are far less innocuous!" Mrs. Campbell raised her eyebrow at Cate.

"Which are?"

"The most commonly agreed upon theory is Douglas involved himself in the black arts!"

"The black arts?" Cate repeated as a question.

"Yes. The rumors spring from the strange goings-on during and after the castle's construction. His unexplained wealth suddenly became explainable."

Cate raised her eyebrows, encouraging Mrs. Campbell to expound on her comments.

Mrs. Campbell leaned closer to Cate, her eyes darting around the room. "Human sacrifices, ritual killings, strange disappearances, devil worship."

"What?!" Cate exclaimed.

Mrs. Campbell nodded her head slowly. "Someone died in an 'accident' during the castle's building. Of course, no one believes that story. Most believe he was sacrificed by Douglas and his coven to appease dark powers."

"That's a bit far-fetched, isn't it?" Cate said.

Mrs. Campbell shrugged. "Is it? Considering the events that occurred here during those days? I'm not certain it is!"

"The accidental death?"

"The accidental death, strange noises, haunting sounds, Douglas disappearing mysteriously then reappearing, others doing the same. Odd shifts in the weather, unexplained winds, storm clouds appearing over the castle with no warning. Screams heard in the wee hours of the morning carrying all the way to town! Orders for odd materials by Douglas with peculiar explanations citing weird experiments. The evidence is endless."

"That's hardly evidence," Cate countered. "More likely conjecture based on things townsfolk couldn't explain."

"Well, people then didn't think scientifically like we do now but... there usually is a bit of truth to rumors. And there is the one story that persists throughout the ages."

"Oh? Regarding Douglas's ties to the dark side?"

"There's no specific mention of devil worship or murder, but the tale is bizarre, to say the least!"

"Do tell!" Cate prodded.

"The story begins shortly after the castle's completion. Douglas entertained several guests in the castle. Townsfolk reported the castle lit from the inside well into the night as he treated his guests to lavish dinner parties. Around this time, townsfolk reported strange happenings in the town. Mysterious attacks of madness, sick animals, dying crops.

"Then the tales take an even stranger turn. On one moonlit night, a few men walked home from the pub. As they did, a storm came out of nowhere. It centered over the castle. Black clouds blotted the moon from the sky. Booming thunder resounded, louder than anyone had heard before. Lightning brightened the night sky."

"Sounds frightening, though the storms here can be quite powerful," Cate noted, recalling the previous night's storms.

"Ah, but that's where the story gets interesting. The men swear the lightning shot from the ground up to the sky."

Cate scrunched up her face at the twist. Mrs. Campbell nodded at her. "Yes, lightning bolts shot from ground to sky in a dazzling display. A fireball burst from near the castle and flew around the estate. A tree suddenly burst into flames with no warning. Winds formed a tornado-like funnel that twisted and twirled toward the castle. Then, without warning, everything stopped. The clouds cleared, the fire extinguished, the lightning and thunder ceased, and the winds died. The moon returned, and the night quieted as though nothing had happened."

Cate raised her eyebrows. "That's quite a tale. Though two gentlemen returning from the pub after a night of drinking may not be the best source of information."

"That's where it gets even more intriguing," Mrs. Campbell explained. "Though those two gentlemen insisted they witnessed something incredible, their story would have likely been written off as fable."

"But?" Cate prompted.

"But around the time the men departed from the pub, the reverend's wife suffered a horrific nightmare in which she witnessed the destruction of Dunhaven Castle. She awoke from the nightmare and raced from her bed to the window to ensure the castle still stood. She, too, witnessed the fantastic events on the castle grounds. She woke her husband, and he also witnessed them.

"When the men retold their strange tale, the MacAlistairs admitted they witnessed the same events. Bolstered by their account, others came forward. In total, over one hundred people in Dunhaven beheld those bizarre events and their stories never wavered. Each of them told the exact same tale with the exact same details. It is those unwavering details that have persisted through centuries and part of the reason Dunhaven Castle's reputation lingers as haunted… or worse, even to this day."

"That's quite a story!"

"And every word true!" Mrs. Campbell insisted.

Cate smiled at her. "Even if it isn't, it makes for a fantastic opening chapter for my book!"

Mrs. Campbell grinned at her. "Yes, it does!"

Cate pondered it a moment. "Did Douglas entertain many guests on the estate? Related to his... black magic?"

"Oh, in those first days of the castle, Douglas entertained often! In fact, I'm certain he had quite the list of visitors from wealthy Americans to high-ranking noblemen!"

"Hmm, how interesting. Anyone in particular?"

"Bankers, shipping magnates, statesman, noblemen. Some even say your Thomas Jefferson stayed here!"

"What a colorful history the castle has! I can't wait to continue my research into that era. Well, I shouldn't take up too much more of your time, Mrs. Campbell. With the application due, I'm sure you're itching to get at it and get your ideas recorded."

"That I am, though I'm never too busy to share tales for your book!"

"And, as always, you are a wealth of information!"

Mrs. Campbell beamed at Cate as she gathered her materials. "I will forward you a copy of the application as soon as I've prepared it. We should begin planning even before the announcement so we can hit the ground running should we be selected."

"Sounds like a plan!" Cate said as she stood from the loveseat.

Mrs. Campbell gathered all her materials and Cate walked her to the door. The horn sounded as she pulled down the drive.

Cate spun on her heel and collected Riley and Bailey from the library before retrieving the tea tray to deliver to the kitchen.

"Is the ninny gone?" Mrs. Fraser inquired as Cate set the tea tray near the sink.

"What did she think of the cookies? Did she say?" Molly asked with hope in her voice.

Cate set a teacup in the sink and lifted the saucer in her hands. She spun to face them. "Untouched," she said as she eyed the uneaten cookie. "Sorry, Molly."

Molly's shoulders slumped. "You're better off!" Mrs. Fraser informed her.

"Better off from what? Did I just spot Mrs. Campbell's car leaving?" Jack inquired as he entered the kitchen.

"Yes, you did," Cate informed him.

"Aye," Mrs. Fraser confirmed. "Another linen crisis."

"And she didn't even try my cookies!" Molly moaned.

"Her loss is my gain!" Jack joked as he grabbed the cookie from the saucer and stuffed it into his mouth.

"But you're no help!" Molly protested. "You've already tried them! I needed an outside opinion."

"You're better off without hers," Jack said.

"Told you," Mrs. Fraser said with a nod. "Well, did you get your linens sorted, Lady Cate?"

"We did. I went with her suggestion after she second-guessed it then confirmed it was a perfect choice. And she had another request."

"No," Jack whined. "Another? What now? Palm trees? Bring a beach grain by grain for a luau?"

"No," Cate answered with a chuckle. "Not related to my anniversary party. She's vying for..."

Mrs. Fraser gasped. "The Presidents' Ball!" she exclaimed.

"Yes!" Cate responded, impressed by Mrs. Fraser's guess.

"What's The Presidents' Ball?" Molly inquired.

"Association of Historical Society Presidents annual charity event," Mrs. Fraser answered as Mr. Fraser joined them in the kitchen. "Isla has been vying for that role for as long as I've known her."

"Is it a big deal?"

"To her, it is," Mrs. Fraser confirmed. "I imagine she figures she'll be a front-runner with you as her host. And I suppose it is quite a big deal, in general. It's a large-scale event. Whatever town it's held in gets a big tourism boost."

"Ugh," Jack groaned. "Dunhaven will be crawling with tourists. Our sleepy little hamlet invaded by foreigners."

"Hey, I'm a foreigner!" Cate exclaimed.

"But we like you, Lady Cate," Jack replied with a wink.

"It would be a big boost to the town," Mr. Fraser chimed in.

"Aye," Mrs. Fraser agreed. "It would be. I suppose I hope she gets it."

"I'm surprised you offered to host, Lady Cate," Molly said.

"A snap decision I'm certain I'll regret at some point, but it seemed important to her and the town so I accepted. And I hope you'll all be my guests at the event!"

"Oh, I won't turn you down, though Isla will be livid when she sees us 'servants' there!" Mrs. Fraser said with a chuckle.

Jack sighed and stared at Mr. Fraser. "Another party to prepare the grounds for," he lamented.

"At the rate she's going, we'll just have to maintain. Mrs. Campbell's got a party a month here, so we're always in tip-top shape anymore!" Mr. Fraser commented. "Though for an event of this nature, I suppose we'll want the banners again."

"Dinnae count your chickens before they're hatched," Mrs. Fraser said. "She's not got the job yet!"

"With Lady Cate as host, we're bound to be a favorite."

"I don't understand why," Cate admitted.

All eyes turned to her. Jack scoffed at the question. "American history professor turned Scottish countess," Jack answered. "Who wouldn't want a colorful character like you hosting?"

"Colorful character?! Hardly!" Cate exclaimed.

"Aye, he's right, Lady Cate," Mrs. Fraser confirmed. "You'll be the talk of the ball. New blood. You'll be the most interesting host in the last thirty years!"

Cate frowned at the statement as she considered it. "Following in the line of the MacKenzies, I suppose."

"At least you haven't summoned any spirits to gain that reputation," Molly said.

"According to Mrs. Campbell, Douglas had a more sinister reputation than that!" Cate claimed.

Molly spun to face her. "More sinister than devil worship?"

Cate nodded her head. "Ritual killings, human sacrifices."

Molly gulped at Cate's admission. Mrs. Fraser scoffed. "That woman and her gossip," she said with a shake of her head. "Dinnae give it a second thought, Miss Molly. That woman tells fantastical tales just to hear herself talk."

"She told me another one, too," Cate announced.

"Oh?" Mrs. Fraser inquired.

"Yes. About a strange occurrence on the castle grounds shortly after its construction. A storm from nowhere, lightning from the ground to the sky. Fireballs flying around the estate. A tree bursting into flames and a tornado. She said hundreds of people witnessed this happen including the reverend and his wife."

Molly's eyes grew wide, and her mouth fell agape.

"Aye, that story's true," Mrs. Fraser confirmed.

"You didn't tell me about that!" Cate protested.

"There's a reason I omitted it."

"Because you didn't want to frighten Molly?" Jack teased.

"Nay, because that story is nonsense."

"But you said it was true," Cate countered.

"Yeah," Molly chimed in. "Fireballs and tornados Cate said, and you said it was true!"

"The account is true. Over one hundred people reported witnessing those strange events on the estate. But she's left out the reason."

"Because this joint is haunted?" Molly questioned.

"Nay, Miss Molly. The town had just finished a spring fair celebration. They later found out the pork pie turned before they ate it. Everyone who ate it experienced the strange phenomenon. It was the result of bad food, nothing more."

"Mass hallucination from bad pork? I'm not sure I believe that," Molly said with a wrinkled nose.

Mrs. Fraser gave her a hearty laugh. "Think of the alternative. Fireballs flying about, a fire that extinguishes itself, lightning bolts from the ground to the sky. Pshaw! Rubbish! Foolishness!"

Molly pressed her lips together and knit her brows. "I guess you're right."

"Of course, I'm right," Mrs. Fraser said with a nod. "The very idea of such nonsense occurring is for children's books."

Cate held in a chuckle. If Mrs. Fraser ever realized the capabilities housed under this castle's roof, she'd faint dead away just as Jack's grandfather suggested.

"Well with that settled, and everyone aware of Mrs. Campbell's latest venture, I will grab my lunch and excuse myself!" Cate said.

"Ah, the announcement was just a sneaky way to retrieve your own lunch tray, was it?" Mrs. Fraser asked of Cate.

"You caught me," Cate said as she held her hands up. "Guilty."

"Good thing we like you, Lady Cate," Mrs. Fraser said with a wink as she handed the tray off.

"Have a good lunch, everyone!" Cate called as she disappeared down the hall with her tray and two dogs in tow.

CHAPTER 5

Cate stared at the gibberish in the notebook again. She toggled between the written words and the information on her laptop. After searching several websites, she concluded this may be over her head. Breaking a cipher, even a centuries-old one, may not be achievable on her own.

Cate clicked off the current website and typed the web address for Aberdeen College. She searched the faculty roster for Dr. Ken Matthews. After finding his email address, she opened a new email and typed a message.

> *Hi Ken - I'm not sure if you remember me. We met on a few occasions while I was at Aberdeen College. I used to work in the History Department. I've since moved to Scotland (long story) and am working on a book about the history of Dunhaven Castle, my new home.*
>
> *I've come across some journals from the castle's builder, but they seem to be encrypted. Code-breaking is NOT my strong suit but Molly Williams reminded me it is yours! Would you be able to provide any help to get me started on trying to decipher these materials?*

Thanks! Cate Kensie

Cate blew out a long breath as the email left her outbox. She slouched in her chair, stretching her arms overhead as she considered what to fill her afternoon with as she awaited a response.

Cate stared out the window, pondering how to identify the man who haunted her dreams. As she considered how to research guests on the estate in the 1700s, her laptop chimed. Cate glanced at the screen, surprised to see a return email from Ken Matthews.

Hi Cate! Or should I say, Lady Cate? You're somewhat of a local legend on campus now. The story of your inheritance spread fairly quickly after your departure.

How interesting to find encrypted journals from a past era! I am happy to help if I can. Would it be possible for you to send a scan of a page or two so I can see what we're working with?

My mind is already listing the most likely possibilities. I may be able to rule a few out by seeing the text.

I hope you are enjoying Scotland.

Ken

Cate scanned the email, and a smile formed on her face. Maybe now she could make some progress. The only problem was sharing the information with Ken. What if the information shared gave something away about the castle's secret?

Cate pondered it for a moment. Would Douglas's first journal mention the secret on the first page or two? Cate weighed the odds. She'd never decrypt this without help.

Cate snatched her cell phone from the desk and toggled open her camera app. She snapped a picture of the first page. She shuffled through a few pages and snapped a picture of another random page from the journal. Two non-consecutive pages should make any information indecipherable for Ken.

Cate clicked the reply button on Ken's email and typed back to him.

Hi Ken - Thanks for your help! I've attached two pictures to this message with samples from the first journal. If you could point me in the right direction (or to an online solver!), I can decrypt these myself. I'm just not sure where to start!

Thanks again. I'll owe you one!

Cate

Cate drummed her fingers on the laptop after sending the email. Perhaps Ken would respond as quickly as he did the first time. Within seconds, her laptop chimed, and a new email popped into her inbox.

On it! I've already got a list of ideas to run through. With any luck, I'll hit on something in my initial list and have more information for you soon!

Ken

Cate appreciated the man's fervor. Like so many of her colleagues, they were like kids in a candy store when faced with a puzzle in their field. She hoped to have answers soon.

With Ken on the case, Cate shut her laptop. She'd need a new project to fill her time as she waited for answers from him.

Cate stood and stretched as she pondered her options. Perhaps she'd poke around in Douglas's office for any other information she could scrounge.

She opened the secret passage and turned on the lighting. Cate wandered down the wooden steps and into the cool laboratory space. She glanced around the room as she considered where to begin.

The stack of drawings near the desk caught her attention. She meandered to them and grabbed the first few sheets from the top. Cate stared down at the drawings. Outside of the sketch, she could make no sense out of any words scrawled on the paper. She shuffled to the next page. Similarly, each written word was no more than a random selection of letters in Cate's eyes. She sighed and flipped to the next page.

After thirty minutes, Cate found herself on the floor with papers sprawled around her in every direction. Outside of the nonsensical labels, the papers shared one additional characteristic in common. Each was numbered on the backside in the bottom right corner. The location matched the numbers in the journal. Using them, Cate pieced together the order in which the drawings were created.

While it didn't help her decipher anything, Cate felt she'd made some progress. As she collected the papers into an ordered pile, she studied a drawing. She decided her next task would be to match the drawings with any of the inventions she'd placed on the shelves. Then, if she could decipher the code, perhaps she could make some sense of each of them.

The drawing, labeled number one, contained an illustration of the large wooden desk in the room's center. Cate examined it. Why draw the desk in the room? Had Douglas designed it? If so, why encrypt its design? Did it hold some secret?

Obscure labels pointed to various areas on the piece. Cate scurried across the floor to the desk and studied the marked areas. They appeared decorative in nature. Several arrows pointed to drawers on the desk. Cate glanced inside a few of them but found nothing unusual.

Stumped, she returned to inspecting the drawing. "Oh, if only I could read these!" Cate bemoaned.

"Talking to yourself, Lady Cate?" Jack inquired from the stairs.

Startled, Cate jumped. "I guess you caught me," she said with a chuckle as she recovered from her surprise. "I didn't even hear you coming down the stairs."

"Lost in thought?"

"Yes," Cate admitted.

"Any luck deciphering those journals?"

"No, that's why I'm down here on the floor. I sent a message to a former colleague and I'm waiting for an answer. I figured I'd move to a new project to pass my time."

"What project? Cleaning the floor with your pants?"

Cate shook her head at him. "No. I found all these sketches with the journals. They are encrypted, too, but I figured I would try to sort through them and match them with the objects they belong with. Then if I decipher the journals, perhaps I can decipher these and find out what each of these inventions of his are!"

Jack stared at the large glass bowl across the room. "I'm not sure I want to find out," he murmured.

"Anyway, the first sketch is of this desk."

"Really?" Jack inquired. "Douglas designed his own desk?"

"It appears that way. I can't read anything on here, but he must have designed it for a reason. All these pieces are marked. I can't read their labels, but I was trying to determine what they mean."

Jack joined her near the desk. Cate climbed to her feet and shared the drawing with him. Jack glanced from the sketch to the desk.

"Perhaps it marks specific decorative items he wanted?"

"But why mark the drawers?"

Jack studied one of the marked drawers. He pulled it open and peered inside. He ran his hand around the drawer's interior.

"Anything?" Cate questioned.

Jack shook his head with a frown. "Not that I noticed."

"No false panels or anything?"

"Nope."

Cate scrunched up her face as she studied the drawing again. "I really wish I could read this," she murmured.

Jack grabbed the paper from Cate and took a closer glance at it. He flitted his eyes between the sketch and the marked components. Cate peered over his shoulder at the drawing. She bent down, her brow furrowing as she studied a decorative element marked on the drawing. Carved wooden leaves adorned a corner piece. She pressed her fingers against the brown leaves. They did not budge.

Cate poked at the carving. She narrowed her eyes at it before changing strategies. Her fingers wrapped around the piece and pulled. The wooden rectangle pulled away from the desk. Cate stood and stared at the piece.

"You broke it, Lady Cate," Jack teased.

Cate glanced at the picture before she reached to the freed piece again. She grasped hold of it and turned. A grinding noise filled the room, followed by a loud clank.

"Well, that did something," Cate said.

"Aye, lassie, but what?"

Cate pulled the drawing from Jack's hands and set it on the desktop. She pointed out the mechanism she'd just engaged. "Okay, this one has been activated. At least I expect so. These other marked pieces must engage some sort of mechanism within this desk."

"What mechanism?"

"I'm not certain," Cate admitted. "But I'd love to find out."

Jack raised his eyebrows. "Oh, please don't tell me you object," Cate groaned.

"For once, I don't. I can't imagine this could be that dangerous."

"Good," Cate said with a smile.

"Until we trigger whatever mechanism is inside the desk and the castle is swallowed by a sinkhole," Jack joked.

"Funny," Cate said.

She identified another leafy panel marked on the sketch on the desk's corner. Cate grasped it between her fingers and pulled. It came away from the desk easily. Cate turned it in a similar manner as she had the first. Nothing happened.

Cate frowned at it. She tried to turn it the opposite way, but it didn't budge.

"Hmm," she murmured. "Nothing happened."

Jack narrowed his eyes at the object before he glanced back to the drawing. "Wait!" he exclaimed. "Look at the label."

"What about it?" Cate inquired.

"The first one you turned has three letters. The second one you tried has five letters."

"So?" Cate asked, knitting her brows in concentration.

"This one," Jack said, pointing to another labeled decoration, "has three letters. And this one has four."

"I'm still not understanding how the number of letters factors in," Cate admitted.

Jack pushed the decorative panel back into place. "Let's try this one," he suggested. He grabbed the panel labeled with three letters. He pulled it and twisted it to the side. A scraping noise resounded, ending with a clank. Jack grinned at Cate. "And there's the second piece."

"Great job!" Cate said with a smile. "How did you know that one would work?"

"I'm a genius," Jack responded.

"Funny, come on, how did you know?"

"It disturbs me that you don't believe I'm a genius, Lady Cate," Jack said with an exaggerated frown.

Cate shot him a glance. "I realize you are very intelligent. You have saved a man from the death penalty without ever setting foot in law school. What I mean is how did you figure it out?"

Jack pointed to the labels. "Each of these has three random letters. This has five, this has four. I surmised these are numbered elements, indicating the order to engage each. You used this one: three letters labeling it as 'one.' You got lucky picking the first one. The only other one with three letters is this one which I figure is labeled 'two.' Now I suggest we try this one. Five random letters which I believe suggests the label 'three' which also has five letters."

"Way to go, Jack!" Cate grinned at him. She reached for the marked panel, released it from its spot against the desk, and turned. The familiar whirring and clanking filled the air.

"Last one!" Jack exclaimed as he repeated the process with the fourth. This produced a grinding noise followed by a clank, then a hiss.

"Now what?" Cate questioned.

They both leaned over the drawing. "The drawers?" Jack suggested.

"But what about them?" Cate mused aloud.

"One label has three letters, one has four, and two have five."

"Five, six, seven and eight?" Cate proposed.

"That's a safe bet, I'd say," Jack answered. He pulled open the drawer labeled "five." The drawer slid further than it had before. "Whoa!"

"That's further than it slid before."

"Aye, it is. And what are these marks?" Jack questioned.

Cate squinted down at the tiny markings. "Numbers!" she exclaimed.

"Numbers?" Jack questioned.

"We must have to open each drawer to a certain number to activate whatever mechanism is built into this."

"What numbers? Five, six, seven and eight?"

"We can try it, though I'd bet that's not it."

Jack positioned the other drawers to match their labels. Nothing happened. "You were correct, Lady Cate. That's not it."

"That's far too easy," Cate admitted.

"Of course, it is," Jack moaned. "Any other ideas?"

Cate pondered the question for a moment. "Birth year, the year the desk was created, the year it was designed, the year the castle was built, the year Douglas married," she rattled off.

"Okay, let's start trying them. What's the date on the drawing?"

Cate glanced at the unreadable title and the date scrawled under it. "1792," she said.

Jack lined up the drawers to that year. "Nothing," he said.

"Try 1791," Cate suggested. "Castle completion year."

"Okay," Jack replied as he pushed the final drawer in to 'one' rather than 'two.' "Nope."

"Uh," Cate mumbled as she processed dates. "Try... 1788." Jack glanced at her with a confused expression. "When Douglas married Olivia."

Jack moved the drawers to reflect the date. Nothing happened.

"1767, Douglas's birth year." Nothing.

Cate squinted into the distance. "1770."

Jack repositioned the drawers. A popping noise sounded. "Haha!" Jack exclaimed. "You got it! How did you come up with that date?"

"I'm a genius," Cate joked.

Jack gave her a wry glance. She shrugged. "Olivia's birth year."

"Good going, Lady Cate. Now, what made that noise?"

"I'm not sure," Cate answered. They glanced around the perimeter of the desk. Cate sank to her knees and glanced underneath. "Here!"

Jack joined her on the floor, sticking his head between the two columns supporting the desk's thick wooden top. He removed his cell phone from his pocket and toggled on his flashlight. Cate pulled open the piece of wood protruding from the back panel.

As the wooden door creaked open on rusty hinges, Jack shined the light into the new opening. Dull metal reflected the light. "It's a safe!" Cate exclaimed.

"This guy loved security," Jack breathed as he reached to pull the metal box from the desk's hidden chamber.

"What in the world did he hide in here?" Cate murmured.

Jack grunted as he struggled to pull the heavy safe from its hiding spot. "What is this made out of?" he squeaked as he clenched his teeth.

"Let me help," Cate offered. She reached in to assist in lifting the metal box. "Oof!" She breathed as they pulled it free from its location and dumped it on the stone floor.

Jack wiped his forehead before they slid the safe out from under the desk. He frowned at the metal box. Round metal buttons covered the surface of the rectangular metal box. "How do you open it?"

"This is a strongbox," Cate explained. She knelt up and pulled open one of the desk's drawers. She pulled a metal ring with two keys, one large and one small with a pointed tip. "One or more of these buttons should have a small divot. We use this pointy key to trigger a mechanism that will open a panel where we use this large key."

"That's quite a knowledge of ancient safes you've got there, Lady Cate. Were you a former safecracker?"

Cate checked several buttons before she inserted the pointy key. "Just a humble historian," Cate promised. A panel snapped open, revealing a keyhole. Cate fitted the key into the keyhole and turned it. She tugged at the key to remove it.

"There must be another," she mumbled. Cate searched the other buttons. Jack followed her progress as she found another trigger. A second panel popped open, revealing a second keyhole. Cate used the key to unlock this bolt. She pulled at the door. "Still stuck."

Cate searched and found a third divot near the bottom of the strongbox. After unlocking the latch, she pulled the door open.

Jack toggled on his flashlight again. "I hope it's something expensive after all this!"

Jack and Cate peered into the box's interior. Cate's mouth hung agape as she held her breath and identified the objects inside. Within seconds, she closed her mouth, a frown forming. Jack made a face. "That's it?" he griped.

Cate reached inside and withdrew the two items. "A piece of paper with a list of numbers and a bunch of metal rings hanging around a bar mounted on a horizontal stand," Jack assessed as Cate set the objects between them.

The items left Cate speechless. She stared at them. She reached out and touched one of the disks on the stand. It spun around on its pin.

"It's not what I expected," Cate admitted after a while.

"Not what you expected? It's junk!" Jack cried. "What is it?"

Cate shrugged. "Ancient calendar?" she joked.

"Well, that had a lackluster result after all that work. Why did he go through all this trouble to hide this?"

"No idea, but it has to be something important," Cate

insisted. "I have no idea what, though. Well, at least we solved it."

"Way to look on the bright side, lassie," Jack said as he climbed to his feet. He extended his hand to pull Cate to her feet. She scooped the items from the floor. "Taking your bounty with you?"

"Yep! We worked hard for this. I'm going to take a closer look at it. See if I can find anything interesting."

"You do that, Lady Cate. I am going to clean up before dinner. At least we've killed the time between meals!"

"I'm glad I could assist with that," Cate said. "And at least I found a new toy to play with while I wait to hear anything back on the journal encryption!"

* * *

The heaviness of her dress's fabric weighed on Cate as she bolted down the hall on wobbly legs. Her heart raced, and she puffed from exertion. As she rounded the corner, she searched for an escape. Her mind clouded as she spun in every direction, finding herself trapped. A tear rolled down her cheek, and she bit her lower lip.

Footsteps approached. A moan escaped Cate's lips as she continued her frantic search. She spotted a wall sconce. Cate lunged toward it, pulling on it with all her weight. It slid down the wall and triggered a mechanism.

A panel slid open. Cate ducked inside. She shoved it shut, collapsing against it and exhaling a deep breath.

Her posture stiffened as the footsteps closed in on her location. "Catherine," a voice sang. "Where are you?"

Cate glanced around as her eyes adjusted. She swallowed hard as she searched the darkened space for a hiding spot or an exit. She backed away from the hidden panel; her hand tracing the stone wall next to her.

A thud sounded behind her and Cate froze. Her assailant pounded against the wall. "Are you there, Catherine?" he called.

Cate's breath caught in her throat, and she backed further away from the hidden panel. The passageway sloped sharply downward. She followed it into the blackness below.

The air turned chilly and damp. Water dripped in the distance. Cate wrapped her arms around her waist as she shivered against the cold.

A scraping sound echoed throughout the chamber. Cate twirled to face the secret panel. Light streamed in from the open entryway. The figure of a man stood limned against the bright glow. Cate backed another step away.

"Catherine!" his voice called into the chamber.

Cate shrunk against the wall as she continued to inch away from the opening. Her back struck another wall. She pressed into the corner as the man stepped inside the passage.

Without warning, the man spun on his heel and faced opening. He cursed and raced from the passage, disappearing into the hall beyond.

Cate breathed a sigh of relief, though she did not budge. Her bottom lip quivered as she strained to listen for sounds in the hall. Was this a trap? Was the man lying in wait for her just beyond the exit?

Cate held her breath as she listened. Her brows knit, and she squeezed her eyes shut in concentration. Within seconds, Cate snapped them open. Her eyes darted around the space. She frowned and tilted her head as she strained to listen again.

In the silence of the room, one sound stood out. Breathing. Cate listened as the rhythmic noise filled her ears. She wasn't alone in the chamber. Cate's heart skipped a beat, and she strained her eyes to search the darkness for the hidden individual.

Cate found no one. "Hello?" she called, her voice breathy and strained. "Is someone there?"

The breathing ceased for a moment. A rustling noise filled the air. Cate recoiled, squeezing closer to the wall. "Who is it?" she demanded again.

A burst of bright blue-white light exploded in front of her. Cate squinted against it as it pierced her eyelids. "STAY AWAY!" she screamed.

"Stay away, stay away," Cate murmured as she thrashed in the sheets.

She shot up to sitting and gasped for breath. She swallowed hard as her heart began to slow.

Another nightmare. Cate grabbed her journal and jotted down all the details she recalled. Who was the man she fled from almost every night? And what was the meaning of the latest development? Who was the other person hiding in the secret passage?

CHAPTER 6

Cate settled at the library's desk and opened her laptop. She scanned her work area, strewn with Douglas's journals as the laptop booted. With a sigh, Cate wondered if she'd ever decipher them. Perhaps Ken would provide some help.

As the laptop's screen lit, Cate swiped at her trackpad. She navigated to her email. Her pulse quickened as she discovered a new email from Ken Matthews. Cate clicked to open it. Time seemed to slow as she waited to read his response.

Hi Cate! I hope you're doing well. I wanted to update you on my progress. (This is fascinating, by the way!) I ran your text through a few text analyzers. What I can tell you so far is that it's not a simple substitution cipher (you may know this as a cryptogram).

My text analysis has not shown that this follows the standard patterns expected in the English language. To explain a bit further, in the English language, we'd expect to see one letter making up 11-13% (this would be an "e"), 6.3%-8.7% as another ("t") and so on. So, if this was a substitution cipher, the one letter that substitutes for "e" should show up 11-13% of the time.

Now, I did adjust for the fact that this was 1700s English based on the information you provided, but even with the Old English taken into account, the text still doesn't come up with the correct percentages expected for letters.

This also rules out a Caesar cipher. This is basically a substitution cipher but instead of random substitutions (e.g. q for e, u for t), this one shifts the alphabet. For example, we may shift 4 letters to the left, meaning A would be coded as E, B as F, C as G and so on. Again, we'd notice the basic percentages of letters that show up in the English language (albeit shifted).

That's probably far too much information about the math behind it for your taste, sorry. Force of habit. Anyway, those are two of the popular ciphers from the 1700s. Which leaves only a few other options, all of which are harder to break. The fortunate thing is without technology, ciphers were quite limited, though some of them still prove difficult (or impossible) to break!

The one that's next to check on my list is the Vigenère cipher. It's a series of twenty-six Caesar ciphers, and encryption is based on a keyword. This cipher is designed to hide the letter frequencies, so that would fit with the text analysis I performed. Vigenère ciphers CAN be broken especially if we can identify the key's length. I've got some tricks up my sleeve I can use to establish this, but I figured I would check in to see if there's any identifiable keyword in your journals. If there are, this will be easy!

If not, I'll proceed with the two attack plans for breaking the Vigenère!

Ken

Cate parsed through the email. Ken's enthusiasm for the subject leapt off her screen. Unfortunately, Cate lacked his enthusiasm for the intricacies of code-breaking. With little idea what a Vigenère cipher was, Cate wondered if she may have overlooked the keyword Ken's email mentioned.

She grabbed the first journal from the desk and paged through it. She searched for any prominent words that suggested keyword status. She found none. She searched the other twelve journals, finding no traces of the keyword.

Cate swiped her laptop's trackpad to revive her laptop. She tapped the "Reply" button and began her email to Ken.

Hi Ken - I'm doing well. Thank you so much for all your work on this so far. I'm sorry it hasn't panned out yet.

I searched all through the journals and didn't see anything that may be the keyword you asked about. Each journal begins with "The Journal of Douglas MacKenzie" before it descends into indecipherable gibberish.

I don't suppose that's the key? Is the key in plain English? I searched through for an English word but maybe I overlooked something if the key is encrypted too.

Sorry for all the questions. This is not my area of expertise (as you can tell). I'm just not sure what I should be looking for.

Thanks again, Cate

Cate sent the email and checked her watch. At quarter after ten in the morning in Scotland, it would be only just after 4 a.m. across the pond in Aberdeen. She'd have a while to wait for a response.

Cate spent another thirty minutes searching through the journals. After finding nothing, she performed an internet search on Vigenère ciphers, hoping that learning about them would assist her in finding the keyword.

She poked around a few sites, learning a little more about how the cipher worked. None of the sites pointed to how to identify the keyword. Cate pinched her lips together. Another dead-end for the moment.

She glanced around the room as she blew out a puff of air. An alert sounded on her computer, drawing her attention back to it. Cate glanced at the screen. A new email stared at her from Ken Matthews.

Wow, Cate mused, Ken was an early riser.

Hi Cate - No problem, I'm having a blast! Great puzzle to solve! I'd doubt the journal title is the key, but I'll run it (and any variants) through my decryption software to see if it produces text.

The key wouldn't be encrypted. It should be a normal word that we will use to determine which shifts to use to encrypt each letter.

Let me try these words and phrases and see what I come up with. I'll get back to you soon (give me about an hour)!

Ken

An hour, Cate ruminated. Perhaps in an hour, she would have an answer. A nagging feeling suggested the answer would be no, but Cate held out hope one of those words would produce something.

Cate rose from her chair and faced the fireplace. "How about a walk, boys?" she suggested to the two dogs lounging near the fireplace.

They leapt to their feet and followed her from the room. Cate spent an hour and a half enjoying the early signs of spring in Scotland. A day with mild temperatures and sunshine provided ample reason to stay outdoors as Cate ticked the minutes down to the next response from Ken.

As they returned to the castle, they passed the side garden. Both dogs raced toward their new favorite location. "I can't believe you two are so obsessed with this spot," Cate said with a laugh.

"Talking to yourself again, Lady Cate?" Jack inquired as he rounded the corner.

"No, talking to the outdoor experts," she qualified, motioning toward the two dogs.

"Oh? And what have our intrepid expert explorers discovered today?"

"Nothing," Cate said with a shrug. "They've been interested in this spot near this bush for days now. I don't see a thing there."

Jack stooped and examined the spot. Riley glanced to him, then back to the mysterious dirt patch. "What do you see there, Sir Riley?" he questioned.

Riley pawed at the ground. Jack knelt next to him and peered closer. "Ohhhh, yes," he muttered.

"What is it? Do you see something?" Cate inquired as she peered over his shoulder.

"Aye," Jack admitted.

"What?"

"A giant... SPIDER," Jack exclaimed, tossing a leaf Cate's way.

Cate shrieked and stumbled backward a few steps. She brushed at her clothes to rid herself of any unwanted visitors on her sweater.

Jack stood as he held in a laugh.

"Is it on me? Where is it?" Cate cried.

Jack shook his head, still holding in his chuckling. "No, no, Lady Cate," he answered as he swiped a green leaf off the ground. "You've dodged it."

Cate narrowed her eyes at him. "THAT was NOT a funny joke!" Cate groaned.

Jack snickered before sobering. "Okay, okay, it wasn't. Sorry."

"It's okay. I'll forgive you."

"Next time I'll say it was a snake. THAT will be funnier."

Cate shook her head at him. "Come on, you three jokesters," Cate said to the two pups and Jack. "Let's head back in. I've got to check my email."

"Check your email? Waiting on an important email from the party czar?"

"No. I emailed a former colleague about the encrypted journals. He's not hit on any solutions yet. And don't worry, I was careful about what I sent. I only sent the first page and a few random early pages. I'm figuring he wouldn't disclose the secret within the first pages."

"Let's hope not. Anyway, with no solutions in sight, we're still safe."

Cate nodded. "I'm afraid without Ken's help, I'd never break that code. Even with his help, a lot of this is over my head."

"I'll admit I am interested to learn what's in those journals myself."

Cate grinned at him. "It could answer so many questions."

"I agree. It could lend us great insight!"

"Heading in for lunch?" Cate inquired as they neared the kitchen door.

"You bet! I'm starving!"

Jack held the door open for Cate and the dogs to enter. She collected her lunch tray and carried it upstairs. With any luck, an email awaited her. An email containing a solution to her cipher.

Cate ushered the dogs into the library and carried her tray to the desk. She shoved the tray onto the desk's top, nudging the journals toward the edge. Cate sniffed at the aromatic tomato basil soup as she opened her laptop.

She tapped the keyboard, signing into her email account. No new messages awaited her. She frowned at the page before refreshing it twice, to be sure. No new emails popped into her inbox. Perhaps this was good news. Perhaps Ken hit on something. Time would tell. For now, Cate would have to wait.

Dejected, she carried her lunch tray to the cozy armchair near the fireplace. Perhaps when she finished her lunch, she'd have an answer, she mused.

Halfway through her meal, her laptop made the characteristic chime, indicating a new email. Cate raced to the desk to check. A bolded email topped her email list. Cate smiled at the sender's name: Ken Matthews.

She toggled it open on her screen.

Hi Cate - Sorry for the delay, I wanted to try a few other things. As you may have surmised, nothing has worked out so far. I tried all the combinations of "The Journal of Douglas MacKenzie" as the keyword and came up with nothing.

I ran through a few different techniques to elicit the key's length (which would help us to break the code) but, again, I came up with nothing.

This doesn't mean it's not a Vigenère but what it does mean is we can't solve it without the keyword. I wanted to check back with you on the off chance you've identified anything else that could be the key. I'm not giving up yet. But is there anything else that may point to a clue to deciphering the text? Even if you don't expect it's related, send it over. A fresh set of trained eyes may be able to come up with something workable.

Thanks, and sorry I've not found anything thus far! Ken

Cate pouted at the screen. Though grateful for Ken's help, her frustration mounted with each negative result. Cate opened the first journal again, determined to scour it for a keyword. She had to find something!

Cate flipped through the first journal again. If the keyword was anywhere, it would be in the first journal, she surmised. Cate scoured every inch of the pages for the thousandth time but found nothing. She let the book fall to her lap. The pages fanned shut as she propped her head up with her hand. Cate stared down at the journal with its front cover open. *The Journal of Douglas MacKenzie*, she read as she stared at it.

Her eyes flitted to the inside cover. She focused on the numbers scrawled on the cover. Cate knit her brows and squinted at them. Could they help?

Cate sat straighter and clicked the Reply button on Ken's email.

Hi Ken - Thanks for your help so far. I have been over every inch of the journal and haven't found any keywords BUT I did find something curious. In each journal I have found, there are twenty-five numbers scrawled on the inside cover. Could they be the keyword? Or related to it? I realize it's not a word, but it's the only thing I can come up with.

I've attached a picture of the inside cover from two of the journals for your reference. Does this help at all?

Cate

Cate pressed send, then drummed her fingers against the desk. In five minutes, she gave up on staring at her inbox while willing the email to appear. She yawned, a sudden burst of tiredness overcoming her.

Her mind turned to another journal. Her own. She'd experienced another nightmare last night. Why was she suffering from them? What did they mean? Perhaps if she couldn't solve the mystery of Douglas's journals, she could make progress on her own.

Cate pushed back from the desk and navigated upstairs to her bedroom. She retrieved the notebook from her night table. As she tucked it under her arm, she recalled the frightening details summarized inside.

They were only silly dreams. Why did they terrorize her? As she contemplated the question, a loud ticking echoed in the room.

Cate grabbed at the timepiece hanging around her neck. She opened the cover. The second hand crept around the watch face. Cate's jaw dropped. She hadn't triggered the mechanism. She glanced around the room. What was happening? Her bedroom contained a time rip accessing 1925. Was she in the 1920s?

She swallowed hard as she considered her options. Cate raised the timepiece, intending to use it to return to the present. Her eyes widened as the second hand sped up and kept normal time.

Cate stood unmoving for a moment. She tore her eyes from the watch face and glanced around the bedroom. She recognized her things. Riley and Bailey's beds lay near her bed. Her cell phone charger poked from behind the night table lamp. A discarded cardigan hung limply over her armchair.

She was in her time. Cate ran a shaky hand through her hair as her heart settled back to normal speed. Had she imagined the incident? Was her mind playing tricks on her? Was this the product of an overtired imagination?

Cate bit her lower lip as questions flooded her mind. She shoved them to the back of her brain. It was a fluke. A trick of her mind. A reaction to the memory of her nightmares.

Still, she felt a sudden urge to leave her bedroom. Cate hurried from the room and weaved through the hallways toward the library. As she stepped into the hallway from a back set of stairs, she bumped into Jack.

"Ahoy there, Lady Cate," Jack greeted her with a salute.

"Hi, Jack," she said.

"Uh-oh, that doesn't sound like Lady Cate! Say, you're not

still sore at me over that spider hoax? I really do apologize, Cate."

Cate waved at him. "No, it's not that."

"Then what is it?"

"Just tired I guess," Cate admitted. She waved her journal in the air. "Another nightmare last night. That on top of no leads on Douglas's journals even with an expert helping me and I'm just indulging myself in a pity party."

"Oh no," Jack moaned. "No. Lady Cate, please. No more parties. Soon, Mrs. Campbell will be asking us to erect a stone fountain of a weeping woman in the back garden. And install a rain machine to ensure nasty weather for the event."

Cate giggled at Jack's ridiculous assessment of Mrs. Campbell's party planning requests. "Okay, pity party concluded!" Cate agreed.

"Another nightmare, huh? Care to discuss it?"

Cate shrugged. "I'm not certain I do, to be honest. These are becoming tedious. As usual, I was being chased. I reached a dead-end, but I managed to open a secret passage and I hid there."

"Did your friend find you?"

Cate rolled her eyes. "He's NOT my friend. That much is obvious. He terrorizes me every time I come across him in my dreams. Anyway, he opened the passage and called to me. I hid in the shadows. Something else caught his attention, and he disappeared. I waited there for a few more moments to determine if I was safe. While I waited, I heard something. Breathing. Someone was hiding with me in the secret passage. I called out to them. They didn't answer but a blinding light exploded in the space and then I woke up."

"A blinding light?" Jack queried.

"Yeah," Cate answered.

"Like a flashlight?"

"No," Cate said, with a shake of her head. "No, not like that. The light was blue-white. Almost ethereal."

"LED flashlight?" Jack suggested.

"No," Cate insisted. "No, it was like an orb of light. It was strange." She shrugged again. "Anyway, this marks the first time another person has shown up in my dream outside of my strange stalker."

"And you didn't spot the person or have any way to identify them?"

"No, none. I never saw them, only heard the breathing." Silence passed between them for a moment. "Then there's another strange thing."

"Oh?" Jack inquired, shooting Cate a questioning glance.

"Two nights ago, I had one of my now infamous nightmares. Afterward, I couldn't sleep, as usual. As I laid in bed pondering the meaning of my dream, I swore I heard the watch slow down. When I checked it, the second hand sped up and kept normal time. I assumed I imagined it."

"Product of an overstimulated and tired mind, perhaps," Jack agreed.

"That's what I thought, too. But..."

"But?" Jack inquired.

"When I went to retrieve my dream journal just now, I could have sworn it happened again. I panicked because I hadn't even been touching the timepiece. And when I checked, the second hand crept by like I had slipped into 1925. Then, without warning, it sped up and everything was normal. My sweater was draped over the chair, my phone charger was on the night table, the dogs' beds were near my bed."

"And you are here with me in the good-old present day!" Jack exclaimed.

"Yes, here I am. But why did the watch slow twice without me triggering it?"

Jack shrugged. "Are you certain it slowed?"

Cate considered the question for a moment. She nodded slowly. "Yes. The first time, no, but this time, I'm sure."

"And you're certain you weren't rubbing it? You discovered the anomaly because you had a habit of rubbing the watch."

Cate wrinkled her forehead in thought. "Ah," she responded with a shrug. "I don't think so. But perhaps I was. I don't remember doing it. But, I suppose, I don't remember NOT doing it either."

"With all these nightmares, you're overly tired. Perhaps you did it without realizing it. A nervous habit."

"I'll bet you're correct," Cate said with a nod. "I did have a bad habit of rubbing the watch like a worry stone. Perhaps it's cropped up again."

"Keep an eye on it. If it happens again, let me know. I'll have Pap check it out just to be sure."

"Okay. And I'll try to pay careful attention to my nervous tics. Pun intended!" Cate said with a wink.

Jack's jaw dropped. "Did you just make a terrible pun joke?"

Cate grinned and nodded. "I did!"

"Lady Cate," Jack said with a chuckle, "you're spending too much time with me and picking up my terrible humor."

"Maybe soon you'll pick up my love of time travel," Cate said with a wink.

Jack raised his eyebrow at her.

"Don't answer," Cate said.

"Deal. Well, I'll let you return to your journals, whichever you choose to study."

"Thanks! With any luck, Ken will have some answers for me when I get back to my laptop. And I can toss this journal to the side and forget about it for a while. At least until I have another nightmare."

"Good luck!" Jack said as they reached the library doors.

"I'll see you for dinner," Cate said as she ducked into the library.

Cate hastened to the desk and set her journal down. She toggled her laptop on and checked her email. A new message from Ken awaited.

> Hi Cate - Okay, this changes everything! That's not a keyword for sure which means we're at a dead-end with the Vigenère cipher. BUT I did a bit more research into ciphers of that era. Turns out, there's another one from the time period invented by Thomas Jefferson. It wasn't as popular as the others. In fact, it didn't gain popularity until it was reinvented in the early 1900s!
>
> I digress, though. My point is: when coupled with the numbers you sent me, I began to wonder if this encryption was a Jefferson disk cipher. The numbers would indicate the order the disks should be placed on the encoder/decoder. The order itself is the cipher key. It tells you how to decrypt the message.
>
> This would also explain why nothing we've tried so far has worked (no keyword length clearly apparent with the Vigenère and no frequencies matching for the substitution ciphers).
>
> Now, given the numbers (one through twenty-five) it appears this is a Jefferson cipher with 25 disks. That's smaller than the original version invented by Jefferson (which had 36), but still with 25, this will be extremely difficult to crack without the disks themselves.
>
> This means we're at a standstill unless you've got the decoder ring. I've attached a picture of what one looks like. Have you found anything like this with the journals? If you have, I can explain how to decrypt/encrypt.
>
> Let me know and I'll keep my fingers crossed you've got the decryption tool right there with you!
>
> Ken

Cate clicked the thumbnail in her email to view the picture. She gasped as she stared at it. Cate leapt from her chair and raced across the room. She retrieved the object she'd found yesterday in Douglas's hidden desk strongbox. She counted the disks, her heart pounding as she counted twenty-five.

Cate quickly clicked the reply button.

Hi Ken - Thanks for the information! Unbelievably, I just found an item that looks like that yesterday! It's got twenty-five disks and each one of them has the alphabet on it in some random order. I've attached a picture.

I'm fairly sure this is the decoder you mentioned in your previous email. I'd be ever so appreciative if you could explain how to use it to decode the journals.

THANK YOU!

Cate

Cate glanced at the stand containing the disks. Her pulse still raced from the discovery. With any luck, she'd soon be able to decipher Douglas's journals. What would they tell her, she wondered? What secrets did they hold?

Cate performed an internet search on the cipher Ken mentioned in his email. She browsed a few sites. Pictures similar to the one Ken sent appeared on them. Cate read about the history of the cipher and its strength against attacks until her email chimed.

She switched browser tabs and discovered a new email from Ken.

Hi Cate - YES! That MUST be the key! We'll find out shortly once I have you try decryption on one of the journals.

I'll reference the first picture you attached for instructions.

You should be able to open the axle and remove the disks (this allows for reordering of the disks, which can provide unique cipher keys). Each disk should be numbered somewhere. You'll want to place the disks on the axle in the order noted in the cipher key. The cipher key (I think) is the list of twenty-five numbers you sent me.

In the first image you sent, the numbers are:

7 13 3 1 20 19 23 21 18 17 6 9 22 11 8 25 10 14 15 12 2 24 16 5 4

Arrange the disks on the axle so they sit in that order (4 on the right end and 7 on the left).

Now you've got the decoder set up to decode the message. This is where you'll need to do a bit of work.

Turn the disks to match the letters in the journal you're trying to decrypt. Without moving them, check the other rows on the disk. One of them should spell out a message. Often, the user selected the row above or below the cipher row to create the encrypted text, so it may be just above or below the row you created.

Sometimes, they used a larger shift in rows (maybe two or three). The good news is they would have been consistent with their choice so once you find the correct row, you'll just use that row over and over to decrypt.

I hope that makes sense. I've included a few reference sites that explain this (maybe better than I did!). If you need more help, let me know. We can also set up a video conference and I can walk you through it.

Let me know if you're able to decipher anything!

Ken

Cate read through the email twice before grabbing the decoder. She fiddled with the axle until it sprung free of the stand. Cate slipped the disks off the ring, spilling them into her lap.

She grabbed one and studied it. As Ken suggested, a number adorned one side. Cate cleared a spot on the desk.

She began to line the disks in the order listed on the first journal's interior cover.

Cate spread the disks across her lap as she sorted through and searched for each number. After ordering them, she threaded them back onto the axle and snapped it shut. She turned to the first page of encrypted text in the journal.

Cate spun the disks on the axle to match the letters on the page. She worked left to right to input the nonsensical letters in a row at the top of the wheel. Once she finished, Cate took a deep breath and checked the row just above her input. Gibberish, she reflected. She pursed her lips and tried the next lineup. The line began BQ. It did not provide a solution.

Cate abandoned the lines above and tried the line below her cipher row. She scanned the row. Her heart skipped a beat. Cate snatched a blank piece of paper from the desk drawer and copied the letters from the journal with the word breaks. Underneath, she copied the letters matching the code.

J IDUP ZTHBESL VGPR XDVPMSD YI
I HAVE CREATED THIS JOURNAL TO

A smile spread across her face. She'd done it! Well, she reflected, Ken Matthews had done it, but with his help, she would now be able to decrypt the journals! Before she responded to inform Ken, Cate tried another twenty-five characters from the journal.

She rotated each wheel to match the letters in the journal. Cate jotted them down on her paper before she transcribed the plaintext from the row below it.

RIIPXGXVZ SFL DENRHQRF GQ OIT
CHRONICLE AND PRESERVE MY EXP

The twenty-five characters ended mid-word, though, from the other words in the phrase, Cate was certain she was decrypting the text correctly.

She set her pen aside and pulled her laptop closer to type a reply email to Ken.

Hi Ken! I read through your email a few times before I tried it. After a bit of work, I found the appropriate plaintext English! I was able to decrypt almost the entire first line. It appears Douglas began the journal to keep a record of his experiences as he began his life in the castle.

I'm sure this will prove fascinating for me (not only from a historical perspective but since Douglas is my ancestor!). Thank you so much for your help with this! I'd never have gotten this decrypted without your expertise. I really appreciate the time you took and how quickly you got back to me!

Well, back to decoding for me! With thirteen journals in twenty-five-character chunks, I've got my work cut out for me! At least it will keep me out of trouble!

Thanks again! I owe you one.
Cate

Cate sent the email and returned to her decryption task. As she finished decoding the first sentence, Cate wondered if typing may be faster. Copying each letter and its matching plaintext proved tedious. Cate pondered skipping the copy of the journal text, wondering if she could write the transcription only. She nixed the idea in case she made a mistake, which she figured would be likely given the sheer volume of text she must work through.

While eager to continue her translation, Cate opened a word document and began to type the first page of ciphertext into it. Cate frowned as the work went slower than she hoped. Transcribing gibberish did not make for easy typing, she lamented. And she itched to get to the transcription.

Cate stopped typing after the first page and decided to translate the text before continuing her copy task. She added the fifty characters she had already decoded, then continued with her decryption.

After a few moments, she had deciphered the first sentence.

I have created this journal to chronicle and preserve my experiences as I search for answers.

Pleased with her work, Cate smiled at the screen. "Well, Douglas," Cate said aloud, "what experiences do you have to share?"

As she pondered her question, a chime sounded from her laptop. Cate toggled open her email and found a new email from Ken.

Hi Cate - That's great! How exciting! I'm so glad I was able to help solve it. I wonder why he encrypted the journals? Maybe he's got a reference to a secret treasure or something and you'll be famous for discovering it! I can ride on your coattails as the man behind your big discovery.

Anyway, as you mentioned, twenty-five-character chunks of text will take you quite a while to decode! Not to mention, I'm sure it will be a tedious exercise to work through. On that note, I've got an idea. I'm not sure it will pan out, but I've got an email out to an associate I've worked with a few times about automating this.

I'm not sure if he'll be able to help but he's a fantastic computer programmer, and he has some knowledge of modern encryption. That would really speed things up for you, so I'm hoping he can help! I'll let you know as soon as I hear from him.

Ken

Cate chuckled as she read the first few lines. In addition to Ken's obvious excitement, he referred to a secret treasure Douglas may have discussed within the pages of the journals.

He had no idea how correct his assessment was, Cate mused. Unfortunately, Cate would never be able to share those details with Ken.

The rest of his email intrigued her, though. She glanced at the stack of journals on the desk. His assessment would prove correct if she had to decrypt them by hand in twenty-five-character chunks. An automated computer program could accelerate her translation exponentially.

Cate replied to Ken and thanked him for pursuing the program, telling him she would keep her fingers crossed since it would expedite her encryption.

Cate glanced to the document on her screen containing the journal's first page then to her timepiece. Dinner approached. Cate's eyes flitted to the outside. The sun's light was already waning. As eager as she was to continue her work, she closed her laptop.

Her stomach grumbled in agreement with her decision to abandon work for dinner. She'd spend the next day engrossed in the journals, she promised herself. Besides, perhaps Ken would strike gold with his associate, and she could speed up the entire process.

After spending the evening with her staff, as was her custom, Cate found her mind relaxed enough to sleep. As she eased back into the pillows, she hoped the dinner also had the power to stave off any nightmares.

CHAPTER 7

Cate stretched as she crawled from her bed the next morning. The sun had not yet risen as she stepped into a steamy shower. Her refreshed mind swam with questions. What would she find in Douglas's journals? Would Ken be able to assist her with hastening the process? What experiences would Douglas recount? How did he discover the time travel anomaly? Would she now be able to read the text on his invention sketches? What would they reveal?

Questions crowded Cate's mind. Of course, without automated help, it may take months or longer to answer them, Cate thought as she slipped into her clothes.

Both dogs still lounged in bed when she returned to retrieve her shoes. "Look at you two sleepy heads!" Cate exclaimed. Riley repositioned his head without lifting it to stare at Cate. "Staying in bed, are we?" Bailey's tail wagged, but he refused to rise from his snug spot amidst the covers.

"All right!" Cate said as she finished pulling on her boots. "I'll go for a walk myself!"

At the mention of the "w-word," both dogs leapt to their

feet and raced to Cate's side. "That's more like it!" she said as she rubbed both their heads. "Come on, boys, we may still catch the sunrise!"

Cate stepped from the castle into the cool spring air. Streaks of red painted the horizon. She strode down the path to the loch with both dogs in tow. As the red sun peeked over the distant moor, she settled on the loch's bank.

Her thoughts lingered on the castle's first proprietor again. She wondered if Douglas's experience matched hers when she had first arrived at the castle. She glanced back to the large stone-clad structure behind her. Its towers and turrets rose high above the rolling hills. Its walls held a life-changing secret. Had Douglas reacted with the same enthusiasm Cate did?

There was only one way to find out. Cate stood and brushed the dirt off her legs. The sun, now fully risen, promised to bring a warm spring day to the area. She may have to take the laptop outside to work and let the dogs frolic in the bright sunshine the day promised.

Both dogs raced ahead of her to the castle. Cate pushed through the door into the fragrant kitchen. The aroma of cinnamon filled the air.

"... told you which I preferred," Mrs. Fraser said as Cate popped through the door. Both dogs scurried to Jack's side to greet him.

"But what about..." Jack began, his voice cutting off as Cate stepped inside.

The conversation stalled, and all eyes turned to her as silence fell over the room.

"Good morning, everyone," Cate said. "Seems I know how to make an entrance." No one answered. "Or kill a conversation," she added. A tangible pall hung over the room, and Cate swallowed hard. Everyone's strange behavior disturbed her.

"No," Molly said with a wave. "We weren't talking about you... anything... We weren't really discussing anything important."

"Well, that's... good," Cate said. "Though I am sorry to have interrupted your conversation about nothing."

"No problem, Lady Cate," Molly assured her.

Cate offered a wide-eyed grin at them. She bit her lower lip and glanced around the room at each of them. "Are you all serious? You're really not going to tell me what you were talking about?"

"Nothing!" Molly answered as Jack stated "cookies," while Mrs. Fraser answered "dinner."

"O-okay," Cate stammered.

"We were discussing having no cookies for dinner. None! Nothing!" Molly filled in.

It seemed obvious they were hiding something, though Cate couldn't fathom what or why. She decided to leave it go. Whatever they were concealing may not be her business. "Well, cookies or not, I'm sure we'll survive," she responded.

"Got your breakfast, Lady Cate," Molly announced. "Ready?"

"Yes!" Cate replied. "I'm hungry after that early morning walk!" She reached for the tray.

"I'll carry it," Jack offered, grabbing the tray from Molly. "There are a few estate items I'd like to run past you while we make the trek."

"Okay," Cate agreed. She called the dogs to follow her. Aware of the routine, both bounded ahead. Cate offered Jack a nervous smile as they continued down the hall toward the staircase leading to the main level. "Weird vibe in there," she said with a chuckle.

"Huh? Really?" Jack said. "I didn't notice anything." Jack cleared his throat. "Anyway, about that estate business..."

"Right," Cate said, her discomfort growing over the

conversation she'd interrupted. "Estate business. What's on the menu? Roofing? Plumbing? Or..."

They reached the staircase and began the climb to the main level. "Actually," Jack whispered as they reached the top. "I just wanted to find out if you made any progress on your projects?"

"Ohhhhh," Cate answered. "I have!"

Jack raised his eyebrows, prompting her to continue.

"Yeah, Ken Matthews, a former colleague of mine from Aberdeen College, helped me. He did a ton of analysis on the cipher bits I sent him. None of the standard channels produced any results. But then I sent him a picture of the numbers written on the inside of the cover. It gave him another idea about the cipher that might have been used to encrypt it. Remember the old-school calendar we found?"

"The letter wheels from the safe in the safe in the safe."

Cate chuckled. "Yes. It's an encoder-decoder wheel for a Jefferson disk cipher! You thread the wheels on it in the order given in the journal. Next, you input the letters from the journal, and you read the lines above or below that one. The one that makes sense in English is the plaintext."

"Okay, I think I've got the idea. Did it work?"

"It did!" Cate exclaimed as they reached the library and Jack set the tray on the table near the fireplace. "I tried it last night before dinner. I decrypted fifty whole characters, too!"

Cate retrieved her laptop from the desk and popped it open as she carried it to Jack. She opened her document and showed him the decrypted line.

"I have created this journal to chronicle and preserve my experiences as I search for answers," Jack read.

Cate grinned at him. "And so it begins!"

"I must admit, I am a teensy bit interested in his experiences," Jack admitted.

"Because you're starting to like this time travel stuff."

"I wouldn't go that far, Lady Cate. But I am curious to learn how this all began," Jack admitted.

"And we soon will! Well," she qualified, "maybe not soon. Translating this in twenty-five-character chunks is slow-going."

"Oh, good!" Jack exclaimed.

Cate wrinkled her nose. "Good?"

"Yeah, it'll keep you busy in this time period for a long, long time!"

"With any luck, it won't!"

"Got a plan to speed translate, do you?"

"Maybe," Cate said. "Ken mentioned a friend who may be able to help automate this. I'm waiting on an email to determine if that's an option or not. If it is, we may be able to discover Douglas's experiences much faster!"

"Oh, Lordy," Jack said with an eye roll. He backed to the door. "Hey, send me a copy of that translation once you have it. I really do want to read through it."

Cate gave him a half-smile. "Will do."

He stepped through the door but spun to face Cate again before disappearing down the hall. "Oh, Lady Cate, one more thing."

"Roofing?" she questioned.

Jack chuckled. "No. For once, I have no real estate business. Any more nightmares?"

Cate shook her head. "Nightmare free last night! Maybe the journal decryption relieved them!"

Jack held up his hand, sporting his crossed fingers. "Have a good breakfast, Lady Cate."

"You too!" Cate called.

Cate set her laptop next to the tray and plopped into the armchair. After a spoonful of her oatmeal, she clicked on her email program. Cate found several emails, including one from Ken Matthews. She clicked to open and read it.

> *Hi Cate - I got a response from my guy and he's happy to help. He considered it a fun challenge to create the program. He thought the easiest way would be to create the numbered disks within the program and the line offset to the plaintext, then all you'd need to do is input the order you want the disks in and enter the text and it'll spit out the decrypted text.*
>
> *In order to do that, he'll need to get the details of the disks. We considered it easier for you two to communicate directly so he could gather the details he needs and give you any support for any bugs you may find in the program. Is it okay for me to pass your contact information along to him?*
>
> *Ken*

Cate clapped her hands in excitement, rousing both dogs from their lazy morning near the fire. "Sorry, fellas! It looks like Ken's friend can help me after all. Got a little overexcited, I guess!"

She typed a return email, giving her permission to send her details along. Cate eyed the decryption ring across the room. Given the new development, this would prove much faster. Was it worth it to continue decoding by hand?

What if the program took months to construct, she ruminated? Then it may be worth it to continue. Cate's mind overanalyzed the situation, as usual, creating backup plans for her backup plans.

As she finished her breakfast, she decided she'd wait to continue her decryption until she had a better handle on when the program may arrive. She had plenty of smaller pieces of text she could work on.

Cate's mind turned to the stack of technical sketches still

in the office downstairs. They each contained encoded text. Maybe she could work on those.

Her lips formed a frown as she pondered how difficult it may be to decrypt them without knowing the order of the disks. As she recalled Ken's statements about the difficulty of breaking the cipher, a new thought popped into her mind.

She dropped her spoon into her bowl and set them back on the tray. She hurried across the library to the desk. Cate shoved the journals aside, searching for a specific item.

Buried under three journals, Cate struck gold. She pulled the paper out and studied it. "Ah-ha!" she exclaimed, rousting the dogs a second time. Riley cocked his head at her. "This list," she explained to them, "that we found with the decoder gives the disk order for decrypting the drawings downstairs, I'd bet. They were all numbered. I'd bet these numbers correspond to each drawing!"

Cate chewed her lower lip as she stared out the window, her mind racing. She could make good progress on those sketches while she waited for Ken's contact to reach out to her.

She considered grabbing them, but the bright sunshine persuaded her to postpone her work. "Let's go for another walk, boys!" Cate proposed.

* * *

Cate approached the gardens in the rear of the castle. She spotted Jack tending to the rose bushes there. "They should bloom in time for your party, Lady Cate," he shouted.

Cate sauntered to him, fingering an infant leaf springing from the plant. "If I remember correctly, they were in bloom when I arrived."

"You remember correctly."

"I remember because I found you tending to them after

you pulled a disappearing act on me. Little did I know I was in 1856, and not the present time."

"I'm glad we cleared that up. Speaking of the past, I'm shocked you're out walking and not working hard on your journal decryption."

"Cabin fever, I suppose. It's such a beautiful day. And to be honest, I am waiting for an email from Ken's associate. He's agreed to create a computer program to decrypt the journals. So, I'm just being lazy and hoping he creates it before I have to tackle those journals twenty-five letters at a time."

"Ahhhh," Jack said with a nod, "lazy Lady Cate. You've gone soft! You're losing your edge!"

Cate held her hands up in defeat. "I know," she said with a chuckle. "And on that note, I suppose I'd better get back and at least do SOME work."

"Good luck, Lady Cate."

"Thanks! Come on, bo..." Cate's voice cut off mid-word. She frowned and scratched her head. "Where did those rascals go?"

"Uh-oh," Jack answered. "The last time Sir Riley pulled a disappearing act outside, he found a new friend."

Cate nodded. "If there's another dog hiding out on the grounds, I may have to rename this place Dunhaven Rescue Castle." She called for the dogs. "Well, I suppose before I continue my work, I'll search for those two imps."

"Need help?"

"I'm sure they're around here somewhere," Cate assured him. "If I can't find them, I'll be back."

"Okay. Golly, I hope they haven't found any other secret passages."

Cate chuckled as she meandered away. She searched the rolling hills for the two small pups. She called to them again, peeking behind bushes and glancing over shrubs.

"Riley! Bailey!" Cate called as she rounded the corner. Two shrill barks sounded from the side garden.

Cate headed toward the noise. "Oh, Riley and Bailey! What have you done?!" Cate exclaimed.

Muddy smudges covered their faces and front paws. Cate stared at the culprit in front of them. A shallow crater dented the earth. Disturbed dirt sat in a pile around it.

Riley nosed the cavity and Bailey scratched more dirt from it. "Stop that!" Cate scolded. "Look at you two. You're filthy! Come on, you both need baths!"

Cate took two steps away. Neither dog followed. "Riley, Bailey! Let's go!" After another forlorn glance at the partially dug hole, the two dogs trotted after Cate. She collected both into her arms before pushing through the kitchen door and into the house.

"What happened here?" Mrs. Fraser asked as Cate entered with the dirty dogs.

"They decided to dig a hole in the side garden," Cate responded.

"Uh-oh," Mrs. Fraser scolded. "Young Jack won't be happy with you digging holes in his landscaping."

"Neither is Cate," Cate replied. "These two are going straight into the laundry tub!"

* * *

With clean pups, Cate headed to the library and settled the two dogs by the fireplace. She swiped at her laptop's trackpad to wake it. She found several emails awaiting her. Cate clicked into the first from Ken. He wrote he would pass Cate's email along to his associate and to expect an email from Damien Sherwood who would create the program for her.

Cate scanned the other emails in her inbox. A smile

crossed her face as she spotted one from Damien Sherwood. She clicked to open it.

> *Hi there, Lady Cate or Dr. Kensie or Lady Kensie or whichever you prefer, I'm not sure how to address someone in your position, what with both a title AND a Ph.D. At first, I thought the education trumped the title, but then I wasn't sure. Anyway, let me know which you prefer!*
>
> *My name is Damien Sherwood, Ken Matthews may have mentioned I would be emailing you. He contacted me about writing a program to help you with some decryption. I took a look at the materials he sent over and it seems fairly straightforward to achieve. I will need two pieces of information from you first! Specifically, I'll need the order of the letters on each disk. To make this task easier, I created a spreadsheet with the disks listed (twenty-five, right?) in each row. In the first position, I put the letter A. We'll use that as our anchor letter. Then, fill in the rest of the row with the order of the letters after A. (When I say "after," I mean if you have the disk so "A" is in the 12:00 position, list the letters going clockwise around).*
>
> *The second thing I need to know is the offset from the ciphertext to the plaintext. Let's again work clockwise. So, tell me how many letters beyond the ciphertext moving in a clockwise position gives you the plaintext.*
>
> *I hope this all makes sense. Once I get this information, I'll get this guy up and running for you (I've already started putting together some of the backbones of the program!). I should have it for you in a few hours or by tomorrow at the latest!*
>
> *If you have any questions, let me know!*
> *Looking forward to hearing back from you.*
> *Damien*

Cate grinned at the email. She clicked to download the spreadsheet Damien attached and popped it open. Dozens of cells filled her screen. Damien had already typed in numbers representing the twenty-five disks. He placed an "A" in the first column, next to each number. Columns across the top listed spaces for letters two through twenty-six.

Cate appreciated his organization. She grabbed the axle containing the disks and clicked it open. The disks slid off into her lap as she spun it sideways.

Cate sorted through disks in search of the first. She spun it until she located the "A" then input each letter after it into the spreadsheet.

She spent the next hour working through the spreadsheet. She double- and tripled-checked each row before saving it and opening a reply email to Damien Sherwood.

> *Hi Damien - Please, call me Cate. I really appreciate your help on this! Codebreaking is NOT something I'm very familiar with (though I have managed to decrypt fifty characters!). And working twenty-five characters at a time is very tedious.*
>
> *I've filled in the spreadsheet as you described and attached it.*
>
> *In terms of ciphertext to plaintext, the plaintext is one row below the cipher row on the disks.*
>
> *If you need any additional information, please let me know. There's no rush on the project, so please take your time. In the meantime, can you let me know your fee for the program?*
>
> *Thank you! Cate*

She attached the spreadsheet before sending the email on its way. Cate stared at the mess on her desk. Disks and journals lay sprawled across it. She grabbed the journals and stacked them in order next to the desk. She wouldn't tackle those until she received the program from Damien. It would speed the process tremendously.

Instead, she'd try to decode the sketches. She studied the list of drawings and the associated disk order. She threaded the disks onto the axle in the order listed for sketch one. As she slid the last one on, her laptop chimed to signify a new email. Cate glanced to the screen, finding a response from Damien.

Hi Cate - Thanks, everything looks good. I'll get started right away. One other thing that might be helpful would be to send a sample of the ciphertext and the plaintext that matches it (I think you said you had a small bit done). Then I can double-check my program before sending it over to you. Wouldn't want any crazy stories popping up because of my incorrect program, haha!

To answer your question, no charge. I'm happy to do it! It's a nice little challenge. I think it'll be fun!

D

Cate raised her eyebrows at the message. No charge? She'd definitely need to send Damien something for this. She'd put her thinking cap on if he continued to refused any fee. She opened her text document containing her decoded message and copied the cipher and plaintext into a message back to Damien.

With the message sent, Cate needed to retrieve the drawings from the office below. She pushed back from the desk and crossed the room. She opened the bookcase and stared into the darkness below. She pondered if she could hurry down and grab the sketches without needing the lights.

Cate took two steps into the blackness before reversing her course. She plugged the lights in before continuing downstairs. The sketches sat in the middle of the floor where she'd left them, except for the desk sketch. It laid where she and Jack discarded it on the desk's top.

Cate grabbed it first, figuring she could use it for practice since they'd already cracked it. As she picked up the sketch, she heard a loud ticking. The timepiece, tucked under her sweater, couldn't have come in contact with anything to have triggered the mechanism.

Her brow furrowed as she grasped the chain and pulled the timepiece toward her. As her hand clasped it, the office plunged into darkness.

CHAPTER 8

Cate's breath caught in her throat. Had one of the dogs knocked the plug loose? She glanced around as her eyes adjusted to the absence of light. Cate toggled on her cell phone's flashlight and took one step toward the stairs when noise sounded overhead. An unfamiliar voice carried down the stairs and reached her ears.

Cate's heart skipped a beat at the sound. She swallowed hard as she processed the situation. The voice, with a light Scottish accent, did not belong to Jack or Mr. Fraser. Another Scottish accent answered. She quickly doused her flashlight's beam.

The bookcase scraped against the floor as someone pushed it shut. Footsteps sounded on the stairs, which she noted no longer creaked. A dim, bobbling light glowed in the stairway.

The urge to hide overcame her. She gnawed her lower lip and glanced around the darkened space. As the light approached, Cate scurried toward the desk. She ducked under the top and curled into the space between each pedestal. As she settled as far from view as she could, she spotted the desk sketch on the floor. In her mad scramble to hide, she had dropped it. Her heart pounded as she weighed her options. Footsteps scraped on the stone floor. She couldn't risk retrieving it now.

Cate pulled her legs close to her chest and held her breath. The footsteps approached her hiding spot. A thud sounded overhead as their owner set something on the desk. By the smell of it, it was an oil lamp.

A figure reached down to the floor and snatched the paper Cate dropped moments earlier. "What the devil is this doing out?" he questioned. He slapped the paper against the desk's top as he approached it. Cate shrank back further. He stood mere inches from her.

With a trembling hand, Cate grasped her timepiece. The second hand crawled across the face. She'd slipped back in time.

"These are the types of incidents I'm referring to," the voice continued as Cate weighed her options.

"Misplaced paperwork?" the other voice answered.

"No, no, no, of course not. This sketch was filed away. How did it get out?"

"Merely a trick of your mind, surely, Douglas."

Cate's eyes widened. Douglas? Was this Douglas MacKenzie? Had she slipped back to the 1700s?

"There are too many tricks of the mind here. There is something more."

"What do you propose?"

"I have several theories. However, I do not wish to impart them until others have reviewed the evidence and offered opinions."

"Evidence?"

"Careful observation. Experimentation. I have kept track of all incidents, every detail." The man shuffled and pulled open a drawer. Cate spied the item he removed: a brown leather journal. She heard it thud against the desk above her. "I am keeping a journal. I've filled one already."

"May I peruse it?"

"Yes." The man bent again and opened a door on the desk. He withdrew the cipher wheel. "You will need this. I have encrypted the entire thing."

"Encrypted?" the other man inquired.

"Yes," Douglas responded.

"Was that really necessary?"

"If my theories prove correct, yes. This is larger than the both of us, Jaime," Douglas responded. "We must ensure this secret does not fall into improper hands."

Jaime, Cate reflected. Jaime Reid? Jack's ancestor? This must be Douglas MacKenzie and Jaime Reid, the castle's original proprietor and his estate manager.

Cate heard the journal's pages fan. "Perhaps you should recount the tales to me yourself," Jaime suggested with a chuckle.

Douglas joined in with a laugh. "Not up to the game, old man? If you prefer to be regaled with the tales minus my enhanced security, join me in three days hence for my dinner party. Bring Aria, Olivia would love it." He bent and shoved the cipher wheel into the desk's cabinet.

"You plan to share them at the dinner table, do you?" Jaime inquired.

"Of course not, though I do plan to share them. Grayson arrives in two days. My hope is he can shed some light on the strange goings-on."

"You plan to share these odd and unusual tales, yet you suggest extreme caution."

"Grayson is no stranger to the odd and unusual."

"If the incidents represent something as monumental as you suggest, perhaps we should leave well enough alone," Jaime suggested.

Douglas groaned with a sigh. "You've no sense of adventure." Silence fell between them.

"All right, Douglas. I shall plan to attend."

"Good man," Douglas said. His feet shuffled away from the desk. He circled it and clapped Jaime on the back. "Now about that estate business..."

"That we can discuss outside the confines of your dingy lab."

The voices began to fade as Cate overheard their shoes clatter against the wooden stairs. The room descended into darkness as the light faded away. Douglas chuckled. "This space is far from dingy..."

The bookcase doorway scraped against the floor as it opened and closed. Silence fell over the room. Cate breathed a sigh of relief. Her head fell back against the pedestal behind her as she gulped her fear down. She stayed still for several more moments, too afraid to move lest someone spring out at her.

After several moments, she surmised the coast was clear. She'd heard nothing. She perceived no presence. Cate crawled from under the desk. Her head rose slowly, and she risked a glance. The darkened room revealed no one. She toggled on her flashlight.

Cate grasped the desk's sketch from the blotter. She couldn't leave it. She stuffed it into her cardigan's front pocket.

She pulled the timepiece into her hand. She stared at its face. How had it activated? Cate rubbed its face, intent on returning to her time. Nothing happened.

Cate's heart sank, and her stomach turned. She tried again. Nothing. Blood rushed into her ears as she swayed on unsteady legs. Somehow, she had returned to the 1790s. And now she was stuck here.

Her mind swirled with questions. They crowded into her

brain all at once. What would she do? How would she return? Could she? One question settled among all the rest. She blanched as panic hit her. And brought tears to her eyes. What would she do if she couldn't get home?

Cate spun as she searched the darkened space for answers. She placed her hand against her forehead. "Think, Cate, think!" she whispered to herself.

Perhaps she needed to move to where she had been when the timepiece slowed. She hurried around the desk and tried to find the spot she'd stood in when she'd slipped to the bygone era. With shaky hands, she rubbed the watch's face again. The secondhand continued to crawl.

A sob escaped her. She chewed her lower lip as she considered the few options that sprung to mind. Could she navigate to the back hallway? The one that provided universal access to the watch wearer's time. Perhaps. Would it work? Maybe. With few other options, it was worth a try. Though escaping from this secret area may prove tricky. She had no idea who may be waiting on the other side of the bookcase at any time.

There must be a way to tell, Cate ruminated. Douglas wouldn't leave that to chance. He must have built in a peephole so he could enter and exit his laboratory discreetly. Cate nodded to herself. She'd search for the eyehole and use it to make her escape.

Cate turned toward the stairs. Bright light blinded her. She squinted against it, raising her hand to shield her eyes.

"Lady Cate! Are you there?" Mrs. Fraser's voice called.

Cate knit her brows, her pulse quickening. Her heart leapt into her throat.

"Lady Cate?"

"I'm here!" Cate squeaked out. She cleared her throat, attempting to steady her voice. "Coming!"

Cate swallowed hard as she glanced around the room.

Jack's temporary lighting glared into the space. The paperwork she'd come to retrieve sat stacked next to her. Riley wandered down the stairs and stared at her. A tear fell to her cheek as she spotted him. He meandered over, pausing to stretch mid-walk. Cate bent to collect him into her arms. He offered her a warm lick to the cheek.

Cate wiped the tear away as she sniffled. On shaky legs, she wobbled to the staircase and ascended it. With each step, Cate attempted to compose herself. She hoped her upset did not show. As she reached the top of the stairs, Cate plastered a smile on her face. She stepped into the room, finding Mrs. Fraser fussing over her tray.

"THERE you are," she said. "I thought you planned to stay in that dungeon forever!"

"Sorry," Cate breathed. "Got caught up with my work."

Mrs. Fraser frowned at her. "You'd better be careful with that work," she warned, waving a finger at Cate.

Cate gulped. How did she know? "You're going to work yourself sick! You already look awfully pale, Lady Cate."

Cate offered a nervous chuckle. She had no doubt she was white as a sheet after her experience.

"Not enough sun, I guess," Cate said with a shrug.

"And too much work. That makes Lady Cate a dull girl! Now, take a break and eat your lunch. My roast beef sandwich will give you some strength."

"Thanks, Mrs. Fraser."

Mrs. Fraser smiled at her and, with a nod, spun on her heel and strolled from the room. Cate collapsed into the armchair and sank her head into her hand. After a moment, she blew out a long breath. "It's okay, Cate. You're okay."

"Talking to yourself again, Lady Cate?" a voice inquired behind her.

Cate leapt in her seat, flailing her arms in the air. She nearly knocked her lunch tray from the table. She shut her eyes for a moment and pressed her hand to her heart. "Oh, Jack," she murmured. "You startled me."

"My apologies, Lady Cate. Wow, Mrs. Fraser wasn't lying," he said as he approached her. "You are terribly pale." He carried a steaming cup on a saucer. "She sent hot tea up. Said you needed it. She was afraid you were coming down with something."

"Thanks," Cate said with a nod.

"You okay?"

Cate bit her lower lip and glanced at him. She shook her head. "No."

Jack sank into the armchair across from her. "Cate, what happened?"

"Ah…" she began in a shaky voice.

"Is she okay?" Molly inquired from the door.

They spun to face her. "Yeah, yeah, I'm fine, Molly. Thanks."

"I didn't mean to startle you. I came up to see if you needed anything else with the tea."

"No," Cate answered. "The tea's fine and the sandwich. I just need some food. I'm fine!"

"Okay," Molly said. She hovered in the doorway.

"Oh, I had a quick estate question I'd forgotten to ask Lady Cate," Jack fibbed.

"Well make it quick, your lunch is getting cold, and Lady Cate needs to eat."

"I will, thanks," Jack said with a grin.

Molly smiled at them as she disappeared down the hall. Jack hurried across the room and pushed the doors closed. "Cate, what's wrong?" he asked, his forehead wrinkled with concern.

Cate sipped at the hot tea, her nerves settling with each sip. "Remember I told you I thought the timepiece slowed twice without my interacting with it?"

"Yes."

"Well, it did it again." Jack raised his eyebrows at her. "And this time I got stuck in the 1700s."

"WHAT?!" Jack exclaimed. He leapt from his seat and paced the floor. "Tell me every detail."

Cate nodded. "Well..." she began.

A knock sounded at the door and Molly stuck her head in. "Are you going to be much longer? Mrs. Fraser said your hot roast beef will soon turn to cold roast beef. I can bring your lunch up if you plan to stay awhile."

"That might be best, Molly. Thank you," Cate agreed. "This is going to take more discussion than we anticipated."

"Okey-doke! I'll run it right up," she said with a grin.

Jack collapsed into the armchair next to Cate. He wrung his hands as he waited.

"I'll wait until Molly brings your lunch," Cate mentioned.

Jack nodded without speaking. Within a few moments, Molly had the second lunch tray delivered. "Here we are. I hope it's nothing too serious!"

"No, just unexpected," Cate fibbed. It was only half a fib, she figured.

"Enjoy and don't work too hard!" Molly said as she left the room.

Cate waited as Molly pulled the doors closed behind her before speaking again. Jack beat her to it. "Okay, start at the beginning," he prompted.

Cate nodded. "Okay." She blew out a long breath before launching into her tale. "I told you earlier Ken helped me to decrypt the journals. And that he asked someone to automate the process. His contact got in touch with me and will have a program for me soon."

Jack perched on the chair, bobbing his head up and down to acknowledge her statements. "How does this relate to being stuck in the 1700s?"

"Given that this guy, Damien, is going to provide me with a program to speed decryption of the journals, I decided I would work on decoding Douglas's sketches while I waited since they seemed less tedious. I went downstairs to retrieve them. Oh, I never got them." Cate's mind began to feel less frazzled as she talked through the circumstances.

"While I was there, the timepiece started its loud ticking. I grabbed it to check, and the lights went out. I heard voices. Unfamiliar voices. So, I hid under the desk. Two men came down the stairs and spoke to each other. They called each other Douglas and Jaime."

"Douglas and Jaime?" Jack questioned. "As in Douglas MacKenzie and Jaime Reid?"

"That's what I'm assuming! Douglas was discussing writing the journals! He told Jaime he experienced strange things and wanted to get to the bottom of it. Jaime asked about them but seemed less than keen on decoding the journals when Douglas suggested it. Douglas told him to come to a dinner party he was hosting in three days. He planned to explain it to someone else then. What was his name?"

Jack rubbed his forehead and shook his head. "Wait, wait, wait, back up a minute. Why did you activate the timepiece?"

"I didn't!" Cate exclaimed. "That's what I was getting at. I went down to retrieve the papers and without warning, I was in 1790-something. I never touched the timepiece. That's the third time it's happened. And this time I can confirm I didn't absentmindedly rub the watch. It was under my cardigan. My hand was nowhere near it!"

Jack's jaw went slack. He swallowed hard. "So, it activated itself?"

Cate shrugged as she took the first bite of her sandwich. "I guess? I'm not certain. All I know is I was studying the desk schematic one second and the next the room plunged into darkness, and I was in the 1700s."

Jack shook his head as though he could not comprehend it. "Okay, I'm sorry, one minute you're glancing at the desk drawing the next you're in the 1700s without ever touching the timepiece?"

"That's right."

Jack shook his head in disbelief. "You're sure you weren't touching it?"

"Positive," Cate answered.

"Okay, okay, so then what happened again?"

"Douglas and Jaime had a brief conversation. They were discussing strange incidents, and Douglas said he was recording it all in journals. He invited Jaime to a dinner party in three days. He told him he planned to discuss the incidents with someone else. Someone familiar with strange goings-on. Who? What was his name?" Cate questioned aloud.

Jack bit into his sandwich and considered Cate's statements as he chewed.

"Grayson!" Cate exclaimed.

"What?"

"Grayson was his name. Douglas planned to tell someone named Grayson. I need to jot that down."

Cate scurried to the desk to retrieve a pen and make a note of her discovery.

"Okay, so, then what happened? Did you use the timepiece to return mid-conversation from your hiding spot?"

Cate shook her head as she returned to her armchair. "No, they left after a bit. I waited until I heard nothing before I climbed out. I had dropped the sketch of the desk and needed to retrieve it before I returned. This is where the story gets weird."

"THIS is where the story gets weird?" Jack questioned in an incredulous tone.

"I climbed from under the desk and grabbed the sketch.

The timepiece was still slow. I rubbed it to activate it and return here. But it didn't work."

Jack's eyes went wide. "It didn't work?"

"No," Cate confirmed. "It didn't work. I tried it again and still nothing."

"How did you get back?" Jack inquired.

"I wasn't sure what to do. I wondered if I could make it to the back hall to try the universal time rip but then, suddenly, the lights lit and I heard Mrs. Fraser calling me."

Jack shook his head again. "So, you didn't activate the timepiece in either instance, yet you slipped through a time rip and back? How?"

Cate shrugged; her eyebrows raised. She shook her head. "I… I don't know."

Jack rubbed his chin. "Cate, this isn't good."

"I know!" she agreed. "It's not good. And this is the third time it's happened. Is the timepiece broken? Malfunctioning? Is it no longer controlling the rips? Are the time rips morphing?"

Jack shook his head, his eyes wide. He paused, searching for an answer. "Perhaps Pap can help. At the very least, he should check the timepiece."

"Good idea," Cate agreed.

"The sooner the better," Jack proposed.

Cate nodded. "Okay."

"We'll go right after lunch. I'd go now but I don't want to raise any suspicion with the others."

"Right," Cate said with a nod. They ate for a few moments in silence before Cate added, "I can't believe this happened. I'm still shocked I was somewhere in the 1790s for a few moments."

"You're damned lucky, Cate. You could have been trapped there!"

"I realize that. I do, but for once, I had no control over it. I didn't ask to go back. I didn't even impulsively try the timepiece there to determine if a rip existed."

"Yet now we know one does," Jack answered. "And it goes somewhere into the 1790s."

Cate nodded. "Early in the 1790s, I'd guess. Around when Douglas started the journals. And he was about to have visitors. A man named Grayson." Cate stared ahead as she parsed through the information again. "Oh! My accidental trip did tell me one thing."

"What?"

"The voice haunting me in my dreams belongs to neither Douglas nor Jaime!"

"So, we were correct in that assumption," Jack responded.

"Yes! But we still can't identify who it is," Cate lamented.

"If the timepiece is malfunctioning, we may have bigger problems on our hands," Jack replied.

Cate sighed as she finished the last bites of her roast beef sandwich. Jack's assessment was likely correct. The mystery of the malfunctioning timepiece took precedence over her nightmares.

Jack finished his meal, and they returned their trays to the kitchen before making the excuse of errands in town. They arrived at Stanley Reid's cottage on the outskirts of Dunhaven shortly after.

Jack let himself in through the front door, calling out to the older man. Cate followed him into the living room. "Jackie?" Stanley called.

"Yes, and Lady Cate," Jack replied.

Jack's grandfather ambled into the room from the kitchen. "Lady Cate! To what do I owe the pleasure?"

"Nice to see you, too, Pap," Jack joked.

"It's good to see you, Jackie, but it's far better to see Lady Cate!" the older man quipped. "Can I offer you a cuppa?"

"I'd appreciate that," Cate responded. Despite recovering

from her earlier scare, her nerves remained raw from the experience.

Stanley motioned for them to follow him to the kitchen. He bustled about the small room as he set the kettle on the stove and retrieved teacups. "What brings you by? Another mystery?"

"No," Jack countered. "Well, yes, although it's more of a problem than a simple mystery."

"Oh?" Stanley inquired as he set cookies on a plate.

Jack swallowed hard before he launched into the story. "Cate ended up in the 1790s earlier today. Without activating the timepiece."

Stanley ceased laying out cookies. He twisted to face them. His brows knit together. "What?"

Cate nodded. "It's true. I went into Douglas's secret office and the next thing I knew I was in the 1790s. I hadn't touched the timepiece. It slowed on its own. And that's not the first time it's happened."

Cate described the other two instances to a stunned Stanley. He sank into the chair across from her as she finished the tale.

"Ever heard of anything like this happening before, Pap?" Jack inquired.

His eyebrows raised, and he shook his head in response. He blew out a long breath as he struggled to find words to respond. "Ah... I... No, I've never heard of anything like this," Stanley admitted.

"Would you mind taking a look at the timepiece to determine if anything is wrong with it?" Jack asked.

"Not at all," he answered.

The kettle screamed its alert across the kitchen. "How about that cuppa first?" Cate suggested with a smile.

Stanley returned her smile. "Whatever the lady wants, the lady gets," he said.

"I'll get it," Jack offered.

"Now, explain this time travel trip again," Stanley said to Cate as Jack poured the steaming water into their mugs. "Every detail."

"Goodness, you two really are alike," Cate said with a chuckle as Jack settled at the table again.

"We are, though I am more roguishly handsome," Jack responded with a grin.

"Obviously, I'm the humbler one," Stanley retorted. He sipped at his cup of tea. "Now, you ended up in Douglas's time. How?"

Cate recounted the details of her experience. His brow furrowed as he considered her tale. "And the timepiece didn't work to return either?"

"It didn't. At least not when I attempted to use it. Perhaps it was a delayed reaction?" Cate questioned.

He rubbed his chin. "I've never heard of anything like this. It certainly never happened in Lady Mary's or Lady Gertrude's time."

"Perhaps the timepiece is reaching the end of its life," Cate suggested.

"Let's take a peek and determine if anything is malfunctioning on it," Stanley said.

Cate handed the timepiece to him. She and Jack followed the older man into his living room. He attached a magnifier to his desk and removed a jeweler's toolset from his drawer. With exceptional care, he opened the timepiece. The mechanism inside whirred away. Jack peered into the magnifier next to Stanley.

"Anything?"

The older man cocked his head at several angles, moving the timepiece under the magnifier multiple ways.

"The mechanism controlling the general keeping of time seems to be working properly," he murmured.

"But?" Cate inquired, reading further into his comments.

He closed the watch and handed it back to Cate. He pulled his glasses from his face. "But," he answered, "beyond that, I couldn't say."

"What do you mean, Pap?" Jack questioned. "I thought you took care of this and kept it in working order for both the previous owners?"

"I did. But our maintenance never went beyond basic repair or the cleaning of it. We never had a problem with the time travel component."

"Is the time travel component working?" Cate asked.

Stanley puckered his lips and glanced between Jack and Cate. "That I can't help with. No one understands how that element works."

Cate's eyebrows squished together, and she glanced sharply to Jack. "What do you mean?"

"I mean, no one beyond perhaps Douglas and possibly Jaime understands how this timepiece controls the time rips."

"What?" Jack questioned. "He never told anyone? Never passed on the secret in case something like this happened?"

"Not to my knowledge, no," Stanley admitted. "No one understood how he managed to harness the power, only how to operate the timepiece."

"Well, that's just great!" Jack fumed, throwing his arms in the air. "So, we've got a malfunctioning time travel instrument interacting with time rips all over the castle."

"It's now vital that we decrypt Douglas's journals," Cate said with a sigh. "Perhaps those along with his sketches will tell us how he managed to control the time rips with the timepiece."

Stanley raised his eyebrows. "Have you made any progress on that?" he questioned. "Jack told me about your find."

"Yes," Cate responded. "A former colleague of mine

helped me identify the cipher and how to decrypt it. And, in the good news column, he put me in touch with someone who promised a computer program to make decoding it much faster. I'll make it my priority to work on those. Perhaps we'll find something there."

"I'm sorry I can't be of more help," Stanley said with a shrug. "The secret of that timepiece went to the grave with Douglas and Jaime from what I understand."

"Are there any elements inside the timepiece that aren't in a normal watch?" Jack inquired.

"No," Stanley said with the shake of his head. "That's what makes it even more enigmatic. There're no special components, no extra pieces. How this timepiece interacts and controls the rips is a mystery."

"Until we find out, perhaps you shouldn't wear that," Jack said to Cate, glancing at the timepiece hanging around her neck.

Cate considered it as Stanley responded. "It wouldn't matter."

"Because the timepiece could interact with any time rips near it wherever I leave it?" Cate suggested.

He shook his head. "No. No, it's not that. Because the watch controls the time rips. They stay closed unless you open them by activating the timepiece. But from what you've told me, the timepiece is no longer doing that. They are opening and closing at random, regardless of the timepiece's presence."

Cate's eyes widened as her jaw dropped open. Jack's eyebrows raised as he blinked in disbelief. "So, what you're saying is," Cate answered, her voice slow as she pieced together the puzzle, "the time rips can open and close at any time sucking in anyone in their vicinity and sending them to another era."

"And we now have no control over this at all," Jack finished.

Stanley stood and swallowed hard. "That's exactly what I'm saying."

Jack ran his fingers through his hair. "You can't be serious."

Cate sank into an armchair, speechless from the latest development. "What are we going to do?" she asked.

"I don't know," Jack admitted.

"Just a moment," Stanley cautioned. "All is not lost yet."

"Are you kidding, Pap? We've got a castle full of people with time rips opening and closing whenever they want and no means to control it! This is a disaster waiting to happen."

"No," Stanley argued, "the timepiece is still controlling them somewhat. You're not slipping in and out of eras at every turn. And when you do, it corrects, eventually. It's still exhibiting some control."

"Not enough," Jack said with a sigh and a shake of his head.

"No, I agree. But they are still held somewhat at bay. We need to determine how the timepiece does that. Perhaps then we can rectify the situation," Stanley suggested.

"And you're sure you have no idea?" Jack inquired. "No mention of even the slightest clue of how this thing works?"

Stanley shook his head. "No, none. As I said, this secret seems to have gone to the grave with Douglas and Jaime. No one understood how they harnessed the power with a simple timepiece."

"I can't believe they told no one," Jack said with a sigh.

"It's likely," Cate chimed in. "Randolph didn't seem to possess an understanding of it either beyond the existence of time travel and the timepiece's relevance to it."

"Perhaps he recorded it in the journals," Jack suggested.

"So, you'll need to decode them and see if it provides any answers," Stanley said.

"That seems a tall order," Jack lamented.

"Maybe Damien will have the computer program for me, and we'll find an answer in Douglas's journal."

"If not, we may be doomed."

Stanley raised his eyebrows at them. "What?" Jack inquired.

He shrugged. "Well...."

"If you've got something to say, Pap, say it," Jack encouraged.

"The journals aren't the only source of information."

Jack screwed up his face. "What are you suggesting?"

Stanley shrugged again. "You seem to have found access to Douglas himself."

Jack's eyes went wide and his jaw slack. "You aren't actually suggesting we travel back in time with a malfunctioning timepiece."

"To be fair, it seems to be malfunctioning only when it's not in use," Cate argued.

"We don't know that," Jack countered. "And I don't want to find out mid-trip that it doesn't work."

"Better than finding yourself suddenly stuck in the 1790s without ever having intended to travel there," Cate retorted.

"All right, all right, just calm down, you two," Stanley said.

Jack rubbed his face with his hands. "Okay, you're right," he answered. "Let's start with the journals and go from there. If we can't get them translated fast enough or they don't give us any information, we..." He paused. "I can't believe I'm about to say this. We head back to the 1700s and search for answers there."

"Agree," Cate answered. "I'll check for that program as soon as I get home. I'll do my best to decipher everything in the next few days. If there's no concrete information in those, we may need to consider attending that dinner party Douglas mentioned."

Jack shut his eyes and shook his head. "I can't believe time travel may be our BEST option."

"Speaking of Douglas," Cate said to Stanley, "do you know anything about a man named Grayson who visited the castle in the 1790s?"

Stanley glanced around in thought. "Name doesn't ring any bells. Do you have a last name?"

"No," Cate admitted. "Douglas mentioned wanting to tell Grayson about the unusual events at the castle in his upcoming visit. I was curious about his involvement in this."

"Sorry, lassie, it doesn't ring any bells."

Cate shrugged. "Oh well, I suppose we should head back, and I can get a start on those journals.

"Do you think you should stay at the castle, Cate?" Jack inquired.

"Where else would I stay?" Cate answered.

"Anywhere," Jack answered. "Just not there!"

Cate shook her head. "I can't do that! There's Molly and Mr. and Mrs. Fraser to consider. How would we explain it to them?"

"Gas leak?" Jack offered with a weak smile.

Cate shook her head again. "That story won't pass muster."

"The lassie's correct. You can't avoid the time rips. Your best bet is to seek a solution as quickly as possible."

Jack frowned and took a deep breath. "Then I'm afraid unless there is a clear answer in those journals, we will be attending a 1790s dinner party in three days."

CHAPTER 9

Cate and Jack returned to the castle. Silence filled most of their return ride. "I'll start on the journals even before I receive that program from Damien," Cate murmured as they traveled.

Jack nodded, providing no additional response.

"I should recover the sketches from Douglas's office, too." She paused for a moment. "Though I'm loath to go down there."

"I'll go with you," Jack offered. "At least then if you get stuck, you won't be alone."

"Thanks," Cate said with a nod.

Cate stared at the castle rising on the hill. Nothing appeared amiss. Inside the walls, though, danger lurked. Trouble brewed under the surface. Cate's new home had become perilous. Perhaps this had been the source of her nightmares. Perhaps they were a warning.

"I'm sorry, Jack," Cate said as the turmoil bubbled to the surface of her mind.

Jack glanced sideways at her. "For what?"

"This," Cate said with a shrug. She gestured toward the

castle looming on the hill in front of them. "The danger, the uncertainty. I..."

"Cate," Jack interrupted. "It's not your fault."

"Perhaps if I hadn't been so headstrong in jumping around in time since we discovered the secret this wouldn't have happened."

"And perhaps it's just an anomaly regardless of the timepiece's previous usage. Perhaps the rips are modifying in some way as you suggested. We know so little, you can't blame yourself for this."

Cate nodded. "Cate," Jack continued. He reached over to grab her hand. "It's not your fault. And besides, those trips were worth it."

Cate's brow crinkled, and she glanced at him. "They were?"

"Certainly. We saved a man's life on one and we caught a jewel thief on the other!"

"I thought you hated time travel and thought it was best to leave well enough alone. Not mess with the past and change things."

"Sometimes I'm a stick-in-the-mud," Jack admitted.

Cate chuckled at his comment.

Jack continued, "Someone very wise once told me the universe has a way of correcting itself. So, perhaps we can't irreparably damage things. And besides, my duty is to protect my MacKenzie counterpart. If I don't do that now, I've really failed as a Reid."

Cate squeezed Jack's hand. "Thanks. I'm glad you've had a sudden change of heart. Because we might be visiting another time period and meeting more of my ancestors."

"And mine!" Gravel crunched under the tires as Jack swung the car onto the drive.

"By the way, speaking of visiting the past, what's with

your interest in the man named Grayson?" Jack asked as he pulled the car parallel to the castle.

"Douglas mentioned him. He said he's no stranger to unusual things. I wondered if he was the man haunting my dreams."

"Ahhh," Jack answered as they climbed from the car.

"Let's grab those drawings and I'll get to work."

"Okay," Jack agreed.

They navigated the castle halls to the library. The bookcase remained open from Cate's previous trip downstairs. The blackness beyond yawned at them as they entered. Cate plugged the lights in, hovering at the top of the stairway.

"Ready?" Jack asked.

Cate shook her head but responded, "Yes."

"That doesn't look convincing at all."

"Let's just do this as quickly as possible."

"Deal!" Jack exclaimed.

Jack held out his hand. Cate grasped it, and they hurried down the wooden stairs, hand-in-hand. Cate raced to the pile of sketches and scooped them up in her free hand. "Okay, let's go," she stated.

She preceded Jack up the stairs. As they hastened into the library, both Cate and Jack blew out a sigh of relief. "Made it," Jack said.

Cate nodded as she pulled the plug, dousing the lights in Douglas's office. Jack pushed the bookcase shut. "Don't go back down there until we have to, okay?"

"Okay," Cate said with a nod.

"Wow! No objections from Lady Cate!"

Cate shook her head at him, a smile forming on her lips. "Don't get used to it."

"Good luck with the journals," Jack offered as he approached the doors.

"Thanks, with any luck, all we'll need to do is wind the thing backward and blow on it twice and it'll be fixed."

Jack stopped in his tracks. "Wind it backward and blow on it?" he asked with a chuckle.

"Don't say anything," Cate warned.

Jack held up his hands as a smirk formed on his face. He motioned his lips were sealed as he backed from the room.

His levity lifted Cate's spirits a bit. The tense situation weighed on her, though she hoped a solution lay in the stack of journals at her feet. Cate piled the sketches next to her laptop.

Before she began, Cate toggled her laptop on and checked her email. Her heart sank as she found no new messages from Damien Sherwood in her inbox. It didn't matter, she reflected. She had to make a start on the information.

She pushed her laptop away and pulled the stack of sketches over. Cate shuffled through them. She located the sketch showing the timepiece. She identified the number in the corner and matched it to the disk orientation written on the list she'd retrieved with the decoder disks.

Cate reordered the disks and began her translation of the marked components. Perhaps one of the marked pieces controlled the time rips. She dialed the wheels around to form the first cipher. The row underneath read: CASE SCREW.

Cate puckered her lips, certain this wasn't the component controlling the time rips. She tried another. It read CROWN WHEEL. She jotted it down and moved on. The next decrypted item read REGULATOR. Cate's pulse quickened. Regulator, her mind questioned? Perhaps this component regulated the time rips! She put a star next to it and tried the next. A smile crept across her face as she decoded this piece: ESCAPE WHEEL PIVOT.

Cate raised her eyebrows at the last two names. This

MUST have something to do with the time rips! Cate grabbed her phone and tapped around until the line rang.

"Lady Cate!" Stanley answered on the other end. "Long time, huh?"

"Hi, Mr. Reid," Cate said. "Funny. You may rival Jack with your joke-telling skills."

"I think I've got that young laddie beat by a mile! What can I do for you?"

"I found a sketch of the timepiece," Cate explained. "Encrypted. I've been decrypting it and I stumbled upon a few components I wanted to run past you as potential time rip managers."

"Go ahead, Lady Cate, what have you found?"

"Okay," Cate said, shifting the phone to her left hand as she pulled her notes closer. "The first piece says 'regulator.'"

"No, that's a standard component for a timepiece like that."

"Oh," Cate said, a note of disappointment in her voice. "Okay. The next one I saw that might relate is 'escape wheel pivot.'"

"No, this allows the time to move forward by a fixed amount of time."

"Really?" Cate questioned. "Both of those are standard components?"

"Indeed, they are, Lady Cate."

"Any others?"

"I haven't decrypted any more, I thought I'd hit upon something. Do you mind waiting while I try a few more?"

"Not at all!" Cate input a few more, checking each with Stanley.

"I'm sorry, Lady Cate, all those are standard pieces of a pocket watch."

Cate sighed. "Shoot! That leaves us nowhere!"

"Sadly, it does. It appears Douglas did not list the components controlling the time rips on the sketch."

"No," Cate lamented. "Well, I won't take up any more of your time. Thank you for your help!"

"No trouble at all, lassie. If you stumble upon anything else, don't hesitate to call."

Cate thanked him and ended the call. She tossed her phone on the desk in an expression of her frustration.

Cate checked the time on her timepiece, which apparently contained no components beyond those in normal pocket watches, as Stanley mentioned. She frowned at it as she noted the later-than-expected hour.

Cate dug through the sketches in the hopes of making some progress today. She found a few other drawings with limited text. She spent most of the late afternoon decrypting them but found nothing to help with their current predicament.

With a huff, Cate shoved the paperwork to the back of the desk. She took a brief break with the dogs outside before dinner.

Upon her return to the library, Cate rushed to her laptop to check her email. Nothing new popped into her inbox. Cate frowned at the laptop as the library doors opened.

"I'm just finishing up," she promised, assuming Molly or Mrs. Fraser delivered her tray.

"Don't stop on my account," Jack's voice answered her.

Cate spun in her chair. "Are you trying out a new job?" she inquired as he waddled across the room and struggled to set the tray on the table.

"If I am, I'm sure I'm failing miserably," he said as he nudged the tray further onto the table.

Cate chuckled at him. "Is anything the matter downstairs?"

"No," Jack admitted. "I volunteered to bring the tray up since I wanted to discuss something with you."

"I haven't made any progress if that's what you hoped to ask about. I decrypted the timepiece sketch, but it revealed nothing but normal watch components. I called your grandfather and discussed each piece with him, and we found nothing beyond what a normal watch would contain."

Jack grimaced. "That's too bad, though that wasn't what I wanted to discuss."

"Oh," Cate answered, her brows furrowing.

"I'm not comfortable with you being in this castle with these haywire time rips. I told everyone there was some problem with a potential water leak. Said we'd noticed it in Douglas's office. I wanted to keep an eye on it until we could determine the source and repair it so I would be staying in the castle."

"Oh!" Cate exclaimed. She gave Jack a soft smile. "I appreciate that very much."

"I probably can't do much, but it makes me feel better being here."

"Somehow it'll make me feel better, too."

"I'll just run home and grab a few things and be back. Molly's preparing my usual room."

"Great. Thanks, Jack."

Cate dug into her dinner as Jack departed. His presence in the castle may help her sleep tonight. Cate considered swapping bedrooms since hers contained a time rip. However, they did not have an exhaustive list of all the time rip locations. She worried about slipping into an unidentified time rip and returning to a time with which she was unfamiliar. At least the rip in her bedroom led to a time she'd already visited.

As evening turned to night, Cate dawdled in the library with a mystery novel. She kept a constant eye on her email, hoping one from Damien Sherwood popped into it any second. Nothing came.

Cate retired to her suite. Both dogs leapt onto her bed, more than ready to go to sleep. Cate was less inclined. She eyed the bed with a frown as she kicked off her slippers. Would she lay awake or fall asleep and have another nightmare? Either way, the night promised misery for her.

Cate crawled into bed and shut off the lights. Moonlight painted the room and cast long shadows on the floor. In the darkness, Cate strained to listen for any sounds, especially the characteristic ticking of her timepiece.

After an hour of tossing and turning, Cate rose from her bed and shuffled to her sitting room. She collapsed on the chaise. Worry crowded her mind, along with potential scenarios and questions. Would the time rips continue to misbehave? What if they ended up in another time period? Would they find a solution before something tragic happened?

Cate's mind spun in an endless cycle of unanswerable questions. She pulled her laptop onto her lap. Perhaps a movie would relax her mind. Or at least pass the time. As she toggled on the display, she wondered if Jack had any luck sleeping in the castle tonight.

Cate's display brightened the room. Her email program still sat open on the screen. Cate swiped at her trackpad. As she pushed the pointer toward a new tab, the email list updated. A new email topped her inbox.

Cate's heart skipped a beat as she recognized the sender: Damien Sherwood. Cate selected the email to open it.

> *Hi Cate! Attached is a shiny new program for you! I tested it and it seems to work fine. If you have any issues let me know!*

Once you open it, you'll first need to tell it the order of the disks. There are drop-down boxes to select the disk number. Once you have that in, click DECODE! That will open an interface with two windows. The first (on the left) is where you'll enter your ciphertext. Then click the GO! button and it will give you the plaintext in the right window.

I wanted to get this to you asap, so I didn't spend a lot of time checking efficiencies (I'll keep working on it). So, for now, maybe only do a page or two of text at a time. It should work fine with more, but it'll be really, really slow, and might take a long time to complete. It'd be faster to work in small chunks and copy the results over to a larger document to compile everything. Well, I'm sure you don't need to be told that! You're obviously very intelligent and capable.

Anyway, good luck and have fun! I hope you find some interesting things encoded in the text! Let me know if you have any questions or problems!

D

Cate's pulse raced as she downloaded the program file. After a brief install, a window popped up on her laptop.

DECODER EXPLODER appeared in colorful letters across her screen. Cate chuckled at the program's name. As it loaded, she carried the laptop down to the library, where the journals still sat in a stack next to the desk.

As promised, the first screen requested the order of the disks. Cate pulled open the first journal and input the disk order before clicking the DECODE button.

The next window presented itself. A blank page stared at her, awaiting a text input.

Cate opened her word document as she flipped to the first page of the journal. She copied the text and input it into Damien's program. Cate waited with bated breath after clicking the GO! button.

After a few minutes, text appeared in the right-hand window along with a pop-up window declaring success. Cate dismissed it and copied the plaintext into a new word document.

I have created this journal to chronicle and preserve my experiences as I search for answers. Strange encounters have met much of my brief time within Dunhaven Castle. I often ponder over the warning I received when walking the property prior to the castle's construction.

"Cursed," the old woman said. Her tattered clothing hung loosely on her frame. One crystal blue eye stared at me from a wrinkled face. The other eye clouded over in a grotesque fashion. Her wrinkled skin sagged on her face and neck. She pointed a gnarled finger at me. "Dinnae you build here. You and your kin shall be CURSED!"

I ignored her. Perhaps I should not have. Indeed, odd occurrences followed us from acquisition through building, eventually enveloping us as we settled into our new home.

Strange weather patterns were reported by townsfolk on the site we proposed for building. As the foundation was laid, a load of bricks shifted without warning, killing a poor soul crushed beneath their weight.

During construction of the west wall, one worker disappeared. Of course, foul play was suspected, but no traces of him, nor his body, could be found.

This would prove minor compared to the disturbances we would endure as residents of the finished castle.

The page ended. Cate hurried to input the next page of text. Within a few moments, she read the next piece of the entry.

It seemed to begin with minor instances. A vase out of place. A book moved. Then, occurrences became more disturbing. As the intensity increased, I vowed to determine the source of these hauntings. I have recorded and will continue to record all instances on these pages.

After living with these happenings for over one year, I have concocted several theories regarding their origins. I shall also detail these within the pages of my journal.

I shall begin at the beginning.

Good fortune smiled upon me, the son of a country doctor. Several wise investments allowed me to rise in wealth and station. Perhaps my wealth cursed me. I sought to create a grand home for my family, one worthy of the newest title I carried: Earl of Dunhavenshire.

At the center of Dunhavenshire sat the small town of Dunhaven, my home as a youth. I left Dunhaven a man of simple means; I returned an earl. Determined to erect the grandest building overlooking the town, I was immediately drawn to the hill overlooking the hamlet.

Even as a child, the hill held a reputation among the townsfolk. Tainted land, they called it. Strange manifestations occurred there. Weather shifted suddenly, without warning.

Hushed whispers suggested the undead roamed the grassy knolls. Others suggested underground rivers flowed with blood. Even more, advocated the existence of a gateway to Hell.

The rumors did little to sway me from my desires to build a structure such as Dunhaven had never seen and such that would never be rivaled by the small town for centuries to come.

"There are other properties to consider," Jaime Reid informed me as we discussed the prospect.

"There are none that hold my interest," I insisted.

"Lord Mackenzie," he countered before I interrupted him.

"If we are to work together, Mr. Reid, you must understand I

am a man with specific ideas and desires. I am not easily put off by nonsense and superstition."

"Still," the man urged, "consider the others. What holds you back on them? Why do you desire the piece of land you mentioned?"

"Simple," I explained. "The land sits at the highest spot overlooking the town."

"And you, as Lord of the county, desire to be a constant reminder to the town of your presence and authority?" he inquired.

"I desire to be a constant source of inspiration. I left this town a pauper. I returned a lord."

Jaime smirked at me. He did not agree yet he did not challenge me on it.

Jaime and I had been school chums before my departure. "You threatened you would, and you have done it, Douglas."

"And I intend to make good on my promise," I assured him.

"We were but children, Douglas. I expect nothing."

"I am a man of my word, Jaime. Do you recall the promise I made?"

"I do."

Under a cloudless azure blue sky, we lay in the field. The cool grass beneath us tickled our bare feet. I had sworn there to make something of myself. "I shall be more than a simple country doctor," I vowed.

"'Tis nothing wrong with a country doctor," Jaime countered. "It is an honest living."

"Indeed, it is," I agreed, "yet it is not very grand."

"Perhaps stability is preferential to grandeur."

"Perhaps stability is an excuse for complacency," I suggested. "Have you no grand aspirations?"

Jaime shrugged. "I strive to make an honest living to provide for my family."

I rolled to my stomach and faced him. "Have you no dreams beyond that?"

He shrugged again. "I suppose not."

"Well, I have," I informed him. "Mark my words this day, Jaime Reid, I shall strive for more than the mundane. I shall be someone one day. Everyone shall know my name. They shall say 'there is Douglas MacKenzie, a man among men!'"

Jaime let out a belly laugh as I continued. "I shall, Jaime. You shall see. And when I do, I shall always remember our friendship. I shall take you under my wing and ensure your family is provided for with that honest living."

Our conversation flitted through my mind as I responded. "And now I have achieved my success and returned to Dunhaven a man among men! And my offer stands. Your family shall be provided for easily with the sum I offer you."

"To build and oversee a castle on cursed land?"

"To build and oversee a castle on PRIME land," I argued. He hesitated. "Oh, Jaime, those rumors are merely the prattling on of superstitious townsfolk. Join me. Take the first step on this adventure with me!"

A smile crossed his face, and he extended his hand to me.

"A wise choice," I said with a grin as I gave him a strong handshake.

Perhaps Jaime had been correct. Perhaps not. Perhaps this, too, is part of my destiny.

CHAPTER 10

Cate's body trembled. She stiffened, her head darting up and her eyes snapping open. She squinted against the light in the room as she searched for the source of the disturbance.

"Cate," Jack's voice whispered. "Cate!"

"Huh?" Cate murmured as she began to awaken.

"Hey, sleepyhead," Jack said with a grin. "What are you doing down here?"

Cate glanced around the room, recognizing the library. Her laptop, its screen blank, sat on the desk in front of her. Douglas's first journal lay open next to it. She blinked a few times before turning her attention to Jack, who knelt at her side.

"Uh," she mumbled. "I couldn't sleep. I planned on watching a movie but when I opened my laptop, I found an email from Damien with the decryption program, so I decided to head down here and start working."

Jack smiled at her as he pushed a lock of hair out of her face. "Care to share your discoveries over one of Mrs. Fraser's shortbreads?"

Cate brightened at the offer. "There's not much to share, but I won't say no to a shortbread!"

Cate stood. "I'll bring them to you. Why don't you curl up on your armchair and relax?" Jack suggested.

"I'm not going to fight you on that suggestion," Cate answered. "I'm exhausted."

Jack grinned at her as she slid into the chair. He disappeared and returned a few minutes later, shortbread tin in hand.

Jack sank into the armchair next to Cate. "Okay, have you fixed the timepiece yet?"

Cate grabbed a cookie from the tin and scoffed at the statement. "Not even close."

Jack dropped his head onto the chair behind him in a dramatic display. "You've GOT to be kidding! You haven't solved this yet?"

Cate giggled, despite her exhaustion. "Nope, sorry. I fell asleep way too fast. I only decoded about five pages."

"So, this Damien guy's program works, huh?"

"Like a charm! I decoded everything I already had typed in. But focusing on that gobbledygook made my eyes cross and apparently put me right to sleep!"

"Okay, so no solutions yet. Did you find anything else interesting though?"

"In my estimation, I did!" Cate raced to the desk and retrieved her laptop. She detailed her findings to Jack.

"Cursed. CURSED!" Jack shouted in his best "old woman" voice.

Cate chuckled. "Not funny, they probably did assume it was cursed!"

"You laughed, didn't you?"

"I did, yes."

Silence fell over them. Cate finished her cookie and

snapped the lid on the tin. She stretched and yawned. "I guess I should get back at it," she suggested.

"You should get some rest."

"I'm okay. I had a little nap there," Cate insisted. "And I really need to make more progress on these. I've got thirteen journals to get through and..."

"Cate," Jack interrupted. "You need to get some sleep. The journals can wait."

"No," Cate argued. "We need to figure something out before this time rip problem gets worse."

"We'll handle it, Cate. We can deal with this. Get some rest. Start fresh tomorrow."

Cate bit her lower lip as she glanced at the stack of journals. After a moment, she nodded. "Okay. I am tired. I'll call it a night and start first thing tomorrow morning."

Jack smiled at her. "Good night, Lady Cate."

"Good night, Jack. Oh, you'd better put this tin back before Mrs. Fraser finds it missing!"

"Don't worry, I'll put it back before I return to bed. There's no way I'm getting us caught!"

***

Morning came sooner than Cate hoped. Her alarm screamed in her ears as she groaned. "Ugh," Cate moaned as she climbed to her feet. At least, she reflected as the hot water cascaded over her in the shower, she'd slept without a nightmare. Cate frowned at the current solution to her predicament. Perhaps she'd find a resolution for her nightmares within the pages of Douglas's journals.

Following breakfast, Cate settled in the library for another work session. Before she began, she typed an email to Damien and informed him the program worked like a charm.

She settled in for a long session of tedious typing. After five more pages, Cate decided to take a break from transcribing and decrypt the new entries. She dug into the entries as the program output them.

Jaime and I toured the property the following day. I stood on the hill and overlooked the property. "Here," I asserted.

"Here?" Jaime inquired.

"On this very spot!" I declared.

Jaime spun as he scanned the area. "It is the highest spot. View of the town below. Though, perhaps..."

"Perhaps nothing. It shall be this spot!" I tapped my cane on the ground.

"Cursed!" a gravelly voice growled from behind us.

I spun to face the sound. The old woman stared at us. Her leathery skin wrinkled across her forehead and cheeks and around her colorless lips. One eye, crystal blue, stared at me from beneath that wrinkled forehead, the other milky and clouded. "Cursed," she repeated.

"Whatever are you on about, old woman?" I inquired of her.

"Cursed, this land is. Dinnae build here. You shall bring a terrible scourge on your family."

"Foolhardy rumors, nothing more," I assured her.

She shook her head. "Nay," she snarled at me. "Bad, this land. Cursed. You shall suffer a terrible fate if you continue with this folly."

"I do not give in to foolish gossip. Now, begone, woman, allow us to conclude our business."

"You have been warned," she muttered.

"She will not be the last person to say these things," Jaime said as she wandered away.

"I am certain she will not be. I care not. Now, where shall we place the stables?"

My mind often returns to that moment. I have spoken with the woman several times since that day. She maintains her warning. And I have grown to believe it.

We began construction on the castle three months to the day from when Jaime and I stood on that hill. I have already mentioned the unfavorable circumstances surrounding the castle's construction. I am certain one if not both of these incidents are related to the quirks we continue to experience.

After the castle's completion, we took up residence in the fantastic space. Not long after, we began to feel the effects of the castle's peculiarities.

I still recall the first night in our new home. Unable to sleep, I roamed the halls. Moonlight cascaded through the leaded windows. How wrong that old harridan had been! The only scourge brought upon us with this castle was that of a beautiful, stately home. Olivia and I had discussed at length the guests we'd invite to our new home, the parties we should throw, the generations of MacKenzies who would grace these halls.

As I sauntered through the back hall, I spotted a wayward shadow. I squinted into the darkness. It appeared to be the figure of a person. "Hello!" I called. We were not yet fully staffed, though we had brought several staff members from our previous home to the castle. I assumed it to be one of them, perhaps unable to sleep and wandering the halls.

I received no response to my inquiry. "Hello?" I called a second time. The figure stood unmoving at the hall's end. Hidden in the shadows, I could make out no more of the person than his or her form. I took a step closer. A rhythmic noise filled the air, which I guessed to be breathing. "See here, who are you?" I demanded.

After two more steps, the figure backed from me. "Stop! Who are you?"

Shadows surrounded the figure as I continued my approach. I hurried down the hall but found no one. I continued around the corner, glancing into the next hall. Empty. I rushed to each door and peered into the darkened rooms. I found no one in any of them.

I returned to the hallway and stalked to my original spot. I stared into the darkness where the figure stood. Perhaps my eyes deceived me, I reflected. The moonlight cast strange shadows. I must have mistaken the distortions as a figure. Still, the old woman's words rung in my mind. I pushed them aside. They were likely the source of my hallucination.

Cate leaned back in her chair. Douglas's first experiences within the castle walls echoed her own. Odd to share so much with a man separated from you by centuries. Cate stretched as she contemplated the latest round of entries.

She switched to her email before continuing her decryption. A message from Damien awaited her.

Hi Cate - That's awesome, I'm so glad it's working! I'm still playing with the efficiencies and if I get something better, I'll send a new version to allow you to decrypt more text at once.

Are you learning anything interesting from the journals? You don't have to answer that. I was just curious what was so important the author felt the need to encrypt it. Though, I suppose it could be out of some odd eccentricity. Well, anyway, I'm rambling.

Keep decrypting!
D

Cate smiled at the email as she clicked the reply button.

Hi Damien - The program is working great! I'm working my way through the journals. The longest part of the process is typing in the random letters! No rush (or even need) for a more efficient program, the current version is more than sufficient and MUCH faster than working twenty-five characters at a time by hand!

> *To answer your question, Douglas (my ancestor and the castle's builder) was quite an eccentric! He was an intellectual and an inventor, so he had some interesting quirks. This seems to have been one of them! So far, the stories have been entertaining at least! It makes the work to get them worth it.*
>
> *Thanks again for all your help!*
>
> *Cate*

With a deep sigh, Cate turned to the next page in the journal and began the tedious task of typing more ciphertext into Damien's program. After deciphering several more entries, Cate continued to read Douglas's experiences.

> *It would not be long before I had more fodder from what I initially thought to be my overactive imagination. As I entered the library, intent on working in my hidden laboratory, I noticed a vase out of place. I would attribute a minor event such as this to Olivia or one of the servants changing its location. However, the hour was too early. I had read only the night before in this room. The vase had stood on a bookshelf near the armchair I occupied. On this morn, I found it across the room on a side table.*
>
> *I approached it and studied the object. How had it moved across the room? I had been last to bed and awake before any servants came from below stairs. How had this moved? I chided myself for my silly behavior as I descended to my lab. Vases did not move on their own. There existed some reasonable explanation, I assured myself.*
>
> *I descended the stairs into my study. When I returned to the library, the vase had returned to its original location. My brow furrowed as I stared at the object in its original location. Befuddlement filled me. As I considered the matter, the library doors opened.*
>
> *"Oh, excuse me, m'lord," Lucy, one of our maids, muttered as she entered. "I came to tend to the lighting of the fire."*

Lighting the fire, my mind pondered? Then no one had entered the room prior to this. I must be sure. "Lucy, has anyone been in the room tidying before you?"

"No, m'lord," she assured me. "'Tis only half-past six. No one has begun daily chores yet."

"Thank you," *I mumbled to her as my eyes fell to the vase. How had it completed its journey 'round the room without human assistance? My mind could find no answers.*

I had almost forgotten the incident until I experienced it again. This time within the confines of my own laboratory. Weeks later, I descended the stairs to find my work in disarray.

I had left my papers stacked in a pile on the right side of my desk. When I returned the following morning, they lay scattered across my desk. I stood with my jaw agape. I had not left my work in this manner. Few people were aware of my lab's location or how to enter it. Hidden by a bookcase in the library, my lab sits deep within the heart of the castle. I had hidden the lab and its entrance from almost everyone except those involved in its construction. Outside of Jaime, no one on the estate knew the location, not even Olivia.

I narrowed my eyes at the mess as I set the lantern on the desk and collected the papers. I would speak with Jaime about it. There must be an explanation, I assured myself.

But I would find none. When I inquired later, Jaime insisted he had not entered my lab nor parsed through my papers. Who had, I queried?

"I've little idea, Douglas," *he answered.* "Though there is surely a reasonable explanation."

"Name it," *I challenged.*

"You forgot the state in which you left them. You worked late and assumed you had tidied them, but you hadn't."

"Nonsense," *I argued.* "I left them neatly stacked on the right side of the desk. Not the left, not the center, not sprawled."

"Douglas, papers do not move on their own," *Jaime assured.*

I pursed my lips at him, unable to argue, though still unsatisfied by the explanation.

Unexplainable events would continue to present themselves. More items moving about with no explanation and no human intervention. I began to wonder if I was going mad. Or someone was playing an elaborate game with me. The incidents occurred with such regularity, I became accustomed to them and paid little attention after a while.

Even with the ever-moving articles, castle life became routine. I stopped questioning the occurrences and began to settle into my new home.

Then things became more disturbing.

Cate frowned at the "cliffhanger" in the journal. "Of course it would stop there," Cate lamented aloud as she turned the page to continue her typing. A knock sounded at the door, and the door popped open.

"Lunchtime!" Molly sang as she flitted into the room.

"Already?" Cate questioned. She checked her timepiece.

"Lost in your research again, huh?" Molly asked with a laugh.

"Yes. It's fascinating. I'm reading through journals from Douglas."

"Devil-worshipper Douglas?" Molly teased.

"Yes, him," Cate replied.

"Has he sacrificed any animals or small children yet?"

"No," Cate assured her. "Just detailing his early life in the castle."

"You know I'm only teasing, right?" Molly inquired.

"I know," Cate said with a smile. "And you know he wasn't a devil worshipper, right?"

"Yeah, I know! What a fanciful tale though, huh? I bet he really hated the town gossips that spread that around."

"I can imagine that would be frustrating, though Douglas

seemed to be a good sport. An eccentric. Perhaps he even enjoyed the rumors and found them entertaining."

"He'd be a way better sport than I would be!"

"Of course, I could be completely wrong. Perhaps he hated the rumors and was an old curmudgeon who frowned down at the town every day."

"Perhaps you'll find out in those journals! Enjoy your lunch!"

As Cate ate, she checked her email, finding a new message from Damien.

Hi Cate - Wait, there's a castle involved? That's cool... and creepy. Is it haunted? Sorry, I had to ask, haha!

Here's a new version of Decoder Exploder with better efficiencies. If your eyes (and fingers) can stand it, you can now input multiple pages into the program (I'd say no more than five for best results) to decrypt at once!

Enjoy!

Damien

Damien's first line made Cate giggle. If he only understood the extent of what these castle walls housed. Ghosts, however, did not haunt these halls.

Cate responded to thank him for the new, more efficient program and to assure him there were no ghosts. As she finished her lunch, another knock sounded at the door.

"Come in! Perfect timing, I've just finished."

"Oh, good. I'd hate to interrupt your lunch," Jack's voice said.

"Jack!" Cate exclaimed, spinning in her seat to face him. "Are you trying out tray retrieval as a new job?"

"I'm here to check on our 'leak,'" he responded. He slid through the opening in the door and pushed it shut behind him. "Anything from the journals about the time rips and how the timepiece controls them?"

Cate shook her head with a sideways frown. "Not yet. He's describing his first few months in the castle and the odd occurrences he experienced. He hasn't even mentioned the timepiece yet."

Jack frowned. "But," Cate added, "Damien just sent a new version of the program capable of translating more text at one time, which may speed things up a tad. Though my typing is woefully slow with the random letters. But I'll do my best to make progress this afternoon. Right after a quick walk with these guys!" Cate motioned toward the two dogs at her feet.

"I'll walk you out," Jack offered.

Cate stood and ushered the dogs from the room and into the hall. "How far have you made it in decrypting the journals?" Jack inquired.

"Only about fifteen pages," Cate admitted with a sigh.

Jack didn't respond. "I should be able to…" Cate's voice cut off. "Jack!" she exclaimed.

Cate blinked several times, her eyes growing wide. She reached out, attempting to grasp Jack's hand.

"Cate?" he questioned. "What's happening?"

"I'm not sure," Cate admitted. She focused her attention on Jack, who faded in and out of her vision. He disappeared for seconds at a time, only to reappear next to her. Her pulse quickened, and her heart pounded. Lights flickered. Noises distorted. Dimensions stretched.

As Jack reappeared, Cate reached a trembling hand toward him. Jack's hand squeezed hers tightly, and he pulled her closer to him. After a moment, the hallway settled. Cate glanced around. Candlelight flickered throughout the space. They were alone. Both dogs were missing from their new surroundings.

She focused her attention on Jack. "Where are we?"

Jack swallowed hard. "I'm not sure."

Cate stalked a few steps away, keeping a tight hold on Jack's hand. "Candles," she murmured.

"Somewhere without electricity," Jack confirmed.

Cate pulled the timepiece from around her neck. The second hand crept along. Jack groaned. "As I suspected," Cate said.

"So, we're stuck somewhere!" Jack exclaimed.

Cate nodded. "Yes, keep your voice down. We don't want to call any attention."

"Perhaps we should find somewhere to hide," Jack suggested.

"No," Cate countered. "We need to stay here. If we want to return, we need to stay near the rip we came through."

"You don't know that for sure."

"No," Cate admitted. "I'm not certain, but it makes sense. If we move from this spot, we may be stuck here."

"Can you try to activate the timepiece?"

"I'll try," Cate answered. "Put your hand around mine so if it works, we can go back together."

Jack wrapped his hand around Cate's, and together they rubbed the timepiece's face. Nothing happened. They tried twice more.

"It's no use," Cate said with a sigh. "It won't work. This is exactly what happened the last time when I got stuck in Douglas's time."

"You planned to try the back hall, the universal rip. Should we try that?" Jack inquired.

Cate pondered it for a moment. "I don't..." she began. Bright lights flashed for an instant before blinking out. Cate inched closer to Jack. He wrapped his arm around her. The lights flashed again before dying. Cate squeezed her eyes shut as they flared again in an almost blinding display.

Tiny paws pressed against her leg, and a cold nose nudged at her hand. Cate's jaw unhinged, and she slid her eyes open to slits. Her heart skipped a beat, and tears formed in her eyes. "Riley!" she cried as she spotted the tiny pup standing on his hind legs. Bailey stood next to him. "Bailey!"

Jack sucked in air and glanced around. "Are we back?"

"Yes," Cate said, scooping both boys into her arms as a tear fell down her cheek.

Jack slumped against the wall, a sigh of relief escaping him. Silence filled the hallway. "You okay?" Cate inquired.

Jack ran a shaky hand through his hair. "Yeah, yeah, I think so," he responded.

"Let's get some air," Cate suggested. She ushered the dogs down the hall after setting them down. Cate reached for Jack's hand and tugged him toward the door.

They exited into the fresh, warm spring air. Jack blew out a long breath. "Feel better?" Cate asked.

"Yeah. Nice fresh Scottish air does the trick every time," he said with a weak smile.

Cate squeezed his hand and smiled at him, giving him another moment to recover. "That was..." he began, his voice trailing off.

Cate nodded. "Yeah, I understand. All too well."

Jack shook his head as he stared at the horizon.

Cate said, "I'll keep working on the journals. I'll try to speed up my decryptions..."

Jack shook his head again, holding up a hand to stop Cate. "That's not going to work, Cate. Even if you work twenty-four seven on those things, it'll take a while to get answers."

"But perhaps the answers are in one of the early journals. We can hope..."

"We need to do more than hope. We need a solution, and I don't like pinning all my hopes on the journals containing the information we need. What if you translate all of them and find nothing? Then we're days behind pursuing anything else."

"So, what are you suggesting?" Cate questioned, her brow furrowing as she glanced at him.

Jack turned to her and studied her face for a moment before speaking. "We need to travel to Douglas's time and search for answers."

Cate nodded but didn't respond. Jack's brow crinkled. "I figured you'd be happy about that suggestion, Lady Cate," Jack teased.

"I guess I'm still in shock," Cate admitted.

Jack nodded. "I understand. That experience was enough to shock anyone."

Cate glanced up at him. "No, I meant because you actually suggested time travel as the solution to a problem." She pursed her lips in a half-grin at him.

He narrowed his eyes. "Very funny, Lady Cate. I didn't realize you hoped to join me on the comedy circuit."

"Anyway, you're right. Douglas somehow harnessed these time rips. He's the best source of information we have."

"Do we just go back and ask him?"

Cate shook her head. "He doesn't realize or understand the scope of what's happening yet. Let's get the lay of the land first and go from there."

"Now I'm in shock. Cate Kensie suggesting caution? What did that slip in time do to us?"

"Perhaps it switched our personalities," Cate joked.

"Are you looking forward to time traveling?"

Cate pondered it for a moment. "Yes, I have to admit I am. A brand-new castle and the chance to meet its builder. Yes, it's an exciting moment!"

"And I'm dreading it, so we're still us."

Cate chuckled at the admission.

Jack continued, "And I hope we can trust that bloody watch to behave itself and return us when we want!"

Cate glanced down at it. "As much as I'm looking forward to the occasion, the 1790s is not where I want to stay on a permanent basis."

"When do you want to do this?" Jack inquired.

Cate considered his question. "It would be nice to attend his dinner party. The one he discussed with Jaime. He's planning to discuss the occurrences with someone named Grayson. With others there, it might be easier to blend in. The focus won't be on only us. And we may get information if he's planning to share it with the people in attendance."

"What are the chances he shares it with two newcomers there?"

"Perhaps small, but maybe we'll learn something by overhearing it. At least we can assess Douglas and his mysterious guest who has experience with the strange and unusual."

"Do you imagine this Grayson is the character chasing you around in your sleep?"

"I'm not sure. But one or two spoken words from him may be enough to tell me. That's another reason I'd like to get to that dinner party."

"It may be a tall order. It's in, what, two days?"

"Yes," Cate admitted. "Day after tomorrow. We'd need to move fast. Visit tomorrow and hope we score an invitation."

"What's our cover?"

Cate shrugged. "The old distant cousin bit?"

"Again? We've gotten caught every time with that one!"

"Last time we got caught because Randolph told Rory the story about us. Douglas should never have heard of us before. Plus, posing as a married couple explains away my American heritage in the easiest way possible."

Jack pursed his lips and narrowed his eyes. "I imagine there's another reason you suggested it."

Cate glanced at the horizon, her brows furrowing. "It makes the most sense for a man and woman traveling together, particularly in that era?" she suggested.

Jack smirked at her. "Oh, come on, Cate. I'll bet you enjoy posing as my wife. I do make a fine husband if I say so myself." He raised his eyebrow at her and offered her a sly grin.

"Yes, that's it," Cate said with a chuckle. "You've caught me. I love posing as your wife. It's the entire reason I love time travel, in fact."

"That explains so much," Jack joked.

"Are you planning to go with the lawyer bit again or do you prefer to avoid that profession?"

"Eh, I may as well continue. I am quite a good attorney after all," he reminded her.

"Very true. You're almost as perfect an attorney as you are a husband."

"Oh, you flatter me too much."

They turned their attention to the yard where the dogs frolicked in the luscious spring grass. "I suppose we have our plan," Cate said after a few moments of silence. "What time tomorrow?"

"Afternoon? Following lunch, perhaps," Jack suggested.

"All right. Tomorrow after lunch, we make our first trip to the 1790s!"

CHAPTER 11

Cate collected the dogs and returned to the library. Despite their upcoming time travel trip, she preferred to make more progress on the journal decryption. Given the new, more efficient program, she spent the afternoon copying ciphertext.

It took her several hours to recreate the text from the first journal before she began decoding it. Cate read the next set of entries before her dinner.

> *The matter of moving vases and unkempt paperwork seemed a harmless quirk of the castle. I had grown accustomed to it and paid no mind to the odd and ongoing circumstances.*
>
> *Two months passed before the next incident. This event would raise the stakes along with the hairs on the back of my neck.*
>
> *On the night of the twenty-fifth of October, I roamed the halls as the midnight hour approached. I had always struggled with sleep, and tonight proved no exception. At least in a castle this size, I possessed plenty of space to amble about in an effort to relax my mind.*

I strolled through the foyer and toward the library. As I strode down the hall, the sound of music reached my ears. I stopped and strained, listening for more. Lilting orchestral music floated down the hall. No orchestra played in my home at this hour! What could produce the sound?

I stepped toward it, following the sound as I navigated through the halls. I arrived outside the ballroom. Closed doors met my gaze. I narrowed my eyes at them. Did they hide the source of the noise? How could they, my mind questioned? Yet I could not deny the irrefutable sound of music emanating from behind those wooden barriers.

My heart leapt to my throat as I inched toward the doors. I know not what I expected to find beyond them that produced such a reaction, yet my body urged caution as I approached.

I stood mere fingerbreadths from the door. My hands reached for the knobs. My fingers caressed the cool handle. My close proximity now revealed another sound coupled with the music, chatter. Voices floated through the air with the music. The din of an ongoing party lay behind those doors.

I swallowed hard as I twisted both doorknobs and flung the doors open. My brow furrowed as I stared at the scene inside. My footsteps echoed as I stepped into the darkened space. The ballroom was empty. No guests chatted; no musicians played. Weak moonlight streamed through the many windows, revealing only empty floorboards.

No. I had heard music. I had heard voices. From where? What was the source? I rushed into the hall. Perhaps I had miscalculated the location. I strained to listen, but only silence met my ears. Where had the odd music come from?

The incident haunted me for several days, though I mentioned it to no one, fearing they may accuse me of being mad. I returned to the ballroom twice after. I searched for information, for some sign of a gathering. I found none.

I decided after three days to remove the incident from my mind. I would not dwell on it. Perhaps it had been the product of an overtired mind, I assumed. At least that is what I imagined Jaime would tell me had I imparted the information to him.

The occurrence would come to the forefront of my mind a fortnight later. Though I was not involved personally, I recount it here as more evidence. Elsie, a maid in our service, fell ill. Wilson, our butler, brought the girl's condition to my attention. He had dismissed her from her duties for the day and sent her to bed. The nature of her illness, however, prompted him to discuss the matter with me.

"Sick in the head?" I queried after he informed me.

"Yes, m'lord, quite. Babbling on with nonsense."

"Is she delusional with fever?"

"She appears to suffer from no fever, m'lord."

"What nonsense was she babbling?"

Wilson licked his lips and swallowed hard as he prepared to impart the news. "Well, spit it out, man," I encouraged.

"She... She returned to the kitchen mid-morning, pale as a ghost. She collapsed into a chair at the table in the servant's hall and told a most fantastical story. She had been tidying the sitting room. When she entered the foyer, she spotted a woman in the hall on the opposite side. The woman she claims to have seen dressed in a most obscene manner, most unbefitting of a lady. I, myself, was shocked at the description and will not repeat it. Elsie then asserts the woman..." He paused.

"Yes?" I prompted.

"M'lord, she says the woman vanished into thin air!"

I mulled over the story Wilson conveyed. "What shall I do, m'lord? Do you prefer I dismiss her entirely from her position or should she be seen by a doctor before we settle on a course? Of course, the doctor's fee may be deducted from her wages."

"I would like to speak with the girl," I responded.

Wilson's eyebrows raised at my request. He stammered for a moment before he said, "Of course, m'lord. I shall fetch her at once."

"No," I countered. "If the girl is ill, I shall go to her. Please, lead the way."

Wilson led me to the servant's quarters, collecting our housekeeper, Mrs. Carter, along the way. We descended upon the poor girl in her chambers.

"Elsie," Wilson said as we entered. "Lord MacKenzie would like to speak with you."

Elsie lay under a sheet, her face as pale as it. Her hands still trembled as she clutched at the fabric. Her eyes darted around as we approached. As she spotted me, she flung the sheet away and attempted to climb from her cot. "M'lord!" she squealed in surprise.

"No, no, madam, please, there is no need to rise on my account," I assured her. "I understand you are ill."

She nodded as she settled into a seated position on the bed.

"Though the source of your illness is not physical. Is this correct?"

Elsie bit her lower lip and lowered her eyes. "A figment of my imagination, m'lord. I am certain it's nothing more than that. I shall be able to perform my duties for the day." She glanced to Mrs. Carson, who offered her a nod. She had been coached, I deduced.

"Please, may I speak with the girl alone for a moment?" I requested.

"Of course, m'lord," Wilson agreed, ushering Mrs. Carson from the room.

"There," I said in what I hoped to be a soothing manner, "now you may speak freely."

"I have spoken freely, m'lord. I suffered from some delusion, though I am certain it shall dissipate. And it shall not affect my work."

"You do not need to worry about disguising the incident. I wish

to learn the truth." She glanced at me as she again bit her lower lip. *"I do not believe there to be some defect in your character. I, myself, have experienced something similar and wish to learn the circumstances of your encounter so I may compare them."*

"Something similar, m'lord?" she squeaked.

"Indeed," I assured her. *"As I wandered the halls late one eve, I heard music and voices. When I followed them, I found no identifiable source. Yet I am certain I heard them. I did not imagine it."*

"I did not imagine the woman either, m'lord. She was there! She was real!" Elsie exclaimed.

"Please, tell me all the details you recall."

She nodded, and her forehead pinched in recollection. *"I tidied the sitting room. As I departed to move to my next duty, I stepped into the foyer. In the hall beyond, I spotted movement. I glanced in that direction and saw the figure."*

"A woman," I prompted.

She nodded in response. *"Yes, m'lord. A woman. In a most curious choice of clothing."*

"What do you mean?"

"She wore trousers, m'lord."

"Are you certain it was not a man?"

She shook her head. *"No, m'lord. A woman. With her hair flowing down her back, not pulled up. And wearing trousers."*

"Could it perhaps have been her underthings? Was she undressed?"

"If so, I have never in my life laid eyes upon underthings like these, m'lord." Color rose into her cheeks as we discussed the matter.

While I hoped not to embarrass her, I preferred she continue. I lifted my eyebrows to prod her, and she added, *"They were dark trousers, tight to her skin. And a brightly colored woolen top."*

"Did she wear shoes? Was she barefoot? Do you recall?"

"She wore riding boots," Elsie responded.

I pursed my lips as I considered the information. "Where did this oddly dressed woman go?"

Elsie swallowed hard. "Well, m'lord, as I stared at the curious scene, the woman... simply vanished!"

"Through a doorway? Into a room?"

"No, m'lord. As I followed her journey down the hall, a bright light flashed. It blinded me. When it subsided, the woman had disappeared."

I nodded. "All right, Elsie. Is there anything else you can recall?"

Elsie furrowed her brow again as she considered the question. "No, m'lord. Except for the bright light, it only flashed for a moment. She couldn't have disappeared through a door in that time."

I smiled at her. "Thank you, Elsie. You should rest given your shock. You may take the day off and return to your normal duties tomorrow."

"Thank you, m'lord. It is most gracious of you."

I offered her a curt smile and a nod before spinning to leave the room. "Oh, m'lord?" she called after me.

"Yes?" I inquired.

"Do you believe... that is, do you imagine... Was that woman a ghost?"

"No, Elsie, I do not believe so. There is some reasonable explanation. We shall find it. Your candor in explaining your encounter helps toward this goal. Do not let it trouble you further."

She nodded as she pulled the bedcovers over her. I stepped into the hallway with Wilson and Mrs. Carson. "I have given Elsie permission to remain abed. She will resume her duties tomorrow. You may leave the incident rest. I do not wish this tale to spread throughout the staff."

"Very good, m'lord. I shall see Elsie rests and the staff does not repeat the story."

"Thank you, Wilson."

I pondered the information as I walked the halls, intent on returning to my office. Instead, I found myself in the foyer. I peered into the hall opposite the sitting room. What I expected to find, I do not know. It remained vacant at this hour. I strode down the hall and examined the floor and walls. No secret passages existed here. The woman could not have disappeared into a hidden passage. Though the music and voices I heard could not have vanished either, yet I could not find the source. Were these incidents related?

I would not wait long before another event confronted us. As November waned and gray skies filled our days, I sat reading in the library one afternoon. As I read, I overheard voices in the hallway outside. I did not recognize them. I rose from my chair and crossed the room. The voices continued on the opposite side of the door.

I threw the doors open and peered into the hall. I found it empty. I swung my head from side to side, glancing up and down the length of it. Not a soul graced the area.

Incidents like this would continue. Phantom noises, disembodied voices, footsteps with no owners. All these would haunt the castle halls on an increasingly regular basis.

Lily, one of our chambermaids, would also become the victim of these manifestations. She claimed a man roamed the halls near the west bedrooms. When she called to him, he fled into the hallway overlooking the back gardens. There, he disappeared after consulting an object clutched in his hand.

The poor girl never recovered from the sighting. She remained abed for two days before we found her meager belongings missing and her bed not slept in one morning. A simple note propped on her pillow read, "I cannot bear another moment in these cursed halls."

Rumors began to spread like wildfire through the staff and into the village. The old woman's curse rang through my mind on a regular basis. What misfortune had I brought upon my family, I wondered?

The occurrences happened so frequently, I mentioned them to Jaime. He suggested there was a reasonable explanation, though, after a lengthy discussion, we could arrive at no logical conclusion. This is when I began to document the incidents.

I have recorded all known instances of these strange manifestations and their locations. I shall continue to monitor them and record them in these journals.

Cate sighed as she reached the end of the first journal. She had learned no more about the workings of the timepiece. It appeared in Douglas's time, the time rips also opened and closed at random, as they were doing now.

How had Douglas tamed them? So far, she was no closer to a solution.

* * *

Cate sat at her desk, pouring over Douglas's second journal. She finished inputting several pages and pressed the button to decrypt them. The progress wheel spun in a colorful circle. As she awaited the results, she drummed her fingers on the desk.

The program completed its run. Deciphered text appeared on the screen. Cate leaned in to read it.

Strange incidents continue to manifest. We cannot ascertain the source of these disturbances.

As Cate read, the cursor began to move backward, deleting the text as it went. There must be some bug in the new program, Cate assumed. She attempted to stop the deletion by pressing the escape key. It did nothing to halt the progress of the cursor. It continued to march backward, erasing all text in its path. Cate pressed a random selection of other keys before swiping at her trackpad. She clicked the button to close the program. She attempted to minimize the window. Nothing worked. The program failed to respond. As soon as it finished whatever it was doing, Cate would send an email to Damien and ask him about it.

When all words in the decrypted text disappeared, Cate attempted to close the program again, but it remained frozen.

The cursor blinked at her on the blank page. After a moment, words appeared. Character after character paraded across the screen.

Hello, Catherine...

With a gasp, Cate leapt from her seat and backed several steps away. The library door creaked open on its hinges. Cate spun to face it. Emptiness stared back. A grinding noise sounded on the opposite side of the room. Cate's breath caught in her throat as she twirled toward the sound.

The bookcase slid open. A figure stood in the cavity.

"Hello, Catherine," his British accent called to her.

Cate's pulse quickened as she recognized the voice. She raced toward the open door and into the dark hall beyond. Her footsteps pounded along the hall's runner as she fled from her assailant.

As she neared the foyer, she skidded to a halt. Her mouth gaped open, and her eyes widened as she stared in front of her. A wall blocked the normally open passage into the foyer. Candles burned in sconces, their feeble light flickering in the large hall. Cate glanced downward. Her tunic and leggings transformed into a light pink gown. A full, floor-length skirt with lace ruffles hung from a tight silk and lace bodice.

"Don't run from me, Catherine," the voice called behind her.

Cate's heart pounded in her chest as she flung herself against the wall. She pounded her fists against it in a desperate attempt to escape. She tugged on one of the sconces, and the wall swung open.

Cate pushed through it and fled across the foyer and into the sitting room. She closed and locked the double doors behind her. As she inched several steps back, Cate ran her hand over her clothes. She now wore a drop-waist peach dress with a sailor's bow.

Her brow crinkled. "Amelia's dress?" she questioned aloud as she recognized the dress her great-grandmother gifted her when she visited 1925. Was she now in the 1920s?

"Why do you run from me, Catherine?" the voice asked from behind her.

Cate whirled to face him. He strode through the shadows across the room, his features indistinguishable in the darkness.

"Who are you?" Cate asked as she backed toward the door. Her fingers reached behind her, searching for the key. She struck cool metal and her fingers tightened around the head as she turned it. The lock unlatched, and Cate spun to fling the doors open.

She fled across the foyer and up the main staircase. Her steps slowed, hindered by the sudden appearance of a domed hoop skirt. She reached a hallway of bedrooms. The man rounded the corner behind her.

"I will always find you, Catherine," he warned.

Cate ducked into one of the bedrooms, closing and locking the door behind her. The handle turned and twisted as he attempted to open the locked door. The door shook as the man pounded against it.

The noise ceased. Cate held her breath as she strained to

listen for sounds beyond the room. An earsplitting boom resounded moments later, knocking Cate down. The room plunged into darkness. The door creaked open, and the silhouette of a man stood inside.

The man stalked toward Cate. She crawled backward on her rear as he approached.

He reached for her. She squealed as icy hands grasped her shoulders. "I will always find you," he hissed as he drew her closer to him.

* * *

Cate gasped and lashed out at her assailant. She attempted to shake loose of his grasp.

"Cate! Cate!" Jack's voice called.

Cate opened her eyes and glanced around the room. "Jack?" she breathed, her voice hoarse with sleep.

"It's okay, you're okay," Jack soothed, still keeping a tight hold of her.

"What happened?" she inquired.

"I found you asleep at your desk again. You were whimpering and moaning. I assume you had another nightmare?"

Cate nodded as she pushed her hair behind her ears. "Yes," she admitted.

"Come sit over here," Jack directed, motioning toward the armchair across the room. "You're still shaking."

"I'm okay," Cate insisted as she stumbled to the armchair and slouched into it. "It just takes me a few minutes to recover from the physical effects."

Jack sank into the chair next to hers. "What happened this time?"

"Same thing, more or less. I'm being chased by the same man. Only this time the new twist was I seemed to be jumping around in time. I started in my normal clothes then

I had a dress from the 1790s, then the 1920s and then the 1850s."

"So, basically, you're melding the reality of these misbehaving time rips with your nightmarish friend."

"It seems so."

"Any more information about him? Did you see him this time? Or the other person you were hiding with?"

"No. I was alone this time. And he's always hidden in the shadows. Just beyond my field of vision. It's so frustrating." Cate's head fell into her hand as she sighed.

They sat in silence for a few moments before Jack asked, "How are you feeling now?"

"Better," Cate admitted.

"Can you sleep?"

"If not, I'll do a little more work."

"No, that's a terrible idea."

"I haven't gotten anywhere yet and I've decrypted the entire first journal. He describes all the weird stuff happening around the castle, but not even a hint of how to control the time rips. I don't even think he knows what's going on yet."

"It's fine. You'll keep working on that and we'll go back to Douglas's time later and start working that angle. We'll figure this out, Cate. But you must rest. Starting tomorrow, we'll have extra hours in our days. You'll need the sleep."

Cate nodded. "You're right."

"Of course I am," Jack teased.

"Okay, I'll head to bed and get back on those journals in the morning. With any luck, we'll find something to help us during our trip."

"There's the spirit, lassie. Now off to bed with you."

* * *

As Cate eased into her desk chair, memories of her nightmare flooded back to her. She hoped she had better luck decrypting the journals than she'd had in her dream. An overwhelming urge to glance over her shoulder coursed through her as she opened the second journal. The decryption program loaded on her laptop as she studied the numbers on the journal's interior cover.

With the program loaded, Cate updated the order of the disks for decoding. She opened a document and began to copy the encoded text. She hoped to make it through at least one-quarter of the journal before their trip to Douglas's time.

After an hour of typing, Cate set the program to work. Within minutes she had text from Douglas's next entry.

> *I continue to keep a careful record of the strange manifestations within the castle walls. I have even begun to explore the areas in which they occur on a regular basis.*
>
> *I, myself, have been party to a number of these strange incidents. On several more occasions, music has filled the air with no identifiable source. In each instance, the music emanates from the ballroom. Noises typical for a large party always accompany it. In every instance, I am unable to locate anyone. I have even attempted to spy through the keyhole.*
>
> *To make sense of the events, I have also begun to record everything surrounding the occurrences. Each time I have heard the music, I have been in the foyer and hall leading to the library. My first journal confirms this to be the case for the first incident of this type.*
>
> *However, not all incidents occur in this way.*
>
> *As we approach spring in Dunhaven, I now have a diverse array of odd and somewhat disturbing events to study. In addition to the music I overheard, several servants insist they have encountered figures wandering the halls. They claim these people,*

when followed, disappear, either dissipating in a brilliant flash of light or turning a corner and vanishing.

Until December, I had never experienced anything beyond the sound of music floating through the halls. However, on one chilly winter night, something rather different presented itself.

I gazed over the frost-covered back garden. Moonlight cast a bright glow across the winter landscape. An otherworldly silence filled the air. It was this quiet solitude that drew me to this parcel of land.

It was also this quiet solitude that made the incident apparent. Hushed voices cracked the silence. Distinct whispers filled the air. Who else was awake at this hour, I wondered as the voices reached me?

I strained to listen. It sounded like a male and female conversing, perhaps arguing. Were two members of the staff engaged in a clandestine meeting? I followed the noise, creeping down the hallway as noiselessly as possible.

Their voices grew louder as I approached the corner leading to a hallway of bedrooms. I made out a few words as I hid.

"... should go before anything else happens," the male said.

"No! We need more information!" the female answered.

"At what cost?"

"Shh!"

"What is it?"

"I heard something."

I pivoted around the corner, intent on determining the identity of the conversants. An empty hallway met my gaze. I scanned it, searching for any signs of life. I found none.

"Hello?" I called.

I received no answer. I squinted into the darkness but found nothing. I ambled down the hall, checking in the various bedrooms, but discovered no living souls.

This incident was my first to involve more than scattered, unintelligible voices and music. In this case, I could identify two speakers and even part of their conversation. I had been in the back hall overlooking the back garden, NOT the foyer or near the library.

This marked the second incident that occurred in or near that back hallway. This is where I had also spotted the figure.

As the year came to a close, I would encounter more bizarre incidents. One week after I overheard the whispered conversation, another strange happening occurred.

I traversed the hallways in the mid-afternoon. My brothers, Alistair and Duncan, and their wives visited for the holiday season. I hoped to invite them for a winter walk around the property. As I turned the corner, I spotted a woman. Her clothing shocked me. Her dress, several inches above her ankles, hung in a boxy form around her figure. Her hair, cut short, fell only to her chin. She proceeded down the hall in front of me and into a bedroom.

I dashed after her and flung the door to the bedroom open. I scanned the room. Emptiness greeted me. Where had she gone?

This incident forced me to confide again in Jaime. He could offer no explanation. I began to wonder what sort of specters roamed the halls of my new home.

As the new year rang in, I began to search the halls for more apparitions. Convinced a reasonable explanation existed, I scoured the castle for more signs of these ghosts. More evidence of their existence continues to pour in. Misplaced items. Phantom voices. Figures that roam the halls, then disappear. Brilliant flashes of light with no source.

I have lost count of all the events but have kept a record of all of them within the pages of one journal, which I have devoted to simply detailing each occurrence, its date, location, and other pertinent details.

In these pages, I began to parse through the information I have at hand.

I have now encountered multiple individuals wandering the

halls. I have noted several patterns occurring. Attire on the individuals varies from location to location. Though WITHIN a location, clothing is consistent. Women in the bedroom hallway always wear dresses above their ankles. Men there wear trousers and coats much different from the current style.

Women in the hall off the foyer often wear trousers! Men there wear odd, loose-fitting trousers and shirts that bare their arms.

I have spotted some figures in clothing closer to our own, though dissimilar enough to be obvious to me.

These patterns suggest some ordering of the events. That they do not occur randomly.

I have read much on the subject of spectral disturbances, hauntings, and ghosts. Often, phantoms are described as appearing in the same clothing. For example, a woman appears in the same red dress to all who see her. And she appears over and over in that dress.

This is not the case in our manifestations. A variety of similarly styled clothing appears even on the same individual. This suggests the passage of time wherever these souls are, rather than the specter being stuck, glued to the earth in some form.

I postulate they are not ghosts. Ghosts imply a departed soul, someone who has lived and died on this earth and whose souls remain tethered to this world. My theory is that these sightings are of individuals who have yet to live. It may sound wild, and I dare not say it aloud to anyone as yet, but I wonder if I am in some way peering into the future.

I plan to discuss these events with a man with considerable knowledge of an otherworldly nature. For the first time since we settled here, we have welcomed guests beyond family. My dear friend, Grayson Buckley, and his wife, Celine, both have experience with unexplainable supernatural events. I hope to determine if he has any explanations for these occurrences.

I shall broach the matter at a dinner party tomorrow evening. I have also invited Aria and Jaime, a voice of cautious reason to temper the wilder discussions. One other couple shall be in attendance. Cousins of mine have arrived in town only today.

I shall only bring the matter up to the men of the party, as the subject may prove too vexing for the ladies. In particular, I am concerned about our newest additions to the party. While I am certain my cousin, Jack, will take the matter well in true MacKenzie style, I fear shocking his wife, Catherine.

CHAPTER 12

Cate's heart leapt into her throat as she read the last line. She stared wide-eyed at the screen. Douglas's journal entry discussed his upcoming dinner party, the same party she and Jack hoped to attend. It outlined the attendants and mentioned Jack and Catherine MacKenzie. This must refer to them!

As Cate considered the entry, detailing the past but also seeming to detail her future, a knock sounded at the door. Cate leapt from her chair, her nerves on edge.

"Lunch!" Molly announced. Cate breathed a sigh of relief. "Still hard at work, huh?"

"I've made it all the way to journal two!" Cate announced.

"Wow! Any child sacrifices yet or have we only made it to animals?" Molly inquired with a wink.

"Just discussing entertaining at the castle in the early days," Cate fibbed.

"Eh," Molly murmured, "that sounds… far less interesting but much safer."

"It is fairly interesting," Cate admitted. "It's fascinating how different life was back then. How entertaining others provided entertainment, too!"

"I suppose without any modern amenities, it would! No TV or radio or email for easy contact. Events were probably a fanfare for everyone involved."

Cate nodded in agreement. "I think I'll do a bit more work over lunch and learn a bit more about Douglas's life."

"Yeah, get it in before Jack steals you away for those estate headaches after lunch."

Cate chuckled. "I'd hardly call them headaches. Not when I live in a place like this!"

"Good outlook. Enjoy, Lady Cate!"

"Thanks, Molly. Have a great lunch."

Cate spent the majority of her lunch typing additional text into a document. Her progress remained slow; her mind continually returning to the last piece of decrypted text she read.

Molly collected her tray as Jack entered the library. "Ready for that estate business?" he inquired.

"You bet!" Cate exclaimed as she closed her laptop.

Molly skirted through the door, tray in hand and Jack closed the doors behind her.

"Got my clothes ready?" he asked.

"I do, but first, you need to look at this," Cate said. She popped the laptop open again and pulled up her decrypted document.

"Did you find something on the timepiece?"

Cate shook her head as she handed the laptop off to Jack. "Here," she said, pointing to the screen, "here he is postulating about what the cause of the strange apparitions and phantom music and all that is. Start there and go to the end."

Cate bit her lower lip as she waited for Jack to finish reading the entry. She shifted her weight from leg to leg as she watched his eyes scan the text. After a few moments, he ran his fingers through his hair, and his eyes went wide. He glanced up at Cate. He drew in a deep breath. His lips moved but no words came out.

Cate nodded in understanding. "That was my reaction, too," she answered.

Jack swallowed hard. "Is this… is this us?"

Cate shrugged one shoulder. "How could it be anyone else? Jack and Catherine MacKenzie? Jack, Douglas's cousin. Who else could it be?"

"It must be us," Jack admitted. "But this is… bizarre."

"It gave me a shock when I read it, too."

"A shock? Cate, we're reading our futures!"

"And our pasts, technically," Cate added.

"Well, THE past, OUR future if we're going to get technical. This is wild!" Jack closed the laptop and set it on the desk. He paced the floor for a few moments. "Cate, I'm not sure you should continue decrypting these journals."

"What?" Cate exclaimed. "The solution to our problem may be in these! I have to continue!"

"I'm not certain that's a wise idea. You've just read our future."

"Yes and no. We realize we're going to the dinner party. Is that a shocking surprise? It's the outcome we hoped for."

"But what if we learn something we shouldn't. What if he continues to detail events in our lives?"

"I'll stop then. If we continue to come up in these journals, I'll stop reading. But this could contain the answers. We agreed to work both angles!"

"Until you started reading our futures, Madame Fate."

Cate gave him a wry glance. "Very funny, Jack."

"The implications of this…" Jack began.

"Let's not dwell on it. It may prove overwhelming."

"Perhaps we should dwell on it! Overwhelming or not!" Jack argued.

"Why? We'll drive ourselves crazy. And end up in an endless discussion of fate and predestination. The fact is, I found mention of us in journals from Douglas. It matches what we plan to do. Let's leave it at that and get after doing the thing we intended. Let's secure our invitation to this dinner party."

"Just a minute," Jack said.

Cate raised her eyebrows at him.

"This other fellow mentioned. Grayson Buckley. That's the name you overheard during Douglas's conversation with Jaime, isn't it?"

Cate nodded. "He mentioned a Grayson, yes. He didn't give his last name but that must be him. It's got to be the same dinner party discussed in the journal."

"Do you imagine he's your dream guy?"

"My dream guy? I thought you said you were the man of my dreams."

"Well, with my roguish good looks, my charming nature and my stellar sense of humor, I assumed so. I'm hard to resist. But apparently, some other bloke's been chasing you around in your sleep. Perhaps I should be jealous."

"You forgot your overwhelming modesty. All joking aside, that's what I'm hoping to find out. Which is why we must secure an invitation to that dinner party! Now, let's go!"

Jack blew out a long breath. "All right. I'll meet you outside your bedroom suite when you're ready."

Cate and Jack parted ways to dress for their immersion into 1792. Cate swept her hair up, allowed several tendrils to frame her face. She slipped into the centuries-old clothing. She adjusted the striped dress and fussed with the blouse top. The overskirt in the rear trailed behind her as she ambled to the door.

Cate pulled the doors open as she gathered the train over her arm for the trek to the library and Douglas's laboratory.

She found Jack pacing the halls in his cutaway overcoat topping his shirt, vest, and dark breeches.

Cate bit her lower lip as she held in a chuckle. "I'm ready," she announced.

Jack spun to face her. "Are we sure we can't wear normal clothes?" Jack questioned.

Cate giggled. "I'm certain. You look... great!"

"In my tights. Oh, yes, I look fabulous. I must say, you look sensational as always. This outfit gives new meaning to my nickname for you! M'lady!" he said with an extravagant bow.

Cate curtsied. "Thank you, kind sir."

"Well, I guess there's no delaying it!" Jack held out his arm to Cate.

They navigated to Douglas's secret study. Cate held out the timepiece and, with a shaky breath from both, they activated it. As the temporary lighting dimmed to darkness, Cate glanced around.

"I guess we made it," she whispered.

"Yeah," Jack agreed. "Now we need to sneak out of here, through the library and out of the house."

"There's a spy panel at the top of the stairs. I found it after I was trapped here. We can use it to make sure the coast is clear."

"We should have brought a flashlight," Jack complained as they stumbled toward the stairs leading to the library.

"I'm not certain introducing modern conveniences into this era is wise. I can't believe a Reid suggested such a thing."

"I'm a MacKenzie at the moment, remember? Wild and impetuous."

"Right," Cate said with a giggle. They reached the top of the stairs.

"At least those things don't creak in this time period. They'd be a dead giveaway."

Cate inched the spy panel open and peered into the library. "Empty," she reported. "Ready to make a run for it?"

"Yes, let's get this party started," Jack confirmed.

They unlatched the secret panel and slid the bookcase open. Cate took another glance around before they emerged into the library. Jack shut the bookcase and they raced across the room.

With the door open a crack, Jack peered into the hallway. "Clear," he whispered. He grabbed Cate's hand as he pulled the door open wider. They dashed down the hall and out the side door.

Jack breathed a deep breath as they inhaled the fresh outside air. "Made it," he declared. "Now, let's hope we can get back in through the front door."

They strolled around the castle and approached the heavy wooden entry doors. Jack drew in a deep breath as he used the lion's head door knocker to summon the butler.

A tall, wiry man pulled open the door. "Yes?" he inquired in a nasally tone.

"Mr. Jack MacKenzie and his wife to see Lord Douglas MacKenzie," Jack responded.

The man raised his eyebrows at them as he glanced between Jack and Cate. "Are you expected, sir?"

"Yes, we are. I have written ahead so my cousin may expect my arrival."

The man bowed his head at them and gestured for them to enter the foyer. He signaled to the sitting room. "You may wait inside. I shall inform his lordship at once."

"Thank you," Jack answered.

They strode into the sitting room. "Another era, same sitting room," Jack noted.

"Yep. Let's hope third time's the charm."

They waited for several tense minutes. Jack fussed with

his cravat. "This is like a noose around my neck," he complained.

"Here, let me see," Cate said. She adjusted the collar, loosening it and fluffing it.

"Thanks," Jack said as he wiped a bead of sweat from his brow.

"Don't sweat this one, Jack," Cate replied with a wink. "We know how it works out."

He offered her a half-smile as the doors burst open.

A tall man stood in the open doorway. His dark unruly curls tamed back into a low queue with a ribbon. He narrowed his eyes at Jack and Cate. After a moment, he raised one eyebrow as he strode across the room.

"Jack MacKenzie, I presume?" he inquired as he eyed Jack.

"Indeed, sir," Jack said with a slight bow. "In the flesh. What a pleasure to meet you, Lord MacKenzie."

"Doulas MacKenzie," he said, extending his hand. "Very pleased to make your acquaintance. May I offer you a drink?"

"No, sir, thank you. May I introduce my wife, Catherine?"

Cate offered Douglas a smile. "Mrs. MacKenzie, how very charmed I am to welcome you to my home."

"Thank you, Lord MacKenzie. How very gracious of you to take the time to make our acquaintance."

"Please, sit! Are you certain I may not offer you a drink?"

"Very kind, sir, but no," Jack said as he and Cate sank onto a loveseat near the fireplace.

"Wilson tells me you assumed you were expected. I am very regretful to inform you of having no knowledge of your arrival."

Jack glanced to Cate. "I am terribly sorry, m'lord. I sent word ahead of business in the vicinity and my intentions on visiting. I am most regretful the correspondence did not arrive."

"As am I! I should have had rooms prepared and waiting to welcome family! As it stands, you shall be forced to wait until one can be readied."

Cate noted the release in Jack's posture at Douglas's invitation. In true MacKenzie style, the man proved gracious and welcoming. "Oh, how kind of you, Lord MacKenzie, however..."

Douglas waved his hand in the air. "Oh, please, call me Douglas. As proud as I am of my title, it isn't meant for family!"

Jack offered a slight smile. "Douglas. Again, how kind of you, however, it is not our intention to impose on your household."

"No imposition at all! Do you imagine I built this home for only myself? It is to be shared and whom better to share it with than one's family. And you come at a most fortuitous time! We are entertaining friends. It will prove most delightful to expand the house party! Olivia shall find it most acceptable, I am certain."

"Your invitation is very kind."

"Then you accept it, yes? Yes, yes, you do. Now, who is our common relative? Are you Uncle Frederick's son? No, no, he had no son Jack," he said as he placed his finger on his lip.

"No, sir," Jack answered. "I'm Broderick's grandson. Our grandfathers were brothers."

"Ah, of course, Broderick's grandson, yes," Douglas responded. "Good, good. Wonderful to have that side of the family in! How is your father?"

"Getting on, though still doing well enough. Same with Mother."

"Excellent. And what brings you to Dunhaven?"

"Business," Jack answered. "My law practice does a great

deal of land management. It often involves travel on behalf of my clients."

"An attorney! Good man! Where did you study law?"

"Oxford," Jack fibbed.

"And you work with land management? Scouting property in Dunhaven? I warn you, I have the best property in the county!" Douglas let out a loud laugh.

"I would concur. It is a beautiful plot and a beautiful castle. The moment I realized my business would bring me to the area, I sent word ahead to visit. I am sorry you did not receive my post."

"No matter. As long as you aren't trying to purchase the property, there shall be no trouble at all!"

Jack held up his hands in defeat. "I wouldn't dream of it."

The butler entered the room, taking a post near the door in silence.

"Oh, Wilson!" Douglas said as he glanced toward him. "Have you everything prepared?"

"Indeed, m'lord. I had a bedroom prepared in the west hall for Mr. and Mrs. MacKenzie."

"Excellent! Thank you, Wilson," Douglas said as the man departed. "Shall we send for your things?"

"That isn't necessary," Jack replied. "We had them sent ahead, though there was a delay. The bags should arrive tomorrow."

"Well, then we shall see you have what you may need for this evening! We shall not be dining formally. The Buckleys are arriving late this afternoon. We shall host a formal welcome dinner in their honor tomorrow evening. We would be most pleased if you would attend."

"We will be looking most forward to it," Jack answered. "Again, thank you."

"I apologize about dinner this evening…"

Jack interrupted Douglas's response. "We are quite tired

from our travels. We shall be most happy to retire to our rooms with a light meal and rest. And on that note, we should take up no more of your time this afternoon."

"No trouble at all," Douglas answered. "Though I am certain Mrs. Mackenzie would like to put her feet up."

Cate smiled at him. "Thank you. The journey has been a little taxing. I would very much like to retire."

"I shall have Cook prepare a light meal for you to be sent up. And I shall have Wilson fetch anything else you may need."

Everyone stood as Douglas rang for Wilson, instructing him on attending to the items he mentioned.

Before arranging for clothing and their meals, Wilson showed Cate and Jack to their room. Cate sank onto the bed as he departed. She raised her eyebrows at Jack.

"Well, we did it!"

"Indeed, we did," Jack agreed. "It was easier than I thought. Either we're getting better at time travel or the MacKenzies are just incredibly nice people."

"Both?" Cate surmised in a questioning tone. "We MacKenzies are incredibly nice."

Jack narrowed his eyes at her as he chuckled. "Very true, Lady Cate, very true."

"I suppose we have a few hours to kill here while we make it look good."

Jack flopped onto the bed next to Cate. "Yep. We'll eat our meager meal before we 'retire' for the evening. Then we're off the hook until tomorrow night."

"Well, off the hook for time traveling. I plan to continue working on those journals."

"Reading more of our future? I'm still disturbed by that, you know. It's just odd reading about it."

"I must admit, I found it jarring, too."

A knock sounded at the door. "I'll get it," Jack offered. He bounded off the bed and pulled the door open.

A maid carried a tray with sandwiches and a decanter of wine. "May I bring you anything else?" she asked in a thick Scottish accent.

"No, thank you," Cate answered. "This is perfect."

Another knock sounded, announcing the arrival of a second maid. She delivered nightclothes for both Jack and Cate.

Jack bit into one of the sandwiches as the door swung shut behind both maids. "Mmm, these are good. Here, try one!"

He handed a wedge to Cate. "Eat up, gotta make it look good," Jack said with a mouth full of sandwich.

"I'll leave the bulk to you," Cate said as she nibbled a corner. "We just ate lunch!"

"So? This is dinner!" Jack answered.

"First dinner," Cate reminded him. "We'll still have a second dinner when we get home."

Jack raised his eyebrows at her as he poured himself a small glass of wine. "I know. I can't wait! Mrs. Fraser's making tuna salad melts!"

"You and your stomach," Cate said with a shake of her head and a chuckle.

As she nibbled on the light fare, Cate wandered to the window.

"Anything exciting?" Jack answered as he joined her.

"A carriage," Cate answered. A cloud of dust billowed down the front drive as a horse-drawn carriage trundled down the gravel path.

"The Buckleys?" Jack inquired.

"I'm not certain," Cate said with a shrug, "but if I had to guess, I'd say so."

Four chestnut horses rounded the circular fountain

before the coachman urged them to a stop outside the front door. The household waited outside as their guests arrived.

"That must be Olivia," Cate said, pointing to the woman next to Douglas. Dark brown curls cascaded around one shoulder from her swept-up style. Her fair skin revealed delicate features with deep-set eyes.

"Why are they all out there?" Jack inquired, pointing to the staff. "Mr. Smythe asked us to be there when you arrived, but I assumed that was because you were the lady of the house and our new employer."

"It's a custom," Cate informed him. "It's the lady of the house's decision, but it's often to make the guests feel welcome and to give a special feel and presentation of the entire household. Kind of a way to make them feel important and give them a grand entrance."

"Hmm," Jack murmured. "These Buckleys must be special people."

"I need to research them when I return home. I didn't have the chance before we came here."

Douglas stepped forward as the coachman opened the carriage door. A tall man with dark hair stepped from the carriage. Cate studied him as he strode forward, grasping Douglas's hand in a firm handshake. A broad smile formed on his lips, and he clapped Douglas on the arm.

"Is that your guy?" Jack questioned.

Cate shrugged. "I wouldn't know unless I heard him speak. It could be."

"Douglas seems to know him well," Jack surmised.

"He referred to him as his good friend. They must be close if Douglas would mention the ongoings in the castle to him and seek his advice on it. He also said he has knowledge of the supernatural. I wonder what that means?"

"Knowledge of the supernatural?" Jack repeated. "Is he a witch-hunter or ghost-hunter or something?"

"I'm not certain. I wish he would have expounded on that in the journal. It could mean so many things."

"Perhaps he's one of those hysterical reverends. Like the Salem people, burning witches at the stake and the like."

"And Douglas plans to tell him he sees ghosts in the house because he'll perform some ceremony to drive them away?" Cate offered as a question.

"Could be. He'll be sorely disappointed when that doesn't work."

"That doesn't add up," Cate said after a moment.

"Why not?"

"Douglas figures out the secret. He creates the timepiece to control the time rips. He has to realize it's not ghosts. He mentioned as much in his journal. No, he wants the Buckleys' opinion for another reason. But what?"

Silence fell between them as they continued to watch the scene unfold outside the castle. The man waved his hand back toward the carriage. He reached toward the inside. A gloved hand grasped his and a woman emerged. Her light blonde hair was swept up under a sapphire blue hat. Even at this distance, her sparkling blue eyes were piercing. Her porcelain skin and rosy cheeks lit up as her full lips formed a smile.

"Wow," Cate murmured. "She's beautiful."

"Yeah," Jack answered after retrieving another sandwich. "Real looker, if you like blondes. She looks kind of young, doesn't she?"

"She's probably seventeen, eighteen," Cate answered. "Not abnormal for this era."

"He looks close to thirty!" Jack exclaimed.

"Again, not abnormal. And if he is my nightmarish friend, judging by his accent, he's likely high ranking in the nobility."

"Ah, married him for the money, huh?"

Cate shrugged. "Might not be the only reason."

"Huh?"

"He's a handsome guy. She really scored if he's a high-ranking nobleman with that face."

Jack froze and stared at Cate for a moment. "Lady Cate! I can't believe what I'm hearing. As your husband, I'm terribly jealous over your gushing about this man."

Cate chuckled. "I'm hardly gushing," Cate answered. "Just making a point. She could have married him for money or looks, perhaps both. Assuming he's my well-bred friend."

The couple chatted for a few moments with Douglas and Olivia before Olivia motioned toward the interior of the castle. The two women stepped forward, Douglas and Grayson followed them. The female staff retreated around the corner to a servants' entrance while the men began to unload the carriage.

"Douglas told Jaime that Grayson was no stranger to odd and unusual phenomena. Wonder what that means?"

"Perhaps we'll find out tomorrow at dinner."

Cate wandered back to the bed and plopped on it. "You okay?" Jack questioned. "You're not daydreaming about your dream guy, are you?"

Cate shot him a wry glance. "No, I'm not. Just anxious to get to tomorrow's dinner."

"You've got a long wait," Jack said as he sank onto the bed next to her.

"I know," Cate said with a sigh. "I just feel like we'll finally make some progress on this time travel thing. Plus, I can hear Grayson Buckley speak and find out if he's the one haunting me."

"And you can ogle him up close and in person."

"Oh my goodness! That's the last time I comment on someone's appearance with you around!"

"Not someone. Some other man's appearance," Jack corrected. "And your dream guy no less."

"I'm starting to think you really are jealous."

Jack changed the conversation's course. "What's your gut say? Do you expect he's your guy?"

"Why would a good friend of Douglas be chasing me? There's no reason for it, so I can't imagine it's him. Then again, I can't figure out who else it would be. Perhaps we'll never find him and he's just a figment of my imagination."

"He's quite a figment. He visits you every night. There must be some reason behind it."

"We shall see," Cate answered before sipping her wine.

"Until then, we may as well enjoy this!" Jack said as he filled Cate's glass then his own.

"Wow! Are you actually enjoying time travel?"

"It's growing on me," Jack admitted. "Maybe it's not so bad." He grinned at her.

They spent another two hours waiting for the household to settle before they snuck to Douglas's secret lab to return to their time. Jack breathed an extra-long sigh of relief as they slipped back to the present.

"Whew, I have spent the entire trip worried that thing wasn't going to work!" Jack exclaimed.

"It did! Your grandfather was right. Well, we spent about four hours in the past, so it's been sixteen minutes here. I have plenty of time to decrypt more of Douglas's journals."

"And I have plenty of time to feed the shrubs in the back garden before second dinner."

"Check in after dinner? We can discuss anything I've found and plan for tomorrow."

"Sounds good, Lady Cate," Jack agreed. "See you then!"

CHAPTER 13

They parted ways after climbing the stairs into the library. After greeting the dogs and slipping into her modern clothes, Cate settled into her seat at the library's desk to continue her work with the journals.

Before tackling the rest of journal two, Cate performed an Internet search on Grayson Buckley. The search turned up little. Cate tried a few alternate searches including Celine Buckley, Grayson and Celine Buckley and Buckley 1792. The final search produced a Wikipedia article on a town named Bucksville in the state of Maine.

> *Bucksville, Maine is a small seaside town on the Maine coast with a population of 564. It was founded by the Buckley family in 1754. The Buckley family is still the largest landowner in the town and its surrounding areas, owning both personal property and commercial ventures including the town's shipping fleet and cannery.*

Cate scanned the second paragraph of the article and

glanced at the location shown on the map. It gave no confirmation of a connection to Grayson Buckley.

Unable to dig up any information on the couple staying at the castle centuries ago, Cate turned her attention to the journal. She spent the better part of the afternoon copying the remainder of the journal's contents.

She spent another forty-five minutes decrypting the ciphertext. As Cate's dinner arrived, she settled into her armchair with her laptop balanced on the wide arm to read

the rest of journal number two.

The arrival of Grayson and Celine brings hope that I will soon discover the answer to our strange manifestations. However, I have grown suddenly reluctant on the morn of our dinner party to bring the subject to conversation. It is not fear over the resulting discussion nor any explanation (or lack thereof) that may be offered. Perhaps I am taking advantage of my guests by thrusting this discussion upon them shortly after the eve of their arrival.

Still, I suppose the task must be done. And what better time than our welcome party when I shall have not only Grayson but Jaime in attendance. My cousin, Jack MacKenzie, will also be present. A man of the law, perhaps he will offer insight the others cannot.

I shall pen a summary of the conversation and any discoveries or theories provided from it following our dinner party.

The conversation was struck over brandy and cigars following our meal. Olivia and the ladies went through, leaving us to discuss business. After a brief discussion of our recent fortunes, I posed a question to the group.

"Gentlemen," I began, "I hoped to trouble you all with a delicate matter I have stumbled upon in the months since we have taken

residence within these walls. Jaime is already aware of some of this, but I shall begin fresh for you, Jack, and you, Grayson."

"Certainly," Grayson answered.

"I must ask before I begin that this discussion remain in confidence. Though rumors will abound despite my best efforts, what I am about to reveal I ask you do not reveal to anyone outside of your circle."

"That sounds ominous," Jack answered me.

"Indeed," Jaime said as he refilled our brandies. *"It may, in fact, send you fleeing from this castle if you are faint of heart."*

Jack raised his eyebrows at Jaime's admission. He turned his attention to me. "Now, I am more than curious."

"As am I. Proceed, old friend," Grayson imparted.

"Thank you, gentlemen. Since we arrived, we have been party to strange occurrences."

"Even prior to your arrival," Jaime interjected. "From the onset of the property acquisition through the building if we are to present all the facts."

"Quite right," I agreed. "As we surveyed the property, an old woman insisted the land was cursed and would bring nothing but woe to my family should I build here."

"Certainly, you did not believe her?" Grayson questioned.

"We would not be sitting in this castle if I had. Though I have often wondered if the woman may have been correct."

"What has happened to make you wonder that?" Jack asked.

"Many things." I retrieved my first journal from the buffet where I had placed it earlier and waved it in the air.

"Douglas has kept a record of the happenings," Jaime informed them.

"It began with small occurrences. A misplaced item, a missing thing. Vases moving across the room, papers appearing and disappearing from different spots."

"Vases floating across the room?" Jack inquired.

"No," I corrected. "The vase would be positioned here." I

motioned with my hand at a vase on our buffet. "In the next instance, here." I motioned to a spot across the room. "In the time between which I had spotted it there, no one had entered the room, yet the same vase had moved there."

"I see," Jack said as he leaned back in his chair, his finger rubbing his chin in thought.

"What else?" Grayson prompted.

"You suspect more?" I inquired.

"You did not ask for our discretion over a transient vase," Grayson said.

"Clever," Jaime replied.

"Indeed," I answered. "And the reason I asked for his input." I swallowed another gulp of brandy before imparting more of my story. "The next incident would go beyond a transient vase, as you put it, Grayson. As I roamed the halls late one night, the sound of music reached my ears. I followed it to its source. My ballroom. As I approached, the sounds of a lively party emanated from behind the closed doors. Chatting, laughing, music.

"I inched to the doors. And all the while, the music and chattering continued. I flung them open." I paused, a bit for dramatic effect and also to read the expressions on the others' faces.

"And?" Jack questioned, his eyebrows raised high in anticipation.

"Nothing," I reported. "An empty room."

"And what of the music?" Grayson questioned.

"Absent, as was any strains of conversation," I responded.

Jack puckered his lips at the admission.

"Hearing things in your old age?" Grayson quipped.

I narrowed my eyes at him. "Hardly. These incidents would continue. In one instance, I overheard part of a conversation between two individuals."

"Two individuals? Did you see them? Or merely hear their voices?" Grayson inquired.

"In the events I've just described, no, I did not spot them."

Grayson raised his eyebrows at me. "Have there been others where you have seen people?"

I nodded. "Several to this moment. To be completely candid, the first apparition was not spotted by myself."

"Who?" Jack inquired.

"A chambermaid. She had taken ill one day, and Wilson said it was not a normal illness. I inquired after the girl's condition to find she had insisted she spotted a woman in the front hall."

"Another of the staff, perhaps," Jack suggested.

I shook my head. "No, the woman she described could not have been a member of this household, staff, or family."

"How do you know?" Jack asked.

"Her attire," I responded. "It could not have been the attire of anyone within this house. The woman she described wore trousers!"

The room fell silent for a moment at the admission. "Tell them about the others," Jaime instructed.

"I questioned the girl about the details and recorded them. Though we would have many additional occasions by which to assess them. On several more occasions, I along with other members of the household would encounter other apparitions."

"Were they always of the same trouser-clad woman?" Grayson asked.

"No," I responded. "There were several different individuals. Some men, some women. All dressed differently and with different appearances."

"A variety of ghosts?" Jack said in a questioning tone as he scratched his head.

I pointed at him. "A starting theory that I postulated myself. I began to take careful notes to test the hypothesis." I patted the journal on the table in front of me. "I recorded every instance and began to notice a pattern."

"A pattern?" Jack questioned.

"Indeed. The people we spotted in similar attire were always in *the same area. And these occurrences tended to happen when I had been in specific areas of the castle."*

"Tell them your theory," Jaime prompted.

"One may assume specters roamed these halls when considering the incidents separately and occurring at random. However, when the information is studied, it presents a rather different picture. Ghosts, as you suggested, Jack, are an implication of a past individual still lurking on the property in some alternate form.

"My theory is quite the opposite." I paused and scanned their faces. "I propose we are viewing some window into the future."

My theory reduced my companions to silence. Grayson grasped his brandy glass and stood. He stalked from the table, his eyes narrowed, and his lips pursed. I allowed them a moment to consider my proposal.

Several more minutes passed before I prodded the group for some response. "Has no one any response?" I inquired.

"I must say, sir," Jack began, "it is a most fantastical theory. I am not certain what to make of it. I have never encountered anything of this nature."

"And you, Grayson?" I said, turning to him. He stared out the window. "Have you encountered anything of this sort in your dealings?"

He remained silent for a moment. He puckered his lips and raised his eyebrows as he stared into his brandy. "Not much," he admitted. "I'll give your theory consideration, run it past Celine. Perhaps she has had an experience of this nature. Shall we join the women?"

"Just a moment," I said. "I would like to hear Jaime's reaction. The theory is new to him, also." I spun in my seat to face Jaime.

He swallowed hard and leaned forward in his chair. "I am afraid it has rendered me rather mute," he answered. "Though my initial sentiments lie close to Jack's statements. Most fantastical. Could it even enter the realm of possibilities? To glance into the future?"

> "Grayson, you may be the best of us to answer that," I suggested.
>
> He swallowed the last of his brandy. "Anything is possible," he responded. "Shall we?" He motioned toward the door.
>
> "Of course," I answered. We left the conversation behind in favor of rejoining our wives for after-dinner drinks.
>
> I must admit, the result of the conversation befuddles me. I did not expect an answer but rather a more spirited discussion about the nature of the strange manifestations. While Jaime always errs on the side of caution and even Jack suggested several plausible theories, Grayson's silence on the matter baffles me. With his experience with supernatural occurrences, I expected some idea or at least an assessment of mine. I have never known him to be so mum on a subject. Perhaps it was the addition of our fourth member, Jack, that prompted his reticence. I shall make it a point to discuss this further in private.
>
> Until then, I have no more answers than I had before the conversation.

Cate sighed as she closed the laptop. She had learned nothing new other than Douglas planned to discuss the thus unidentified time-rips with his male guests.

A knock sounded at the door. Jack and Molly entered. Molly collected Cate's dinner tray and said her goodnights before heading off for her final duties of the day.

Jack collapsed into the armchair next to Cate. "How'd the research go?" he asked after they were alone.

Cate frowned at her closed laptop. "It didn't," she admitted. "I tried a search on our newest housemates Grayson and Celine Buckley."

"And?"

"Nothing. I found an obscure article on a town in Maine founded by a Buckley family but I'm not sure if they are related. I didn't delve too deep into searching records. If we can finagle more information from them, it would give me a starting point for more research."

"Anything else on our future?"

Cate offered him a smile and a chuckle. "The entirety of his final entry in the second journal is the discussion you'll have following dinner." Jack raised his eyebrows. "It should be an interesting conversation for you," Cate said with a wink.

"What, that's it?"

Cate shrugged. "You didn't want to know too much about your future."

Jack shook his head at her. "All right. I'll go in unprepared. Nothing but genuine reactions here."

"Guess we have our mission then. More information on the Buckleys and one wild, but genuine conversation."

"1792, here we come!"

* * *

Cate paced the floor of her sitting room as she waited for the sunrise. Unable to sleep since she experienced another nightmare and with her upcoming time travel trip, she climbed from her bed in the wee hours of the morning.

She settled on her chaise after rising to note the details of her nightmare. Again, she was chased by an unidentifiable man. Again, she raced through the halls with her heart pounding. Again, she found herself unable to sleep afterward.

Instead, after recording the details, she had turned her attention to fretting over their upcoming trip. She had found nothing in Douglas's journals to assist with the growing problems of the time slips. Would they make progress tonight? If they didn't, what would it mean for them moving forward? Would the time slips continue? Would they grow worse? Would they become what Douglas described in his journals?

Who were Douglas's mysterious guests? What supernatural experience did they possess? What was Douglas referring to? And would Grayson Buckley be identified as the man haunting Cate's dreams?

Cate's mind spun out of control. Questions crowded in. Questions with no answers. She had hours to wait before their journey would begin. Cate and Jack planned to travel back in the late afternoon to prepare for their dinner. Prior to leaving yesterday, they had left a note for Douglas informing him they planned to travel to town early and request their luggage be sent on to the castle then finish some business in the area.

With their excuses made for earlier meals, they would spend most of their day in the present. Cate planned to work on Douglas's third journal. She hoped she could keep her mind focused on the work.

Her nervous energy drove her outside for a walk following her breakfast. She spent the early morning hours at the loch. After pondering her questions again while waterside, Cate meandered up the path toward the castle. Riley and Bailey raced ahead of her. She was in no hurry to return, frustrated with the events of late.

As she approached the castle, Jack emerged from around the corner. He carried a dog under each arm. Cate's eyes widened at the sight.

"Riley and Bailey! What have you two gotten into?" Cate eyed the two dogs. Mud covered their front legs and faces.

"Dug another hole in the garden," Jack said.

"I'm sorry," Cate answered as she hurried to relieve Jack of the dogs.

"No problem. The little rascals seemed to thoroughly

enjoy their hole digging. I've got Sir Riley," he answered as he passed Bailey to Cate. "I'll carry him in for a bath."

"Thanks," Cate said.

They entered through the kitchen door.

"Uh-oh," Molly said as she spied them with the dirty dogs. "A few cute pups got themselves in trouble again."

"Yep," Cate replied. "And they're going to get a bath for their antics!"

"Ooooooh! Naughty puppies!" Molly teased. She grabbed Riley from Jack's arms. "Need a hand?"

"I've got it," Cate answered. "You two have enough work already!"

"Nay," Mrs. Fraser argued, "Miss Molly can help you bath the pups. And then I've got a nice juicy bone for them. A reward for their bath!"

Cate chuckled. "They are only getting their bath because they dug another hole in the back garden!"

"No matter to me," Mrs. Fraser insisted. "I plan to spoil the little monkeys."

"Your plan is working. This is their third time with their dig-fest!"

After their baths, Cate settled the dogs in the library with their prize. She spent what was left of her morning inputting cipher code from journal number three. With her mind distracted, she made slow progress.

After lunch, Cate packed several items to be laid out in their bedroom in the 1790s before preparing for her trip. She pulled her hair into a style similar to Olivia's with curls cascading over her shoulder. After dressing in her day dress, Cate gave both Riley and Bailey a kiss on their head and promised to be back as soon as she could.

She met Jack in the hall, and they returned to 1792. They skipped the front door, sneaking straight to their bedroom from Douglas's lab. Cate unpacked the items she brought as Jack hid their suitcase under the bed.

"That should do the trick," Cate said after completing the task. "Time to dress for dinner."

"I will be in the sitting room area," Jack said, stepping through the double doors and into the sitting area in their suite.

"You sure you don't want to change first?"

"No, thanks. I'd rather not spend a second longer in the ancient monkey suit than I have to."

"Because that ensemble is so much more comfortable?" Cate inquired of his breeches and overcoat.

"Much," Jack insisted. "Like my comfy pj's."

After they both dressed for dinner, Jack escorted Cate to the castle's front sitting room. Cate's pulse quickened as they trekked through the halls and descended the main staircase. Soon, one of her questions would be answered. Was Grayson Buckley her nightly visitor?

They proceeded into the sitting room, finding only Douglas and Olivia inside. "Ah, Jack, Catherine!" Douglas said. He poured brandy into a glass and handed it to Jack as they approached the sofa. "Can I get you something, Catherine?"

"Sherry, please," Cate answered as she eased onto the couch.

Douglas poured the cocktail and handed it to Cate before he introduced them to Olivia.

"Jack and Catherine MacKenzie, this is my wife, Olivia."

Jack bowed to her before he joined Cate on the sofa. "Lady MacKenzie, it is a pleasure to meet you."

"Olivia, please!" Olivia said in an even and easy tone.

"And how was your morning business, Jack?" Douglas inquired. "I was shocked to find you'd already gone this morning when Wilson delivered your note! And Catherine, too! You must be quite the adventurer!"

"Yes," Olivia chimed in, "I quite expected you'd like to rest after your journey."

"I wanted Catherine to experience a bit of the Scottish countryside," Jack answered. "I did not give her much choice about joining me. The business proved fruitful."

"Excellent," Douglas responded. "And how did you find the surrounding area?"

"Beautiful," Cate answered.

"Is it much different than where you are from?" Olivia questioned. "You are American, yes?"

"Yes," Cate said. "Quite different, though I was raised in the city, not the country."

"And were you able to sort your luggage? Wilson did not seem to think it was delivered."

"Yes," Jack answered. "We had it sent on this morning."

Douglas rose from the couch opposite Jack and Cate as Jack finished his statement. "Welcome! Wonderful timing!" he said with a broad grin.

Cate twisted in her seat as Jack stood. A dark-haired man with spectacles escorted a red-haired woman. "Come in, come in!" Douglas encouraged, pouring additional cocktails for each.

He joined everyone near the fireplace. "Please meet my cousin, Jack MacKenzie, and his wife, Catherine. Jack, Catherine, this is my estate manager, Jaime Reid, and his wife, Aria." Cate smiled as she noticed Jack's posture stiffen as he gripped the hand of his ancestor. Greetings were given all around before the couple who had arrived in the carriage yesterday appeared in the doorway.

"There they are!" Douglas said, welcoming them into the room. "Come in, I have several introductions to make. Jack, Catherine, Jaime, Aria, please meet one of my oldest and dearest friends, Grayson Buckley, and his wife, Celine. Gray, Celine, this is Jaime, my estate manager, and Aria."

"Yes, I believe we met once, Mr. Buckley," Jaime said as he shook Grayson's hand. "At a gathering in London, though I am not certain you've met my wife, Aria. And I haven't met Mrs. Buckley."

"And this," Douglas said after Jaime finished, "is my cousin, Jack, and his wife, Catherine."

Cate's heart rose into her throat as she waited to hear the man speak.

CHAPTER 14

"Pleased to meet you, sir," Jack said as he grasped Grayson's hand. Cate offered a smile.

Grayson Buckley smiled broadly at him. "Certainly a pleasure to meet Douglas's family." Cate's chest collapsed in a long breath at hearing him speak. American. Not the man haunting her nightmares, she noted.

"Grayson, you and Catherine share a common nationality. I may begin to worry about an insurrection," Douglas said followed by a boisterous laugh.

"Oh? American, are you?" Grayson said, his stormy blue eyes studying Cate.

Cate nodded. "Yes. I, too, hail from the other side of the pond."

"Whereabouts?"

"Philadelphia," Cate fibbed. "And you?"

"Massachusetts, north. A small town named Bucksville. I doubt you've heard of it. You're from a far more civilized region," he said with a laugh.

So, he was related to the family she'd read about in the

Wikipedia article, Cate mused. Perhaps she could use this knowledge to track down more information on him.

Wilson announced dinner and they filed into the dining room. As was custom, Olivia took her seat one place left of the head of the table, Grayson found his place to her right at the table head. Jack sat to Olivia's left. Aria sat on Jack's other side. Cate found herself placed between Grayson and Jaime with Celine next to Douglas, who sat opposite Grayson.

Cate glanced to Olivia for her cue on the direction of her first discussion. Olivia faced Grayson to begin a conversation. Following her lead, Cate turned to her right to talk to Jaime.

"Good evening, again, Mrs. MacKenzie," Jaime said with a broad grin. Cate couldn't help but notice how similar his smile was to Jack's.

"Please, call me Catherine," Cate instructed. "Have you lived in Scotland your entire life, Mr. Reid? Your accent is distinctly Scottish, it reminds me of Jack's."

"Indeed, I have. And please call me Jaime. I grew up in the town of Dunhaven. With Lord MacKenzie."

"Oh!" Cate exclaimed as she pretended not to know. "I did not realize Lord MacKenzie grew up in the area."

"Aye, born and raised in the town of Dunhaven. We were schoolmates."

"How interesting!" Cate responded. "And have you worked with him since?"

"No, Lord MacKenzie left the area, made his fortune then returned. He hired me on then."

"And do you enjoy the work? Managing the estate?"

"I do," Jaime answered. "I find it most interesting. And what about you, Catherine? How are you enjoying Scotland? Do you find it a large change from Philadelphia?"

"I am enjoying it very much. There is a vast amount of

natural beauty to be appreciated here. It is quite different from my urban life."

"How did you meet Jack?"

"We were seated together at a dinner party my aunt hosted while Jack was in town on business. How did you meet your wife?"

"Aria is also a resident of Dunhaven. We knew each other for much of our lives. It was a good match since we both wished to stay in the area near our families."

Cate smiled at the statement as she caught Olivia turn toward Jack out of the corner of her eye. This signaled for everyone to turn their attention to the person on their left for conversation.

"Hello again, fellow American," Grayson said as Cate turned toward him.

"Hello," she said with a smile. "I hope no one suspects we are planning a revolution. Seating the two Americans next to each other is quite a risk."

"Indeed," Grayson said with a chuckle. "We may be making them nervous."

"Good fortune for them we are separated from your wife. Is she also American?"

"No," Grayson informed her. "French, actually. Though, she lost most of her accent after our marriage."

"Oh, how interesting. And what does one do in Bucksville, Mr. Buckley?"

"Grayson, please," he said with a broad grin. "My family owns a fleet of fishing ships there."

"And is the town very large?"

"No, quite small. Very similar to Dunhaven. And nothing compared to what you're used to in Philadelphia. In fact, my father would argue that Philadelphia is woefully overcrowded."

Cate chuckled at the comment, more because of the definition of overcrowded in the 1790s. As they finished their conversation on their hometowns, the staff arrived with the first course.

The conversation turned to include the entire table.

"How are all our visitors enjoying Dunhaven?" Olivia prompted as she lifted her soup spoon to her mouth.

"I am enjoying it very much," Cate assured her with a smile.

"As am I," Celine answered. "The countryside is most beautiful. It reminds me of Massachusetts."

"And do you enjoy it there? It must be quite a change for you," Douglas followed up.

"But a welcome one," Celine answered.

"Celine is originally from France, though she spent most of her life in Martinique," Grayson explained.

"Oh, the island? Was life very different there?" Aria inquired.

"Yes," Celine admitted. "Island life is quite different in some ways, and in others, no different."

"Do you miss it?" Jack questioned.

Cate glanced at Celine as she answered. "No," she responded. "After my father's death, Martinique held no charm for me. I much prefer Massachusetts. Or wherever my husband may be." She shot a glance to Grayson with a smile.

"Oh, yes, terrible shame about Marquis Devereaux," Douglas answered. "Our deepest condolences, Celine."

"Thank you," she answered with a curt smile.

"Grayson, how is your cousin, Alexander? Still enjoying life across the pond?" Douglas asked, changing the subject.

"Indeed. He is quite well. The exterior of his new home was nearly complete when we departed. He anticipated it to be finished before winter set in. Then they would begin work on the interior."

"And it is a replica of your estate here, is it not?" Olivia inquired.

"Yes, of the country estate. He has copied every detail. A piece of England in his new home, he says."

"How interesting," Cate added.

"Yes. If you and Mr. MacKenzie venture back to your home, you must visit with us. Though I warn you the journey to upper Massachusetts may prove arduous."

"Thank you," Cate replied. "I am certain the excursion is well worth it."

The conversation turned to the weather and the surrounding area. Cate learned little more about the Buckleys or the time rips. Douglas's plan to bring it up after the ladies left the party meant she would likely learn nothing.

As the meal ended, Olivia suggested the women retreat to the sitting room, leaving the men to discuss business. The ladies settled on the sofas near the roaring fire.

"How long were you at Grayson's home, Celine?" Olivia inquired as they settled.

"We stayed a short while. Gray's mother fell ill. We departed shortly after her recovery."

"And after all your traveling for your honeymoon. You must be quite worn out!" Olivia answered.

"I do not mind," Celine answered. She turned her attention to Cate. "Catherine, it seems you do a fair amount of traveling also."

Cate nodded and smiled. She swallowed hard, trying to compose herself. The women's ice-blue eyes seemed to gaze through her. "Yes. Jack's business requires a fair amount of traveling. Though I do not mind it either."

"I am afraid Aria and I are rather homebodies," Olivia admitted.

"Yes, I have barely traveled to London," Aria admitted. "Though I believe I much prefer the Scottish countryside. I am afraid I am not fond of larger cities. I suppose it is what one becomes used to."

"Grayson's father expresses a similar sentiment about cities," Celine answered.

"Douglas and I traveled a fair amount, though I prefer to remain settled. At least at this stage of life."

"You certainly have a lovely home to remain settled in," Cate offered.

"Douglas spared nothing when it came to the building of Dunhaven Castle," Olivia answered. "The result is quite lovely. I wondered, or rather worried when he told me of this grand plan what the outcome may be."

"It is quite lovely," Cate agreed.

"I agree," Celine added.

Olivia paused a moment then sighed. "I hope the loveliness outweighs the oddities."

"Oddities?" Celine questioned.

"Yes," Olivia informed her. "Some of the castle's occupants, including Douglas, have experienced strange events. The town is stirring with rumors of a haunting or cursed land. One of our maids claims she saw a woman wandering the halls. She fled in the middle of the night, leaving a note behind calling Dunhaven Castle a cursed place."

"Surely nonsense," Cate said. "Stirred by the enormity of the castle. It must produce illusions."

"I quite agree," Olivia answered. "I hope the matter soon is closed with a simple explanation."

The conversation ceased for a moment before resuming, turning to spring blooms and flower shows. The men rejoined them after another forty-five minutes. Conversations remained light until the post-dinner drinks broke up.

After wandering through the upstairs halls to make it appear they were going to bed, Cate and Jack snuck to Douglas's secret lab and returned home.

They returned to their time exactly thirty-two minutes from the moment they departed. Jack breathed his customary sigh of relief.

"Whew!" Jack exclaimed. "Another successful mission."

"How did your post-dinner discussion go?" Cate inquired.

"Wow, right into it, huh? Do I at least get to change my clothes?"

Cate raised her eyebrows at him. "Okay, okay. I'll let you get out of the monkey suit."

"Thanks. And besides, shouldn't you already know the outcome, Madame Fortune?"

"I want to hear it from the horse's mouth."

"I hope you'll return the favor and let me in on the secret women's meeting."

"Of course. The floral shows will blow your mind."

"Ooooh, I'll change as fast as I can!"

They parted ways with the plan to meet in the library after changing their clothes. Cate wandered into the room long after Jack had slumped into his favorite leather armchair. Riley bounded toward him and leapt into his lap. Bailey followed, choosing to remain on the floor but propped his front feet on Jack's legs for a petting.

"Hello, boys," Jack said. "I'm glad you missed us even though we were only gone for half an hour."

"Crazy, isn't it?" Cate said with a sigh as she collapsed into the chair next to Jack.

"And exhausting. So, post-time travel analysis. What have we learned?"

"We have learned that Grayson Buckley is NOT the man haunting my nightmares."

"Right, he's American! I did not see that coming! So, he's innocent."

"He is," Cate answered.

"You don't sound happy about that."

Cate sighed as she considered the statement. "I guess I'm not. We've ruled out Grayson Buckley, the only suspect we had for this guy's identity. So, we're no closer to finding who this is. Which means we're no closer to solving that mystery."

"We're also no closer to solving the mystery of the time rips turning into time slips," Jack added.

"Nothing came out of your meeting of the minds following dinner?" Cate inquired.

"I'm going to point out again that you know the outcome of this conversation. You've read it already, haven't you?"

"Perhaps his account wasn't accurate. Besides, I'd love your take on what happened."

"Douglas laid out the odd events, beginning with misplaced items. Then he overheard phantom music and conversations. And finally, the events escalated to physical manifestations. A maid witnessed a woman in the front hall and then Douglas also began to see people."

"Did anyone offer any explanation?"

"I went with the standard haunting scenario."

"And Douglas did not agree."

"He did not. It's almost like you know what happened."

Cate narrowed her eyes at him. "Please, continue."

"Douglas said ghosts were windows into past lives, but he believed the events they experienced were windows into the future."

"How did Grayson Buckley react to that?"

Jack shook his head and pursed his lips for a moment before speaking. "He didn't say much. He offered to run it past Celine, then suggested we join the women."

"Did his reaction seem odd?"

Jack shrugged. "I suppose in thinking about it, yes, it did. Though perhaps he doesn't know anything about it."

"This is the man Douglas pinned most of his hopes on. He wanted to run this past Grayson because of his supernatural experience. What does that even mean? And why was Grayson so quiet on the subject?"

"In retrospect, yes, it seemed like he wanted to avoid the subject. Perhaps he didn't want to speak candidly in front of Jaime and me. And, yes, Douglas asked if Grayson ever ran across anything like this in his 'dealings.' That's an odd statement. What type of dealings does someone have that involve time travel?"

"That's exactly what I wondered!" Cate answered. "What supernatural dealings do the Buckleys have?"

"You talked to him at dinner. Did he say anything interesting?"

"Not much. He is from Bucksville. I found a Wikipedia article about the town before we left. Maybe I can use that to track down more information about him."

"And his wife is from Martinique."

"Yes, and the daughter of a Marquis! She must be someone. What supernatural dealings could they have? Perhaps he's referring to the island customs, voodoo."

"Voodoo? Like pins in dolls?"

"It's a bit more subtle than that, but yes. Caribbean islands were well-known for voodoo customs."

"Could be that, then. But why would Douglas assume that could help with his glimpses into the future."

"I'm not sure," Cate admitted with a sigh.

"Did you learn anything interesting from the women?"

"Not really. Olivia mentioned the supposed hauntings. She hoped it would die down soon. Rumors are abounding in town."

"That's it? Nothing else?"

"Not really," Cate said with a shrug. "Though…" Her voice trailed off as she crinkled her brow.

"What?"

"It's nothing," she said as she waved her hand in the air to dismiss the idea.

"What? Come on, Cate. Don't hold back now."

Cate shrugged again. "It's probably stupid but... there's something odd about Celine."

"She's French. It's how they are."

Cate giggled at the statement. "That's not true. No, it's something else. She asked me a question and when she looked at me it was like she could see right through me."

"It's the voodoo."

"I guess time will tell."

"Well, if you get any odd pains anywhere, we'll know who to suspect first."

"Very funny," Cate said with a groan. "I certainly hope not."

"I certainly hope we get more information and soon. The way Douglas talked, the uncontrolled time rips seem to escalate. We need a solution and fast."

"I'll work more on the journals tomorrow. I'm not sure I can concentrate after our double day."

"Tomorrow's a new day, Cate. Get some rest. Besides, it's nearly time for dinner!"

"Second dinner, you mean," Cate corrected.

"Yep, second dinner. The best part of time traveling. Repeat meals!"

"Speaking of time traveling..."

"We should go back tomorrow. We need to keep searching for answers."

"I agree," Cate answered. "I'll translate journal three in the morning, and we can travel back for dinner again. How's that?"

"Works for me," Jack said with a groan as he pushed himself out of the armchair. "I'd better be heading down for that second dinner."

"Enjoy," Cate said as he moseyed across the room.

* * *

Cate ran through the castle's halls. She stumbled down the main staircase in a desperate attempt to flee. She pushed through the sitting room doors, tugging her dress' train behind her. With wide eyes, she searched for a hiding spot.

Footsteps followed her. Cate raced across the room and sank behind the sofa. She crawled under the slim console table, realizing its narrowness would fail to hide her completely.

Men's shoes clacked across the hardwood floor. They stalked into the room slowly and deliberately. The noise stopped. Cate held her breath. Her pulse raced and her hands trembled as she bit her lower lip.

The footsteps commenced again. They approached her hiding spot. She spied legs coming around the sofa. The man stopped again. After a moment, he spun, his footsteps receding across the room.

"Soon, Catherine, soon," the man said. His footsteps departed into the foyer. As the front door banged shut, Cate awoke.

Another nightmare, Cate reflected as her heart returned to normal speed. This one came with a warning. The man's words rung in her mind.

Soon, Catherine, soon.

CHAPTER 15

Cate set her cup of tea next to her laptop. She'd balanced a few shortbreads on the saucer, a preemptive reward for her decryption work this morning. She nibbled on one as she popped her laptop open.

She'd spent yesterday morning entering ciphertext from the third journal into a document but hadn't decrypted it yet. She planned to begin that process now. With any luck, she'd learn more about how to control the time rips, the curious Buckleys, or anything that may help them.

Cate copied several pages of text into the decipher program and clicked the "GO!" button. A colored circle spun around and around as she waited for decoded text to appear. Cate took another sip of tea and enjoyed more of the shortbreads. Molly's latest batch tasted fantastic. She made a mental note to pass her sentiments along to Molly when she saw her next.

After another few moments, text filled in on her screen. Cate copied it to her decrypted document. She started another round with the program as she read the next journal entry.

> *Having a laboratory in the castle is simply glorious! I have spent several days working on my inventions. With my own space, Olivia can no longer lament my materials lying about. It has caused something of an awakening in me. Ideas now swirl in my mind constantly. I have the room to draft their sketches and work on multiple projects at once.*
>
> *And I have finally begun on my larger projects! Projects for which our previous abodes did not provide sufficient space. Indeed, my stairway project is shaping up quite nicely, though it has produced no results yet. And my seclusion chamber is nearly ready for use. I wonder if results will be more readily forthcoming from it.*
>
> *I shall try it soon. Jaime insists I should not, but I cannot see the harm in it. Today's project is something quite different. I am attempting to produce a light source without fire. I believe it would be a most useful invention as using flame for light can be tedious.*

Cate's brow furrowed as she read the start of the entry. She glanced at the journal from which she'd copied it. Cate paged to the back cover. Had she selected the wrong journal? Was this not the next journal?

Cate spied the small "3" penciled into the bottom corner of the interior back cover. She checked the other journals but found no other threes among them. This must be the correct journal. The opening entry made no mention of Grayson Buckley, the time rips, or anything related to the final entry in the second journal.

Cate scanned the remaining text in the passage. It discussed Douglas's first attempt at creating a lightbulb and his findings. No mention of anything that could help them existed in what she had decrypted.

Behind her text document, the decryption program announced the completion of the next set of text. Cate skimmed the text. She offered a frustrated sigh as none of it related to Douglas's discussion of the time rips.

As she considered her next move, Cate reached for her teacup. She took a sip, but no warm liquid reached her lips. She frowned down at the empty cup and saucer. Perhaps a refill would assist her in planning.

With her empty cup and saucer collected, Cate wandered the halls to the kitchen, lost in thought. Why had the journal jumped? Why did Douglas behave as though the time rips were suddenly unimportant? Why did his focus shift? And would she find more in the subsequent journals? Perhaps she should decode a portion of each of the remaining journals to determine if any additional information existed in them.

Cate resolved to try that tactic as she moseyed down the hall to the kitchen. She found Mrs. Fraser and Molly enjoying their cuppa. "Oh, Lady Cate! I could have collected the teacup," Mrs. Fraser said as she entered.

"I'm actually looking for a refill," Cate answered.

"Research going that good, huh?" Molly joked.

Cate nodded. "That's about the size of it." She set the kettle on with fresh water to boil. "Oh, Molly, this latest batch of shortbread is really good!"

"Thanks!" Molly exclaimed.

"Aye, I quite agree, Lady Cate," Mrs. Fraser answered. "The next test is to bake them with no supervision!"

The tea kettle whistled on the stove and Cate poured herself a fresh cup. As she dunked the tea bag into the steaming water, Jack entered.

"Okay, she's all ordered. I got the one you liked and..." His voice stopped mid-sentence as he stared at Cate. "Lady Cate! What are you doing here?"

"My, that's some greeting. It is HER castle," Molly teased.

"Aye, it is," Jack answered. "But I don't often find her in the kitchen of her castle mid-morning."

"Just making a cuppa," Cate responded.

"Didn't you have one already?"

Mrs. Fraser guffawed. "When did you become the tea police?"

Jack ran his fingers through his hair and offered a nervous chuckle. "No tea police here," he said with another chuckle. "Just... well, anyway."

"So, what did you get ordered?" Cate inquired.

"Huh?" he questioned.

"When you came in you said you had gotten something ordered."

"Oh, right," Jack answered. "Manure. Yep, ordered the manure for the garden."

Cate knit her brows and frowned. "Not a pleasant conversation, you're right," Jack added.

"It's not that. You mentioned you got the one someone liked. Who likes manure?"

"Oh," Jack said with another nervous chuckle. "I meant the one the flowers like."

"Oh," Cate answered. "Got it. Yes, the plants probably do like manure. Well, I'll leave you to your day!"

"Okay, bye!" Jack said. Cate offered him a confused glance, her eyes narrowed as she collected a few more shortbread cookies and returned to the library.

She spent the rest of the morning copying excerpts from half of the remaining journals. None of them mentioned any references to the timepiece, time rips, time travel, or the Buckleys. Cate slouched in her desk chair. Unless something changed in the second half of the journals, they'd learn nothing from these. Their only hope remained with traveling back to Douglas's time.

The news would not sit well with Jack, she reflected, as a knock announced her lunch. She left the journals in favor of her favorite armchair during the meal.

Jack joined her following lunch. Molly departed with the lunch tray as he sank into the armchair next to Cate.

"Ordering that manure really wore you out," Cate teased.

"Aye," he admitted.

Cate narrowed her eyes at him. "What?" he questioned.

"That conversation just seemed... strange."

"Strange? No, just... I never talked to Gertrude about manure."

"I see," Cate murmured.

"Anyway, how's your research going? Anything to help us?" Jack responded before Cate could say anything further.

"Well..." Cate began. Molly's reappearance in the library interrupted the conversation.

"Molly?" Cate questioned. "Is everything okay?"

Molly stumbled into the room. Cate's lunch tray remained clutched in her hands. White knuckles wrapped around each handle. Her jaw hung agape. Her eyes stared ahead without seeing. Her skin, normally golden and warm, was an ashy white.

"Molly?" Cate asked again as she climbed from her chair. Jack followed Cate as she approached Molly who stood unwavering in the doorway. "What's wrong? What is it?"

Molly's bottom lip quivered as she attempted to form words. Jack tugged the tray from her hands and set it on the desk as Cate guided her to an armchair.

Molly eased into it, still staring straight ahead. Her brows pinched together, and she frowned. Cate glanced at Jack as she perched on the chair's arm. She rubbed Molly's shoulders. "What is it, Molly? Are you not feeling well?"

Jack rejoined them, sinking into the chair next to Molly. "Molly, are you okay?" he questioned.

Molly took a deep inhale. Her eyes darted around the room before settling on Cate. She grasped Cate's hand then glanced between Cate and Jack. "I think… I think I just saw a ghost."

"What?!" Cate exclaimed. She shot a look to Jack. "Where?"

"I-In… in the hall," Molly stammered.

"Okay, Molly. Take a deep breath and calm down. Then tell us everything."

Molly nodded and pushed her hair behind both ears. She took a deep breath and blew it out before she continued. "I picked up your tray and stepped into the hall. I started down the hall toward the kitchen and… there she was!"

"She?" Jack questioned.

"Yes, she. Wearing a long dress. Old-fashioned. And her hair was swept up." Molly waved her hand behind her head to demonstrate.

"What was she doing?" Cate inquired.

"Walking. Just… walking. Toward the foyer."

Cate nodded. "Did she see you?"

Molly shook her head. "No, I froze. I didn't know what to do. I… I…"

"It's okay," Cate said, grasping Molly's hand and squeezing.

"I'm not crazy!" Molly burst out.

"I didn't say you were," Cate replied.

"Bu-but you said the castle wasn't haunted, but I think it might be!" Molly cried.

"Let's not jump to conclusions just yet," Cate soothed.

"I saw a ghost, Cate!" Molly shouted. "I'm sorry," she said in a trembling voice. "I'm sorry. I just… I saw something, Lady Cate. I saw… No, not something. A woman. I saw a woman."

"Funny trick of the lighting?" Jack suggested.

Molly shook her head but didn't respond. "We believe you," Cate assured her. "But I wouldn't get too worked up just yet. If you see her again, please tell us. I want to keep track of this."

"What are we going to do if she's a ghost?" Molly breathed.

"Let's cross that bridge when we come to it," Cate said.

"She didn't harm you," Jack answered. "Even if she is a ghost, and I'm not saying she is, it may just be a nuisance, not a problem."

"Yet," Molly added.

"Molly, let's not get too worked up. This could be anything."

Silence fell over the group. Cate glanced at Jack. He gave a slight shrug.

"Let me get you a cup of tea," Cate offered.

"I can run down for it," Jack said.

"No," Molly insisted. "No, I... I'm okay. You're right. I saw something. I don't understand what it was, but I definitely saw something. But it's no reason to panic. It's an old house. It could be anything. And even if it was a ghost, so what?! So I live in a haunted castle. At least I live in a castle."

Molly stood on wobbly legs. She took a deep breath as she steadied herself. Cate leapt to her feet with her arms outstretched toward Molly in case she fainted.

"I'm okay," Molly insisted as color returned to her face. "I better get this tray downstairs. Mrs. Fraser will be wondering what happened to me."

"I'll walk you down," Jack said.

"No, no, I'm okay. I don't need an escort."

"Are you sure?" Cate asked. "If you'd feel better with someone going with you, one of us can walk you down."

Molly shook her head and firmed her jaw. She squared her shoulders. "I'm good," she stated with a nod and a sniffle.

"Okay, if you're sure," Cate said.

"I am," Molly assured her with a smile. She retrieved the

tray from the desk and stood in the doorway. After another deep breath, Molly disappeared into the hall. Cate snuck to the door and popped her head into the hall. She followed Molly's retreating form.

As Molly vanished around the corner, Cate returned to the armchairs. Jack raised his eyebrows at her. "That's not good," he said.

"No kidding," Cate answered as she collapsed into her armchair.

"These time slips are growing worse. Tell me you found something in those journals."

Cate shook her head. "Nope. Nothing."

"Nothing?" Jack sighed as he paced the floor. "How far are you from finding something do you think? Is he mentioning anything close to a solution?"

Cate remained silent for a moment. "That's where things go from bad to worse."

"What do you mean?" Jack questioned as his pacing ground to a halt.

Cate glanced up at him, fixing her eyes on his. "Douglas's writing has ceased to mention manifestations, time rips, time travel, Grayson Buckley or anything relating to our problem entirely."

"What?!" Jack cried. His eyes darted around the room as if searching for an answer. "What is he detailing in the journals?"

"His inventions. Journal three discusses his attempt to make a lightbulb." Cate sank her head into her hands with a deep exhale.

"Oh, you're kidding. Are they out of order? Did you miss a journal?"

"I checked! And I started to randomly pull excerpts from the remaining journals. I made it through half. Not a single reference."

Jack collapsed into the armchair next to Cate. He shook his head in disbelief. Jack's head dropped onto the chair behind him.

"I'll keep checking both the other journals I haven't tried and more excerpts from the ones I checked already," Cate continued.

Jack shook his head at her statement. "We can't depend on those," he admitted. "We need another solution. We've got to step up our game in the past."

Cate paused before responding. "But how? Douglas has his suspicions, but it doesn't seem like he's formed any final conclusions yet."

"Perhaps we can nudge him in that direction," Jack suggested. "I could tell him I agree with him. That I've been considering it and have concluded he is correct."

Cate pondered Jack's suggestion. "We could try. I'd be interested in finding out Grayson Buckley's response to that. Both you and Douglas judged his behavior to be odd."

"Perhaps he deems Douglas is crazy."

"Douglas seemed to expect Grayson to be his biggest ally in this. Or at least for him to offer some solution, perhaps even have some experience with these situations."

"If I reopen the subject after dinner tonight, perhaps we'll get a clearer picture. If he ignores it again, we may have something. If not, perhaps we'll finally figure out what supernatural experience this guy has."

"Okay, there's our plan. Our very weak plan," Cate said with a sigh.

"At least it's a plan. We'll try our best to push Douglas's discovery so we can find out how he controlled these time rips and hopefully use that information to fix our problem."

"Before Molly sees another ghost."

"Aye, before Molly or anyone else ends up in a time period not their own."

"Meet you around four to head back?"

"Sounds like a plan," Jack agreed.

* * *

Cate pulled on her eighteenth-century attire as worry creased her brow. Would they make any progress today? If they didn't, what would happen? In both other instances when she and Jack had investigated in the past, it hadn't spelled disaster if they failed. This time it may. The future of the castle may depend on their success. If they failed, the time slips could worsen. The castle could become uninhabitable, leaving anyone who chose to stay in it prone to trips to other centuries with no warning.

Cate finished fastening her dress and fussed with her hair. For the first time since her arrival at the castle, reluctance to time travel coursed through her. She feared failing. They would not fail, she promised herself. They could not. She pushed her shoulders back as she cemented the idea in her mind. They would solve this.

Cate gathered her train and navigated to the library where she found Jack. "Ready?" He inquired.

"Yes," Cate said, resolute. "Let's go solve our problems."

"There's the spirit, lassie," Jack said with a grin as they descended into the laboratory.

"Well, I suppose the burden lies on you. It is you who will be privy to those secret meetings of the male minds."

"Complete with billowing clouds of cigar smoke and decanters of brandy," Jack answered. "And don't discount your work, Lady Cate. Flower shows are serious business!"

Cate narrowed her eyes at him as she suppressed a giggle. She held out the timepiece. "Here we go!"

They activated the timepiece and the second hand slowed to a crawl. The lights blinked out, replaced by the blackness characteristic of the closed-off, secret room. They snuck from the lab, through the library, and into the foyer before climbing the stairs to their bedroom.

Once inside their bedroom, Cate discovered a note addressed to them both. She flipped open the folded paper.

Jack and Catherine - I hope your business is progressing well. You are going to run poor Catherine ragged with your traipsing about the countryside! I jest, though I'm certain Olivia would enjoy seeing Catherine for tea.

I do hope we shall see you today for dinner. We have another guest joining us. Quite unexpected but it should prove most entertaining for the group! I should very much like for you to meet him.

If you return in time, please do not delay in presenting yourselves for dinner.

- Douglas

Cate read the note aloud as Jack peered over her shoulder at it. "Ohhh, a mystery guest!" Jack exclaimed. "Wonder who this guy is Douglas is so interested in introducing us to?"

Cate pursed her lips as she considered the note. "Another relative?"

"I hope it's not someone who needs a land attorney."

Cate giggled at the prospect. "Tell him you have too many clients already."

"Good plan, Lady Cate. Plus, my real talent lies in criminal law, not land."

"If it's a relative, I hope it's not someone who knows the family well. Our cover could be blown!"

"Let's keep our fingers crossed it's someone who needs a land attorney." Jack held his hand out. "Sorry, fellow, my client list is full," he practiced.

"Convincing! Well, I suppose we shouldn't delay dressing for dinner!"

"Don't want to be late to meet my newest client," Jack joked.

After changing for dinner, Cate and Jack arrived at the sitting room to await the meal. Olivia, Douglas, Aria, and Jaime awaited them.

"Good evening, Jack and Catherine!" Douglas greeted them. "I am so pleased you could attend!"

"We received your note," Jack replied. "I am glad my business concluded in time."

"As am I. We are most fortunate…" The arrival of Celine and Grayson Buckley interrupted Douglas's statement. "Celine, Gray, good evening."

"Good evening, Douglas," Gray answered with a broad smile. "I understand we have more company this evening."

"Indeed."

"Additional family?" he inquired.

"No," Douglas admitted. "Though I am most enthusiastic about this unexpected development!"

"Care to elaborate?" Jaime inquired.

"In due time, my good fellow, in due time." Douglas poured cocktails for everyone. It appeared he intended to keep mum regarding the surprise dinner guest. Not family, Cate ruminated. Their cover should remain intact then. She pondered as she sipped her sherry who could induce this giddy reaction from Douglas.

As the dinner hour neared, Wilson entered from the foyer and offered a slight nod to Douglas. "Won't you all excuse me?" Douglas said in a gleeful tone. "Olivia, would you please?" He motioned for her to join him in the foyer. With a grin on his lips, he hurried from the room with Olivia.

Cate stood and approached Jack. "Moment of truth," she whispered.

"At least he's not family," Jack breathed.

Cate gave him a nod, her eyebrows raised to acknowledge the win.

Within a few moments, Douglas returned with another man. The man stood a bit taller than Douglas. Perfectly tailored clothing evidenced his lean form. His dark hair, tied back in a queue, topped his chiseled, regal features.

Cate witnessed a shared glance between the Buckleys. Were they familiar with the new arrival, she wondered?

"Ladies and gentlemen," Douglas announced. "We have the wonderful fortune to have a duke join us under our roof. If you would all join me in welcoming Duke Marcus Northcott! Duke Northcott, please." Douglas motioned into the room. "Allow me to fix you a cocktail and introduce you to our other guests."

Duke Northcott offered a tight-lipped smile as he surveyed the room.

"Who the heck is this character?" Jack whispered to Cate as their eyes followed him across the room.

Cate glanced to the Buckleys again as she answered. "I'm not sure." She narrowed her eyes as she noted the set expression on Celine Buckley's face. Her husband wore a matching unimpressed look. "But it seems as though our new friends, the Buckleys, know him."

Aria and Jaime joined the Buckleys near the fireplace as Douglas handed a scotch to Duke Northcott. They spoke a few words before Douglas motioned toward Cate and Jack.

He sauntered toward them with Duke Northcott in tow. "Duke Northcott, I am so pleased for you to make the acquaintance of my cousin, Jack MacKenzie, and his wife, Catherine."

The man's dark eyes flitted to Jack then focused on Cate. He studied her, a smile bordering on a smirk formed on his lips. His stare disconcerted her, but she forced a smile onto her face. Jack's hand hung in the air as the Duke ignored it, directing his attention solely on Cate.

She offered him her hand, which he accepted. His fingers brushed hers, sending a shiver down her spine. Cate ignored her instinctive response. "A pleasure to meet you, Duke," she said.

His eyes met hers. "Hello, Catherine," he said in a crisp British accent. Cate's heart leapt into her throat and blood went cold. Her stomach somersaulted and her knees went weak. Her hand trembled in his and her lower lip quivered as she struggled to pull herself together.

That voice. That haunting voice. The same voice from her nightmares. In two words, she had identified the man who had chased her, tormented her, haunted her for months. Duke Marcus Northcott.

CHAPTER 16

Cate swallowed hard as she forced a weak smile onto her lips. Jack cleared his throat and thrust his hand out further. "Duke Northcott, how fortunate we are to dine with you," he said.

Duke Northcott offered him a displeased glance and murmured, "Yes."

"Allow me to introduce you to the rest of the group," Douglas offered, signaling for the Duke to move toward the group near the fireplace.

"Friendly guy," Jack murmured. Cate gulped the rest of her sherry as she spun away from the newest member of their group. "Cate? Are you all right?"

Cate shook her head without answering. She bit her lower lip, her forehead creasing. "What is it? Are you sick? Do you need to sit down?"

Cate met Jack's gaze. "It's him."

Jack's brows knit for a moment before his eyes went wide. "Him? As in the guy in your nightmares? That's him?" Jack whispered.

Cate offered a clipped nod. She swallowed hard.

Jack studied the man across the room as he greeted Jaime, Aria, Grayson, and Celine. "Our new friends seem to share your sentiments regarding Duke Northcott," Jack commented.

Cate twisted to face the scene as she recovered from her shock. "Celine looked less than pleased when Douglas announced him."

Jack surveyed the scene a moment longer. "Who is this character? Why would he be lurking around your subconscious?"

"And what history does he share with the Buckleys?" Cate added.

"Would you prefer to go? I could make our excuses. Say you felt ill. Caught the vapors," Jack said with a wink.

Cate shook her head and squared her shoulders. "No. We need answers. We must see this through. Perhaps we'll get a twofer! Solve both mysteries in one fell swoop."

"You sure?" Jack inquired.

Cate nodded and let out a deep breath. "Yes." She narrowed her eyes at the Duke as he chatted with Olivia and Douglas. "I need answers. WE need answers."

"If you want an escape just shout "PICKLES" and I'll make an excuse."

Cate swung her head to face Jack, an incredulous expression on her face. "Pickles?"

"Yeah. It'll be our signal word."

Wilson entered and announced dinner before Cate could respond to Jack's escape word plan. The group entered the dining room and found their seats. Cate's muscles stiffened as she noticed her seat to the left of Duke Northcott.

She met Jack's eyes across the table and offered him a grimace as she stepped toward the table. The chair slid in behind her. She turned to find Duke Northcott easing it toward her. She offered him a curt smile as she lowered to her seat.

The man took his seat next to her. Olivia turned to her left to speak with Grayson. Cate breathed a sigh of relief as she faced Jaime for their pre-dinner conversation.

"Good evening, Mrs. MacKenzie," Jaime said.

"Mr. Reid," Cate greeted him. "And how are you this evening?"

"Splendid," he responded. "A most fortunate turn of events to welcome a Duke!"

"Yes, Douglas seems thrilled with the development," Cate agreed.

"Aye, to welcome a Duke to his humble country estate in the highlands!" Cate held in a chuckle at the description of the large, ornate castle as humble.

"Duke Northcott is well-traveled. He should provide a most entertaining evening," Jaime babbled. His enthusiasm brimmed over the visit.

"It seems the Buckleys are acquainted with Duke Northcott," Cate began when Olivia turned to her right to speak with Jaime.

Their unbalanced party had left an awkward conversation between Douglas, Duke Northcott, and Celine, though from the corner of Cate's eye she noticed Celine remained silent. As they turned, Celine took the opportunity to speak with Jack, seated to her right.

Cate swallowed hard and forced a smile onto her lips as she faced Duke Northcott.

"Good evening again, Catherine," he said. Cate found the tone of his voice disconcerting. After hearing it on a near-nightly basis, the mere sound garnered a fear reaction from her. She fought to keep her heartbeat steady and not shiver as he spoke.

"Good evening, Duke," she answered. "I trust your travel here was pleasant?"

"Rather tedious, however, I am most pleased to have arrived in this unique location. I imagine your journey to have been quite a bit more taxing."

Cate's brow furrowed at his statement. "Your accent," he continued. "You are also American."

"Also?" she questioned.

"Yes, Buckley is also an American."

Cate noted the tone he used as he spat out Grayson's name and the lack of salutation that accompanied it. What history did they share, she wondered?

"Oh, yes," Cate answered. "Yes, though we are from very different parts of the country."

"Oh? You are not also from Massachusetts?"

"No, Philadelphia."

Duke Northcott narrowed his eyes at her. "Hmm," he murmured as though weighing her statement for its truthfulness. "And you married a Scotsman."

"I did, yes."

"An odd lot, you Americans. And how remarkable that two Americans should arrive at Dunhaven Castle at the same time."

"A happy coincidence in my opinion."

He narrowed his eyes at her statement. "Yes, well, you Americans are rather easy to please. Though…" He paused as his dark eyes studied her face. "There appears to be something unique about you, Catherine. I should look forward to speaking with you further during my stay."

Cate suppressed a shudder at the statement. The serving of the first course postponed any further conversation, much to Cate's delight.

The dinner proceeded with light conversation. Celine remained quiet for much of the meal. Grayson interjected comments here and there, mainly aimed at Douglas. Duke Northcott's descriptions of world travel dominated much of the conversation. True to Douglas's word, his colorful stories passed the time despite Cate's trepidation about the man.

Halfway through the meal, she began to wonder why her subconscious mind seemed so terrified of him. He possessed an old-fashioned charm that made him rather likable. Still, she reflected, something about him distressed her. What?

She glanced up as she pondered the question to find Jack's eyes on her. He raised his eyebrows at her. She nodded to answer his silent question. She was okay.

As the meal ended, Cate found herself relieved to leave the men behind and escape Duke Northcott's side. As they settled in the sitting room, Cate's mind remained in the dining room. Jack planned to broach the subject of the manifestations haunting the castle with Douglas. What response would he receive, she ruminated? Would Duke Northcott's presence hamper their plan?

Aria and Olivia chattered about the Duke's colorful tales about a remote region in Africa. Their voices provided little more than background noise for a distracted Cate. Celine also remained silent.

Within moments, Grayson entered the room. The other men trailed behind him.

"Oh!" Olivia exclaimed, unprepared for the sudden entrance of their male counterparts.

Grayson stalked to Celine. "How are you feeling, darling? Would you prefer to retire early?"

"Yes, if you wouldn't mind. Olivia, I am so terribly sorry, but I am rather under the weather."

"Not at all!" Olivia responded. "I do hope you are feeling better tomorrow."

"Thank you," Celine answered as she clutched Grayson's hand and stood.

Jack entered as the two crossed the room to depart for the evening. He shot Cate a confused glance. She answered with a shrug.

"Leaving?" Douglas questioned as he entered with Duke Northcott.

"Yes, please accept our apologies," Grayson responded. "Celine has been feeling unwell. I suggested she rest."

"Of course. I hope you improve soon, Celine," Douglas said.

Jack poured himself a drink as the Buckleys said their goodnights to their hosts. Cate joined him at the drink cart. "That was quick," she whispered. "I'm guessing you had no luck."

"Not a shred, "Jack answered. "I didn't even get the words out before I was interrupted."

"Grayson seems intent on getting Celine out of here."

"Is she that sick, do you imagine?"

"No," Cate answered. She narrowed her eyes as she followed the departing forms of Grayson and Celine Buckley. "No, I don't think she's sick at all."

The group spent another forty-five minutes chatting before Duke Northcott announced his departure. Cate and Jack spent another few moments with the remaining group before taking their leave, feigning fatigue from their business earlier.

"Should we head straight to the library?" Jack inquired as they stepped into the foyer.

"Yes," Cate agreed. "While the remaining group is still accounted for."

As they proceeded toward the library, angry, hushed whispers carried down the hall. Cate ceased walking mid-step. She held her finger to her lips and signaled for Jack to listen.

The voices seemed to come from around the corner. Cate

tiptoed toward the other hallway. Jack crept behind her. She ducked into a parlor and hurried across the room. Two large double doors on the adjacent wall opened into the other hallway. She eased the door open a crack and peeked out. Jack hovered behind her, peering over her head.

"Is that…" he began.

"Celine Buckley," Cate answered. "With Duke Northcott."

Celine's posture was stiff and her jaw set. "Why did you follow me here, Marcus?" Celine demanded.

"You already realize the answer to that question, Celine," Duke Northcott answered.

"Leave, Marcus. Stop making a fool of yourself."

Duke Northcott grasped her by the arm and dragged her toward him. Cate shrank back from the door, her eyes wide as his quick and fierce actions startled her.

"Do not presume to tell me what to do, Celine. I shall be thought no more a fool than you who cannot settle in one place for more than months at a time. People will begin to wonder, dear, what you are running from?"

"Or who," Celine spat at him.

"Unfortunately for you, my reputation precedes me. It opens doors for me. Yours does not."

"You overestimate your appeal, Marcus. Though you always have." Celine wrenched her arm from his grip. "There is nothing for you here. Go."

Duke Northcott straightened his cravat and smoothed his jacket. A smirk crossed his lips. "Au contraire, my dear. There is something odd here. There is a reason you came here."

"To escape you!"

Duke Northcott rolled his eyes at the statement. "When will you cease this charade and take your rightful place? Your behavior is childish."

"I will NEVER stand beside you."

"Very well, Celine. Insist all you'd like but you know the score. I shall not leave unless you are at my side. Besides, something draws me here. There is something that intrigues me. And I shall not leave until I determine what it is. I suggest you learn to manage your emotions, though, unless you plan to embarrass Buckley by leaving every dinner party early."

Celine set her jaw. "There is no managing my enmity toward you!" she hissed before she stormed down the hall.

Duke Northcott stared after her for a moment before he retreated in the opposite direction. "Wow," Cate whispered.

"Yeah, no kidding," Jack answered.

"Those two definitely have a history."

"Must be a humdinger, too!"

"Come on," Cate urged. "Let's get back home and discuss what we've learned so far!"

They checked the hallway before darting down it to the library. They descended into Douglas's unoccupied laboratory and returned to the present. After changing into their normal clothes, they met in the library to discuss the dinner party and their next steps.

Jack collapsed into his favorite armchair with Riley in his lap. Cate collected Bailey and eased into the chair next to him.

"Well," Jack began. "One mystery down, two to go."

Cate reflected on his statement. "Duke Marcus Northcott," she murmured. "So, he is the man haunting my dreams."

Jack nodded. "That's the one solved."

"But why?" Cate questioned.

"And that's one of the mysteries yet to be solved. The other is the time rips and how to control them."

"Yeah, what happened at your man meeting? Grayson popped in way earlier than anyone expected!"

"I'm afraid that may be my fault," Jack responded.

Cate raised her eyebrows. "Really? What in the world did you say?"

"Nothing!" Jack exclaimed.

Cate puckered her lips at him, prompting him to continue. "Really, nothing! We settled at the table after you ladies left. Well, most of us did. Grayson wandered around the room and settled in front of a window to glare out of it."

"Glare out of it?" Cate questioned.

"That's putting it mildly. If looks could kill, whoever stood on the other side of that window would have been dead.

"Anyway, I started to bring up the discussion from last night. I got the words, 'Douglas, about your theory from last night' before Grayson interrupted me."

"What did he say?"

"We shouldn't dwell on that. Not with someone as illustrious as Duke Northcott in our midst. I propose, gentleman, we disband and rejoin the ladies. And with that, he was out the door. Douglas seemed a bit puzzled, and he stammered around a bit but suggested we follow Grayson's lead."

"So, you did not speak about anything involving the time rips at all."

"Not even for a second," Jack admitted.

"Ugh," Cate groaned. "This is frustrating. We're making no progress on ANY front!"

Jack nodded as he stared at the crackling fire in the fireplace. "We need to keep at it. Before Molly ends up in another century again."

Cate sighed. "I suppose we're back at it tomorrow with another dinner party."

"Should I try to bring it up again?"

Cate pursed her lips in thought. With a shrug, she answered, "Maybe?"

Jack slid his eyes toward her. "You okay?"

"Yeah," Cate admitted.

"You sure? You seem... distracted. Perhaps your midnight visitor is still rattling around in your mind?"

"That's another front we need some progress on. I'm going to do a little more research on him and both Buckleys. See if I can find anything. Why is he chasing me around in my sleep? Who is this guy? And what is his connection to me?"

"Did you learn anything from him during your dinner conversation?"

"Nothing other than he's quite a snob. And he seems to hold a heavy dislike for Grayson Buckley."

"Not surprising. It sounds as though he has a history with Grayson's wife."

"Unrequited love? You imagine he was after her and she turned him down for Grayson Buckley?"

"It seems likely," Jack answered. "Celine asked him why he followed her."

"And he told me they were well-acquainted."

Jack raised his eyebrows. "Ooooooh, now we get all the bawdy details!"

"And he seemed to be quite surprised that Grayson and I were not acquainted."

"Really? He can't possibly think America is that small. He's well-traveled, he seems to have a good understanding of the world."

"Yes, I found it odd, too. He acted almost as though I was being disingenuous with him."

"All right, so tomorrow's plan is to learn more about this Duke Northcott guy and see if we can push the time rip conversation to a place where we can gain some information."

Cate nodded in agreement. "And in the meantime, I'll

continue to work on researching these people and deciphering a few more excerpts from the journals."

"Sounds like a plan. Same time, same place tomorrow?"

"Same time, same place!"

* * *

Cate pulled her laptop onto her lap after dinner. Her eyes threatened to close with each blink, but she was determined to seek information on the people visiting the castle in 1792. With a deep sigh, Cate pulled up her search engine and began to search for information on a variety of topics surrounding the people she and Jack had recently met.

Her previous searches on Grayson and Celine Buckley had resulted in very little. She used the additional facts they'd learned, however minimal, to tease any information she could from the internet.

Douglas had mentioned the Marquis Devereaux's untimely death. Cate entered his name into her search bar. The first result was a Wikipedia article detailing the governors of Martinique in colonial times. Cate scanned the list finding Marquis Gaspard Devereaux listed from 1774 to 1786. She clicked his name and scanned the brief article.

Outside of detailing his major accomplishments as governor, the article also described his untimely death. The man was murdered on 1 August 1786 as he traveled to board a ship bound for France. A seaman murdered him in a botched robbery.

While intriguing, the article provided no information about Celine or any of the others. With heavy eyelids, Cate pushed the laptop closed. She'd try when she was fresh in the morning. Despite the early hour, Cate's extended day caught up to her. She took one final walk with the dogs as the setting sun painted the western sky.

***

Cate stared at her laptop the next morning. She'd performed a variety of web searches to seek information on her new old-fashioned friends. Outside of a handful of obscure references, she found nothing.

Cate stared out the window with her chin cupped in her palm. She'd need to try a new avenue. She toggled her laptop screen on again and navigated to several historical records databases.

She began her search with Grayson Buckley. After several moments of searching, the database returned a birth record from the year 1760. The details on the record appeared to match with the Grayson Buckley she'd met.

Cate searched for his death certificate but found none. She expanded her search beyond the state of Maine, formerly Massachusetts, to cover the entire United States. After several moments the screen showed NO RESULTS. She tried again, this time using a worldwide search. The search wheel spun in an endless circle before the screen indicated a failed search.

Cate sighed and dropped her head between her shoulders. Missing records were not surprising though the result, or lack thereof, still proved frustrating.

She moved on to Celine Buckley née Devereaux. Cate found no records of her birth in Martinique. She tracked down a record in Lyon, France, but again, she found no death certificate. Where had Grayson and Celine lived at the end of their lives, she pondered?

Cate moved on to the third person of interest: her nightmare companion. She searched the United Kingdom for records on Duke Marcus Northcott. The search returned none. Cate knit her brows. No records at all, she ruminated? A man of his ranking surely was recorded. She expanded the search to other likely areas for his birth. She found no record of the man. Odd, Cate brooded, no documentation about Duke Northcott's life could be found. It was as though he didn't exist.

Cate sighed as she slouched in her chair. At a dead end with the investigation of the people of 1792, she moved on to processing excerpts from the remaining journals. After an hour of work, she had decrypted portions of three more journals. None of them mentioned the time rips or the timepiece.

With a frustrated groan, Cate slammed the laptop shut. She rubbed at her tired eyes. "Time for a break," she announced to Riley and Bailey.

Cate rose from her chair and stretched. She rolled her head around, easing the kinks from her neck. "How about a walk, boys?"

Riley leapt to his feet and raced to Cate's side. Bailey climbed to all fours and leaned into a stretch before trotting toward them.

Cate strode down the hall and out the front door with both dogs in tow. They wandered to the loch.

Cate perched on the bank as the dogs frolicked nearby. She stared out over the calm water. It reflected the surfaces around them like a mirror. Cate spotted the castle's image in the pond. Was she losing her home, she wondered? What would happen if they made no progress with controlling the time rips? Her mind went one step further. What happened if she made no progress in determining why Duke Marcus Northcott haunted her dreams? Would she not only lose her home but her mind as well?

As tears threatened, Cate stood from the bank and called the dogs to her. They would solve this problem. With a determined stride, she set off toward the castle. She wound through the back garden. Jack pounded in a few stakes to train a set of rose bushes.

"Good morning, Jack," Cate called to him as the dogs dashed ahead to greet him.

"Good morning, Lady Cate," he answered. "On a break?"

She nodded without speaking. "Well, that doesn't sound good. Any progress?" Jack inquired.

Cate shook her head. "Not really," she admitted. "I can't seem to find any information on any of our new friends. And I worked on three of the six remaining journals and found no references to the time rips or the timepiece."

"I wasn't holding my breath on the journals giving us any information, but I thought at least you'd find something interesting on the Buckleys or that Duke. He seemed fairly well-known."

"That's where this gets weird," Cate said. "It's not that I can't find anything interesting, it's more that I can't find anything at all."

"What do you mean?"

"I mean there are no records of them. Nothing."

"None of them?" Jack inquired.

"I found a birth record for a Celine Devereaux in Lyon in 1770 and one for Grayson Buckley in 1760 in Massachusetts, now Maine. But I can't find any death records on either of them."

"Is that odd?"

Cate shrugged. "Given the years they lived in, it's not entirely surprising that records are missing. But I'm surprised to find nothing on them. Especially with their wealthy status."

"And how about our newest snobby friend, Duke Northcott?"

"He's even stranger. I can't find a single record on him anywhere. It's like he never existed. And that's even more surprising than the elusive Buckleys. He's a Duke. His lineage would have been kept track of! Those types of things were important to people in that era."

"And still is to some!" Jack exclaimed. "But you're right. This is odd."

"So, we're stuck. Yet again."

Jack shook his head. "We're going to have to step up our efforts in the past. I hate to pin all our hopes on Douglas, but he's all we've got."

"I agree one hundred percent, but we've got no choice. We have to get our information straight from the horse's mouth."

"And hope it solves our problem."

Cate nodded in agreement. "So, I'll see you at four for the next round."

"Yep," Jack agreed.

"All right, until then, I'll try the last few of the journals. Come on, boys, let's…" Cate's voice trailed off as she glanced around. Neither dog was in sight. "Now, where did those two get off to?"

"Probably chasing each other around the garden," Jack suggested.

Cate narrowed her eyes. "Or digging around in it."

Jack winced. "Oh, yeah. They have their spot they love to dig."

"And I'd bet that's where they are," Cate said with a sigh. "I know two pups who are going to need a bath."

"Need help fetching them?" Jack questioned.

"No, finish your roses. I can get them."

"Well, it's almost time for lunch," Jack responded. "I'll finish this after."

Cate began her walk to the side garden in search of the dogs. Jack trailed behind her. "Ah, now I understand," Cate teased. "Lunch is calling your name."

"Darn right, Lady Cate," Jack answered.

They rounded the corner and strode across the lawn toward the side garden. "Riley! Bailey!" Cate called.

Cate navigated to their favorite spot. There they found two dirty dogs. Riley crouched over a small indentation in the earth while Bailey pawed at it further.

"THERE you are!" Cate exclaimed in an exasperated tone. "What is it about that spot that is so intriguing?"

"Perhaps another dog buried a bone there in another era."

"Maybe. If we ever solve the mystery of the misbehaving time rips, this is the next one we need to solve."

"Lady Cate, I will happily solve this mystery if we can stop slipping in and out of other eras," Jack said with a grin.

"You grab Riley, I'll get Bailey."

"And straight to the washtub for you both," Jack said as he scooped a dusty Riley into his arms.

CHAPTER 17

Cate spent her early afternoon hours translating more passages from the remaining three journals. The selected excerpts she processed made no mention of anything beyond odd experiments.

Cate sighed as she tossed the final journal onto the desk. She closed her laptop and headed to her bedroom to change for their upcoming trip to 1792. With any luck, they'd learn something there.

When she was dressed, Cate met Jack in the library, and they returned to the past. "Whew," Jack said as they arrived in their bedroom in 1792. He tossed himself across the bed. "I get nervous every time we have to use that timepiece."

"It seems to be working for normal time travel."

Jack picked his head up to stare at her. "Say that again."

"Huh?" Cate asked.

"Normal time travel. I never thought I'd hear a statement where we referred to time travel as normal. Yet it oddly makes sense."

Cate chuckled despite the dire situation they discussed. "I

get nervous every time Molly retrieves my meal tray. I may have to walk it back to the kitchen myself."

"And incur the wrath of Mrs. Fraser? You're taking your life in your hands there, Cate."

"Better that than have Molly slip into who-knows-when again!"

"That doesn't solve the problem, anyway. You could slip into who-knows-when and then what?"

"And least I'd know what happened!" Cate countered. A moment of silence passed between them before Cate asked, "Hey, you're not wandering around the castle at night, are you?"

"Me?" Jack inquired in an incredulous tone. "No way. You couldn't pry me out of my bed with those time rips opening without warning! Are you?"

"No," Cate responded. "Not since the last time you found me asleep in the library. Although, a time rip exists in my bedroom that has opened twice already so if I don't show up for breakfast one day…"

"Look in the 1920s," Jack answered.

Cate nodded. "How you'll get there is another story."

Jack crinkled his brow. "That's a good point, Lady Cate. What if you did disappear? We'd have no way of retrieving you. You're the only one who has access."

Cate sighed. "I'd love to duplicate this," she said, dangling the timepiece in her fingers, "but we have no idea HOW it works."

"No, we don't. But with any luck, we will soon, lassie. But not if you don't get dressed for dinner."

"Jack Reid. The picture of optimism. Whoever would have thought?"

"Time travel changes a man."

* * *

Cate and Jack changed for dinner and convened with Douglas, Jaime, Olivia, and Aria in the sitting room. Absent from the room were the Buckleys and Duke Northcott. Perhaps one or both of them departed, Cate mused.

"Ah! Jack, Catherine, welcome!" Douglas greeted them. "Catherine, I am beginning to worry about you."

"Oh?" Cate inquired, uncertain of his meaning.

"It appears my cousin, Jack, is running you ragged every day! You're both gone before breakfast!"

Cate smiled at the comment. "I quite enjoy seeing the countryside." Douglas raised his eyebrows at her. "I'm an American," Cate continued, "we are quite sturdy stock!"

Douglas burst into laughter at Cate's comment. "And very good sports," he replied. His eyes turned toward the open doors. "Ah, here is the lion's share of our remaining party."

"Don't let Northcott hear you say that," Grayson answered. "He would argue he, himself, is the lion's share of any party."

Cate turned her gaze to the door as Grayson and Celine entered. Behind them trailed two men. Both tall, one with sandy blonde hair, the other with medium brown. The man with the brown hair glanced to Cate and offered a shy smile.

"And how are you both settling in? I trust your rooms are sufficient?" Douglas inquired of them.

"More than sufficient, very comfortable, Lord MacKenzie," the blonde answered. "Thank you again."

"No trouble at all, sir! What a joy to fill these rooms with our friends!" Douglas responded. He turned to Cate and Jack. "Catherine, Jack, please meet our newest arrivals! We have been most fortunate to receive so many unexpected but cherished guests! This is Michael and Damien Carlyle, Celine's cousins. Michael, Damien, this is my cousin, Jack, and his wife, Catherine."

Everyone greeted each other and Douglas offered drinks

to the newcomers. Cate noted their American accents. She sipped her sherry as she eyed the newest members of their party. Michael and Damien Carlyle, she repeated mentally. Two new names to search. Perhaps these cousins would provide her with some lead.

Jack raised his eyebrows at her as the conversation flowed in the room. She returned the gesture. "Curiouser and curiouser," she whispered as they sat together on the loveseat.

The arrival of Duke Northcott interrupted much of the cocktail conversation. Cate surveyed the reaction of the Carlyles to his arrival. From their stiffened postures and lack of conversation, she judged them to share the same sentiments as their cousin, Celine. Their sudden appearance almost seemed as though she had summoned them for support. Of course, Cate reflected, that idea was ridiculous. In 1792, it would take months for word to even reach the American shores, let alone for them to travel to the highlands of Scotland.

"May I introduce you to Celine's cousins..." Douglas began as Duke Northcott entered the room.

He offered a smirk, adding, "We are acquainted."

"Oh. I hadn't realized," Douglas answered.

"More Americans," Duke Northcott grumbled. "We are beginning to be overrun, Douglas."

"Indeed, indeed," Douglas said with a hearty laugh, though Cate deemed Duke Northcott's comment less of a joke and more his actual sentiments.

Wilson announced dinner and everyone filed into the dining room. Much to Cate's relief, she found her seat between the brothers Carlyle. As Olivia chatted with Duke Northcott to her right, Cate and Michael discussed life in America.

"Also, an American," Michael noted as Cate turned toward him.

"Yes. From Philadelphia. And you?"

"Damien and I hail from New York," Michael answered.

"And you are cousins of Celine's?" Cate inquired.

"Yes. Rather distant, though since she has recently spent some time in the States, we have had the opportunity to spend more time with her."

"She is originally from France, is that correct?"

"Correct, from Lyon."

"Life for her in the States must be quite different from both France and Martinique."

"I would imagine so, yes."

"And what brings you to Scotland, Mr. Carlyle?" Cate questioned.

"Business," Michael responded. "Damien and I are furthering our fortunes with various investments."

"What is your business?"

"Ship-building, mainly, though we are expanding our interests," Michael responded.

Cate smiled at the response as Olivia turned, prompting her to begin her conversation with the man on her left, Damien Carlyle.

Damien smiled at her as she turned toward him. "Good evening, Damien," she greeted him.

"Hello," he said. "How fortunate to meet you."

Cate furrowed her brow at the statement. "Because we are both Americans. We share that in common," he explained further.

"Ah, yes," Cate answered. "And you are from New York?"

"Yes, New York. Though we have recently spent a great deal of time on Gray's family's estate in Massachusetts."

Cate nodded. "I have never traveled that far north."

"You would very much enjoy it, I presume," he said. "Perhaps one day, you shall."

"Perhaps," Cate answered. "How fortunate you were able to travel to Dunhaven when your cousin is visiting."

"Yes, very. Gray mentioned a business venture to pursue when they left Massachusetts for Scotland. Michael and I decided to pursue it and traveled behind them."

"Was your journey very taxing?"

"No, we enjoyed calm seas for most of the voyage."

"How fortunate. Which ship did you travel on?"

Damien's eyes widened and he glanced away from Cate. He stammered for a moment before Wilson arrived with the footmen to serve the first course. They did not return to the conversation. His hesitance stuck in Cate's mind. Why had he reacted so strangely, Cate wondered?

As light conversation proceeded through the main course, Cate's mind dwelt on the new circumstances surrounding them. The arrival of the Carlyles threw another monkey wrench into the works. The larger party meant less ability for Cate and Jack to discuss the time rips with Douglas. And by extension, less chance they would retrieve the information they needed.

The rate at which new guests arrived, they would never have the opportunity to discuss this with Douglas. Cate found the dinner tedious given the new arrivals.

At the meal's conclusion, Grayson suggested everyone reconvene for nightcaps in the sitting room. It seemed he hoped to avoid the private conversation amongst the men once again this evening. No one objected.

As they filed from the dining room, Jack rejoined Cate. "Well, this is going to be tricky."

"You've read my mind," Cate breathed. "The Carlyles are a bit strange. And their presence doesn't help our cause."

"No. Neither does Grayson Buckley actively destroying any chance we have to discuss the time rips."

"We need a new plan."

"Yeah, and fast. But for now, it appears our night is a bust."

The group spent another hour making stilted conversation over post-dinner drinks. During the course of the nightcaps, Cate swore she caught Duke Northcott staring at her more than once. His gaze unnerved her more than she liked to admit.

After a tedious sixty minutes, the party broke up. Cate and Jack followed the other guests upstairs and navigated to their bedroom. They waited several moments before sneaking downstairs. After creeping down the hall and into the library, they accessed Douglas's lab and returned home.

"Whew," Jack exclaimed as they slipped back to their time.

"Not quite the sentiment I am ready to express but I suppose it's good to be home," Cate said with a sigh.

"Yeah, I'm frustrated, too," Jack answered.

"Change and discuss?" Cate asked.

"Yeah," Jack answered.

He took a step toward the wooden staircase leading from the lab when a quiver raced through the room. Jack stopped in his tracks and spun to face Cate.

Cate stared at him. He seemed to shimmy in front of her. "Jack!" Cate shouted.

"Cate?!" he exclaimed.

Cate rushed toward him and grasped his hand. He pulled her close to him as the room shuddered around them. The lights flickered on and off, then began to appear and disappear. Darkness consumed them over and over.

Cate clutched at Jack, wrapping her arms around him. After a moment, darkness surrounded them. In the dim light, Cate glanced around then at Jack.

"Are we stuck?" he inquired.

"I think so," Cate said in a shaky voice. She pulled the timepiece from around her neck and listened. "I don't hear any ticking. I can't see the face to confirm it's slow, though."

"So, we're back in 1792."

"Yeah," Cate agreed.

"And the timepiece won't work, right? This is what happened to you before and it didn't work."

"Right."

"So, now what? Do we just wait here until the time rip opens again?"

"We could try the universal rip. I never assessed whether or not that portal would work."

"Okay, let's try…"

A scraping noise sounded above them. "Shh!" Cate warned.

They glanced upward. Light shone at the top of the stairs.

Jack glanced at Cate, his eyes wide. "We need to hide!" Cate whispered. Cate searched the room for a hiding spot. "There!" She pointed to a partially built wooden staircase. She pulled Jack toward it and crawled underneath. Jack followed her. Together, they crammed into the tight space as footsteps descended the stairs.

"…interesting turn of events," Douglas's voice echoed throughout the space.

"Quite. A bevy of unexpected guests," Jaime responded. "Olivia must be at sixes and sevens with the sudden change."

The two men reached the bottom step and entered the space. Cate and Jack pressed as far under the wooden structure as possible. They peered between the risers as they held their breath.

"I have explained to her no one expects her to balance the party on such short notice."

"Not to mention the upset to the household, though. The

poor woman must be overwhelmed with her first major house party turning into a widespread event."

"You've no sense of adventure, Jaime," Douglas answered.

"You've too much. How you take these things in stride is beyond me."

"There's not much else to be done, is there? And I do not mind the added company, though it rather impedes the conversations I intended to have with Grayson."

"The arrival of Jack MacKenzie did not stymie your crusade for information. What's changed?"

"Several things," Douglas replied. "The arrival of our additional guests for one."

"Two of whom are related to Celine Buckley. I shouldn't expect them to be shocked or bothered by the discussion."

"Perhaps, though there is Duke Northcott."

"You assume he will find the conversation ridiculous. Perhaps spread a nasty rumor about you?"

"No," Douglas responded. "It is something Grayson said."

"Oh?"

"Yes. He seemed most insistent we do not discuss it in his presence. You witnessed his reaction after dinner yesterday. And this morning he mentioned being cautious in retelling my tales in our expanded company."

"He seems to have a strong dislike for Duke Northcott."

"Yes, I gather it has something to do with Celine."

"A love triangle?" Jaime questioned.

"Something of that sort. I did not inquire after the details as I believe them to be none of my business."

"Indeed," Jaime answered. "And perhaps best left as a private matter. Though given the circumstances, perhaps Grayson's caution stems from his dislike of the man rather than any real concern."

Douglas pursed his lips as he pondered it. "I trust

Grayson's judgment. We proceed with caution until we can discuss the matter privately."

"All right," Jaime agreed. "I shall follow your lead."

"Good. I hope to be able to discuss this further with Grayson soon."

"Please keep me informed in the event he has any conclusions."

"Yes, I will. Well, I suppose I should allow you to depart for the evening. The hour is growing late."

"Aria will thank you," Jaime said with a chuckle.

"Poor woman, I should not have kept you this long! Allow me to walk you out."

The two men disappeared up the stairs. A scraping noise signaled the closing of the secret passage above. The room descended into near darkness. The dim flicker of a single lit wall lantern did little to fight back the blackness.

Silence consumed the dimly light space surrounding them. Cate let out a breath, realizing she'd been holding her breath for much of the conversation.

"Do you suppose it's safe?" Jack whispered after several moments passed.

"Yes," Cate answered. "At least I hope so."

Cate grasped Jack's hand and they crawled from under the wooden structure. "We have to go back, Cate, we have to go back! Should we make a run for the back hallway?"

"I guess so," Cate answered.

"Okay, come on. Be careful." Jack tugged her toward the staircase. They inched along in the shadows.

As they crossed the room's center, a low-pitched vibration resounded throughout the room. Jack stopped dead, causing Cate to bump into him. "What is that?" he inquired.

"I'm not sure," Cate admitted.

The noise sounded a second time before lights burst across the room. Cate squinted at the blinding glare, holding her hand in front of her eyes to shield them. Jack stumbled back a step as the brilliant flash seared his eyes.

After a moment, Cate removed her hand from her forehead. She gasped. "Jack!" she exclaimed, tugging on his arm.

"What is it?" he inquired, his eyes still slits.

"The lights!"

"Yeah, they're blinding!"

"We're back!" Cate cried. "We're back!"

Jack opened his eyes and glanced around. A smile crossed his face. "The lights!" he shouted with a grin. "Come on, let's go before they disappear again."

"Agree," Cate answered.

They dashed to the stairs and climbed them two-by-two. Cate plowed into the library above with Jack right behind her. Each let out a sigh of relief as they glanced around the modern library.

"Oh, wow. Thank heavens," Jack blurted as he caught his breath.

Cate puffed with exertion from their race up the stairs. She nodded in agreement.

"We need a plan, Cate," he said after another moment. "This can't continue."

"I agree. It appears to be getting worse."

"Change and meet here to discuss an updated plan," Jack repeated.

"This time, let's hope we stay in this century-long enough to get that far," Cate responded.

They parted ways to change and returned to the library.

"We made it," Cate said as she hurried through the double doors, finding Jack lounging in his usual armchair.

"Yes, thankfully," Jack answered as Cate slumped into the chair next to him.

"Now for the plan," Cate replied.

"Do you have anything in mind? We need to speed up our

information-seeking before this wobbling between centuries worsens."

Cate's shoulders sagged. "Not really. I can search for records on the two new additions to the group, perhaps. I'm not certain that will help us."

"No," Jack answered. "I'm not sure it will either. We need real information about the time rips. And that Duke guy and why he's stalking you in your dreams."

"The larger problem is the time rips. Let's focus on fixing that problem first."

"I'll take answers on either front, to be honest."

"Let's go over what we've learned."

"That's easy. Nothing," Jack retorted, his voice thick with disgust.

Cate shook her head. "That's not quite true."

"Were we at the same dinner party? The one hijacked by loads of new people so we couldn't discuss anything with Douglas."

Cate offered him an unamused glance. "Yes, smarty-pants, we were at the same dinner party. But we learned several things there and during Douglas's conversation amidst our accidental trip back to 1792."

"Care to enlighten me? Other than Douglas lamenting the inability to learn anything about the time rips, I didn't glean anything. By the way, I am totally on his wavelength with that."

"Douglas confirmed what we already suspected. Grayson Buckley does not want to discuss this with others around. Specifically with Duke Northcott present."

"Right," Jack said. "He neither trusts nor likes Northcott. Due to some love triangle with his wife."

"We also learned that Douglas trusts Grayson's judgment. Implicitly, it seems. He's following his suggestion to keep mum on the subject."

"How does this help us?"

Cate shrugged. "It helps us identify who we can trust. We can trust Douglas. And probably Grayson. Douglas trusts Grayson, so by extension we can trust Grayson."

"What if Douglas is wrong? Perhaps that's why there's no more in the journals about his trusted friend, Grayson."

"Even if that's true, we can still trust Douglas. We've got to speak with him about the time rips."

"But according to Douglas, he hasn't learned anything from Grayson because he's not been able to speak with him about anything because of the new arrivals."

"No, but we can give him support for his theory and perhaps spur him to create the timepiece."

"And tell us how he does it," Jack added.

"That, too," Cate agreed.

"As much as I hate to say this, we need to go back earlier in the day and try to catch him alone."

"I agree, but can we do it?"

"With the time differential, yes. We make the excuse of errands in town or the like. Even if we're gone twenty-four hours, that's only a little over ninety minutes. No one would miss us."

"Okay, so we go back earlier. What if we get nowhere with Douglas? From the sounds of it, Douglas doesn't know anything more than when he brought it up to us a few nights ago."

"Then we move on to Grayson and hope we can trust him. Douglas seems to be waiting on some information from him."

"Do you expect he knows anything?"

Jack shrugged. "I'm not sure. Perhaps not. That may be why he hasn't given any clue to Douglas."

"Someone has to know something!" Cate groaned. "Douglas figured this out! We wouldn't have this timepiece if he didn't."

"And no one seems to understand how," Jack lamented.

"No, not even Randolph, his grandson, knew the secret. Why?"

Jack remained silent for a moment. "Perhaps..." His voice trailed off. "Eh, never mind, I'm just tired."

"What?" Cate prodded.

"Perhaps Douglas never figured it out. Perhaps someone else did and gave him the timepiece."

"Like Grayson Buckley?" Cate inquired.

Jack nodded and pointed at her. "You got it."

"Even more reason to speak with Grayson Buckley," Cate advocated.

"What about his cousins-in-law?" Jack inquired. "Do you imagine we'd have any luck trying to get information out of them?"

Cate shrugged. "I'm not sure. They are a bit strange."

"Strange?" Jack questioned. "What do you mean?"

Cate considered the question a moment as she puckered her lips. "Something just seemed off. Nothing specific, just a gut reaction, I guess."

Jack smirked at her.

"What?" Cate asked.

"Perhaps it's the younger one. What was his name, Darren?"

"Damien," Cate corrected.

"Right, Damien. Perhaps it's his constant grinning at you," Jack suggested.

The crease in her forehead deepened. "So, he's friendly. So what? No, it's not that. Here's an example, I asked him what ship he and his brother crossed on. The question seemed to make him nervous, and he couldn't answer it."

"So?" Jack said.

"So, it's 1792. They would have spent weeks if not months aboard that ship. You would expect they would recall the name. Especially given that he and his brother are in the business of ship-building!"

"Perhaps he's terrible with names. Though I expect it's nerves that has got him tongue-tied not lack of memory."

"He seems friendly enough, but perhaps he's backward," Cate suggested.

"Or perhaps it's the company," Jack countered.

"You mean the Duke?"

Jack rolled his eyes. "No, I do not." Cate pursed her lips. "Oh, come on, Cate. He's always stealing glances your way, grinning at you, nervous when he speaks to you. He's got a crush on you!"

"What? That's ridiculous!" Cate argued. "We've just met. He doesn't even know me."

"It's not. And he's got eyes, doesn't he?"

Cate offered a dubious glance in Jack's direction. "I don't agree. And even so, it's too bad for him I'm a married woman," she said with a wink.

"Darn right you are! Would be a terrible shame to ruin that perfect marriage to that perfect man."

"And all over a dalliance with a ship-builder," Cate joked.

"But perhaps that flirtation can elicit some information," Jack suggested.

"Are you actually proposing that I flirt with Damien Carlyle to get information?"

Jack shrugged a shoulder. "I'm merely suggesting that if the opportunity presents itself, you may try talking a bit more to him. In an effort to impress you, he may slip up and say something useful."

Cate raised her eyebrows. "If the opportunity presents itself, I'll see what I can do. No promises, I still think he's just the nervous type."

"We'll see. All right, so our plan is we return tomorrow, maybe after lunch. We seek out Douglas and speak with him. If that fails, we try to get any information we can from Grayson and his friends."

Cate nodded. "Okay."

"We should also inquire about Duke Northcott. Solving our time rip problem may not resolve your nightmare issues. We need to work on that, too."

"I'll admit he gives me the creeps. I caught him staring at me a few times after dinner." Cate shuddered as she recalled his eyes on her. "He's even more intimidating in person."

"That's why we need more information on him, too. Tomorrow afternoon. We start solving both our issues tomorrow afternoon."

CHAPTER 18

*A*fter eating a second dinner, this time in her own time period, Cate grabbed her laptop from the desk. Despite extreme sleepiness, she hoped to gain some information about the newest arrivals at Dunhaven Castle in 1792.

She forced her eyes to focus on the screen in front of her as she typed into the records database. A search for Michael Carlyle in eighteenth-century New York revealed nothing. A similar search for his brother, Damien, also yielded no results. She expanded the search to include other areas within colonial America but again found nothing. She tried a search of French records, wondering if they hailed from the same area as their cousin, Celine, but she found no evidence of that.

On a whim, Cate entered their names into the search bar of her browser. She turned up little more than a reference to a Michael Carlyle of Carlyle Industries, a multinational and modern corporation, not the shipbuilders of the 1700s. No mention of Damien Carlyle existed.

Cate slammed the laptop shut in frustration. They'd go back to 1792 blind. Again.

***

Cate's cell phone disrupted her morning cuppa just after 9 a.m. The shrill jangling cut through her brooding, pulling her from her ruminating over their lack of information. She grasped the phone and focused on the screen. The caller ID display read Isla Campbell.

Cate swiped to accept the call. "Good morning, Mrs. Campbell, how can I..." Cate began as Mrs. Campbell's excited voice interrupted her. Cate held the phone a short distance from her ear, afraid the noise may damage her hearing.

"Lady Cate!" she shouted on the other end of the line. "Oh, thank HEAVENS you answered. I took a chance calling you this early in the hopes I would not be forced to postpone my announcement. I have the most wonderful, exciting, outstanding news!" Mrs. Campbell paused a moment as she caught her breath.

Before Cate could speak, Mrs. Campbell gushed, "We have been selected to host the President's Ball!"

"Oh!" Cate responded as she processed the news.

"Isn't it simply wonderful? Oh, after all these years, I have finally achieved it! The President's Ball! Oh, we must start planning immediately! I've already created a list of items we'll need to discuss. With your anniversary party only six weeks before the ball, we'll have our hands full!"

"Well, congratulations, Mrs. Campbell! I hadn't expected to hear the news until next week!"

"Oh, thank you, Lady Cate, thank you! I couldn't wait to tell you the news! I had to call the moment I hung up with the selection committee. Apparently, they were so thrilled with our application, we clinched the spot without much discussion! Of course, we were the first to be informed."

"YOU clinched the spot with YOUR application, Mrs.

Campbell," Cate corrected. "I can take no credit for it. I know you poured your heart into it before you submitted it. And your ideas are wonderful."

"Well," Mrs. Campbell said with a chuckle, "I'm sure your name added to it. Though I believe the ideas I've presented are exceptional, particularly compared to some of the previous events."

"I have no doubt they are. You are a master of creating an event."

"Why, thank you, Lady Cate. Now, when shall we begin our planning? I'm tempted to begin today, though I really need to vet through my ideas more carefully and gather some materials. In short, I am unprepared for today as tempted as I am."

"That's fine, Mrs. Campbell. Today is quite busy for me, anyway. Perhaps next week?"

"Yes. Yes, that should work nicely. Perhaps Wednesday if your schedule suits? That gives me several days to gather materials, samples, and the like. It'll give us a nice start."

"That's perfect. Shall we plan for 9 a.m.?"

"Excellent, Lady Cate. I shall see you at 9 a.m.! Have a wonderful rest of your day. I know I will!"

Cate said her goodbyes to Mrs. Campbell and the line went dead as Mrs. Campbell disconnected the call. The woman's excitement was obvious even over the phone.

Cate leaned back in her desk chair as she pondered the event. She imagined Mrs. Campbell flitting around, overseeing every detail. Guests meandered through several areas of the castle as they perused auction items. They commented on the beautiful backdrop the Scottish castle provided.

As they wandered among the displays, the room shuddered. A low boom resounded in the halls. Thunder sounded overhead. Rain poured from the skies. Shouts and startled screams emerged from the crowd as people began to fade away. Specters from previous centuries replaced them, stalking among the group as though they belonged.

The remaining event-goers shrieked in horror as friends and family vanished. Panic ensued. People raced from the castle in various directions. Chaos reigned as people, their faces masks of terror, fled from any exit they could find.

Cate bit her lower lip. They must solve the problem of the time rips before hosting any events. Before tragedy struck. She shook the disturbing images from her mind as she swallowed the last of her tea.

Instead of dwelling on them, Cate traversed the hallways and descended to the kitchen. "Knock, knock," she said as she rapped her knuckles against the door jamb.

"Oh, Lady Cate! Need a refill?" Mrs. Fraser inquired.

Cate shook her head. "No, just returning my teacup."

"There was no need for that. We could have grabbed it when we brought your lunch!" Mrs. Fraser assured her.

"Well, I have some news I thought I'd share, so I made the trek."

"News?" Molly inquired.

Cate nodded. "Yes. I just got off the phone with Mrs. Campbell."

A sigh escaped Mrs. Fraser's lips at the mention of the librarian's name. "What did the ninny want? I suppose to clutter your schedule with a discussion about linens. Or perhaps to debate lady locks versus eclairs."

Cate chuckled at the assessment, all of which was plausible with Mrs. Campbell. "No," Cate responded. "She called to inform me that we have been selected to host the Presidents' Ball."

Mrs. Fraser raised her eyebrows. "She finally did it."

"That she did," Cate said. "And she is more excited than I've ever heard her!"

"I can imagine," Mrs. Fraser replied. "She's talked about hosting this event for years."

"We begin our discussions next Wednesday."

"Next Wednesday?" Molly inquired. "I'm surprised she waited that long."

"Aye, I cannae believe it either."

"She aims to be prepared with various things before the meeting."

"What meeting?" Jack asked as he pushed through the kitchen door.

"Isla has landed herself the Presidents' Ball," Mrs. Fraser informed him.

"Oooohhh," Jack answered, his face a mask of dismay. His shoulders sagged as he processed the news. "You're kidding?"

"Doesn't sound like it," Molly answered.

Jack grimaced, his lips forming a pout. "There will be no managing her on this one," he muttered.

"We'll have to do the best we can," Cate said. "Oh, while you're here, Jack, do you have a minute to discuss something?"

"Aye, whatever you need, lassie. Unless it's a roller coaster suspended from the tower roof for the Presidents' Ball."

"No, it's not that," Cate assured him.

He followed her from the kitchen as she retraced her steps to the library. After a proper greeting to Riley and Bailey, Jack sank into his armchair. "This conversation isn't regarding some outrageous request from Mrs. Campbell for her latest venture, is it?"

"No. So far, no outrageous requests. But we're not meeting for a few days, so that gives her plenty of time to come up with a few."

"Oh boy," Jack groaned. "That's more than enough time. I fully expect a rollercoaster that circles the castle and dives from the turret roof."

Cate chuckled at him. "You may prefer the Dunhaven Castle Coaster to the information I have."

"What is it?" Jack inquired. He snapped his head in her direction and stared at her. "You didn't disappear into another time again, did you?"

"No," Cate assured him. "Nothing that dramatic. Just more of the same. I searched for some information on our newest friends last night."

"And?"

"And nothing. I couldn't find a thing on them. No birth records, no death records. Nothing. It's like they don't exist."

"Like Northcott," Jack noted.

"Yep. So, again, we have nothing."

"Well, we don't have nothing. You've got your beauty and witty charm to use with Damien," Jack said with a wink.

"Oh, right," Cate said. "No worries at all then."

"Only a couple more hours to wait."

Cate nodded without responding.

"What's this? Cate Kensie not looking forward to time travel? Is this the first time I'm less nervous than you?"

"It might be," Cate admitted. "I feel like no matter which way we turn, the walls are closing in on us. When I hung up with Mrs. Campbell, all I could imagine was people disappearing right and left from the party into various time periods. And people from those time periods popping into our party. Partygoers ran screaming from the castle and Mrs. Campbell's efforts were all for naught."

Jack leaned forward in his seat and reached for Cate's hand. He gave it a squeeze. "We'll get through this, Cate."

Cate's face scrunched with upset. "I feel like I'm losing my home."

"That's not going to happen," Jack assured her. "We'll get through this. We'll solve this. Together."

Cate took a deep breath and squeezed his hand. She

nodded and offered Jack a weak smile. "You're right. Douglas figured this out once. We just need to get that information from him."

"And we're going to. In the next few days, if not today."

"Okay! Thinking positive," Cate said, broadening her grin. "See you at one-thirty?"

"One-thirty! Then we get answers!"

Cate spent the rest of her morning decrypting passages from the remaining three journals. Nothing pointed toward a solution to their problem. With a sigh, Cate closed her laptop, leaving any hope of a solution behind.

After lunch, Cate dressed for her trip back and met Jack in the library. "Let's go get some answers!" she exclaimed as they descended into the lab below.

"There's the Cate Kensie I know!" Jack said with a grin.

They activated the timepiece and returned to 1792. They tiptoed up the wooden stairs and peered through the peephole into the library.

"Olivia is there!" Cate whispered.

"Shoot!" Jack hissed. "Any chance we can sneak out without her realizing?"

"The bookcase makes a loud grinding noise when it opens and closes. She'll hear it. We'll have to wait."

They settled on the staircase to wait. "We really can't catch a break, can we?" Jack grumbled. "So much for our big plan to come back early!"

Cate grabbed his hand. "We'll catch one," she said.

The cold dampness penetrated through Cate as they huddled on the stairs waiting for an opportune moment to sneak from their hiding spot. A shiver passed through her, and Jack pulled her closer to him.

"Cold?"

"A little," Cate admitted. "I didn't prepare to be down here this long. I should have brought a sweater."

"A famous Cate Kensie cardigan?"

"Something a little more period-appropriate, maybe," Cate answered.

"With any luck, we won't be down here much longer."

They waited a few more moments before the sound of a door closing reached them. Cate leapt from her seat against the hard wooden stair and peered from the peephole.

"She's gone!" Cate exclaimed as Jack hovered behind her. "Let's go!"

They pushed through the secret passage into the library. "Now to find Douglas," Jack murmured as they stepped into the hallway.

"The office?" Cate suggested.

"Let's try it." The pair hurried through the halls to the castle's office space. They knocked at the door but received no response. Jack twisted the knob and pushed the door open a crack. "Douglas?"

He received no answer. He pushed the door open further. An empty chair sat behind the desk. "He's not here," Cate said with a sigh.

"Any other ideas?"

"Sitting room? I'm not sure."

"We'll head there and try," Jack agreed. They backed from the office and navigated the halls. As they retraced their steps past the library, Wilson appeared in the hallway.

"Oh, Wilson!" Jack called.

"Yes, sir?" Wilson inquired as he ground to a halt.

"We are searching for Douglas. Would you happen to know where he may be?"

"Lord MacKenzie is away on business. He will not return until just before dinner, sir."

Cate's heart sank at the news. They really couldn't catch a break, she lamented. "Is there something I may do for you, sir?" Wilson prodded when he received no response.

"No, thank you, Wilson," Jack answered. "We'll speak with him later."

"Very good, sir. If you require anything, please do not hesitate to ask."

Jack nodded to him, and Wilson continued his trek down the hall away from them. Jack shook his head at the development. "Unbelievable," he muttered.

"Now what?" Cate inquired. "Should we wait for Douglas? Or try to find Grayson?"

"Maybe. Let's... Let's sit down and regroup. Discuss the pros and cons of moving on to Grayson without talking to Douglas first."

"Okay," Cate agreed.

Jack grabbed her hand and pulled her toward the sitting room. As they entered the foyer, the sitting room doors swung open. Grayson, Michael, and Damien strode from the room.

"Oh, Jack," Grayson said. "How fortuitous to run into you. I had hoped to discuss some business with you. Do you have a moment?"

Jack glanced at Cate before clearing his throat. "Well..." he stammered. "Ah... actually, Mrs. MacKenzie and I were about to enjoy a walk around the property."

"Might we ask you to postpone for a short while? My apologies, Mrs. MacKenzie."

"Ah, if I may interject," Damien said, "perhaps I could escort you on the walk. While my company may pale in comparison to Mr. MacKenzie's, we can still take in the beautiful grounds."

"Oh, well..." Cate hesitated as she glanced at Jack. He offered a slight shrug and a nod.

"We'll walk the property tomorrow, dear," Jack promised. "I am certain you'd enjoy company other than mine for an afternoon after all the business I've dragged you on."

Cate forced a smile on her face, uncertain if this idea was the best plan. She glanced at Damien who offered her a wide smile.

"Excellent!" Grayson exclaimed as he motioned for Jack to follow him into the sitting room. "I appreciate your patience, Mrs. MacKenzie."

Grayson clapped Jack on the back and slid his arm around Jack's shoulders as he guided him through the sitting room doors. "Now, we have several questions for a man of your skills, Jack," he said as Michael closed the doors behind them. He offered Cate a curt smile as she gazed at their disappearing forms.

Damien stepped into her line of vision. He still wore a large grin on his face. "Shall we?" he said as he offered his arm to her.

Cate gave him a soft smile as she wrapped her hand around the crook of his arm. "I have not yet walked the property," Damien said as they stepped into the cool spring air. "Though the view from my bedroom window seems picturesque. Quite lovely. Rolling hills and all that."

The gravel crunched under their feet as they stepped onto the circular driveway. Damien scanned the horizon. "Which way? Do you have a preference?"

Cate did not so she suggested the path toward her favorite spot on the property in modern times: the loch. "Perhaps this path."

Damien nodded as they set off around the castle. After a few moments, Cate noticed his eyes sliding sideways to glance at her. She forced her mind to come up with conversation to fill the awkward silence. "So," she began as he said, "Have you…"

"Oh, my apologies," Damien said.

"No, please, Mr. Carlyle, no apology needed."

Another awkward pause passed between them. "You were saying?" Damien prompted.

"Oh, please, I believe you were trying to speak," Cate answered.

"No, no, please. Ladies first!" Damien said with a clumsy chuckle.

"Oh, ah," Cate stumbled as she sought to recall her inquiry. "So, you are from New York but your cousin, Celine, is from France?"

"Yes, just outside Lyon, though she moved to Martinique at a young age. French though, definitely. Not like me. I am American. My brother and me. Both of us. Americans." Cate held in a chuckle at his babbling. Perhaps Jack had a point. Was he nervous?

"How fortunate that she has moved to the States and nearer to you."

"Yes. We visited her once in Martinique, but Massachusetts is much closer."

"Indeed," Cate answered.

Silence spanned the next several steps. "It seems you are very well-traveled," Damien said to Cate.

"Oh, not very, no. Only from the States to Scotland."

"How did you meet Jack?"

"He was seated next to me at a dinner party."

"Oh, in Philadelphia?"

"Yes," Cate answered. "He was in the States on business."

Damien nodded at her. "And your business is ship-building?" Cate inquired.

"Yes, shipbuilding, that's it. That's my business. The building of ships! Big ships, small ships. All sorts of ships." He offered another nervous chortle.

Cate scrunched her forehead at his statements. His behavior seemed odd to her. Something about him struck her as strange though she couldn't put her finger on what it was. They reached the loch and Cate gazed over the water. This spot brought her such comfort in her time. In this year, though, her mind raced in a thousand directions.

How was Jack faring? What questions was he fielding? Could he fake his way through them? Would he learn anything that would help them? How long would she stand here with Damien before they returned? What could they discuss on the return trip? Could she elicit any information from him? Jack suggested she use an opportunity with Damien for this purpose. She felt unprepared to do so.

Cate pretended to gaze out over the water at the moors beyond.

"What a beautiful spot," Damien declared after a moment.

"Yes, quite."

"You've selected well," Damien said.

"I'm certain every path leads to a beautiful spot," Cate answered.

After another moment, Cate suggested they return.

"Oh! All right," Damien agreed after seeming surprised at the request.

As they meandered the path back toward the castle, Cate took a chance with a random question. "Are you well-acquainted with our other guest as well? Duke Northcott."

She studied Damien's reaction to the question. She swore his muscles stiffened and his jaw tensed. Did the dislike of the Duke extend beyond Grayson to the Carlyles as well?

"Yes, we are acquainted," he said in a clipped tone.

"Have you…" Cate began as Damien interrupted her.

"You would do well to stay away from him," he blurted.

The reaction surprised Cate, though she agreed with the sentiment. Duke Northcott unnerved her. But what bothered the Carlyles about him, Cate wondered?

"That is a bold statement, Mr. Carlyle. Is there an explanation behind it?"

Damien stopped walking and spun to face Cate. "He's not a nice man. You'd be wise to stay off his radar."

Cate's brow furrowed at his statement. She gazed at him with narrowed eyes as he resumed walking, tugging her up the path with him.

"How long do you and Mr. MacKenzie plan to stay?" Damien questioned, changing the subject.

"We are uncertain of our plans," Cate answered, her mind still pondering his previous statement.

As they approached the castle and rounded the corner to the front, Cate spotted a large carriage pulled by four jet-black horses stopped in front of the door. Damien's jaw tensed again. He ground to a halt.

"Perhaps you'd care to view more of the property," he suggested.

Cate shook her head. "I should return to ascertain if Jack's business is concluded."

"I am certain it is not. Grayson had several questions to discuss. My bedroom overlooks this side of the castle, and the gardens appear quite lovely. Let us…"

"No," Cate argued. "I am quite tired. I would prefer to return."

Damien hesitated. He glanced at the carriage again before he returned his gaze to Cate. He nodded and motioned for her to precede him into the castle.

They stepped into the foyer. The sitting room doors stood open. The room was empty. Cate's heart beat faster. Where was Jack?

"Catherine!" Duke Northcott's voice called. "Is that you?" She glanced down the hall to their right, noting a man's figure approaching in the shadows. Details of her many nightmares flooded her mind. Damien's reaction added to her sense of fear.

"Quick!" Damien whispered as he grasped her arm and guided her into the sitting room.

He pulled her through the room, his pace fast enough to cause her to trot to keep up. They exited through the other doors into another hall. Damien continued to tug her down the hall.

"Catherine?" Duke Northcott's voice called to her again.

"Come on," Damien encouraged.

Panic filled Cate. Her pulse raced and her head swam. Her breathing turned ragged as they continued their race through the halls.

Damien ducked into the tearoom. He eased the doors shut, locked them and backed away. He held his finger to lips.

Cate's apprehension grew. While the Duke caused unease, so did Damien Carlyle. He was not who he pretended to be. His comment earlier gave him away. He warned her to stay away from the Duke. He warned her to stay off his *radar*. An interesting choice of words, Cate ruminated, since radar would not be invented until the early twentieth century. One question burned in her mind as she stood behind locked doors, hiding from Duke Northcott. Who was Damien Carlyle?

CHAPTER 19

Cate stared at the man in front of her. He took a step toward her, and she inched backward away from him. His brow furrowed at her reaction. He stepped forward again. Cate backed up several steps.

"Stop! Don't come any closer!" she warned.

"What's wrong?" he asked.

"Who are you?" she demanded.

"Damien," he answered.

Cate shook her head. "No, that's a lie. You're not telling me the truth."

"I am," he insisted. "I…"

"No!" Cate interrupted. "No, you're not. Tell me who you really are, Damien Carlyle."

"I…"

A noise interrupted Damien. The doorknobs on the doors Damien locked moments earlier twisted and turned.

"There's no time for this," Damien argued. "We need to go."

Cate shook her head again. "I'm not going anywhere with you until you tell me the truth!"

Pounding sounded on the door outside. "Catherine!" Duke Northcott's voice called.

Damien gulped in air before he rushed to Cate. He grasped her hands. "I can explain. I promise. I'm not lying, not really. But you must trust me. We can't let him find us."

Cate frowned. She had no desire to be near Duke Northcott, but she did not trust Damien. Her eyes darted around the room as she considered her prospects.

"Please," Damien continued, "please, you must trust me. We need to go."

The doors rattled in the jamb as Duke Northcott again attempted to open them. Cate caught her breath as she saw the doorknobs twisting again. Then the room went silent. With slow precision, the key Damien used to lock the doors withdrew from the lock and clattered to the floor.

Damien twisted to identify the source of the noise then spun to face Cate again. "Now or never, you've got to make a call."

Cate swallowed hard. Her stomach rose to her throat and her knees felt weak. She glanced between Damien and the door. After a moment, she nodded. "Let's go."

Damien squeezed her hand in his and pulled her to the doors on the opposite wall. He swung them open and peeked into the hallway. "Clear," he announced and pushed Cate ahead of him.

They hastened down the hall away from the tearoom as the doors burst open. "Catherine!" Duke Northcott called again.

They reached the end of the corridor. A door to a small parlor provided the only exit from the hall.

Damien moved toward it. "No," Cate said. "It's a dead end. We'll be trapped there."

"We're trapped now anyway. Perhaps we can hide."

Cate shook her head. Panic crowded her mind as she

scanned the hall. In her nightmares, this man had chased her all over the house. In one of them, she had landed in this exact situation, stuck in a dead-end hallway.

"Catherine," a sing-song voice called behind them.

Cate groaned as her mind ran through their limited options. Her heart skipped a beat as her eyes focused on an object. The candelabra hung just above her eye level. She reached out and grasped it, tugging hard toward the floor.

The candelabra gave way, sliding down the wall as a panel swung open. "In here!" Cate exclaimed. She hurried inside the dark tunnel. Damien followed her, pushing the panel shut behind them. They inched back a few steps into the darkness.

Damien clutched at Cate's hand as they overheard the door to the parlor swing open on creaky hinges. Cate held her breath and bit her lower lip as she waited in the darkness. She strained her ears for signs of Duke Northcott's retreat.

Instead, another sound reached her ears. Breathing. The breathing emanated from behind her, not next to her. Someone else was hiding in this passage. The scenario was identical to her dream where she hid in a dark passage with another unknown individual.

Cate squeezed Damien's hand. He wrapped his arm around her. Cate stood on her toes and leaned toward Damien's ear. "Someone's here," she whispered.

She felt Damien's muscles stiffen. He ceased breathing for a moment. The slow rhythmic breathing from behind them continued.

Footsteps sounded in the corridor beyond. Damien pulled Cate back a few more steps, bringing them closer to the other person.

"Is someone there?" he breathed.

"Damien?" a woman answered. Cate recognized Celine's voice.

"Celine?" Damien whispered back.

"Yes, it is me."

"Celine, what are you doing down here?"

"Searching for the source of the anomalies."

The footsteps in the hallway outside circled but did not retreat.

"Marcus," Celine huffed.

"Yeah," Damien answered. "He followed us here. He's after Cate."

Cate's brow creased deeper, and a frown formed on her face. She had only been introduced as Catherine. Yet Damien called her Cate, her nickname. Who was this man?

"We must leave. He cannot learn what these walls house," Celine answered.

"I agree. Could you give us some light? Maybe there's a way out of here beyond the secret door."

Celine did not respond. She pondered the meaning of Damien's statement. Perhaps Celine carried a candle or lantern, though Cate did not understand how Damien knew this.

A loud pounding sounded against the wall. Cate jumped at the sound, startled. Her heart skipped a beat before it sped up.

"Celine, come on!" Damien insisted.

"This may not be wise," Celine answered.

"She'll be fine. Come on, we're running out of time."

A bright blue light burst in the dark space. Cate shielded her eyes. What type of lantern did Celine carry that produced this light? Cate blinked a few times and lowered her hands. She peered with narrowed eyes at the light now illuminating the space.

Cate gasped at the scene in front of her. A bright blue

luminous ball floated above Celine's hand. It glowed and crackled with energy.

"Thank you," Damien breathed as he began to search the walls surrounding them.

Cate stood speechless. In her dream, a blue light blinded her before she awoke. Was this the source of that light? What was it? Who were these people?

Cate stumbled back a step as her legs threatened to betray her. "Whoa," Damien said, grabbing Cate to steady her. "You okay?"

Cate shook her head. She attempted to pull out of his grasp. "It's okay, we aren't going to hurt you," Damien insisted.

"Who... What..." Cate's eyes darted around the room. "What is she? Who are you?"

"It's difficult to explain..." Damien began.

"Try!" Cate insisted. "You... first you mentioned radar, which isn't invented yet, then you called me Cate, and now... this! Who are you?" Cate signaled toward Celine's floating ball of light.

"Damien. You know me."

"I don't!" Cate insisted.

"Yes, you do. Just not as Damien Carlyle. But you know me. As Damien Sherwood. You know... Decoder Exploder guy! I'm not from this time. But neither are you, right? You're Cate Kensie, aren't you?"

Cate's mind raced at his words. Damien Sherwood? Her email contact for the decryption program? But how? How had he time traveled here? And why?

The pounding on the wall sounded again. "I'll explain everything but now we need to find a way out of here." He tugged her forward.

Cate shook her head and pulled back again. "No. What..."

Cate began, unable to finish her thought. She motioned toward the floating ball of light.

"She's a very special woman," Damien answered. "And a good friend to have."

"I won't harm you, Cate," Celine said as she placed her free hand on Cate's arm. "Marcus on the other hand may. He is a dangerous man. We must go."

Cate swallowed hard as she glanced between the two of them. A scraping sounded behind them and candlelight began to flood in through the opening panel. Damien cursed under his breath. Celine whipped the ball of light toward the secret door. It exploded against the panel, sealing it shut with a crackle of electricity.

Celine pulled another light ball from thin air and waved it in front of her. "There!" she exclaimed.

Cate squinted her eyes and detected a small opening in front of them. Damien clasped her hand in his and dragged her toward it. Using Celine's light, they navigated through a series of passages, winding deeper underground.

The air grew cool and damp. The walls turned from manmade to natural stone. They continued to follow the winding path. After several more yards, the path sloped upward.

"We must be close to the end," Damien surmised.

"Yes," Celine agreed.

"Wonder where we'll come out."

"Hopefully far from Marcus," Celine answered. "Then we have many things to discuss."

Cate's mind still swam with questions as they climbed upward in the stone tunnel. She began to wonder if she was trapped in one of her nightmares. None of this made sense. Nor was it possible. People couldn't generate fireballs from thin air.

She stopped walking for a moment.

"Are you okay?" Damien inquired. "Do you need a break?"

Cate shook her head and squeezed her eyes shut.

"Cate?" Damien questioned.

Cate opened her eyes and glanced around. Her circumstances hadn't changed. Perhaps she wasn't dreaming. "This can't be real," she murmured.

"She is in shock. She is panicking," Celine assessed. "Can you carry her?"

"No, don't," Damien countered. "She'll be okay."

Cate's eyes grew wide at the conversation. What were they suggesting? She backed a few steps away, intending on retreating through the passage as fast as she could.

"Cate! Wait!" Damien shouted. He raced ahead of her and blocked her way. "It's okay. No one is going to harm you."

"No?" Cate questioned. "What is she proposing to do to me that requires you to carry me afterward?"

"To put you to sleep," Damien said. "That's all. She's got this ability to just touch your cheek and BAM! You're asleep. It can be handy at times. It doesn't hurt, she's used it on me. She…" Cate blinked and shook her head at his babbling. "Anyway," he continued as he noticed the mask of confusion and shock on her face, "she won't hurt you. Let's just get out of this place and then we'll explain everything."

"O-o-okay," Cate stammered.

Damien smiled and nodded to her. They continued up the passage. The walls changed again from natural stone to blocks.

"This looks manmade," Damien noted. "We must be close to the end."

Within a few moments, they entered a large, cavernous space. Still cool and damp, stone walls surrounded them. No obvious exits existed. The remaining three sides looked solid.

"What is this place?" Damien inquired.

Cate's mind churned. She pushed aside the questions plaguing her and focused on the question at hand. Where were they? Her mind combed through the structures on the estate.

"There's a private cemetery on the grounds with a crypt. Could this be it?" she pondered aloud.

"Oh, maybe!" Damien exclaimed. "Is there a way out of it?"

"I'm not sure," Cate answered. "I've never been inside it. I spend most of my time at the loch."

"Wait," Damien said. "Wait, your castle... the one you mentioned in your email is this castle? You own Dunhaven Castle in our time?"

Cate cocked her head as she stared at him. Her mind returned to the oddity of the situation facing her. "Yes. How did you know me?" she questioned.

"I recognized you."

"We've never met."

"No, but the internet is a wonderful thing!" Damien answered. "I searched you when Ken emailed me about you. Your picture was still on Aberdeen College's website. I recognized you the second I saw you."

That explained his odd grins at her, Cate mused. "Okay," she responded. "And you're Damien Sherwood. But how are you back here? In 1792?"

"Michael and I traveled back to help Celine with the Duke. He's really bad news, Cate. I wasn't kidding."

"How? Using the time rips?"

"We can continue this discussion once we've safely returned to the castle," Celine argued. "We must search for an exit."

"Right," Damien agreed. "Can you shine your light in the corners?"

Celine held the fireball higher and stepped toward the

corner opposite them. She and Damien wandered around the chamber, scanning the walls. "There!" Damien shouted.

A small ring protruded from the block above their heads. Damien reached up, grasped it, and pulled downward. A screeching filled the space and a clanking sounded as a portion of the block wall swung toward them.

Fresh air rushed in as daylight streamed into the chamber. Celine extinguished her ball of light and they stepped into the outer chamber. Several stone coffins filled the space. Empty markers accompanied them. Prepared for Douglas and his family, the crypt sat empty awaiting its occupants.

"The castle is this way," Cate said as she stepped out of the mausoleum.

"We should go there straight away," Celine suggested. "We have much to discuss."

"I must find Jack!" Cate exclaimed.

"He is with Gray," Celine assured her.

"Yes," Damien agreed. "Gray will ensure he is okay."

"I'd like to see for myself."

"We'll hurry," Damien promised.

They set off on the most direct route to the castle. As they approached, Cate noted the obvious absence of the carriage and its four jet black horses.

"Marcus has departed," Celine stated, "for the moment."

"I'm sure he'll be back for dinner," Damien said. "Can't wait!"

Cate detected the deep antipathy in their voices. Their history with Duke Northcott must be long and painful, Cate surmised. Celine pushed through the front door of the castle. She crossed the foyer and ascended the stairs.

"Wait!" Cate called. "I must find Jack! He was in the sitting room with Grayson and Michael."

"He will have moved to our suite when Marcus arrived," Celine called without stopping her climb. "Come."

Damien offered his hand to Cate with a wide smile. "Come on," Damien said. "It's okay. I'm sure he's fine."

Cate eyed them both before accepting his hand. They climbed the stairs and followed Celine to their suite. Celine pushed open the doors to a large sitting room.

"Celine, are you all right?" Grayson inquired.

"Yes, I am fine."

"Where is Catherine?" Jack demanded.

"Here!" Cate called as she released Damien's hand and pushed through the door.

Jack offered a relieved sigh as Cate joined him near the loveseat. Damien closed the door behind them. Cate noted Michael standing near the fireplace.

"Did you find anything?" Grayson asked Celine.

"Yes and no," she answered. "Damien was correct."

Grayson side-eyed Jack and Cate before continuing. "Do you imagine they can help?"

"That is what I plan to find out."

Michael tugged at his collar, loosening and removing his cravat. "Can we dispense with some of these formalities now that we're all on the same page?"

"Apparently, I am not on the same page. I'm not even sure I am in the same book! Would someone mind cluing me in on what's going on?" Jack questioned. "We've been discussing odd business questions for over an hour. And we moved to your suite for some strange reason which I still do not fully understand. I am starting to suspect you have an ulterior motive."

"You are correct, Mr. MacKenzie," Grayson admitted.

"Oh, come on," Michael grumbled. "You're not from this century. You're time travelers."

CHAPTER 20

*J*ack's eyes went wide, and he collapsed onto the loveseat behind him. "That does it!" he exclaimed. "We really are terrible at this."

"Don't sweat it," Damien said. "We're not that good at it either."

Jack's jaw went slack at the admission. "You…You are… " Jack's eyes scanned the room as his unfinished sentence hung in the air.

"Time travelers," Damien said with a grin. "Oh, just Michael and me. Celine and Gray are really from this time."

"I hate time traveling," Michael murmured as he shook his head.

Jack glanced up at him sharply. "Me too!"

"Wandering around in centuries that aren't your own. It's just… there are no bathrooms, people died of typhoid and other diseases. What part of this makes you grin like that?" Michael asked Damien.

"It's fun!" Damien countered. "Immersing yourself in another time. When people viewed the world in a far different way."

A smile formed on Cate's lips. "That's exactly what I said!" Cate exclaimed.

"Can we stick to the subject at hand rather than our love or lack thereof for the art of time traveling?" Grayson interjected.

"I still don't understand how you time traveled," Cate said. "Are there time rips in other locations?

"Time rips?" Grayson questioned.

"Yes," Jack answered. "The phenomena Douglas described a few nights ago after dinner. They are the result of time rips. People shifting in and out of their own time and into others."

"Several exist in the castle," Cate explained further. "They all lead to different years."

Celine nodded. "These are the aberrations in time-space I detected. But how did you use them?"

"We control them with this," Cate said, holding up her timepiece.

"A watch?" Michael questioned.

"Yes," Cate responded. "I'm sorry, I'm still confused as to how you two time traveled."

"Through a time portal," Damien answered. "Celine possesses the ability to open time portals."

Cate glanced at Celine, her mouth agape. Damien informed her she was a special woman. He wasn't kidding. Jack slouched further down the sofa as shock settled around him.

"How do you use a watch to time travel?" Michael inquired.

"You go to the location of the time rip leading to the year you want to travel to," Cate explained, "and you rub the face. That triggers the time rip to open and allows you to slip through it."

Damien peered at the timepiece.

"May I see it?" Celine requested.

"Sure," Cate answered. She slipped the chain from around her neck and handed the gold timepiece to Celine.

"Why is the watch stopped?" Damien asked. "Is time paused in your year when you use it?"

"It's not stopped," Jack informed him. "It keeps time in the present. But time there moves more slowly than it does here."

"Really?" Damien said.

"Yes. Fifteen minutes here is only one minute in our time," Cate explained.

"Yes," Celine answered, handing the timepiece back to Cate. "These distortions do not behave as normal time portals. They are distended in some way. It's what twists the passage of time at different speeds."

"Is that not the case when you time travel?" Cate asked Damien.

"No, though Celine can open portals to whenever we'd like so we can, essentially, defy time passage in some cases."

"How does the timepiece interact with the distorted time portals?" Michael inquired.

"We don't know," Cate admitted. "Which is why we're here. There are no extra pieces inside that we could identify. For all intents and purposes, it appears to be a normal pocket watch."

"It is enchanted," Celine answered.

"By whom?" Grayson asked. "Can you tell?"

"Me," Celine replied.

Cate's eyes went wide, and she sank onto the loveseat next to Jack. "So, that's how Douglas did it," she murmured.

"So, your enchantment allows them to control the time rips?" Michael asked.

"Yes," Celine answered. "It keeps them closed until activated. Then, they open."

"Which solves Douglas's problem," Grayson added. "His supposition that he was glimpsing snippets of the future was correct. Though he had no way to control when he would see them. That timepiece gives him the ability to close them."

"Marcus must never find out about this," Celine stated. She glanced at Cate and Jack. "You two should return home at once."

"No," Cate argued. "We can't."

"We'll handle things with Douglas," Grayson assured her. "Celine is correct. The Duke is dangerous. You shouldn't be here."

Cate shook her head again in disagreement. "We cannot leave for two reasons."

"Which are?" Grayson fired back.

"In our time," Jack explained, "something is going on with the time rips. They are popping up randomly. We can't control them anymore."

"Right," Cate answered. "Which is why we're here. To learn how Douglas controlled them so we could solve our problem. And second, we must ensure Douglas invents the timepiece and Celine enchants it, so we can travel to this time in the first place."

Celine pursed her lips at the admission. "The timepiece has ceased to function in the future?"

"Not exactly," Cate answered. "It still interacts with the time rips, but it doesn't always keep them closed. At times, we'll slip into another era despite not activating the timepiece."

"And the timepiece won't work to get us back when that happens," Jack added.

"Yes, that's right. If we don't get this fixed, the castle will become unlivable," Cate said.

"Can you help them, Celine?" Damien inquired.

Celine shook her head. "Not from here. Not from this time. The enchantment that exists on that timepiece works with the aberrations I studied here. It should work."

"So, these time rips have morphed in some way in the future?" Michael proposed.

"It appears they may have if this enchantment no longer holds them closed," Celine responded.

"Then you'd need to study the distortions in the future to create something that would control the new rips," Damien suggested.

"Yes," Celine said with a nod of her head.

"Would you return with us to our time to study it?" Cate inquired, her voice filled with hope.

Damien shook his head. "No need," he said. "We live in that time. We'll just meet you there!"

Jack shook his head. "You and Michael live in that time," he said. "We need her though." He pointed to Celine.

"No, we all live in that time."

"But you said only you and Damien were from our time."

"I mean, technically that's true," Damien answered. "This Celine and Grayson are native to this era, but they also exist in our time period. It's complicated. The point is we can help you. You can return home now, and we'll be there to help."

Cate sank onto the couch again as the complex discussion threatened to cause her brain to implode. "Come on, you time travel, you have to be open to the possibility that things exist that are well beyond your comprehension and knowledge," Damien said as Cate remained silent.

"All right. I'll trust you," she answered after a moment.

"Good!" Damien answered. "Then we'll plan to meet you tomorrow."

"For now, you should go home," Celine repeated. "You cannot stay here. It is far too dangerous with Marcus."

"Who is this guy? Why is he such a concern?" Jack questioned.

"He is a very dangerous man," Celine answered.

"Yeah," Damien chimed in. "He's really bad news."

"Evil," Michael added.

"Which is why you must go and leave the rest of this to us," Grayson insisted.

"But..." Cate began.

"No," Grayson argued. "This is not up for debate. It's far too dangerous. And this secret must be protected. At all costs. We will discuss the problem and solution with Douglas."

"We'll tell him to leave you a note in one of those journals you're decrypting!" Damien exclaimed. "And then we'll see you tomorrow in your own time and we'll solve your problem, too."

Damien took her hands in his. "Trust me, Cate," he said as he stared into her eyes.

Cate scanned their faces. She hated to leave things to chance. She wanted to ensure everything worked properly. What if something went wrong? These people had more experience with this man, though. He haunted her for months in her dreams. Perhaps this was why. Perhaps staying was a mistake and would lead to more trouble. If she continued to have nightmares, she could discuss them with Celine and Damien in her own time. She would trust them. She had to.

She twisted to face Jack. He shrugged at her, suggesting the decision was up to her. "Okay," she agreed with a nod. "I'll trust you. We really need your help. And I've had terrible nightmares about that man. I have no desire to be near him."

"You've had nightmares about the Duke?" Damien inquired.

Cate nodded.

"Even more reason for you to leave," Grayson chimed in.

"Please give Douglas our apologies," Cate said as guilt washed over her. She'd leave her ancestor without saying goodbye. She could visit again when things settled down, she promised herself.

"We will. We will explain everything to him," Celine answered. "Now go. Collect your things and return to your own time."

The group said their goodbyes with the promise of seeing one another the next day. Cate and Jack stepped into the hallway as Grayson closed the door behind them. "You okay?" Jack asked Cate once they were alone.

"Yeah," she said with a slight nod.

"You sure? You're certain you're okay with this plan?"

"I am," she answered with a sigh. "It's not what I would have picked first but I agree we should leave. Duke Northcott spotted me with Damien earlier and chased me through the house."

"What?!" Jack exclaimed.

"It was just like my dream. I felt as panicked as I did in my nightmares. I'd prefer to be away from him."

"All right. Then we'll gather our things and get out of here."

"Plus, I trust Damien. I know it sounds odd, but they are time travelers, and he happens to be from our time. He's the one who helped me with the journals."

"The decryption program guy?"

"One and the same. Odd coincidence, huh?"

"Or not," Jack suggested. "Either way, let's get out of here."

They threaded through the halls, heading to their room. As they rounded a corner into another hallway, Cate spotted Douglas coming toward them.

"Catherine! Jack! How fortunate I bumped into you. I was just searching for you."

"You were searching for us?" Cate inquired.

"Indeed. I hoped to have a word with Jack. Oh, I hope you do not mind, Catherine. I expected you would be resting before the dressing gong, and I could steal Jack for a few moments."

"O-oh..." Jack stammered. "Catherine and I were just..."

"I promise not to take too much of your time, cousin Jack," Douglas promised.

"Go on, dear. I am perfectly capable of returning to our room to rest on my own," Cate said.

Jack smiled at her, and Cate gave his hand a reassuring squeeze. "I promise not to keep him too long, Catherine."

"Take your time," Cate answered.

"See you soon, dear," Jack said as he allowed Douglas to lead him toward the main stairs.

Cate watched as they disappeared around the corner before continuing to their bedroom. Perhaps Jack would be able to pass along a few sentiments before they departed to explain their sudden absence.

Her mind spun with the latest developments as she rounded the corner into the hallway housing their bedroom. With her mind distracted, she failed to notice the man there until it was too late.

Cate stopped short just before she ran into him. A smirk crossed his face. "Hello, Catherine," Duke Northcott hissed.

Cate's eyes grew wide, and she swallowed hard. Her pulse quickened and her knees threatened to buckle.

"Oh my! Have I left you speechless?" he questioned.

"Duke Northcott," Cate said, her voice a hoarse whisper. "You startled me."

"Did I? My sincere apologies, Catherine. Though I hoped to speak with you. Perhaps I would not have been forced to seek you out here had you not disappeared earlier this afternoon."

"Disappeared?" Cate repeated. "I am not following."

He narrowed his eyes at her. "You did not hear me call to

you earlier when I was on the estate?" he said, phrasing it as a question.

"No. My apologies. I did not."

He stared at her as she fibbed about their near encounter earlier this afternoon. She wondered if he could tell she was lying. Perhaps, though there was something else about his eyes. Something that disturbed her. She swallowed hard again.

"Though I cannot imagine what you desired to speak with me about," Cate added as the silence became unbearable.

"Really? Can't you?" He raised an eyebrow at her as he left the statement hang in the air for a moment. "I find you a most interesting woman, Catherine."

He pressed closer to her. Cate inched backward. "Oh," she murmured. "I assure you I am not very interesting."

"Oh, but you are! You do yourself a disservice speaking in that manner."

"Perhaps we can continue our conversation over dinner," Cate suggested in an attempt to end the conversation.

"But that simply won't do," Duke Northcott countered.

"I am very sorry, Duke, but I do not have a moment now. I hoped to rest before the dressing gong."

"You avoid me, Catherine," he said, catching her arm as she attempted to skirt around him. "Why?"

"I do not. I am only tired and wish to rest before dinner."

"There is something very strange about you," Duke Northcott said. She held his gaze a moment. Perhaps he would let her go now. "I am determined to find out what it is."

She forced a weak smile onto her face. "Perhaps over dinner," she suggested again.

"I already told you, Catherine, that will not do." He tightened his grip on her arm and yanked her closer to him. His other hand reached for her face. Her eyes grew wide, and a grimace formed on her lips as she stifled a scream. The cool flesh of his fingertips brushed her cheek. A strange sensation came over her entire body at once. The hairs on her neck stood on end, her stomach somersaulted, her knees buckled, and her vision began to close to a pinpoint. Cate felt her body slumping to the floor as the world crashed around her.

CHAPTER 21

Cate's eyelids fluttered open. She blinked several times to clear her blurred vision. She laid on her side in an unfamiliar room. Candlelight flickered its dim light across the small room from the table next to the bed on which she lay. She inhaled a sharp breath as she recalled the details of her last memory. She stood with Duke Northcott in the hallway leading to her bedroom. He had approached her. They had disagreed about the timing of a conversation, and she had fainted. Where was she now?

Cate pushed up to sitting as she glanced around her new surroundings. Her body ached with fatigue and her mind was clouded. Random thoughts crowded her brain though she could not process them. Still groggy, she attempted to swing her feet to the floor below her. A wave of nausea passed through her as she tried to stand.

She collapsed back onto the bed behind her as she swallowed the bile creeping up into her throat before she attempted to stand again. On wobbly legs, she hovered for a few moments next to the bed before she stumbled across the floor. She fell against the door as she attempted to twist the handle and pull it open. It did not budge.

Her fists pounded against the door. "Help!" she called. Tears streamed down her cheeks, and she choked down a sob. Cate spun to scan the room. A small window adorned the wall across from her. Darkness stared back at her from beyond it. She raced to it and attempted to pull it open. The window was stuck fast.

Cate peered at her surroundings. She spotted lights in the distance on the moor. From the vast area the lights stretched over, Cate assumed the structure was Dunhaven Castle. After another sob, Cate struggled with the window again, rattling it in its frame. It did not open. She scanned the area closer to her. The moonlight cast shadows across the fields. It appeared she was nearer to town than the castle, perhaps on the outskirts. If she could escape, she could run to town for help.

Footsteps sounded on the floorboards outside the small room. Cate's breath caught in her throat. She searched for an object she could use to defend herself. She found nothing in the sparsely decorated room.

The clank of a key sounded, and the door swung open. Cate pressed into the opposite corner, her breathing ragged. A dark-skinned man stepped into the room. He carried a small tray. A teacup and several biscuits sat on it. "Hello, Miss Catherine," he said, his accent sounding South African, "I have brought you some food."

Cate's brow furrowed at the statement. He slid the tray onto the small wooden table near the door and spun to depart. "Wait!" Cate called. "Please wait!"

He turned back, his hands clasped in front of him, a calm expression on his face. "Yes, Miss Catherine?"

"You must help me! I... I do not know how I came to be

here. I must return to Dunhaven Castle. My husband is expecting me."

"I am sorry, Miss Catherine, Duke Northcott requests you to remain here. Please if you would like something more to eat, simply request it from me. My name is Dembe."

"No!" Cate shouted as he departed from the room. The lock engaged, leaving Cate trapped again. She banged against the door as she pleaded for help. None came.

Cate returned to the bed and collapsed onto it. With a frown, she stared at the tray of food across the room. Her stomach growled. She wondered about the time. How long had she been gone? Had Jack sought her and found her missing? Were they searching for her?

She pulled the timepiece from under her dress and stared at it. The second hand crept around the face. Tears stung her eyes as she realized she was not the only one trapped. Without the timepiece, Jack was stuck in 1792. If they never found her, he would be trapped here forever, doomed to live and die in an era centuries before his birth.

She, too, was trapped. She would never see Riley and Bailey again. What would become of them? Of Molly? Of Dunhaven Castle?

Tears rolled down her cheeks. She gave into her panic and wept. After a few moments, Cate swallowed hard and wiped at her cheeks. Crying helped nothing and would solve none of her problems, she reminded herself.

"Pull yourself together, Cate," she told herself. "You need to think."

She swallowed hard again and took a deep breath. Squaring her shoulders, she stood and lifted her chin and strode to the door. She pounded against it. "Dembe!" she called. "Dembe?"

Footsteps sounded on the stairs leading to her second-story room. The lock clanked and the door pushed open. Cate backed a few steps away.

"Yes, Miss Catherine? May I retrieve something for you?"

"What time is it?"

"It is 2 a.m." He glanced at the tray. "You have not eaten."

Cate shook her head. "I do not want it."

"Please, Miss Catherine, eat some food."

Cate set her jaw. "I demand to see Duke Northcott."

"He is not available. He plans to visit you in the morning." The man's cool demeanor rattled Cate. While he seemed kind, nothing she said seemed to affect him. Appealing to him to assist her would not work.

She tried anyway. "Dembe, please. People must be searching for me. They are undoubtedly worried. You must help me. I am here against my will."

"Please, eat, Miss Catherine. It will help settle your nerves."

"Settle my nerves?" Cate shouted. "I have been kidnapped and am being held prisoner here! Tea and cookies will not settle my nerves!"

Dembe opened his mouth to answer when a shadow loomed behind him. "What's this? Catherine awake already?" Duke Northcott skirted around Dembe and stepped into the room.

Cate stumbled backward a step as he entered. "Yes, Duke Northcott," Dembe answered. "She awoke several minutes ago. I brought the food as you instructed." He motioned toward the tray.

"And yet Catherine has not touched her food. Tsk tsk, Catherine. You must be hungry. You've missed dinner!"

"I do not want your food. I want to go home."

"You Americans are always so onerous. You demand this. You insist on that. Though the simple truth is we cannot achieve everything we desire, dear. You must learn this lesson. Now, eat the snack Dembe has prepared for you and go back to sleep. We shall discuss things further in the morning." Duke Northcott lifted the teacup on its saucer and offered it to Cate.

"No!" Cate insisted.

"Oh, come, Catherine. Dembe has gone to great trouble to prepare you a nice cup of hot tea with fresh biscuits in the middle of the night." He picked up a biscuit and waved it at her.

Cate knocked it from his hand. It skittered across the floor leaving a trail of crumbs. Duke Northcott raised his eyebrows at her and set his jaw.

"Obstinance is not a quality I prize in women, Catherine. If you refuse Dembe's treat, then you shall go hungry."

"Then I shall go hungry," Cate stated despite her rumbling stomach.

"How unfortunate for you," Duke Northcott answered. "And for poor Dembe who waited to prepare it."

"And poison it?" Cate shot back.

Duke Northcott roared with laughter. "Poison it? Whatever for, my dear?"

"To kill me," Cate suggested.

"Why would I go through the trouble of bringing you here to poison you? There are so many other more interesting ways in which I could achieve this feat. I'd not resort to the mundanity of poisoning someone with a cup of tea."

Cate's brow furrowed as she considered the question. "Do not tax yourself, dear," Duke Northcott continued after a moment. "Dembe did not poison your biscuits nor your tea. Did you, Dembe?"

"No, Duke," Dembe answered in his soft voice.

"Then why did you bring me here?" Cate demanded.

"As I've already told you, we shall discuss it in the morning. Now, eat."

Cate eyed the teacup perched on the saucer in Duke Northcott's hand. He raised it toward her again. Cate set her jaw as she accepted the saucer. She sipped from the cup at the sweet, creamy English tea. Duke Northcott passed the plate of remaining cookies to her.

Cate set it on the small night table. She sank onto the bed as she nibbled the cookie's corner.

Duke Northcott smiled at her as he caressed a lock of her hair. "Good girl," he said. "I trust you will be able to sleep after you've eaten. I shall see you in the morning. Good night, Catherine."

He spun on his heel and exited the room. Dembe stepped toward the broken cookie strewn across the wooden floorboards. "I'll do it," Cate offered, rising from the bed.

"No, Miss Catherine. Please eat. I shall clear the mess." Dembe removed a handkerchief from his pocket and collected the crumbs and the discarded cookie. "Is there anything else, Miss Catherine?"

"No, Dembe, thank you." He nodded his head and stepped to the doorway. "Oh, Dembe?" Cate added.

"Yes, Miss Catherine?" Dembe asked as he twisted to face her.

"I'm very sorry about earlier." She raised her teacup to him. "Thank you. The tea and cookies are very good."

"I am pleased you are enjoying the meal. Good night, Miss Catherine."

He pulled the door shut and Cate heard the lock engage. She sipped at the warm tea, finding it brought her more comfort than expected. Her mind reeled. Why had Duke Northcott brought her here? What did he want from her? And what would he do to get it?

Her mind wandered through frightening scenarios as she finished the cookies and tea. She set the dishes on the tray and wandered to the window. Light from Dunhaven Castle danced in the distance. Cate pressed her hand against the glass as she stared at it. Her forehead rested against the cool windowpane as she continued to study the lights. They must have noticed her absence by now. Poor Jack. "Jack," she moaned. "I'm sorry."

Another few moments passed before exhaustion crept over Cate. Her eyes became heavy and her limbs felt like lead. Had the tea contained a sleeping draught? Or was her adrenaline from the distressing situation waning?

She wandered from the window and collapsed onto the bed. With drooping eyelids, she stared at the flickering flame of the candle. What would become of her, she wondered, as she drifted off to a dreamless sleep.

* * *

Cate awoke the following morning to bright sunshine streaming through the room's single window. The candle's wick smoked after having burned down to its end. Melted wax stuck to the table under the candleholder.

Cate rolled onto her back and stared at the ceiling for several moments before she rose and ambled to the window. In the daylight, the clear outline of Dunhaven Castle dominated the landscape in the distance.

She scanned the property closer to the house. No defining features stood out. If she could manage to escape, she spotted nothing to hide her flight.

Cate jimmied the window again but could not open it. She crossed to the door and tried the knob. Still locked, she realized, as she tugged against it. She paced the small area between the door and the bed as she considered her options.

A knock sounded and the lock disengaged. Cate spun to face her visitor. Duke Northcott strode into the room.

"Good morning, Catherine!" he said with a wide smile.

"Up and about already? I should have thought after your rather taxing experience last evening you would prefer to sleep late."

"I prefer to be informed as to why I am here," Cate countered. "Why did you abduct me?"

"Abduct is such a strong word. I prefer to say I strongly and enthusiastically persuaded you to leave with me."

"But you didn't!" Cate argued. "You dragged me here, unconscious and against my will!"

The corners of Duke Northcott's mouth turned down as his bottom lip raised in an upside-down smile, forming a mouth shrug. "A rather trivial difference in the description of the event."

Cate's eyebrows shot up and her jaw fell open at the statement.

"Well, shall we put aside the debate on how you happen to be here and go to breakfast?" He offered her his arm.

Cate's expression remained unchanged. "No!" she exclaimed after a stunned moment.

"Oh, really, Catherine! Must you continue to be so obstinate? You surely do not object to a well-prepared meal! Dembe is quite a good cook, I promise."

"I demand to know what is going on!"

"Tsk, tsk," he clicked his tongue at her. "You are in no position to demand anything, dear Catherine. Let us try to be congenial, shall we? There is no reason for this bitterness between us."

Cate blinked at him as she attempted to understand the request for cordiality from her kidnapper. She would learn nothing from him unless she complied with his demands. She bit her lower lip and sighed as she reached for his arm.

"A wise choice, Catherine," Duke Northcott said with a nod.

He led her down a narrow stairway and through another

hallway before they entered a dining room. Cate's eyes scanned every area, memorizing as much as she could, searching for an exit. As they approached the table, he pulled her chair out and seated her before sitting across from her.

Dembe waited in the corner of the room. As Duke Northcott sat down, he scurried from the room and returned in moments with a tray. He set it on the sideboard and lifted two plates which he placed in front of Cate and Duke Northcott.

Cate eyed the poached eggs on her plate with the side of cured bacon. "May I bring you anything else?" Dembe questioned.

"No, Dembe, not unless Miss Catherine requires anything else. She appears unimpressed with her meal."

"No, it looks most appealing, thank you." Cate picked up her fork to begin eating. Dembe retreated to his corner. Cate took a few bites of her food before setting her fork on her plate. "Now will you tell me why I am here?"

Duke Northcott raised his eyebrows at her. "You are a most impatient woman, Catherine," he answered.

"I often find myself impatient when kidnapped, yes," Cate answered.

He grinned at her. "Your sense of humor is most entertaining. Perhaps, first, we shall discuss why you ran from me yesterday and where you managed to disappear to."

Cate returned to her meal, focusing her gaze on her plate. "I do not know what you are speaking of," she insisted.

"Yes, you mentioned that yesterday. I do not believe you. I believe you were very much aware that I called to you. And that you deliberately avoided me. With the assistance of that stooge Damien Carlyle."

Cate's fork clattered to her plate. "What difference does it make?"

"It makes a great deal of difference to me, Catherine. As

I've told you, you are a most interesting woman. Your actions intrigue me."

"I am not that interesting," Cate contended.

"I shall be the judge of that," Duke Northcott countered. "Tell me about yourself, Catherine."

"There is little to tell. I lived in Philadelphia for most of my life until I married Jack. After our marriage, we traveled to this country for Jack's legal practice."

"A Scottish lawyer won your heart? Oh, dear Catherine, you have settled poorly. With your beauty, you could have attained a better match!"

"I love Jack," Cate answered.

"Love is for fools and ladies' novels. And I do not take you for a fool, Catherine."

"I do not agree," Cate said.

He shrugged. "Either way, your marriage is most odd to me."

"Your opinion on my marriage does not concern me."

"Fair enough. What brought you to Dunhaven?"

"My husband's business. He is a distant cousin of Lord MacKenzie and we hoped to visit family whilst here." Cate glanced up to find his eyes on her. She held his glance as she slipped the knife from the table and into the folds of her dress.

After a moment, he raised his eyebrows. "Are you certain that is all there is to the story?"

"What else would there be?" Cate inquired.

He narrowed his eyes at her. "I conjecture there is more." Cate remained silent, tending to the food on her plate. "Why were you walking with Damien Carlyle yesterday?"

"Grayson Buckley requested a moment to discuss business with my husband. Mr. Carlyle kindly offered to escort me on a walk around the property in my husband's stead."

"How well do you know the Buckleys?"

"I have only just met them when they arrived at Dunhaven Castle."

"And the Carlyles?"

"The same," Cate answered.

"Damien Carlyle seems oddly protective of you for someone he's only just met."

"Duke Northcott, I do not know what you are referring to."

"I am referring to your wild fugue through the castle with Damien Carlyle yesterday resulting in your strange disappearance in a dead-end hallway. Where did you go and why is Damien Carlyle so invested in protecting you?"

Cate was running out of answers that skirted the truth. She shrugged. "I cannot answer that. After our walk, Mr. Carlyle offered to show me an interesting trinket he'd spotted in the castle. I followed him to another room to view it. I did not hear you calling to me and I certainly did not disappear."

He held her gaze for a moment before speaking. "No. There is more to the story. There is something odd about you, Catherine. I cannot put my finger on it, but I believe there is something you are hiding."

Cate returned her attention to her plate and finished the final bites of her meal. "I have ways of gaining information, Catherine," Duke Northcott warned.

"There is no more information to gain," Cate informed him.

"We shall see," he answered as Dembe cleared their dishes.

Cate wiped the corners of her mouth and set her napkin on the table. "Shall we?" Duke Northcott asked as he stood from the table.

Cate swallowed hard and rose, anxious about what may happen next. Arm in arm, Duke Northcott led her to the hallway and toward the cottage's front door. "Perhaps you would care to read in the sitting room for a time."

Cate rubbed the back of her neck at the statement, and she did not respond. Her focus remained on the door in front of her. Freedom lay on the other side. It stood mere yards from her. Could she make it? If she could make it to the grass beyond, perhaps she could call for help. Perhaps someone would spot her and help her.

Cate considered her options. This may be her only opportunity for escape. She must try, she determined. Her hands trembled as she slid her arm from his. She shoved him against the wall and raced to the front door. She clutched at the doorknob, twisting and turning it as she tugged. No key sat in the keyhole. The locked door prevented her from any escape. Tears streamed down her cheeks as she realized the situation.

Behind her, Duke Northcott recovered. He smoothed his cravat and jacket before approaching her. He clapped his hands in a slow, methodic manner. "Bravo, Catherine, Bravo."

Cate spun to face him and pressed against the door. Her breathing turned ragged as he stalked toward her. "Oh, do not cry, dear," he said. "It was a brave though gravely miscalculated move." He removed a handkerchief from his pocket and offered it to her, waving it between two fingers. "Take it."

Cate snatched it with a trembling hand. She pressed it to her face, drying her tears. "Let us resolve this matter once and for all. You cannot escape, my dear." He pulled Cate away from the door and swung it open. He motioned toward the outside. Cate smelled the fresh air and felt the cool breeze on her damp cheeks. She glanced to Duke Northcott then through the door. "Well, go ahead, my dear, try to depart."

Cate's brow furrowed and she stepped forward. As she attempted to step over the threshold, she ran into an invisible barrier. She lifted her arm and pressed her hand forward. Her hand could not breach the doorway.

She twisted to face him. "There. You see? It is quite impossible for you to leave. Not until I allow you. Resign yourself, Catherine. You are stuck here."

A fresh wave of panic and nausea swept over Cate. Her breakfast threatened to fly back up her throat. She bit her lower lip, and her hand found the cool metal of the knife hidden in the pocket of her dress. She clutched it, wrapping her fingers around the handle. She had no other options now.

Cate slid the blade from the folds of her dress. She raised her arm high and swung down. Duke Northcott caught it mid-swing. The knife grazed his hand but clattered to the floor as he gripped and squeezed her wrist. Blood trickled from the small cut which seemed to disappear almost as soon as it opened.

"Ow!" Cate shrieked.

Duke Northcott slammed the front door shut. "Do not do something you will regret. I will not tolerate these games, Catherine," he roared at her. "I have been a most accommodating host. Yet you attempt to harm me?" He drove her back against the wall. She crashed into it as he pressed against her.

"Let me go," she wailed.

"Come, Catherine, you have not earned any favors." He yanked her up the front stairs and dragged her down the hallway to her room. He pulled the door open and tossed her inside. She stumbled a few steps before collapsing to the floor in a heap. "There you shall stay until our next conversation. Perhaps by then, you shall have learned to behave." He swung the door shut and the lock engaged.

Cate climbed to her feet as tears stained her cheeks. She threw herself against the door and pounded on it. "Let me go! Let me go!" she cried.

Her sobs went unanswered. She slid down the door and crumpled to the floor. Within a few moments, a sound reached Cate's ears. She sniffled as she lifted her head, straining to hear.

Hoofbeats resounded. Cate pulled herself to standing and hurried to the window. She searched the landscape outside. A carriage approached, pulled by two chestnut horses. The carriage slowed to a halt outside the front door. The coachman dismounted and opened the door for the occupant.

Celine climbed out. Cate's eyes grew wide. She banged against the windowpane. "Celine! Celine!" she called. "Celine, I'm here!"

The woman stormed to the front door, oblivious to Cate's pleas. Cate raced to her door and pressed her ear against it.

"Marcus! Marcus!" Celine's voice called in the foyer.

"Celine," Duke Northcott answered. "What a pleasant surprise."

"Where is she?" Celine demanded.

"Where is who, my dear?"

"You know very well who. Where is Catherine MacKenzie?"

Cate's heart leapt. Jack must have told Celine she was missing. Celine must have deduced Cate's location. She was saved! Cate hammered her fist against the door. "I'm here, Celine! Celine! I'm up here! Help!"

"I have no idea what you are talking about, Celine," Marcus answered.

"Don't you?" Celine countered.

"No, I do not. I am sorry to hear the poor girl is missing. Though perhaps there is a more reasonable explanation than accusing me of some involvement in her disappearance."

"You are the reasonable explanation, Marcus. You chased

her through the house yesterday. You've taken her. Where? I demand to know."

"A tale you've no doubt gathered from that dimwitted ally of yours, Damien Carlyle. I grow weary of these accusations, Celine. First, I am responsible for Elizabeth Buckley's strange illness and now an ocean away, I am the responsible party for a missing woman. It is most likely she's run off to escape that dullard of a husband she has. It really isn't that surprising, Celine."

"That's a lie!" Celine screamed at him.

"It's not," Duke Northcott retorted, his voice calm and measured, bordering on taunting. "He is rather dull. A most useless man if I've ever met one. He may even make Grayson Buckley seem appealing."

Cate overheard a scuffle. "I wouldn't if I were you, Celine. I suggest you depart before you say or do something you'll regret."

"I will find her, Marcus. And she had better be unharmed." Cate heard footsteps retreat from the house.

"Oh, Celine! I hope she is found. What a terrible shame it would be if anything were to happen to a beautiful woman like that!" he called, his voice raised.

Cate rushed to the window. Celine emerged from the house and approached the carriage. She climbed aboard without a glance back. "No, wait!" Cate shouted. "Celine, wait!"

Cate groaned as the carriage pulled away. "No," she moaned. "Come back!" Her bottom lip trembled as she slogged to the bed and sank onto it. Not only did an invisible barrier trap her inside this house, but it also prevented others from seeing or hearing her. How? What sorcery was this? Who were these people? And how could she fight against it?

CHAPTER 22

Cate paced the floor of the bedroom as the sun descended in the sky. Celine had not returned. No one had visited the house. She had watched Duke Northcott depart in the early afternoon. His carriage traveled in the opposite direction of Dunhaven Castle. Where was he going, she pondered?

As the dust settled in his wake, Cate tried the door and window again. She could not budge either.

"Dembe!" Cate called as she banged on the door.

Footsteps climbed the stairs and approached her door. The lock clanked and the door swung open. "Yes, Miss Catherine?"

"Where has Duke Northcott gone?"

"Business, Miss Catherine. He will return in the early evening to dine with you."

"Dembe, please," Cate pleaded, "please, I cannot stay here. I'm frightened."

"Perhaps some tea will soothe you, Miss Catherine," Dembe offered.

Tears stung Cate's eyes. "No, Dembe, no tea. Thank you." Cate stalked away from him to stare out the window.

"I shall bring it in case you change your mind." With that, the man exited. He returned in moments with a steaming cup of tea and set it on the small table before leaving Cate alone again.

As the sun dipped below the horizon, Cate spied Duke Northcott's carriage return. He strode into the house. Thirty minutes later, he knocked at her door.

"And how are you feeling this evening, Catherine?" he inquired as he led her to the dining room.

"Frustrated," Cate answered.

"I am sorry to hear that," he said as she took her seat.

"Perhaps you can alleviate my frustration," she said after a moment.

He raised his eyebrows at her and set down his fork. "What an interesting proposition. Continue."

"Why have you brought me here?"

"My reasons are my own," he answered. "I shall share them when the time is appropriate."

Cate set her jaw as she considered her next question. "If you cannot answer that, perhaps you can explain to me what you are."

"What I am?" he repeated.

"You caused me to faint with only a touch. You have created some sort of unseen barrier that prevents me from leaving the house even through an open door. I scratched you earlier with the knife and you healed immediately. These things are not normal."

"Your intelligence impresses me, Catherine. Even in a frightening situation, you keep your wits about you. You pay careful attention to detail even under these ominous circumstances."

Cate narrowed her eyes at him. "Compliments will not distract me from my question."

He smiled at her. "You do not give up. Admirable. In different circumstances, we may have made fantastic allies."

Cate cocked her head. "I cannot imagine ever aligning with you."

"Never limit your options, Catherine. Life can offer us strange circumstances in which we must accept what we imagined we would not."

"You have not answered my question," Cate reminded him.

"You must accept that there are things in this world beyond what you may expect."

"Such as?"

"Suffice it to say I possess several unique abilities that allow me to navigate the world differently than most others."

"Unique abilities," Cate repeated. "Such as the ability to heal your wounds in seconds?"

"Your interest in me is flattering, Catherine. And your curiosity in these affairs is a most attractive quality."

"I only wish to learn the circumstances that surround me."

"Oh, I do admire you, Catherine. Despite your assumptions to the contrary, I find you a most interesting woman."

Their conversation continued through the meal but did not delve further into Duke Northcott's strange abilities. Cate spent time after dinner reading in the sitting room before Duke Northcott returned her to her room, locking her in for the night.

* * *

Cate woke from a dreamless sleep before the sun crested the moors. With the candle burned down and only minimal light, she laid in bed as the sun rose. Painting the sky like a watercolor, the sun's light brought her some solace. She imagined lounging in her own bed, surrounded by her two buddies, Riley and Bailey.

Tears threatened as she wondered if she would ever see them again. Marcus Northcott's strange abilities baffled her. And what she couldn't explain pushed her mind to explore places she'd rather it didn't.

As the sun rose fully into the sky a quiet knock sounded at the door. The lock released and Dembe pushed the door open. He set a tray of breakfast on the small table near the door.

"Breakfast, Miss Catherine," he announced.

"Thank you, Dembe," she responded as she rose. "Is Duke Northcott not here?"

"Duke Northcott will return for dinner with you, Miss Catherine," the quiet man informed her before pulling the door shut.

Cate eyed the tray and its carefully prepared meal. Perhaps a solitary breakfast was preferable, she pondered, as she took a bite of her poached egg. The downside to the solitude was her wandering mind.

When Dembe collected her breakfast tray, he brought several books to entertain her. Despite her best attempts, Cate found reading impossible. She resorted to pacing the floor, stopping occasionally to stare out the window.

After what seemed like an eternity, Dembe brought her afternoon tea. Cate settled onto the bed afterward. The waiting wore on her. What did this man want from her? What were his intentions? Would she ever escape? Would she see Jack again? Would they return to their time?

* * *

Cate eyes fluttered open as the setting sun painted her room a brilliant shade of red. She pushed up to sitting, pulling her cheek from her tear-soaked pillow. She had cried herself to sleep hours ago after Dembe had brought her a small meal and warm cup of tea.

Cate sniffled as she scanned the room. A large box trimmed with a blue satin ribbon sat on the small table across from her. She rose and approached it. A folded note sat atop the white box.

Cate snatched it from the lid and flipped it open.

My dearest Catherine -

I look very much forward to dining with you this evening. I imagine the conversation we share will be illuminating. Please accept this dress as a token of my advanced appreciation for the evening. I expect to see you in it when I call for you.

~ Marcus

Cate frowned at the note. It read like something from a bad Lifetime movie. She had no desire to dine with the man, though she assumed she had little choice in the matter.

Cate slid the ribbon from around the box and pulled off the lid. A blue satin dress lay inside. Cate ran her fingertips across the fine material. In any other circumstance, this may be exciting. In her current predicament, it was anything but.

Cate pulled the dress from the box and laid it across the bed. She eyed the satin dinner gown. A rich blue color and trimmed with lace, the dinner gown was the picture of nobility in this era. She attempted to assuage her trepidation by distracting herself with the beauty of the dress. Though she could not repress the shudder that passed through her body as she pulled it on.

After dressing, Cate perched on the edge of the bed. She

pulled the timepiece from beneath the bodice of her dress. A sudden urge to hide it overcame her and she shoved it into a pocket of the dress.

The sun sank below the horizon and darkness crept across the sky. Moonlight shone through the window.

A knock sounded on the door. The bolt clanked and the door pushed open. Duke Northcott strode into the room, his hands behind his back. He studied Cate, a smile crossing his lips. "I see you found my gift. I hope you appreciate it. You look lovely, my dear."

Cate did not respond. He narrowed his eyes at her. "Smile, dear. I have paid you a compliment."

Cate forced a weak smile onto her face as she held back tears. Pleased with her effort, Duke Northcott continued. "Good. Now, no woman is complete without some form of jewelry. I find this piece particularly stunning. And a perfect match to your blue eyes." He swung his hands from behind his back. They clutched a velvet jewelry box. He popped it open. A large sapphire necklace lay inside. Diamonds trimmed the teardrop-shaped sapphire.

Cate's eyes widened. No stranger to fine jewelry since her inheritance of Dunhaven Castle, this piece was spectacular. "If you'll allow me." He motioned for her to stand. Cate recoiled as his hands swept her hair away from her neck. The weighty sapphire pressed against her skin as he fastened the necklace behind her. "There." Cate spun to face him. "C'est magnifique, dear Catherine! Shall we?" He extended his arm to her.

Cate accepted it as the strangeness of her circumstances rattled through her mind. In another situation, Cate may find the man charming. When being held hostage, the sentiment was tempered by her discomfort and fear.

Duke Northcott seated her at the candlelit table and took

his seat across from her. Dembe bustled about the room, delivering their first course. Cate sipped at the soup.

"Have you recalled any interesting tidbits about yourself you've forgotten to mention to me, Catherine?"

Cate glanced at him across the table. "No. I have hidden nothing from you."

"I find it difficult to believe a woman like you hides no secrets behind that beautiful facade."

"I am a simple woman. I have no secrets."

"Hmm," he murmured as he returned to his soup. "I visited the castle this afternoon."

Cate set her spoon down and raised her eyebrows at him. He glanced up at her. Satisfied he had captured her full attention, he continued. "The family is in quite a tizzy over your absence. I passed my condolences along to your husband through Douglas. I understand the poor man is quite upset."

"Are you telling me this to torment me?"

"Torment you? I assumed you'd be pleased!"

"Pleased?! Pleased that you've abducted me? Pleased to learn of the upset it's caused? Which part of what you've conveyed do you expect me to be pleased with?"

"Clearly your husband grieves your absence. He must care for you very deeply. I assumed this would please you."

"If you are concerned with pleasing me, you could let me return to him."

He chuckled at her statement. "You are a worthy sparring opponent, Catherine. You remind me of another woman with which I am acquainted."

"I assume the answer to that request is 'no.'"

"You assume correctly, my dear. Interesting or not, you are far too valuable to me to return."

"My husband has no funds to pay a ransom. I am not very valuable."

"It is not money I desire," he informed her. "You are valuable in other ways."

"What ways?" Cate inquired.

He offered a half-smile. "I prefer to keep those to myself for the moment. Unless, of course, there is something interesting you'd like to share with me in return."

Cate sighed and her shoulders sagged. "I do not understand what you expect me to share. I have lived a simple life. I do not have any secrets."

"Yes, so you've said. And perhaps you are being genuine. Perhaps not. Either way, I shall find the truth eventually. I always do."

He stared into her eyes as he spoke. Cate held back a shudder. They spent the rest of the meal conversing about polite topics. Cate found the juxtaposition of polite conversation with her circumstances jarring when she considered it.

After dinner, Duke Northcott invited Cate for a nightcap in the sitting room. Cate sipped at the brandy and stared at the flames dancing in the fireplace. A growing sense of dread filled her with every sip. What intentions did he have for her? At what point would he enact them? Could she play along long enough to keep herself alive to be rescued? Was a rescue even possible?

When she finished her drink, he relieved her of her glass. "You should rest, dear," he said.

"I am not tired," Cate countered. She preferred not to be locked in that bedroom again. And each minute that passed brought her closer to her doom, she fretted.

He offered her a brief smile. "I must insist, Catherine," he said. He approached her and caressed her cheek. Cate opened her mouth to protest, but no sound emerged. Her eyelids and limbs grew heavy, and her vision closed to a pinpoint. Her head lolled to her chest as she experienced the sensation of being lifted into someone's arms.

* * *

Cate's eyelids fluttered open. With bleary eyes, she took in her surroundings. Her eyebrows knit as she failed to recognize the location. Something cold and hard pressed against her back.

"Hello, Catherine," Duke Northcott said as he knelt next to her.

"Where am I?"

She pushed her hands to either side as she slid her eyes around to scan her new environment. Stone walls surrounded her as she lay on her back. Cate's eyes darted frantically as she attempted to make sense of it. Her stomach leapt into her throat as she realized she lay in the family crypt. Duke Northcott had placed her in one of the unused stone coffins.

"No," she cried as she attempted to sit up. Tears formed and escaped from the sides of her eyes.

He pressed her back into place. "Now, now, Catherine. Do not give in to panic. You are a stronger woman than that."

"No," Cate repeated. "Please, don't."

"I am afraid I must. Though it does pain me. You have such potential, Catherine. Perhaps in another circumstance."

Cate breathed raggedly as panic swept through her. She attempted to rise again but with a wave of his hand, Duke Northcott pinned her into place. Cate struggled to move, achieving nothing more than wiggling and squirming.

"I shall miss your feistiness." He reached to her and pushed a lock of hair from her face. His hands fell onto the necklace. "Keep this as a reminder of me."

"No, please," Cate sobbed. "I am valuable. You said so yourself. Please!"

He smiled at her. "Yes, you are. We are about to learn just how valuable. Do not fear, Catherine. If your friends are as clever as I expect them to be, you shall not perish. If they are not, well... let us not speak of that possibility."

He stood and stared down at her. "Goodbye, Catherine. For now. If you do hold a secret, I shall learn it. In time. Though at the moment, I have achieved my goal. Celine's focus is centered on me. I shall cease my cat-and-mouse game with you. For now. I do hope we shall meet again."

Cate's eyes grew wide as he began to push the large stone over the top of the coffin. "No! NO!" she screamed.

Light narrowed to a slit before disappearing entirely as the stone cover came to its final resting place. Tears streamed from Cate's eyes as she pounded against the cool stone above her. "No! No! Please! Duke Northcott!"

Cate bit her lower lip as she wept. She attempted again to shift the stone above her. She pushed at it, trying to move it from every angle. She pulled her knees up until they pushed against the stone above, but she could not budge it.

Cate let her limbs collapse as sobs wracked through her. When tears no longer flowed freely, Cate wiped at her face. She sniffled as she attempted to regain her composure. She took a deep, steadying breath. As she inhaled, her mind pondered the amount of air she may have remaining. Did she have hours? Twelve? More? Less?

Cate's mind spun as she considered the duration of life she had left to live. She attempted to control her breathing, forcing herself to take shallower breaths. She closed her eyes and focused her attention. Her thoughts turned to Jack. He would be stuck here unless he could retrieve her remains. If they found what was left of her, he could retrieve the timepiece and return to their time. He could take care of Riley and Bailey.

The thought of the poor pups left behind brought fresh tears to her eyes. She fought against them, fought to maintain control of her emotions. Duke Northcott suggested she may be found. Was it false hope? No, she insisted. It couldn't be. Someone would find her as he hinted. They had to. She clung to that hope as she began to drift in and out of consciousness.

CHAPTER 23

Cate's head lolled to the side. A haze clouded her mind as she drifted in and out of a responsive state. A scraping noise filled her ears. She attempted to rouse herself, but her lightheadedness prevented her. Cool air brushed past her cheek. Garbled voices sounded overhead. Light and darkness played across her closed eyelids.

"Lift her out," a garbled female voice instructed.

Cate experienced the sensation of being pulled up. Arms wrapped around her, and she floated briefly before her body settled onto a hard stone surface.

"Is she alive?" a male voice posed.

"Come on, Cate, be okay," another clearer voice said. Cate recognized Damien's voice. She fought to regain her senses and open her eyes. Her head rolled from side to side, and she moaned. Warm skin touched hers. Fingers wrapped around her hand and squeezed. "That's it, Cate. Come back to us."

"Find Michael and Jack," Celine's voice said.

"You'll be all right?" Grayson inquired.

"Yes, bring them here. Quickly," Celine answered.

Cate moaned again, squeezing her eyes together. Her lips

moved without forming words. After a moment, her forehead pinched and she forced out, "Damien."

A renewed squeeze of her hand. "I'm here, Cate. Can you open your eyes?"

Cate's eyelids fluttered open. The world blurred in front of her, and her eyes threatened to close. Celine leaned closer to her. "Take a deep breath and listen to the sound of my voice."

Cate concentrated on her voice as she breathed deeply. Celine whispered a few Latin words as she placed her palm on Cate's cheek.

Cate gasped for breath, her eyes opening wide and her muscles tensing. After a moment, she relaxed. Her breathing returned to normal, her vision cleared and her muscles relaxed. She glanced around at her surroundings. She lay in the family crypt next to the coffin that had been her prison only moments ago. Damien and Celine knelt over her. Damien clutched her hand.

As she opened her eyes, he grinned at her. "Hey," he said. "Welcome back."

Cate focused on his face. Her lips trembled and tears formed in her eyes. "Hey," she answered in a shaky voice. A tear escaped her eye and rolled down her cheek. Damien wiped it away.

"Don't cry. You're safe. Nothing is going to happen to you now. It's okay, Cate."

She smiled at him as she fought her tears of joy and squeezed his hand. "I didn't think I was going to make it," she choked out.

"We weren't going to let you die," Damien assured her. "Me, Michael, Gray, Celine, Jack, and his grandfather haven't stopped searching for you since you disappeared."

Cate's brow furrowed at the statement. "Jack's grandfather?" she murmured.

Damien smiled and nodded at her. "Yep. Stanley Reid. Nice fellow, it seems. Extremely worried about you though not more than Jack. Poor guy was beside himself."

"He can't return to our time without me," Cate explained.

"I don't imagine that was the reason for his upset. Besides, he could get home with Celine's help which is how he got Stanley."

Cate's mind swam with the details, and she struggled to keep up with the conversation. "Just rest for a minute," Damien soothed as he patted her hand.

Celine rubbed her cheek. "How are you feeling?" she questioned.

"Better," Cate admitted. "Happy to be alive." She pushed herself up to sitting.

"Careful, easy," Damien warned.

"I'm okay," Cate assured him. "I just…"

The mausoleum door burst open. Jack's figure appeared limned in moonlight. He stopped at the door, peering into the vault. "CATE?!" he exclaimed as he searched for her.

"JACK!" she called, reaching her hand out to him.

He raced to her, skidding to a stop next to her and dropping to his knees. Damien retreated a few steps, allowing him access to Cate. He scooped her into his arms. His pounding heart thudded in his chest against Cate's ear. "Thank God you're okay," he gasped as he held her tightly. She wrapped her arms around him in a tight embrace. "I thought I'd lost you," he said as he released her and cupped her face in his hands. Tears shone in his eyes.

She grasped his hand in hers as fresh tears spilled onto her cheeks. She nodded, unable to speak as she considered the possibility that he nearly had, indeed, lost her. She swallowed the lump in her throat. "Are you okay?" Jack questioned.

"Yes," Cate choked out. "Yes, I'm fine."

"She's okay," Damien chimed in, putting his hand on Jack's shoulder. "We found her in time. She was a little groggy but she's okay."

"Great job, buddy," Michael said, clapping Damien on the shoulder.

Grayson entered moments later with a winded Stanley Reid. Cate could have cried again at the sight of him. "Mr. Reid!" she exclaimed.

He sidled to her and puffed a few breaths before he spoke. "Aye, lassie. You gave us all quite a scare!" Cate reached out and grasped his hand, squeezing it. He returned the gesture. "I am ever so glad you're all right, Lady Cate."

"I'm sorry. I…"

"You don't have to explain, Cate," Jack hushed her. "I'm just glad you're all right."

"No, you don't have to explain," Michael assured her. "We all know who is to blame and it's not you."

"I didn't tell him anything," Cate insisted.

"He does not know the secret?" Jack inquired.

Cate shook her head. "No."

"Great job, Cate," Damien said with a grin.

"Impressive, Catherine," Grayson added. "He is a difficult man to hide the truth from."

"He kept insisting I was hiding something. I just kept denying it. And eventually, he brought me here and put me in that… " Cate stopped before she voiced the word.

"At least he only suspected and did not know you were hiding something," Michael said.

"He said he used me to get to Celine. Why?" Cate questioned.

"It's a long story," Damien assured her.

"One not to be told now. You three must return to your time," Grayson said. "Before any more harm befalls you at the Duke's hands."

"I agree," Celine added. "You must return at once."

"What about Douglas… our time rip problem… " Cate began.

"Douglas understands everything about the time rips, including where we came from," Jack informed her.

"Celine has already enchanted his pocket watch, it's finished," Grayson added.

"And don't worry about your problem," Damien added. "We'll be there tomorrow to help you with it." He rubbed her shoulder and gave her a reassuring smile.

Cate glanced around at all of them.

"Come on, lassie," Stanley said. "Time to go home."

Jack climbed to his feet and offered her his hand. He pulled her to standing. "Easy," he cautioned. "Can you stand?"

"Yes," Cate said as she steadied herself on her feet.

"How do you feel?" Damien asked. "Faint? Can you walk?"

"I can walk. I'm a little shaky but I can make it."

"You sure? I can carry you," Jack offered.

The statement made Cate giggle. "I'm sure. Despite it being 1792, I do not need to be carried to the castle like a damsel in a gothic novel."

"Even so, I'd love to sweep you off your feet, Cate," Jack joked.

"I'm glad to see you haven't lost your sense of humor, Jack," Cate teased.

"We should go," Grayson urged.

The group filed out of the mausoleum. Dunhaven Castle dominated the landscape in the distance, its lights a beacon in the darkness. The sight sent Cate's heart soaring. If she wasn't so weary, she'd have run to the castle.

"What time is it? How long have we been gone?" Cate asked Jack as they trudged up the path.

"Almost one in the morning," Jack answered. "You've been gone over sixty hours. Don't worry, I've been back and made an excuse that you were in town and may be there for hours. If you returned for dinner, you'd be okay on your own."

"Wow," Cate mumbled.

"You sure you're okay, Cate?" Jack asked as Cate stared ahead, lost in thought.

"Yeah, I'm fine. I just... I'm sorry you had to go through that," Cate explained.

"I honestly am not sure how I held it together during that conversation with Mrs. Fraser and Molly," Jack admitted. "But it's nothing compared to what you've been through."

Cate grasped his hand and squeezed it. "I'm fine."

"A fact for which I am very thankful," Jack said, returning the hand squeeze.

"As am I, lassie," Stanley chimed in. "Though I must admit, it gave me quite a rush when we hopped back to another era."

"A rush, Pap, really?" Jack inquired.

"I don't hate time travel as much as you, Jackie," Stanley said with a chuckle. "I rather enjoy it. When Lady Cate isn't missing, of course."

Jack wrinkled his forehead at him. Michael caught up to them and clapped Jack on the back. "I hate it as much as you do, pal. If you ever want to compare notes, give me a call."

"I just might do that, friend," Jack said. "I cannot understand how anyone enjoys this."

"Oh, come on, it's amazing!" Damien replied. "We're living in another culture, basically."

"I agree, Damien!" Cate said. "It's fascinating! Outside of the kidnapping part."

"You two can keep it," Michael said with a roll of his eyes.

"He's a real stick in the mud," Damien complained. Cate giggled at the statement; one she'd often used to describe Jack's resistance to time travel.

"Speaking of keeping things," Jack said. "Where did you get this?" Jack pointed to the dress and necklace.

"From our mutual friend," Cate said.

Jack raised his eyebrows. "He gave you a sapphire and diamond necklace? Is it real?"

"Oh, I'm sure it is," Damien answered.

"It's fairly heavy," Cate added with a shrug. "He told me to keep it to remember him."

"Oh, wow, this guy kidnaps you then gives you a gift to remember him by? What kind of psychopath is he?" Jack questioned.

"Don't ask," Michael called over his shoulder. "You really do not want to know."

"He's right," Damien said with a shudder.

Cate's glance flitted between both men. Both shared an intense hatred for Duke Northcott. After her trouble with the man, she could only imagine what they had endured at his hands.

They continued up the path toward the castle together. The group talked and laughed, relieved the ordeal was over.

As they rounded a bend in the path near a clump of trees, a man strode into the path in front of them. He clapped his hands in a slow, dramatic fashion.

The group ground to a halt. "Well, well, I see the merry band has succeeded in retrieving dear Catherine. Bravo, Celine."

Jack pushed Cate behind him, shielding her from the man. Michael and Damien filled in on either side of him to further cover Cate. Cate clung to Jack as she peered over his shoulder.

"No thanks to you, Marcus," Celine spat at him.

"Au contraire, my dear. After all, I gave you the clue. I had high hopes you would find her. I preferred you did. I rather like Catherine." Duke Northcott peered over the group and waved a hand to Cate. "Good to see you looking so well, my dear."

"We need to get out of here," Damien whispered to Michael.

"I'm all over it, buddy," Michael said, his eyes darting around the area. "Make a break for those trees?"

"What? Are you crazy?" Jack breathed. "We can't leave Celine alone with him?" Cate glanced around. Grayson and Stanley had fallen behind on the trek. She spotted them approaching. Grayson's eyes went wide as he witnessed the scene. He pulled Stanley from the path, hiding him behind a large oak.

"Believe me, she'll be fine," Michael answered.

Damien reached back and grasped Cate's hand as he began to inch toward the grove of trees.

"And where do you think you're going, Mr. Carlyle?" Duke Northcott inquired. Cate jumped as a bolt of lightning sailed from Duke Northcott's hand and struck the dirt next to Damien. He danced a few steps back away from it.

"Stop, Marcus," Celine shouted. She flung a large blue ball of energy toward the man. He deflected it with some sort of ray. Cate wondered if perhaps she had fallen asleep and was trapped in a dream.

He raised his eyebrows at her. "Oh, I think not, dear. I'm only warming up." He cupped his hand. A crackling ball of light formed above it. Lightning blazed inside. Cate stood stunned at the sight. Duke Northcott lobbed the ball toward them.

Michael and Damien reacted quickly. Damien grabbed Cate by the shoulders and dragged her behind a large tree in the grove. Michael tackled Jack to the ground, rolling off the path with him and down a small grade.

The lightning ball exploded in a brilliant flash, charring the ground underneath it. Cate covered her mouth as a squeal emerged. "Get down!" Damien hissed as he pulled her lower.

"Celine!" Cate shouted.

"Shh, she's fine! We've got to go!"

"No!" Cate argued. She attempted to stand and run to Celine, but Damien pulled her down.

She glanced across the path. Michael held Jack at bay, also. Michael emphatically gestured toward the castle as he shook his head, catching Damien's eye. He motioned again toward the castle. Damien nodded.

"We can't run away!" Cate countered. She struggled against Damien's grip. "We must help Celine! We can't leave her."

"All right, Marcus," Celine said. "If you insist on having this out, let's." She narrowed her eyes and swung her hands out to the sides. Her foot stomped on the ground as she let out a shriek.

Cate ceased grappling with Damien as she witnessed the scene unfold. Overhead the skies darkened. Black clouds obliterated the moon and stars. Thunder boomed and lightning tore through the sky. Celine's fingers crackled with electricity.

"As cool as this can be to watch, we need to get out of here," Damien urged. "As you can see, she's quite capable of taking care of herself."

Damien grabbed Cate's hand and pulled her away from the scene. They kept low to the ground as they raced toward the castle. Cate risked a glance back as the battle between Celine and Duke Northcott continued.

Lightning flashed between them. Balls of fire slammed into trees and charred them. Brilliant orbs of light flung in every direction. The dazzling display almost mesmerized Cate. Damien tugged on her arm, urging her to continue.

They hurried to the castle and Damien ushered Cate

inside through the front door. She stood speechless in the foyer for a moment as she reflected on what she'd just witnessed. Booms of thunder and blasts of lightning still sounded, announcing the continuation of the battle outside.

Moments later, Michael ushered Jack through the doors. Jack's face betrayed his confusion and astonishment. "Cate!" he exclaimed. "Did you see that?"

"Yes," she nodded, her eyes wide. "What was that?"

"A battle between two supernatural beings," Michael informed him.

"And something you want to be far, far away from," Damien assured them.

"I'm not sure I can believe what I just saw," Cate responded.

"Me either," Jack agreed.

"You two time travel," Damien answered. "You can't honestly question the existence of other supernatural things."

"Oh, I can and I will!" Jack insisted. "Accepting time travel was one thing, this is completely bonkers."

"Bonkers or not, it exists," Michael answered. "And there is a dark side. One you want to stay away from."

"And one this secret needs protecting from. The fact that it's still hidden in our time suggests your family is very good at it," Damien said. "And now it's time for you two to go home."

"No," Jack countered. "Pap isn't here. I have to find him. Oh, what if he's…"

Douglas emerged from the sitting room with Stanley. "Pap! Thank heavens!" Jack exclaimed.

"Yes, Grayson brought me here before returning to help Celine."

"Oh, Catherine!" Douglas exclaimed. "Oh, how fortunate they have found you. I have been beside myself with worry. I wished to join the search though they maintained I should wait here. Dreadful business, this."

"You three need to return home," Damien said.

"Yes, with a device something like this!" Douglas exclaimed as he brandished the timepiece. Noticeably missing was the inscription. He grinned from ear to ear. "I was most pleased to learn I was correct. Much to Jaime's chagrin."

Cate smiled at him. "It is an incredible discovery, isn't it?"

"Most definitely!" Douglas agreed. "Though Jaime views it as a burden, particularly given the circumstances surrounding us now." Douglas turned serious for a moment. "Oh, Catherine, I am so very sorry about what happened to you. My own progeny stolen from under my roof. Perhaps Jaime has a point." He turned pensive.

Cate clasped his hand in hers and patted it. "I am unharmed, Douglas. And while the secret must be protected, that doesn't mean it can't also be celebrated."

Jaime joined them in the foyer. "Oh, Catherine, thank heavens! I have been worried about you."

She smiled at him. "We found her in the nick of time," Jack assured him.

"Good, quite good." He clapped Jack on the back.

"Does he know?" Cate whispered to Douglas.

"Indeed," Douglas confirmed. "Three generations of Reids from various centuries standing in my foyer. Incredible!"

Cate gazed at the scene. Stanley, Jack, and Jaime talked, smiled, laughed, and shook hands. Despite the gravity of the situation, they were incredibly fortunate.

"I hate to break up the family fun," Michael interjected, "but you three need to go."

Douglas spun to face Cate and took her hands in his. He studied her face, much like a father studying his child. "I wish we did not have to part so hurriedly. Though I hope when all has settled perhaps we may enjoy a more leisurely visit."

"I look so forward to that, Douglas," Cate answered.

"If you can convince Jack. He is, after all, a Reid."

Jack stepped toward him and extended his hand. "Sir, after this visit, I will never view time travel in the same way. And I will likely complain but I will never object to visiting family. You exhibited a phenomenal level of understanding and assistance in a difficult situation. I will never forget it."

"Anything for family, Jack," Douglas said as he grasped his hand. "Now, I suppose you should be on your way."

Cate nodded. "Yes, we should be," Cate lamented, the familiar feeling of sadness creeping over her as she prepared to leave her family behind in another time.

"As I understand it, certain areas lead to and from certain time periods," Douglas said. "Lead the way to your home."

Cate gave an uncertain glance to Damien as she attempted to formulate the words to ask about his help in their own time. Damien beat her to it.

Damien grasped Cate's hands in his. "Don't worry, we'll be right behind you. Well, sort of. We'll see you tomorrow and we'll get you all squared away with your little problem."

Cate nodded again. "Okay, thank you. And thank you again for finding me. I…"

Damien shook his head as he interrupted her. "There's no thanks necessary, Cate. I'm glad you're safe."

"You'll be safer once you're away from you-know-who," Michael reiterated. "And as much as I'd like to continue sharing our mutual hatred of time travel, it's time for you three to leave."

The group said their goodbyes before Cate, Jack, Stanley, Douglas, and Jaime stepped from the foyer. Cate glanced back as they continued down the hall toward the library. Damien nodded and waved as he disappeared into the sitting room. She wondered if she'd actually see him the next day as he promised. It all seemed too strange for her to process.

She and Jack led the way to the library. Jack crossed the room and pressed the stone to trigger the mechanism to open Douglas's laboratory. Douglas's eyebrows raised as the bookcase swung open.

"The time rip is..." he began.

"In your secret lab, yes," Cate finished for him.

A half-smile crossed his lips and he chuckled. "Fitting," he murmured.

The group descended the stairs into the cool air below. Cate held out the timepiece. Jack and Stanley both grasped it with her. "Goodbye, Douglas," she said.

"Goodbye, Catherine. And good luck," he answered.

CHAPTER 24

Cate nodded and the three activated the timepiece. Cate smiled at Douglas just before he disappeared from her sight, replaced by a glaring light standing where he had stood only seconds before.

"Whew," Jack breathed as he pressed his hands over his chest. "It's good to be back."

"Aye," Stanley agreed. "Good to have the lassie back where she belongs." He squeezed her arm and gave her a nod.

"The lassie is quite glad to be back where she belongs, too," Cate said.

"You must be exhausted," Jack stated. "I'll tell Mrs. Fraser you're back but are feeling under the weather and going straight to bed."

"You'd better not," Cate warned. "That will send Mrs. Fraser into a tizzy, and she'll fuss over me to no end. I'll change and let her know myself."

"Cate, you've lived through days and only four hours have passed! You've got to be exhausted."

"Well, yes and no. I'm too wired to be exhausted. I feel like so much has happened. Would you mind if we had our usual post-time travel discussion? Mr. Reid, you're welcome to join us."

Stanley smiled at her. "Thank you, but I'll pass and leave you and Jackie to your discussion. This old man is heading home to sleep off the time lag!"

"I'll drive you," Jack said.

Stanley waved at him. "Bah, I'm not THAT old. I'll walk."

"Pap..." Jack began.

"Take care of Lady Cate," Stanley insisted. "I'll take a stroll through the property to the cottage before a nice long sleep. The fresh air will do me good. I'm glad you're okay, lassie." He winked at them before disappearing up the stairs.

Jack's eyes followed his departure. "He's one tough old bugger. I am wiped out!"

"If you prefer to change and relax, we can postpone our discussion."

"No, like you, I am also wired. Some of the things we witnessed I'm not sure I can process. I'd feel better if we talked about it."

"Okay, sounds good. Usual spot after we change?"

"Perfect. Unless you prefer to rest, I can come to you."

"No, that's fine. I'd rather make everything look as normal as possible for Molly and the Frasers."

"Good idea. Okay, see you soon."

Cate nodded and they parted ways. Cate pushed through the doors into her suite. Riley and Bailey lifted their heads from their fireside spot. Tears welled in Cate's eyes as she spotted them. "Riley! Bailey!" she exclaimed as she rushed to them with her arms outstretched. She gathered both pups to her, showering them with kisses and ear scratches. Memories of her predicament rushed into her mind. She recalled wondering if she'd ever see her two beloved pups again.

She wiped a tear from her cheek as she pushed the

disturbing memories away. She had survived. She would focus on that.

Cate forced herself to stand and change her clothes. The sooner she was back to normal, the better, she figured. Her eyes fell to the large gemstones as she pulled the necklace from around her neck. "Keep this as a reminder of me," Duke Northcott's voice echoed in her head. With a shudder, she dumped the piece in the bottom drawer of her jewelry armoire. Perhaps she could donate it for the auction at the President's Ball.

Before meeting Jack, Cate navigated to the kitchen. She knocked on the door jamb. "Just wanted to let you know I'm back, though I'll handle my own dinner."

"Oh, Lady Cate!" Mrs. Fraser said. "No need. I've just finished preparing your dinner and was going to put it in the refrigerator with a note. You've saved me the trouble."

"Thank you, though you didn't have to do that," Cate answered.

"We didn't want you making cereal for dinner," Molly said with a chuckle. "And besides, with me here full-time, if you're late for dinner, I can always make it whenever you're back."

"Thanks, Molly. Though, again, not necessary. By the way, while I was in town, I got a text from…" Cate stumbled for a moment as she attempted to explain. "A friend. He is in Scotland and may stop in for a few days beginning tomorrow. I apologize for the short notice, he…"

Mrs. Fraser waved away Cate's concern. "No problem at all, Lady Cate. Your friend is most welcome in your castle anytime! Is he a picky eater? Any food allergies?"

Cate shook her head. "No, and he has a guest or two with him. With the short notice, I don't expect you and Molly to be responsible for meals. We can eat in town, or I can order in. Please don't go to any trouble."

"I'm starting to wonder if you dinnae like my cooking, Lady Cate," Mrs. Fraser teased.

"It's nothing like that," Cate assured her. "But with this last-minute development, I don't expect you both to be whipping up meals for a crowd on short notice."

Mrs. Fraser shook her head. "Two or three guests is hardly a crowd. Molly and I are quite capable and if you've no special requests, it should be an easy task. Molly and I will make up a few bedrooms tomorrow morning for them. I'll put them in the hallway near your suite."

"I am indebted to you both," Cate said. "And I can take my meal with me along with Jack's. After my surprise trip into town, we got behind on our discussions about the leak we've been dealing with."

"Dining in the library, is he?" Mrs. Fraser questioned.

"Yes, at my request," Cate said.

"Well, Molly can help you carry the trays. Are you feeling all right, Lady Cate?" Mrs. Fraser asked as Cate slid her tray off the counter.

"Yes," Cate assured her. "Just a little tired, but I'm fine!"

"Be sure you get plenty of rest tonight before your guests arrive! You don't want to catch a cold with all the entertaining you'll be doing."

"I will," Cate promised.

Molly followed Cate to the library with Jack's dinner tray. Both dogs raced ahead of them to greet Jack. "Special delivery," Molly said as she set the tray down for Jack.

"Thanks, Molly," Cate said before Molly slipped through the doors on her way back to the kitchen.

Cate collapsed into the chair next to Jack. He sank back into the armchair and slouched with a long exhale. "Did that just happen?"

"Which part?" Cate questioned.

"Any part. All parts. Every part," Jack answered.

Cate shook her head. "I've been wondering that myself. It's surreal."

"What was going on between those two... what did Michael call them?"

Cate's eyes widened. "Supernatural creatures," Cate answered.

"The guy threw a lightning bolt from his hand!" Jack exclaimed.

"And Celine can open time portals. Oh, and levitate light balls from her hand. She did it in the secret passage when Damien and I were hiding from Duke Northcott there. I nearly collapsed."

"I would have collapsed," Jack said. "I nearly did when she opened the time portal to send me back here. And gave me a charm to return to 1792 with Pap. And the other two with her. Just calm and casual like nothing's amiss. Hey, you two time travel, you should be okay with supernatural things!" Jack mimicked.

"So that's how you got back, huh? I was wondering. I can't believe we met other time travelers," Cate said with a shake of her head. "Though it explains a lot."

"It explains nothing. Things just keep getting more complicated."

"Well, it explains why I couldn't find anything on Michael Carlyle or Damien. First of all, Damien's last name is Sherwood, not Carlyle and second, the information I found on Michael Carlyle from the modern-day is correct. There wasn't a Michael Carlyle in 1792. It also explains the origins of both the warlock story with Douglas and the tales from town about the events on a certain March evening when the skies clouded, and lightning went from the ground to the sky."

Jack shook his head at the turn of events. "Yeah, every tale begins with a kernel of truth, I guess."

Cate nodded. "Those people witnessed the battle between Duke Northcott and Celine. So did we, up close and personal. Thank goodness for Michael and Damien who probably saved our lives."

"I like Michael. He seemed like a good guy."

Cate offered a wry glance. "You just like him because he hates time travel, too."

"Like I said, he seems like a good guy," Jack answered.

"Do you suppose they'll show up tomorrow? Damien and Celine? Michael, perhaps?"

Jack shrugged. "I'm not sure. I don't know what to expect. They insisted they would, and I sincerely hope they do because without them our problem isn't solved. Though I honestly cannot imagine they will just pop up at the door."

"How can Celine exist in 1792 and here? Does she time travel from the past to the future?"

"I suppose we'll find out," Jack answered. "Or not if they never show."

Silence passed between them for a moment while each of them picked at their food. "Are you certain you're okay, Cate?" Jack questioned after a moment.

"Yes," Cate assured him. "I'm okay. Damien found me in time. I mean, I was in and out but…"

"No, that's not what I mean," Jack interrupted. "I mean like mentally also. You spent days with some supernatural creature. Did he hurt you? He didn't throw any lightning bolts at you or anything, did he?"

Cate chuckled at the ridiculous-sounding statement. "No, no lightning bolts. We were talking and then he touched my cheek and I passed out. When I woke up, I was in a bedroom. Frightened but unharmed. He was actually charming in a strange sort of way."

"Charming?!" Jack guffawed. "Are you crazy? This guy kidnapped you!"

"No, that's not what I meant. For a deranged kidnapper, he was quite the conversationalist. An old-fashioned gentleman. I wonder what happened between him and Celine? And Damien and Michael?"

"I shudder to think you were forced into a conversation with that man. I'm glad we are away from him. I hope forever. It's clear both the Buckleys and Carlyles detest him. Or rather the Carlyles and Sherwoods, or whatever. There has to be a strong reason."

"Perhaps we'll learn more tomorrow... if they show up."

"I really hope they do. After all this, I hope our problems are all solved."

"Me too," Cate admitted. "Me too."

Cate laid awake for most of the night. Tension lodged between her shoulder blades as she tossed and turned, unable to sleep. Would Celine and Damien arrive tomorrow? Would she slip away into another era before they came? Would another nightmare of the Duke disrupt her sleep? Perhaps her nightmares stemmed from the danger she faced from him. Perhaps now that she was saved and away from him, the nightmares would cease. They had solved one problem with ensuring Douglas had a method to control the time rips. Had they solved two and relieved her nightmares as well? Time would tell.

Still, the most crucial problem remained unsolved. Time rips opened and closed without warning, swallowing her, Jack, and now Molly. How much longer could they survive like this before tragedy struck?

As the sun rose over the moors, Cate rose from her bed and paced the floor of her suite. Whatever today brought, she prayed it moved them closer to a solution. Following breakfast, Cate took a stroll with Riley and Bailey. She stared out over the calm waters of the loch.

As they returned to the castle, the dogs bounded toward their favorite spot in the garden. Cate shooed them away before they could do any more damage, hurrying them into the castle's kitchen.

"How was the walk?" Molly asked.

"Pleasant, as always," Cate responded.

"Any word from your friends?" Molly inquired.

"No, nothing yet," Cate answered. "Unless they've popped in already this morning!"

"Nay, Lady Cate," Mrs. Fraser answered. "No one's arrived yet."

"Didn't they give you an ETA?" Molly questioned.

"They didn't. I'm not sure they knew how long it would take them to wrap up their business and get to Dunhaven," Cate fibbed. "I'm expecting them this afternoon, but I don't have a definite time."

"Well, either way, we'll be prepared," Mrs. Fraser answered. "I've got lunch planned for everyone and if we don't use it today, we can use it tomorrow."

"Thanks, Mrs. Fraser, you really are the best."

"Spending the day with your journals again?" Mrs. Fraser asked.

"Yes, they are fascinating," Cate said, though she didn't imagine she could focus on any work. "They will make a great addition to my book!"

"Anything about Douglas being a warlock?" Mrs. Fraser quipped.

"Sorry, no candid revelation about him being a warlock."

Molly bit her lower lip. Cate assumed she was fretting over her odd experience from two days prior. Molly had made no mention of her ghost sighting after the initial conversation, but Cate could tell it continued to bother her.

"All just gossip," Mrs. Fraser answered, waving her hand in the air to dismiss the rumors.

"Yep," Cate agreed. "Well, I'll be upstairs, and I'll let you know if I hear anything from Damien!"

Cate wandered upstairs with the dogs in tow and settled in the library. She stared at the journals before paging through them. She opened a document on her laptop to continue typing ciphertext but found herself unable to concentrate. Instead, she opted for pacing the library floor.

Hours wore on as Cate waited for some word from Damien. She sat down at her laptop to email him multiple times before deciding against it. Morning crept to afternoon and Cate finished her lunch. After handing the empty tray to Molly, a knock sounded at the door.

"Got a minute?" Jack asked as Molly skirted past him.

"Yep. Come on in."

"About the leak," Jack said in a loud voice as he pushed the doors shut. Once closed, he spun to face Cate. "Anything?"

Cate shook her head. "Nope, nothing. Not even an email. I keep wanting to email him but I'm afraid of his reaction. What if this was all some kind of weird joke or odd coincidence?"

"He said he knew you, right?"

"Yes, he's the one who sent the program."

"That is an odd coincidence," Jack said as he shook his head. "Perhaps too odd."

"Do you think he was using me to get information or something?"

"To what end?"

"To learn about the time rips? I'm not sure," Cate said with a shrug. "Nothing makes sense anymore. With everything that's happened over the past few days, my mind is swimming. Up is down, left is right. I can't make sense of anything."

"After the past day. We've lived through days, but it's only been a day here."

Cate's eyebrows shot up. "Perhaps that's it. We lived through days. Perhaps when Damien said tomorrow, he meant tomorrow from the day we were living. Which is days from now."

"Days where anything could go wrong," Jack lamented.

Cate sighed. "Yep."

"So, do we just wait for days?" Jack questioned.

"I don't see what other choice we have."

"And what do we do in days if they don't show up then?"

Cate shrugged and opened her mouth to answer when a loud thud sounded at the front door.

CHAPTER 25

*C*ate raised her eyebrows and glanced at Jack. "Could it be?"

They hurried down the hall to the door. Cate's heart hammered in her chest as she placed her hand on the door handle. She glanced at Jack who offered an encouraging nod.

Cate swallowed hard and pulled the door open. Her eyes went wide as a variety of emotions surged through her from shock to relief. Damien, Celine, Michael, and another man stood outside the door. They appeared identical, more or less, to when Cate had seen them less than twenty-four hours ago in another century.

"Hi, Cate!" Damien said with a broad grin. "Long time, no see!"

A moment of lightheadedness passed over Cate as she took in the situation. They had come. Perhaps now they could solve their problem.

"And not a moment too soon," Jack answered.

"Yes," Cate agreed. "Come in, please."

Cate ushered them into the foyer. "The old place looks good," Damien quipped.

"Looks better in this century if you ask me," Michael said. He glanced at Jack. "I assume you have bathrooms."

"That we do, mate, that we do!" Jack answered.

He and Michael shared a knowing glance.

"I hope you don't mind," Celine began. She sounded distinctly American, having lost all traces of any of the slight French accent she carried in 1792. Her blond locks now flowed freely rather than being pinned up in an upswept style and she wore modern clothes. Though nothing else about her had changed. "I brought Gray's cousin, Alexander, to help."

"Not at all," Cate answered. "We appreciate all your help. Gray…" Cate phrased the last word as a question, leaving his name hanging in the air.

"Is at home in Maine," Celine said with a smile, realizing the question Cate implied. "He can access Alexander's reference library if we need information."

She smiled at Celine then turned to Alexander, who extended his hand to shake hers. "Lady Cate," he greeted her in a crisp British accent. "A pleasure to meet you. I was most curious when I learned of your predicament."

"We hope you can help," Jack said. "Oh, by the way, Cate and I are the only two in the house who know the secret so, mum's the word." Jack held his finger to his lips.

"Got it," Damien responded.

"We're pretty good at secrets," Michael assured him.

"Shall we go into the sitting room?" Cate offered.

"I'll let Mrs. Fraser know everyone is here," Jack said. "You can explain the loads of fun we've been having with the time rips."

"Okay," Cate said with a nod.

Jack strode down the hall as the rest of the group shuffled into the sitting room. "He's not staying?" Damien questioned as he sat next to Cate on the loveseat.

"No," Cate said with a shake of her head. "It may appear a bit odd for my estate manager to stay while I'm entertaining."

Damien's brow furrowed. "Oh," he murmured. "I thought... never mind."

Cate cocked her head at him. "What?" she asked.

Damien shrugged. "I thought you two were actually married. It's just... weird to realize you're not and he's your estate manager."

"Ohhhh," Cate responded with a knowing nod. "Yes, we usually pretend to be a married couple when time traveling. It may look odd for a man and woman to be traipsing around the Scottish countryside unwed in past eras."

Damien smiled and nodded. "Good point. You two do a good job of it. Smart!"

Cate returned his smile.

"No more trouble with the Duke?" Michael inquired.

"No," Cate answered. "Since we returned late yesterday afternoon, nothing."

"We were worried he may have followed you here," Damien answered.

"I'm glad he didn't," Celine added. "What can you tell us about the problems you've been experiencing with the time rips? We've filled Alexander in but it's best if you reiterate the details. The last time I spoke with you was over two hundred years ago." Celine chuckled at the last statement.

Cate remained silent for a moment as she processed the Celine's admission. The woman sitting in front of her had lived for over two hundred years. Or was she merely making a joke?

"For us, it was just yesterday," Damien said. "But for Celine, it was two hundred years ago."

Cate nodded and swallowed hard as Damien confirmed Celine's age. She had, indeed, lived for over two centuries.

The fact astounded Cate and she found it difficult to pull her thoughts together.

"Well..." Cate began before pausing as she attempted to collect her thoughts.

"Take your time," Damien said, patting Cate's arm. "It's a lot to take in."

Cate cleared her throat and began. "As Jack and I told you yesterday... or two hundred years ago," she began with a nervous chuckle. "When I arrived at the castle, the time rips were controlled by the timepiece. To open a time portal, we'd activate the timepiece and be able to slip back and forth between eras.

"But then in the last two weeks or so, we've experienced some disruptions with the time rips. They open and close at random and we can't control them with the timepiece. The timepiece still slows to represent the entry into the time portal, but we can't open and close it like usual. Instead, we're just sucked into the other time period and stuck there until we get pulled back."

Celine narrowed her eyes and pursed her lips as Cate spoke.

"Does it happen in every rip location?" Damien questioned.

Cate shrugged. "I'm not sure. I haven't ventured to all the locations where we know time rips exist, to be honest. Though it doesn't always happen where there is a time rip. My bedroom is a prime example. It leads to 1925. Twice I've been sucked back there and returned within a few moments, but I've slept in that room for the past two weeks and all but two times remained in my own century.

"It has occurred in the rip leading to 1792 multiple times as well. And there's something else. It seems to be occurring in places where we didn't realize a rip existed. For example, the hallway leading to the library. We had no knowledge of a time rip there and several people have been sucked back in time. Of course, we do not have an exhaustive list so it may not be a new location."

"Hmm, so that makes it impossible to tell," Damien said. "Unless you spend a decent amount of time in the rip location it may not happen."

"As far as you knew there was no time rip in the hallway, right?" Michael questioned.

"Right. And it happens to everyone, even people without the timepiece. My housekeeper-in-training, Molly, got sucked into a time portal a few days ago. She swore she spotted a ghost. She has no idea a real, live woman stood in front of her and she was in another era."

"I'd like to see the locations, one where a known time rip exists and the other where you didn't realize one existed," Celine requested.

"Sure," Cate agreed. "If you'll follow me, I can show you one of each."

Everyone rose and headed toward the foyer except Michael. "You coming?" Damien inquired as he sat drumming his fingers on the chair's arm.

"Nope," he answered.

Cate furrowed her brow at his response. "It's not very far..."

Michael interrupted her. "I have no desire to be in a location where I could accidentally slip back in time with no way to return. I'll stay right here. Oh, unless you've slipped into another time period here?"

"No, we've never had it happen here," Cate answered.

"Yet," Damien said with a wink and a grin as he left a frowning Michael behind. "He has no sense of adventure."

Cate chuckled at the statement as they joined Celine and Alexander in the foyer. Cate led them down the hall toward the library. She stopped before they reached it. "This is the hallway where we've experienced a lot of activity. Prior to this, we didn't realize any time rips existed here, but both Jack and I along with Molly have slipped into the past."

Celine nodded as she glanced around the space. Cate remained silent for a moment as she watched Celine. After a moment, her eyes flitted around the space trying to determine what Celine was seeing. She seemed to stare at specific areas in space.

Celine narrowed her eyes and reached her hand out. She spread her fingers, twirling them as she swiveled her wrist as though grasping something. Cate scrunched her eyebrows together and stared at the invisible item Celine grasped.

Alexander raised his eyebrows at her. "This wasn't here in 1792," Celine informed him.

"Interesting," he answered as he stared at her hand. "What are you seeing?"

"What are YOU seeing?" Celine asked, directing the question back to Alexander.

"A distortion," Alexander said. "Portals usually have smoother edges. This one is rough, distended."

"And spiked," Celine added.

Alexander narrowed his eyes and leaned closer to her hand. Celine grabbed his hand. "It's easier to feel them."

"Oh, yes," he answered as she guided his hand. "I feel them now."

Cate stared at the scene unfolding, unable to make sense of it. "This is..." she murmured under her breath, unable to finish the statement.

"Weird," Damien finished for her. "Yeah, I know. You get used to it. They are far more perceptive than we are about these things."

"Are the time portals you use invisible?" Cate questioned.

"No, not even to us. When Celine opens a time portal,

you know it. The wind is howling. It sounds like a train coming straight for you and a giant black hole opens."

Cate raised her eyebrows at the description. "Wow. That's... well, I'm not sure I would have gotten Jack into one of those."

Damien chuckled. "Michael only went into one because Gray shoved us through while we were both still in shock over the whole 'witches and warlocks exist' thing."

Cate pursed her lips. "You seem to have lived quite an interesting life, Damien."

"And you don't even know the half of it," he said with an eye roll.

"Where is the other?" Celine inquired.

"In Douglas's lab. This way."

Cate led them into the library. "Wow! Great library!" Damien exclaimed.

"Thank you! I can't take credit for decorating it, but I enjoy it quite a bit."

Riley and Bailey stood and stretched from their spots near the fireplace. They each eyed the newcomers. Bailey sniffed in the air at them before giving a shrill bark. Riley offered a few yips too.

"Oh, dogs!" Damien exclaimed.

"Yep. Meet Riley and Bailey," Cate said. "My two best buddies! Boys, quiet!"

"Are they friendly?" Damien asked.

"Yes," Cate answered. "Just a little barky."

Celine approached them, squatting down and extending her hand. She stared at each of them. The dogs seemed mesmerized by her presence. Both quieted, approached her, and sat as she scratched their ears.

"Now there's a trick worth having," Cate quipped.

She continued across the room and pressed the stone

trigger on the fireplace's edge to open the secret passage to Douglas's lab.

Damien's eyes grew wide, and his jaw dropped. "Wow, cool, a secret passage!"

Cate plugged in the lighting before they proceeded down the stairs. "This was Douglas's secret lab. We discovered it a few months ago. The dogs kept barking at the bookcase. We assumed there was a leak somewhere but then we discovered all this."

"Wooooow!" Damien breathed. He gaped around at the various contraptions Cate had sorted through. "Douglas was quite the inventor."

"Yes, he was. I'm still sorting through his journals and notes, but he was quite a visionary."

"No doubt the time traveling helped," Damien answered.

"It's likely, yes," Cate responded. "This area contains a time rip. This is how we accessed 1792."

Celine nodded. "Yes, I see it."

"Is it like the other? Distorted?"

"Yes, it is," Celine answered.

"And also has a few spikes," Alexander chimed in.

"I studied a few of these when I visited in 1792. Would you mind if we wandered around and observed?" Celine asked.

"Not at all," Cate answered. "Feel free."

"Thanks."

Celine and Alexander departed, leaving Damien and Cate alone in the lab. Damien peered around the space. "You can have a peek around if you'd like," Cate offered.

"Thanks!" Damien replied. "This is so cool. All these inventions in a secret lab!"

Cate didn't respond right away. "Oh, sorry. I didn't mean to treat your home like a curiosity shop," Damien added.

"No, not at all. I treat it like one!" They both chuckled

before Cate continued. "I'm just... I find it interesting you are so fascinated by this."

"Why?" Damien asked as he studied the lightbulb prototype.

"You seem to have lived a life far more interesting than a few secret passages and some strange inventions."

"Ah, you mean the supernatural stuff," Damien conjectured.

"Right. I cannot imagine living with... well, whatever you live with on a day-to-day basis."

"You mean with the fireballs and time portals and stuff?" he inquired as he squinted at the staircase to nowhere.

"Yes, that. And the living for centuries. And the weird touch that makes you pass out. Duke Northcott did that to me twice."

"Yeah, Celine can do that, too. It can be helpful when you can't sleep! But it is super weird."

Cate nodded as Damien continued his exploration of the lab. "So, is Alexander..."

"A centuries-old warlock, too, yeah."

"But you and Michael are..."

"Just humans, yep," Damien said as he completed his circuit of the room.

Cate shook her head. "You say it all so matter-of-factly. I don't understand how you do it!"

"Well, when I first found out, I freaked out. But I've since gotten used to it. You get used to it," Damien replied. "And you have a freak out, albeit a more tempered one, every now and again when you find out about even more strange stuff you never realized existed."

His last statement produced a chuckle from Cate. "It's good to realize you aren't just cool as a cucumber while chaos reigns around you. I feel completely inept at dealing with this. The whole thing makes my brain hurt."

"It takes some getting used to. But at least now you know there are other people in the world dealing with the supernatural... oddities of the world. You'll always have a friend in me... us to use as a sounding board if you need one." Damien gave her an awkward grin and a bit of color rushed into his cheeks. "Shall we head up? Maybe check on Michael?"

"Sure," Cate agreed.

They climbed the stairs into the library and navigated to the sitting room. Cate pushed through the doors with Damien behind her. They found the space empty. Cate's stomach turned over as she eyed the empty armchair across the room.

"Uh-oh," she murmured as she glanced around in search of the man. "Do you think he tried to follow us or went for a walk? Or got sucked into a time portal we didn't know existed?"

"Mmm, probably the former. Celine didn't mention a time portal here. Let's go check around for him," Damien suggested.

As they re-entered the foyer, the sound of loud laughter reached their ears. Cate glanced up the main staircase, following the sound. Michael and Jack rounded the corner from the hall and descended the stairs. The two talked and laughed as though they were old friends.

"There you are!" Damien called.

"Yes, we were just taking the luggage up," Michael said, thumbing toward the upstairs.

"Aye, and having quite the discussion," Jack said as he continued to chuckle.

Michael clapped his arm around Jack's shoulders and pointed his finger at him. "We have GOT to have this guy out to Bucksville. Especially right around the time you start discussing time travel as the solution to any problem we have. He can talk some sense into you."

"Listen, mate, I've got the same problem here," Jack said, motioning to Cate.

"It's not that I mind using it as a method to solve problems, but I cannot fathom what these two enjoy about it," Michael added.

"Neither can I. Though I must admit, meeting my ancestors has been well worth the inconveniences."

Michael gave a half-smile. "Okay, you have a point there."

"We've never met any ancestors," Damien chimed in.

"If you have the chance, take it," Jack said.

"Noted," Michael replied. He faced Damien. "Where are Celine and Alexander?"

"Exploring the castle and studying the time rips."

"Anything so far?"

"They are appearing in new locations than Celine noted in the 1700s and they are distorted and spiked."

"What does that mean?" Jack questioned.

"No idea," Damien said with a shrug. "But I'm guessing the spikes and distortions are what's causing your problems."

"What could cause new rips to appear?" Cate asked.

"What caused them to be there in the first place?" Michael inquired.

"I'm not certain," Cate answered.

"Perhaps they always existed," Jack suggested. "The land was considered cursed."

"Alexander and Celine may have a better idea. We can connect over dinner and determine what they've come up with," Damien suggested.

"Oh, actually, could we keep dinner conversation time rip-free and save it for afterward? Then Jack can join, and the Frasers and Molly won't overhear anything," Cate said.

"Sounds good!" Damien responded.

"Would you like to head back into the sitting room?" Cate questioned.

"Would you mind if we took a look around the castle?" Damien inquired.

"Not at all. Would you like the full tour?" Cate asked.

"Sure," Damien answered with a grin. "If you don't mind!"

* * *

The group gathered in the sitting room following their evening meal. Mrs. Fraser and Molly provided them with hot cocoa and shortbread cookies as an after-dinner dessert as they settled in. After Cate assured her she could take care of the cleanup, Molly agreed to retire for the evening to read in her room.

Jack slipped into the room shortly after Molly's departure. "I hope you didn't start without me," he quipped as he slid into an armchair near Cate.

"We wouldn't dream of it," Cate assured him. "Though I must say I'm more than curious about what you've found."

"As am I, though I'm more interested in whether or not you've found a solution," Jack added.

"A solution, no, but information, yes," Celine answered.

Cate's shoulders sagged a bit at her response. With no solution in sight from the only person who could help them, perhaps their problem would never be solved.

"Don't worry. Celine will find one," Damien assured her.

"What did you learn?" Michael prompted.

"A few things," Celine began. "First, the portals, or time rips, as you call them, remain distorted as they were in 1792. This is what causes the time differential when you travel through them. That remains unchanged. Which explains why whenever the timepiece interacts with one it slows when you slip through."

"Okay," Cate said. "That makes sense."

"The second major thing we learned is that new portals

are opening in locations they did not exist in before," Celine continued.

"Like the one in the hall to the library?" Jack inquired.

Celine nodded. "Yes. That one did not exist in 1792."

"But others did? Beyond the rip we used to access that year?" Cate questioned.

"Yes," Celine confirmed. "Several existed already in 1792, but there are far more now."

"Since they are new, would the timepiece not control them?"

Damien shook his head. "That can't be the problem," he inferred.

Cate glanced at him and scrunched up her face. Damien explained, "If that was the case, you'd only slip into and out of new portals. But you've been slipping into and out of ALL the portals. Even the ones the timepiece used to control."

"Right, D," Celine confirmed. "Which leads me to our third discovery. The spikes surrounding the portals. They weren't there in 1792. The time portals are morphing."

"Morphing? How? Why?" Jack asked.

"We're not certain why, perhaps due to the new portals emerging," Alexander answered.

"Is there a way to re-enchant the timepiece to take the transformations into account?" Cate asked.

"That's what we're still figuring out," Celine responded. "You said this has all occurred over the span of a few weeks?"

"Yes," Cate said with a nod. "Actually, within two weeks."

"Right, Monday marks two weeks since we've noticed the issues. The issue seems to be becoming more prevalent by the day."

"So, this is progressing and fairly quickly," Damien said.

"It seems to be," Cate agreed.

"I'd like to assess where these time rips are tomorrow," Celine answered. "If we can determine how they are morphing, if they are growing, how many are appearing, and whether or not the spikes resorb, we may have a better idea how to combat the issue."

"How is this different from in Douglas's time?" Cate questioned. "He also experienced random openings of the time rips like we are."

"He did, yes," Celine answered. "I enchanted the watch to hold them closed unless he opened them. Those portals were only distended, not spiked."

"So, you need another enchantment," Michael suggested. "One that handles whatever the spikes do."

"Therein lies the issue," Alexander commented. "Other than circumventing the current enchantment at times, we aren't sure what the spikes do."

"Any theories?" Jack questioned.

Celine and Alexander shared a glance.

"Nothing beyond pure conjecture," Alexander said.

"That glance between you suggests more than pure conjecture," Jack countered.

Celine heaved a sigh. "The working theory is that the portals are morphing and melding to become a universal time portal."

CHAPTER 26

"A what?" Cate asked, her eyebrows shooting high.

"A universal time portal," Celine repeated. "It's a…"

"A portal that can access any point in time," Damien finished for her as he stared into space, amazed by the idea.

"You mean… go anywhere in time?" Jack asked.

"Yes."

"How? Would you just slip through the portal and end up in a random era?" Cate questioned.

"No, you'd need a mechanism to control when and where you'd travel to, right?" Damien conjectured.

"Yes, which explains why the timepiece doesn't effectively work," Celine answered.

Jack wiped his brow. "Universal time portal," he repeated. "This is…"

"Amazing," Cate finished for him. "Access to any time you want or need. Absolutely astounding."

"A real game-changer," Damien agreed.

"And a more dangerous secret," Jack added.

"Yes," Celine concurred. "Access to a specific set of years

is one thing but access to any year is another. The secret must be kept as quiet as possible."

"IF that is what's going on here," Michael chimed in. "You said you weren't certain, right?"

"Right," Celine admitted.

"Okay, so assuming you are correct, is there a way you can control the universal portal? Some mechanism like the timepiece that can be used to open and close the portal and control the date you travel to?" Damien inquired.

"In theory, yes, though I'd need to do some research to get everything correct," Celine answered.

"We plan to call Gray after our discussion and research some references in my library," Alexander added.

Damien nodded.

"What if that's not what's happening?" Michael questioned.

"We'd have to determine why the timepiece is failing to control the rips, both old and new. In theory, it should interact with either. If they remain separate, we need to determine how to deal with the spikes to create a device that properly holds them closed unless activated."

"But you believe you CAN find a solution, right?" Jack inquired.

"Yes," Celine answered. "We can find a solution to control this."

"How certain are you?" Jack asked. "I'm sorry," he added, "I don't mean to sound ungrateful or distrustful, but the stakes are high for us. If this continues, it puts everyone in the castle in danger and makes it far more likely the secret will be discovered. Short of shutting the castle down to any outsiders and telling anyone who sets foot inside the truth, there's not much we can do."

"I understand," Celine answered. "But I'm certain. I've seen a universal time portal before. When I saw it, it had already finished its formation. But the descriptions of the melding rips into the universal portal match what we're experiencing here."

"So, you have some experience with this?" Cate asked with hope filling her voice.

"Yes," Celine said. "Not with creating a device to interact with them but with the phenomenon itself. Though I'm confident we can get this under control."

Cate breathed a sigh of relief at Celine's statement. "Okay," she said. "Thank you."

"Yes, thanks," Jack said. "Looks like we wait to see what's happening tomorrow then."

"Sounds like a plan," Damien agreed. "Should we hit the hay for the night? I'm tired! We took a flight here. I haven't used commercial air travel in a while." He stretched and yawned.

Cate giggled as she nodded. "Sure, I'll show you to your rooms."

"Thanks!"

The group followed Cate upstairs and she pointed out their bedrooms. After a brief discussion with Celine about the best location to place a call to Gray, Cate and Jack departed, continuing to their bedrooms.

As they neared Jack's door, Cate sighed. "So, what do you think?" she asked.

Jack shrugged and pursed his lips before answering. "I honestly don't know. I hope they can fix this. They seem to think they can, and they did help Douglas, but maybe they're being overconfident."

"They seem determined," Cate said. "They did show up as they promised. And Celine seems to have some knowledge of what's happening."

Jack shook his head. "Unbelievable," he said.

"What is?"

"She's seen one of these things before. A universal time portal? And there's another one somewhere? And people time travel all the time. These people time travel all the time!"

"I know! My mind is swimming. All this time we assumed Dunhaven held this secret that existed nowhere else. I guess it was a rather narrow view of the world."

"I suppose you're right," Jack answered. "It was rather naive to assume we cornered the market on time travel."

Cate nodded in agreement. "They seem so savvy about all of this."

"Well, I guess when you've been dealing with it for over two centuries, it's second nature."

Cate shrugged. "Michael and Damien are both human, so they couldn't have been dealing with it for longer than they've been alive. They seem to take it in stride. At least Damien does. He talks about it like it's normal."

"Perhaps when you're living with it on a constant basis, it becomes normal. Kind of like us and time traveling. A year ago, I'd have locked you in the looney bin if you'd discussed time traveling to solve a crime, now it's barely shocking."

"Maybe," Cate said pensively.

"You okay?" Jack inquired.

"Yeah," Cate said with a nod and a smile. "It's just that this whole situation is still incredible to me. It's hard to process."

"I understand exactly what you're saying. My mind can't wrap around everything we've learned and experienced in such a short time. And now the universal time portal bombshell on top of it all."

"Right! A universal time portal? I mean, my mind is racing in a thousand different directions at the possibilities of that but at the same time it seems too impossible to believe!"

"Why? We had time portals to specific years, why not one to any year?"

"I don't know why that seems more improbable than the former, but it does. Perhaps they've got it wrong, though."

"Time will tell. Pun intended, lassie," Jack said with a wink.

"You should try your stand-up comedy routine on the newcomers."

"Yeah, they seem to have a great sense of humor for the time travel jokes. Well, perhaps Michael does. He'd get it."

"You really like him, huh?"

"Ah, yes. A fellow man who appreciates the downside of time travel as much as I do. Yes, I like him very much."

"A comrade in arms, is it?"

Jack nodded. "It seems you've found one in Damien. I still think he likes you."

"I think he's just a nice guy who wants to help," Cate countered.

"Well, either way, let's hope he can. Or Celine can."

"I'll keep my fingers crossed," Cate said as she flashed a set of crossed fingers. "I suppose we should head to bed."

"You feel okay sleeping in a room with a morphing time portal?" Jack inquired.

"I guess so. Probably better than I did before."

"Better than before?" Jack questioned.

"Yeah. At least if I disappear this time, Celine can send you back to find me!"

"Good point."

"And besides, your bedroom isn't very far from mine. For all we know, the time portal has already expanded well beyond the confines of my bedroom. You could get sucked back, too!"

"At least we'd be together in 1925 or wherever we got sent," Jack conjectured.

"True. Well, anyway, if I don't show up for breakfast tomorrow, ask Celine for help to come and find me."

"Will do. Good night, Cate."

"Good night, Jack."

Cate continued down the hall to her bedroom suite. Riley and Bailey had already wandered into the bedroom and curled in their beds during her conversation with Jack. "You two are both lazy bones," Cate said as she changed into her nightclothes. The comment earned a sigh from Riley and a sideways glance from Bailey and nothing more. "I don't suppose you two have any insight on whether or not Celine and Alexander can help us."

Bailey's eyes closed to slits and Riley spun onto his back, his front feet reaching high in the air as he settled in for the night. "I guess that's a 'no,'" Cate said as she crossed the room toward her bed. "At least you didn't end up filthy from digging in the garden today."

As Cate crossed the room, she hesitated in front of her jewelry armoire. Her lips parted and her brow furrowed as she stared at the bottom drawer. She shook her head and took another step toward her bed before returning her gaze to the armoire.

Cate took a tentative step toward the jewelry box. Her hand lingered on the drawer's pull. Her mind focused on the contents of the drawer. She attempted to push them aside. She'd rather dwell on her time rip troubles than this, but her mind did not allow her.

Instead, Cate pulled the drawer open and stared at the necklace laying inside. The sapphires and diamonds sparkled against the drawer's black velvet interior. Cate ran her fingers over the necklace. The stones, cool to the touch, mesmerized her. "Keep this as a reminder of me," Duke Northcott's voice echoed in her brain.

Cate lifted the necklace out of the drawer and held it up.

It sparkled in the light; the diamonds dancing next to the sapphires. Cate bit her lower lip. Would she suffer more nightmares about the Duke or had they solved this problem? Why had he given her the necklace? And why was she so drawn to it?

Cate held it up to her neck as she glanced in the mirror. She raised an eyebrow at her reflection. She'd never owned anything so ostentatious. Not even the jewelry she'd inherited was this extravagant. Perhaps that was the draw.

As she stared at her reflection, Cate's mind regressed to her time with Duke Northcott. After a moment, she shook the thoughts loose from her head. No, she promised herself, she wouldn't dwell on it. The events still disturbed her. There was no reason she should be drawn to this necklace. It only reminded her of her frightening experience.

Cate shoved the necklace into the drawer and slammed it shut. She swallowed hard as her fingers lingered on the drawer pull, threatening to open the drawer and retrieve the necklace again. With a determined step, Cate pulled herself away from the armoire and climbed into her bed.

With any luck, she'd have a nightmare-free night again. And with a little more luck, she'd have a safe home tomorrow.

* * *

Cate stretched and yawned as she meandered down the hall for her pre-breakfast walk with the dogs. A night of tossing and turning as she pondered her predicament left her feeling drained. Riley and Bailey bounded in front of her, scurrying down the main staircase's thick carpeting and disappearing into the hallway leading to the library.

Cate raised an eyebrow at their path as she padded down the stairs. This was not the usual circuit to the outside. She plodded down the remaining step and turned the corner into the hallway.

She spotted Riley and Bailey in a perky sit at Celine's feet. They stared up at her as though waiting for instructions. Alexander scratched Riley's head.

"Good morning," Cate called. "You're both up early."

"Good morning," Celine answered followed by Alexander. "Yes, trying to get a handle on where we're at with the time portals today."

"It seems you've garnered a few adoring fans," Cate said.

Celine glanced down at the pups with a smile. "What cute fans to have!" Riley leapt to his hind legs to receive a head scratch from Celine.

"I'll let you finish your exploring. We can discuss your findings after breakfast."

Cate called the two reluctant pups away from Celine's side and out the front door. As she rounded the castle, she found Damien wandering in the back garden.

"Good morning," she greeted him. "Wow, you're all early risers."

"Good morning, Cate," Damien said. "Yeah, I don't sleep much. My mind never shuts off."

"I understand completely," Cate responded. "I'm the same. I had a miserable night last night."

"Worried about the time portals?" Damien inquired.

"Yes, and a few other things."

"Don't worry too much about the time portals. Celine and Alexander will fix it. What else was on your mind? Oh, sorry, you don't have to answer that. I don't mean to overstep," Damien said as they followed the dogs around the castle's exterior.

"No, it's fine," Cate said. "You have a lot of confidence in Celine, huh?"

"I do. She's never let me down and she's well-versed in a good many things like this."

"Sounds like she's at least got some experience with a universal time portal."

"She probably saw one when she was engaged to the Duke."

Cate ceased walking a moment. "Celine was engaged to Duke Northcott?"

Damien nodded as he waited for Cate to catch up.

"Yep. For three years before she married Gray."

Cate's jaw went slack as she processed the information. "I told you it was a long and complicated story."

Cate shook her head. "You aren't kidding." She paused for a moment before adding. "That was the other thing keeping me up last night."

"Our long and complicated story? It could probably fill a book or maybe be a whole series," Damien said with a chuckle.

"While the details of your long and complicated story did cross my mind, it was more Duke Northcott who kept me tossing and turning."

Damien halted and spun to face Cate. "What do you mean?"

"Nothing specific. Perhaps I was just worried I'd have another nightmare about him. Before I went to sleep, I took out the necklace he gave me. Something compelled me to want to see it."

"Compelled you?"

"Yeah, it was weird. And I kept hearing his voice over and over telling me to keep the necklace as a reminder of him."

"Did you have another nightmare after that?"

"No," Cate admitted. "Though I may not have slept enough to have one."

"But you've had nightmares involving him before?"

"Yes, for months. It became almost a nightly occurrence. Though I had no idea who he was. I only realized it was Duke Northcott when I met him."

"What were the dreams like?"

"Varied with the consistent theme of Duke Northcott chasing me."

Damien pursed his lips and narrowed his eyes as Cate continued. "At first they centered around the library. The nightmares began before we found the secret passage to Douglas's lab and the time rip to 1792. Then he began to appear in them. He'd chase me or grab me and begin dragging me away."

Damien halted and spun to face Cate. "Cate, get rid of that necklace. And forget about the Duke."

"I'd love to," Cate admitted. "I'm just not sure my mind will let me. With any luck, the nightmares are a thing of the past. I'm hoping my encounter with him relieved them."

"I'm sorry you had to go through that. If we could have prevented it, we would have. It must have been terrifying."

"It was. I'm trying not to dwell on it." A moment of silence passed between them before Cate spoke again. "Hey, can Celine heal herself? Like if she gets cut or something?"

"Yeah, why?"

"I nicked Duke Northcott with a knife while trying to escape and he bled for a second before the wound disappeared. I've been wondering if I was seeing things."

"Oh, wow! I'm impressed! That was really, really brave, Cate! You went after him with a knife?" Damien chuckled. "I'd have paid to see that."

"It wasn't that impressive. And it obviously didn't work," Cate lamented. "Anyway, I hope I am rid of him."

"He is trouble. If you start having nightmares again, please let me know. The last thing you need is the Duke poking around at you with no one to help."

"I have Jack," Cate reminded him.

"Jack has no experience with that man and is no match for his supernatural powers. Just do me a favor and promise me if you have even a whiff of a nightmare, or he starts pervading your thoughts, or anything involving him, you'll call me. Or text me. Or email. Or whatever form of communication you prefer."

Cate chuckled at his long-winded request. "I promise I will contact you. Knowing me, I will use ALL the communication methods."

"Fine by me, send out an alarm on all channels. Just don't go it alone, deal?"

"Deal," Cate promised. She scanned the horizon. "Where did those two get off to?"

"Uh-oh. I wasn't paying attention, I'm sorry. I didn't see. I hope they didn't go too far or run away!"

"No," Cate said. "They're around here somewhere. And I have a good idea where. Follow me."

Damien followed Cate around to the side garden. A yip sounded from within the bushes.

"Sounds like you were correct," Damien said.

"And I'll bet they're both digging a nice hole right over here," Cate continued as they rounded the hedge.

Cate stopped dead and put her hands on her hips.

She raised her eyebrows and stared at the two dogs as they stood near a growing hole. "Just as I suspected," she said to them.

"Found an old bone?" Damien suggested.

"I have no idea, but they're always here digging around and staring at this spot. Come on, you two, let's go." Cate ushered them back toward the castle with Damien's help. The two entered the dining room for breakfast, meeting Michael, Celine, and Alexander.

Following the meal, Celine suggested they discuss their

latest findings. They agreed to meet in the hallway outside the library after Cate retrieved Jack.

With the two dogs following Celine as though she were a large, juicy steak, Cate slipped down the stairs and started down the hall to the kitchen. Voices floated from inside. By the sounds of it, she'd catch Jack before he went outside.

She quickened her step, determined to catch him before he left. The voices turned from incoherent to intelligible words.

"... have any updates?" Mrs. Fraser inquired.

"Not beyond what I've already shared," Jack answered.

"And you're sure they're doing the special thing on it?"

"Aye, called twice to confirm."

"Good, there is no room for error," Mrs. Fraser chimed in.

"We need to figure out how we can keep this secret," Molly said.

"I agree," Jack began as Cate neared the door. "We've really got to... CATE!"

"No, we can't tell... CATE!" Molly exclaimed as Cate entered.

"Hello," Cate said as she scanned their faces. "Everything okay?"

Everyone murmured an affirmative response, all speaking at once. "What would be wrong?" Molly added with a nervous chuckle.

Cate shrugged in response. "You seemed a bit surprised to see me."

"Well, you've got guests. We assumed you'd be with them. You startled us, is all," Mrs. Fraser said. "Is there something you need? Tea, perhaps?"

"No, thanks, Mrs. Fraser. I just wanted to steal Jack for a moment. About the leak. Celine noticed it this morning, I wanted you to take a peek."

"Oh, sure, absolutely. Let's head up right now."

"Okay. You could finish your discussion first and then head up if you'd prefer."

"Discussion? What discussion, no discussion here," Jack babbled.

"We weren't even talking," Molly added.

"Right," Cate said with a knit brow. "Well, let's head up then."

Jack and Cate proceeded up to the main floor and met the others in the hallway. Michael stood several feet from the group.

"Better safe than sorry," he noted as they passed him.

"So, you've found something?" Jack inquired as they approached the others.

"Yes," Celine said. She strode several feet away, stopping nearer to the library door.

"Yesterday, the time portal ended about here."

"Yes, I remember that's where you were when you said the portal was distended and spiked," Cate answered.

Celine nodded as she stalked several feet closer to them. "Today, the portal ends here."

Jack raised his eyebrows at the change. "That's a growth of several feet."

Celine nodded. "At least," she confirmed. "In less than twenty-four hours."

"What does this mean?" Cate inquired.

"I'm almost one hundred percent certain my theory is correct. This is becoming a universal time portal."

"So, they'll need a new mechanism to control it," Damien commented. "Something that can control where they go when entering in addition to keeping the portal closed."

"Right," Celine confirmed. "And I need to modify the enchantment to hold this shut unless opened. It's a bit trickier with a universal time portal than one leading to the same date in another year, but it's doable."

"What do you need from us?" Jack inquired.

"Some time. We'll need to make sure what we're doing works. As the portal grows, the spikes are lessening. I'd like to get a better idea of the final form. I'll continue to observe this today while we create a solution to control this," Celine answered. "And I'll also need a device that can accept a date input."

"Okay," Cate said with a nod. "Is there anything we can do in the meantime other than find a new device?"

Celine shook her head. "No, we'll keep an eye on all the portals and once we've got a solution, we'll test it out on whatever device you give me and hopefully be all set!"

"Test it out?" Jack questioned. "As in, activate it and time travel?"

"Pretty much," Celine confirmed.

Jack heaved a sigh.

"I'll test it," Damien offered.

"No, no," Jack replied. "It's our issue, we'll test it, but thanks."

"In the meantime, try to relax," Alexander said.

Jack nodded. "Easier said than done."

"And possibly easier outside of the castle walls," Cate suggested. "Would you two like to take a trip into town? There are no time portals there." She directed her final statement to Michael.

"Best idea I've heard all day," Michael answered.

With Jack heading outside for some groundskeeping, Cate, Michael and Damien headed to town for most of the day. They returned just before dinner. The group gathered in the dining room for the meal.

"Any news?" Cate inquired.

"The portals seem to be stabilizing," Alexander mentioned.

"That's good, right?" Cate asked.

"Yes, very. The spikes are receding which means the portals will be less volatile. I expect the spikes will be gone tomorrow."

"Portals?" Damien questioned. "There are still multiple, they didn't merge."

"Yes and no," Celine answered. "I detected a portal in the hallway overlooking your back garden that seemed to be a universal portal in one direction only."

"That's correct," Cate answered. "You can return to your own time from wherever you are in that hallway."

"That portal has merged with the portal in the hallway outside the library. They now form a universal time portal in both directions that spans from the back hallway through the secret passage we used to escape Marcus and into the hallway near the library. However, the other portals still exist and lead to their respective years."

"Are they also less volatile?" Michael inquired.

"They seem to be stabilizing. You shouldn't get sucked into them at random anymore and the original timepiece should still control them without any issues," Alexander explained.

"But it will not control the new one?" Cate asked.

"No," Celine said with a shake of her head. "For that, we'll need a new controller."

"Will this do?" Damien questioned. He pulled a gold pocket watch from his hoodie pocket. "It's not a family heirloom like yours but it's similar. Small, easy to hide, and has a date function."

Celine eyed it over Damien's shoulder. "Yes, that should work."

Cate stared at the gold pocket watch as Damien flipped it open. Similar to hers, though missing the distinctive crosses on the top, it would provide an excellent new controller for the time rips.

"When did you..." Cate began.

"You were speaking to the shop owner in the antique store, and I found it. I wanted to surprise you! I hope you like it."

Cate smiled at him. "Thank you, Damien. I love it. I'll always remember you when I use it."

"Looks like we're set," Celine said. "Alexander and I will work on creating an enchantment to close the universal portal and use the new timepiece as the controller.

It will also work for the old time rips, though you won't need to set the date for those."

"Great! I can't wait to tell Jack. Maybe we'll all rest a little easier now."

CHAPTER 27

When Cate emerged the next morning from her bedroom, she found Jack pacing the hallway outside her suite.

"Hey, everything okay?" she asked.

"Couldn't sleep. I'm anxious. Do you think they can solve it?"

"Celine seemed confident. I guess we'll find out today."

Jack nodded and held up his crossed fingers.

"Let's hope."

"I'll get an update at breakfast. Let's meet in the library hallway after and see where they are."

"Sounds like a plan. Hey, we'll miss you at breakfast today."

"I'll miss you all, too. But I'll schedule one with you once our new friends have departed."

"I'll let Mrs. Fraser know so she's not startled by your request on an off day," Jack joked.

"I can't miss my staff breakfast for the week!"

When Cate reached the dining room, she found herself

alone. She hadn't run into any of her guests outside on her walk with the dogs nor on her way out.

Instead, the new gold timepiece lay at her seat with a sealed envelope next to it with CATE scrawled across it.

Cate pulled the envelope open and flicked open the note.

Cate -

Here is your brand-new time travel device! Celine and Alexander worked through the night to make sure we had this under control.

Michael and I tested it thoroughly with both the old time portals and the new universal one. Works like a charm! We may have scared a person or two when we popped in out of thin air, oops.

Just kidding! The advantage of time travel in the middle of the night is there aren't a lot of people wandering around the halls.

We also noted the time portals are still distended, so your time difference still exists. We tested this too. It still seems to be about one minute in the present to every fifteen minutes in the past. At least some things didn't go haywire!

Anyway, we'll probably sleep in, but rest assured, no one will disappear into any random time portals anymore! See you later, alligator. Sorry that was lame.

See you later, Damien

P.S. I had Celine and Alexander recreate the look of your old timepiece with the new one. No one will suspect you've replaced it!

Cate's heart skipped a beat as she read the note.

She picked up the new timepiece and held it in her hands. The two crosses now graced the top of the pocket watch. She opened the cover, finding the familiar engraving on the inside.

Only the face differed now. A smile formed on her lips as she lifted the original timepiece from around her neck.

Cate opened the clasp and slid the original pocket watch from the chain, replacing it with the new one. She slid the original timepiece into her cardigan pocket. She'd need to discuss with Jack what to do with it.

As she pondered the question, Mrs. Fraser and Molly popped into the room. "Lady Cate! You're all alone!" Molly exclaimed.

"Yes, I am," Cate confirmed. "It looks like everyone is sleeping in." Cate waved the note in the air before sliding it into her pocket. "So, I'm on my own. Mind if I join you for our usual breakfast?"

"We never mind if you join us, Lady Cate," Mrs. Fraser answered.

"Here, let me take something off your hands," Cate said, reaching for the water pitcher from Mrs. Fraser. "I'm terribly sorry you had to drag all this up for nothing."

"The exercise didn't hurt me! It'll keep me spry at my age."

"You aren't THAT old, Mrs. Fraser," Cate countered.

"Tell that to these old bones," she said as they descended the stairs.

"Lady Cate!" Jack exclaimed from his seat at the table. "Fancy meeting you here."

"She got ditched," Molly joked with a giggle.

"It's true," Cate confirmed as she slid into a seat across from Jack. "I found a note saying everyone else decided to sleep in, so it looks like I'll get my regular staff breakfast after all!"

"Lucky us," Mr. Fraser said.

Cate grinned at him as Mrs. Fraser put the final preparations on their breakfast. "I'll put this away for the sleepy-heads to eat later," she said as she stowed the fruit plate and yogurt in the refrigerator.

The group settled in for their breakfast. The tension that hung over Cate for the past several weeks eased away as she no longer worried they may all disappear. She itched to tell Jack the good news.

After the group finished their meal, Cate requested Jack's presence upstairs.

"About the leak?" Jack inquired as they headed out the kitchen door.

"Yep," Cate confirmed. "We may have it under control."

They continued down the hall and ascended the staircase. As Jack pushed the door shut, he twisted to face Cate. "Are you serious?" he whispered.

Cate nodded. She pulled the note from her pocket and handed it to him. "I found this at my seat this morning along with the new timepiece. It seems they fixed the problem."

"And this is the new one?" Jack questioned as he motioned to the timepiece around Cate's neck.

"Yes. I switched them out this morning. I have the old one in my pocket. We'll need to find a safe place to keep it."

"The safe," Jack suggested. "It should be secure there."

"That's what I was thinking," Cate agreed.

Jack stared at the note for another moment. "Hmm," he murmured. "Do you think this is it? Problem solved?"

"It should be," Damien said with a yawn as he stumbled down the main staircase. He smiled at them. "Good morning."

"Good morning," Cate answered. "And thank you!" She held up the timepiece.

"You're welcome. Feel free to test it yourselves, but Michael and I did a pretty thorough analysis last night in a few locations, both old and new."

"We just may do that," Jack answered. "Not that we don't trust you. It's just that…"

"You want to see it for yourselves, so you'll rest easier. No, I understand," Damien answered.

Cate smiled at him. "After a few weeks of time troubles, it would be nice to verify that we're firmly in control again."

"Sure, give it a go!" Damien said. "Oh, one thing I forgot to put in my note. In the old time rip locations, you don't need to set the date. The timepiece will just transfer you to the same date in the other year no matter what you input. In the new time rip, the one that extends from the library to the back hall, you'll need to set the watch's date before activating it. You'll then return to that date at the same time of day as when you activate it. So, for example, if it's 8 a.m. and you set the date for June first, 1834, you'll go back to June first, 1834 at eight in the morning."

Cate nodded. "Got it." She glanced at Jack. "Want to try it now?"

"As much as I don't want to, yes, I do. Like you said, it would be nice to confirm we've got this solved."

"Oh," Cate said as they began to part ways. "Mrs. Fraser has breakfast in the fridge for you."

"Great! I'm starving. I'll just pop down and grab it if you can point me in the direction of the kitchen."

"You can go through the door in the dining room, down the stairs and hall straight into the kitchen."

"Got it," Damien answered. "Thanks!"

Damien spun on his heel and continued down the hall to the dining room. Cate turned to Jack with her eyebrows raised. "Ready?"

"As I'll ever be. Let's test this bad boy out!"

"Wow, you almost seem enthusiastic."

"If Michael was willing to test this out for us, then I should be!"

"Should we start with a new time rip or an old one?" Cate asked as they headed down the hall.

"An old one," Jack responded. "If it works there, I'll feel a smidge more confident that we won't get stuck in the new one."

"Don't trust them?"

"I do, I just can't believe we have a universal time portal and it's working."

Cate chuckled as they entered the library. "Douglas's lab?"

"Sounds good," Jack agreed. "We can easily tell if it's working if the lights go out!"

They opened the bookcase and descended the stairs. Cate held out the new timepiece. Jack wrapped her hand in his. Her eyes flitted up to Jack. He offered an encouraging nod. Cate took a deep breath and focused on the timepiece. In unison, she and Jack rubbed the face to activate it.

Within seconds, the second hand began to slow. The lights flickered then blinked off, disappearing from their sight. Darkness surrounded them.

"Looks like we made it," Cate said.

"Yep," Jack answered, still clutching her hand.

"Good enough or did you want to take a peek around and verify this is 1792?"

"I'm happy to assume it is," Jack answered. "Let's head back and try the universal location. Unless you have an objection."

"No," Cate said. "I trust that it is."

They reset the timepiece and returned to their time. The blaring lights announced their arrival in the correct year.

"Well, we know the return trip worked," Jack said with a sigh of relief.

They climbed the stairs and headed to the hall. "Should we try this here?" Cate questioned.

"Didn't Damien or Celine mention a secret passage?"

"Yes," Cate answered. "It's here." She led him through the halls to the trigger. Cate pulled the sconce on the wall and the hidden panel swung open.

"Perhaps we should duck in there and try it. Less chance of running into someone."

"Good idea," Cate answered. "Oh, do you have your cell phone on you? We may need a flashlight."

"Got it," Jack said as he dug in his pocket and toggled the flashlight on.

They stepped into the dark passage and pushed the panel shut behind them. "What year should we try?"

"An old one," Jack answered.

"Really? Have a fondness for the olden days, huh?"

"It'll be easier to tell if we're actually back in an old time. There won't be any lights on the walls."

"Okay," Cate answered as Jack aimed the flashlight at the timepiece. "How's March 30, 1803?"

"Sounds like a perfect date to me!"

Cate set the date and held out the timepiece.

"Okay, here goes nothing."

Jack pushed out his lips as he stared at the timepiece for a moment before he grasped it. They activated the mechanism and waited as the second hand slowed.

"Seems to have worked," Cate whispered as the second hand crept around the face.

"Yeah," Jack said with a nod. "Now to check if we've made it to where we expected."

"Check your cell phone."

"For what? The latest news from 1803?"

"No. You should have lost your Wi-fi signal when we slipped back."

"Oh, right." Jack toggled on his display. "Yep, it's gone."

"Okay, let's check the hallway."

"Where's the trigger to get out?" Jack inquired.

"I'm not sure," Cate answered. "We wandered through the passage for a while before we ended up in the mausoleum. We never went out this way."

Jack shined the light on the wall near the secret panel. They studied the area before they found a small handhold on the panel. Jack curled his fingers around it and pulled. The panel lurched open a slit.

Light streamed into the passage. Cate peeked into the hallway. Candlelight flickered against the walls. "Candles!" Cate exclaimed in a hushed whisper.

"Yeah," Jack responded, peeking over her head. "So, we've traveled somewhere back in time."

"How can we tell if it's 1803?"

"Find a newspaper and check the date?"

Cate bit her lower lip. That would require them to traipse through the castle. They weren't dressed for the occasion which was only the first issue with the plan.

As Cate considered the plan, a giggle sounded in the hallway. Cate peered into the hall, spotting a small child toddling down. Dark curls adorned his head. He wore a wide grin as he continued to patter toward them.

A woman rounded the corner. "Look! It's Olivia!" Cate breathed.

"I see her," Jack answered.

"And that little boy must be…"

"Finlay MacKenzie, just where do you think you're off to?" Olivia said.

The child let out another giggle before Olivia caught up to him and scooped him into her arms. Another woman followed her. "My apologies, Lady MacKenzie," she said as she collected the boy from Olivia. "He is quite energetic and insisted on finding his father."

"It is quite all right, Nanny Mae. Children are permitted a bit of mischief once in a while."

As they disappeared from the hall, Cate pushed the panel closed. "Well, that confirms what we needed to know for the most part. If that was Finlay MacKenzie we're in 1803. He was born in 1801 and he looked to be about two. That would put us where we thought we were."

"Do you want to confirm the exact date?"

"It's too risky," Cate answered. "We shouldn't be wandering around the castle. Especially in these clothes!"

"What's this I hear? Cate Kensie not being impulsive enough to roam around another century?"

"Is this Jack Reid arguing to parade around another time period?"

"Indeed it is, lassie. I want to be sure this thing works before we use it and get into more trouble than we're after!"

"Okay," Cate answered. "How do you propose we find a newspaper?"

"There should be one in town."

"How are we going to get to town? In these clothes? There has to be a better way."

"I'm sure they have one in the castle, I'm just not sure where. Douglas would have read it, surely."

"That's it!" Cate said, snapping her fingers.

"What's it?"

"Douglas! If we can find Douglas, we can ask him. He's aware of time travel. He knows us. He wouldn't question us showing up and asking the date!"

"Okay, great. The question is: can we find him?"

"We can try!" Cate said. "It was just after eight when we arrived. At this time of the day, Douglas was likely finishing breakfast and heading to his office."

"Let's try there first. We're not far from it."

Cate nodded and found the handhold in the panel.

She slid it open a few inches and they perused the hallway, finding it empty.

"Let's go as quick as possible," Jack said, grabbing Cate's hand.

He led her into the hall. They rounded the corner and

sprinted down the hall to the office. The door was ajar. Jack peered in before pushing through the door.

"Douglas, pardon the interruption," Jack panted as he pushed the door shut behind Cate.

Douglas leapt from his seat, his eyes wide.

"Jack! Catherine!" He studied them up and down.

"Hello, Douglas," Cate said. "Sorry to barge in like this but we needed your help."

"Of course, anything. What is it? Are you in some sort of trouble? Is it Duke Northcott again?"

"No," Cate assured him. "We're not in any trouble. We've had some developments with the time rips in our time and we're hoping to assess whether or not we've got the situation under control."

"Developments? How interesting! What has happened?"

"New time rips have opened. We're investigating where they lead," Cate answered.

"Could you tell us the date today?" Jack inquired.

"Yes, of course. Today is 30 March, the year of our Lord, 1803," Douglas answered.

Jack breathed a sigh of relief and glanced to Cate. She nodded to him with a closed-mouth smile. "Judging by the expressions on your faces, I'd say that answer was what you hoped to hear."

"It is," Cate answered. "Exactly what we hoped to hear. Thank you."

"Yes, thank you, Douglas. For everything," Jack responded. "We won't take up any more of your time. And we'll leave the way we came." Jack offered a wink.

"So soon? Oh, what a shame. I had hoped to visit with you again."

"Perhaps another time when we're more appropriately dressed," Cate said with a chuckle.

"Let's plan for it, Catherine. I do hope to visit with you again."

Cate grasped his hand in hers and squeezed it. "I promise we'll visit soon."

As Cate and Jack prepared to depart, a knock sounded at the door. Everyone froze. "Yes?" Douglas called.

"Lord MacKenzie," Wilson's voice answered. "I have your morning post."

"Oh, of course," Douglas called. "Just a moment." He eyed Jack and Cate. "You must hide!"

"Where?" Cate whispered.

"Behind the door, I shall only open it a crack."

Cate nodded and she and Jack hurried out of sight as Douglas inched the door open. "I'll take them, Wilson, thank you," Douglas said as he reached through the door.

Cate spied the butler's confused expression through the small crack. "Yes, of course, m'lord."

"Oh, Wilson, would you please fetch me a cup of tea."

"Right away, m'lord," Wilson said with a nod as he spun on his heel to retreat to the kitchen.

Douglas slammed the door and spun to face Cate. "Give him a moment to clear the hall, then it should be safe to flee."

They waited a moment before Douglas peeked into the hallway. Finding it empty, he nodded to them. "Go now," he urged.

Cate smiled and nodded to him as Jack grasped her hand and tugged her into the hallway.

Douglas gave her a smile and a nod as she spun to leave the room. "Oh, Catherine?" Douglas called before they stepped from the room.

"Yes?" Cate asked as she twisted to face him.

"I left you a note in my journals as Damien suggested. I hope you found it."

"I'll check for it the moment we're back," Cate answered.

He smiled and offered another nod. "Goodbye, Catherine. And good luck."

"Thank you," she said. "We'll see you soon."

After peeking into the hall again, they snuck to the secret panel and slipped inside. Together, they activated the timepiece and returned to the present.

"Are we back?" Jack inquired as the second hand sped up to its normal speed.

Cate grasped the panel and inched it open. She peered into the hallway. Damien meandered around near the passage.

"Yep, we are," Cate answered. She pulled the panel open and stepped out.

"Whew," Damien exclaimed. "You scared me!"

"Sorry," Cate said. "I figured you were waiting for us."

"I was. Everything go okay with your tests? Went to the right date, returned all right, no problems?"

Jack joined them in the hall, pocketing his cell phone. "Yes," he answered. "Seems to work as you said."

Damien beamed at them. "You should be all set now!"

"Yes," Cate agreed. "Damien, you saved me and my home. Saying thank you feels so trite but thank you."

"Really, no thanks is necessary. I'm glad we could help. And if you have any trouble at all, we're just an email, text, or call away."

"I'm so glad this is over," Jack said. "We can get back to normal life again without worrying about people disappearing."

Michael strode toward them, a bag slung over his shoulder. "Everything working okay?" he asked as he approached Damien.

"Perfectly," Cate answered. "We were just thanking Damien, though the simple words don't feel like enough."

"No problem at all," Michael assured her.

Cate eyed his bag. "Going somewhere?"

"Home," he answered. He pointed to Damien. "I brought your bag down for you, too."

"Already?" Cate exclaimed. "Can't you stay a few days at least? Enjoy the castle a bit? It's the least we can do for all your help!"

"Sorry," Damien answered. "Duty calls."

"Trouble at home?" Jack questioned.

"When isn't there," Michael said with a chuckle and a roll of his eyes. "You ready?" he inquired of Damien. "Celine and Alexander are waiting in the foyer."

"Yep."

"We'll at least walk you out," Cate said.

They navigated to the foyer, meeting Celine and Alexander. Luggage sat near the front door. "Everything okay?" Celine asked.

"Yes, the timepiece works great, thank you!" Cate responded.

"If you have any trouble at all, just contact us," Celine replied. "But you should be in the clear from here on out."

"I told Damien that a simple thank you just isn't enough. We're eternally grateful to you for all your help."

"No thanks is necessary," Celine assured them.

An awkward silence passed over the group. "Are you certain you can't stay a few days?" Cate inquired.

"Yes, our apologies for rushing off, but we do have a situation brewing at home."

"I understand," Cate answered. "Good luck with it. If there's anything we can do to help, please ask."

"Yeah, we definitely owe you," Jack added.

"Thank you," Celine said with a smile.

"Well, it was lovely to meet all of you despite the circumstances we were in," Cate said.

Everyone exchanged their goodbyes, shaking hands with each other. As Damien said goodbye to Cate, he added, "It was great to meet you, Cate. Don't hesitate to call if you need anything. I'm serious."

"Let's plan to keep in touch," Cate answered.

"Deal."

As she stepped away, she overheard the conversation between Michael and Jack. "If you ever need to vent about time travel, text me," Michael said.

"You may be inviting more trouble than you bargained for," Jack said.

"Believe me, you can't hate it more than I do, buddy," Michael retorted.

The two shared a chuckle over their mutual dislike for visiting other centuries before parting ways. Cate and Jack followed the foursome outside, waving as their car pulled down the drive.

They stood for another moment as the car disappeared toward the town of Dunhaven.

CHAPTER 28

"Did that just happen?" Jack asked after a moment.

"Yep, I'm pretty sure it did," Cate confirmed. They waited another moment before Cate spoke again. "Well, I guess it's time to get back to normal around here."

"Sounds like a great idea to me. What's your plan? Long walk to the loch? Reading in the library? Working on your book?"

"First, I'm going to lock this guy in the safe," Cate said, holding up the original timepiece. "Then, I'm going to check the journals for that letter from Douglas. And then, maybe I'll take that relaxing walk!"

"Mind if I tag along on the first two? As protector of the secret, I'd like to ensure the safety of the original timepiece."

"Of course," Cate answered as she strode down the hall.

"You know, as protector of the secret AND you," Jack said as they walked, "you really put me through it this time."

"Sorry about that," Cate responded.

"It's okay. I'm only teasing," Jack said. "But, Cate, if anything had happened to you…"

He stopped and stared into her eyes. His lips attempted to form words but none came.

"Cate, I…" he began.

"Nothing happened to me," Cate interrupted. "Let's focus on that."

"You're right," he said with a nod.

They entered the office. Cate's mind recalled their encounter with Douglas in this room less than an hour ago as she crossed to the wall safe. She typed in the number then pressed her thumb onto the digital fingerprint scanner. The door released and swung open.

Cate pulled the original timepiece from her pocket. "You served us well," she said as she placed it inside the safe.

"Now, it's time for a new era," Jack said as they closed and locked the safe.

Cate sighed. "Well, that should do it! Let's check for Douglas's note."

She led the way to the library. Douglas's journals were scattered across the desk.

Cate plopped into the chair and grabbed the last journal. She scanned the pages for any hint of the note Douglas mentioned.

"Here," Jack said after scanning journal number ten.

"This could be it." He pointed to letters scrawled on the last page of the final journal.

"Maybe!" Cate exclaimed. "This page is blank in all the other journals."

She opened Damien's program on her laptop and copied the text from the page. She clicked the button and waited as the program worked. In moments, decrypted text appeared.

"This is it!" Cate exclaimed as she scanned the first few words.

Dearest Catherine,

I hope you have found this note and are well in your time. The situation still astounds me at times though the good fortune to have met a descendent, however far removed, will remain a high point in my life.

I do regret the trouble you experienced while visiting my time and hope it has not followed you to yours. More than that, I hope it has not soured you on time traveling as I do desire to meet with you again. How extraordinary to share a conversation or break bread with my progeny.

Rest assured, Grayson and Celine Buckley along with her cousins, the Carlyles, have made sure I can control the time rips and have protected me from any harm from the foul Duke Northcott.

Perhaps this will be the end of the rumors of hauntings within these halls, though I doubt it. A new set of gossip abounds in the town already following the night you returned to your time.

No matter, we know the truth. And we shall remain the sole keepers of that truth along with the Reids. The secret shall remain protected through the generations.

Remember, Catherine, only travel for good, never for personal gain, do no harm, and do not travel to a time in which you already exist. Also, there is a distortion in the time rip, causing the time you travel from to move slower than the time you visit. These were the rules imparted to me by the Buckleys and that I shall impart to my heir and on down the line until it is imparted to you.

As a MacKenzie, you have a solemn duty. Though one I view as a privilege. I hope you will, too.

Good luck, Catherine.

And goodbye.

Yours,

Douglas MacKenzie

A smile crossed Cate's face as she read the note.

"And there it is," Jack said. "Looks like the Buckleys solved all our problems!"

"He really was an interesting man," Cate said as she stared at the screen.

"Yes, he was," Jack agreed. "He'll make a great addition to your book, minus the time travel stuff."

"I'll be sure to leave that part out. But his inventions alone are worth several chapters!"

"And now you have time to explore them without worrying about disappearing into another time period!"

"Yep," Cate said with a grin. "But first, I think a nice long walk is in order. What do you say, boys?"

Riley and Bailey leapt to their feet, ready to enjoy the grounds. "I'll escort you out. M'lady," Jack teased with an extravagant bow.

Cate chuckled as she proceeded in front of him and to the front door. As she opened the door, both dogs raced past her and into the yard. They rounded the corner as Jack and Cate stepped on the path.

"We really should make good on that promise to visit Douglas," Jack said.

"Wow, I'm impressed!" Cate exclaimed as they meandered the path toward the side garden. "Jack Reid suggesting time travel."

"It is a gift. And I'd like to live life to the fullest. Particularly since one of us almost didn't get that opportunity."

"I'd really rather not dwell on how close I came to not seeing another birthday. Though, for whatever reason, I kept the necklace Duke Northcott buried me with. Damien told me to get rid of it. I don't know why I didn't. It is a beautiful piece of jewelry. Maybe I'll give it away as an auction item at the President's Ball. But for now… I don't know…" Her voice trailed off.

"I would get rid of that thing long before the ball.

Damien's right. Speaking of, odd people, those Buckleys and their friends."

"Definitely. The lives they must lead are…" Cate's voice trailed off as she tried to formulate an appropriate comparison.

"The stuff you read in books or see on TV," Jack finished.

"Good description," Cate replied.

"At least our lives can now return to normal," Jack said. "Only the odd, controllable time travel trips now."

Cate nodded with a chuckle as the side garden came into view. Her eyes scanned the horizon for the dogs. She stopped in her tracks as she spotted them. Her lips parted as her jaw went slack.

"What is it?" Jack inquired as he noted the expression on her face.

She swallowed hard. In response to his question, Cate raised her arm and pointed toward the dogs.

Jack followed the direction of her finger, his eyes going wide at the sight. Cate stumbled two steps forward as she raised her hand to cover her mouth. "Riley! Bailey! Leave that," she choked out in a shaky voice after a moment.

The dogs dropped the item they play-fought over and bounded to Cate. Cate scooped Bailey into her arms as she continued toward the now-larger hole near the bushes. Jack grabbed Riley and followed her.

"Oh," Cate groaned with a frown. "Now we know why they've been digging."

"Yep," Jack answered.

They approached the discarded "toy" and stood over it, each of them staring down at it. In contrast to the bright green of the springtime grass, lay a collection of white bones. Cate's eyes swept across the object from top to bottom. She identified a radius, ulna, wrist bones, and hand bones that extended to skeletal fingers.

"Someone's buried in your side garden, Lady Cate," Jack noted.

"Yes, but who?"

"Another mystery," Jack answered. "So much for getting back to normal."

Stay up to date with all my news! Be the first to find out about new releases first, sales and get free offers! Sign up for the newsletter now!

* * *

If you loved solving this mystery and want to continue the adventure at Dunhaven, look for Book 5 of the Cate Kensie series coming in 2022! If you haven't read the first three books, now is a great time! Start with *The Secret of Dunhaven Castle* by clicking here!

* * *

Want to her the story from Jack's perspective? Try The Secret Keepers, Book 1 of Jack's Journal!

* * *

Want to learn more about Celine, Grayson, Damien, Michael, Alexander and even Marcus? Read the Shadow Slayers series, a fast-paced supernatural page-turner! Book one, *Shadows of the Past*, is available now by clicking here!

Ready for adventure? Travel the globe with Maggie Edwards in search of her kidnapped uncle and Cleopatra's Tomb. Book one, *Cleopatra's Tomb*, in the Maggie Edwards Adventure series is available now!

Love immersing yourself in the past? Lenora Fletcher can communicate with the dead! Can she use her unique skill to solve a mystery? Find out in Death of a Duchess, Book 1 in the Duchess of Blackmoore Mysteries.

A NOTE FROM THE AUTHOR

Dear Reader,

Thank you for reading this book! *Danger at Dunhaven Castle* was one of the most exciting books for me to write! I love a good crossover and the idea of introducing Cate and her crew to the Shadow Slayers made writing so much fun. Look for Cate Kensie stories coming in 2022!

I hope you enjoyed reading the story as much as I enjoyed writing it! If you did, please consider leaving a review and help get this book and series into the hands of other interested readers!

Keep reading for a sneak preview of *Shadows of the Past*, Book 1 in the *Shadow Slayers Stories* series! You got a taste of these characters already, keep reading to learn more!

All the best, Nellie

SHADOWS OF THE PAST SYNOPSIS

Josie is having terrifying nightmares...

And she can't make sense of them.

During the day she's a typical twenty-five-year-old woman, but at night all she keeps seeing is blood...

On her hands.

When a mysterious man drops an antique music box on her doorstep, Josie is intrigued, especially when he leaves her a note...

And calls her by the name Celine.

Promising her all the answers she's looking for, Josie takes off with the mystery man and embarks on a journey to find out why she's having nightmares, who Celine is and, most importantly, what lies hidden underneath the surface.

As danger is confronted and more information is revealed, Josie is completely unprepared to learn what lies at the heart of these strange occurrences.

And who-or what-she really is...

Shadows of the Past is Book One of the Shadow Slayers Stories series and is a supernatural suspense mystery novel for people who love fast-paced action, secret identities and edge-of-your-seat suspense.

Get *Shadows of the Past* now.

SHADOWS OF THE PAST EXCERPT

"Josie!" Damien called behind her. "JOSIE!" They caught up to her and Damien grabbed her elbow. "Josie, please, wait."

"D, sorry, this isn't the best time. I'm busy trying to get things figured out so we can get back to normal. Now, please, let me go. Go back to the house. Read a book or something and go home on Monday."

"No, Josie!" Damien said, "I will not accept that. No way!" Damien's insistence surprised Michael.

"D, please, I can't explain it now, I can't but I definitely want you and Michael to go. I'm pleading with you to leave."

"Why, Josie? This is beyond bizarre and I'm not leaving without you. I want you to come home with us."

"I can't come home yet, D, I can't."

"Why? Please, Josie."

"There is nothing to worry about. But I can't come home." She turned to leave.

"Josie, come on," he said, grabbing her arm again. "You can't expect us to go home and leave you here. Do you realize how bizarre this looks to ANYONE on the outside of it?"

She pondered for a moment. "I realize how bizarre it is,

yes. It's as bizarre as it was to me when Gray first approached me but it makes sense, it does, but I can't explain it. Now, please…"

"No, Josie," Damien continued, "no. I'm beyond worried about you. I'm exceptionally concerned. This bizarre story about you being someone named Celine who that kid told us lived here when his mother was a kid, these people bringing you here, you going along with it, have they brainwashed you? Are they threatening you or someone in our family?"

"No and no. I'm not brainwashed. They are not threatening me. I am here of my own free will, believe it or not. And I have other things to do. Now, please," Josie said, pulling away from Damien's grip and heading off down the path.

Damien opened his mouth to call after her but gave up, surmising it would be useless. Michael clapped a hand on his shoulder. "Well, we're right back where we started, still no information, but a terrible feeling that something is wrong."

"Something is wrong," Damien said, turning toward him. "And if Josie won't tell us, then I'll confront the guy who brought her here. One way or another we're getting some answers. Come on!"

Keep reading *Shadows of the Past* by clicking here!

Made in the USA
Monee, IL
12 November 2021